Tying the Knot

SUSAN MAY WARREN

Tying
the Knot

TYNDALE HOUSE PUBLISHERS, INC.
CAROL STREAM, ILLINIOS

Visit Tyndale's exciting Web site at www.tyndale.com

TYNDALE and Tyndale's quill logo are registered trademarks of Tyndale House Publishers, Inc.

Tying the Knot

Library of Congress Cataloging-in-Publication Data

Warren, Susan, date.
  Tying the knot / Susan May Warren.
      p. cm. — (HeartQuest.)
  ISBN 0-8423-8118-X (sc)
  1. Emergency medical personnel—Fiction. 2. Minneapolis (Minn.)—Fiction. I. Title.
II. Series.
  PS3623.A865 T95 2003
  813'.6—dc21   2003009960

ISBN-13: 978-1-4143-1384-9
ISBN-10: 1-4143-1384-5

Printed in the United States of America

13   12   11   10   09   08   07
  7   6   5   4   3   2   1

To my Lord
and Savior,
Jesus Christ.
You are sufficient.
Always.

Acknowledgments

Only God could have put this story together—He knows how frazzled I was during the writing of *Tying the Knot*. As usual, in His kindness, He equipped me with a team of encouragers who held me up and brought this work to fruition. I thank the Lord for you every time I think of you.

Andrew, supreme omelet maker and hero of my heart. I'll never forget our first motorcycle ride. "Hold on tight, snuggle closer," you said. I'll never let go.

David, Sarah, Peter, and Noah, my sweet children who consistently offer hugs, cheers, and words of encouragement when I am beating my head on my keyboard. Thank you for putting up with endless burned or cold dinners and for not getting angry when I asked, one overwhelming day, "Do you *have* to eat?" I thank the Lord every day for the blessing of being your mother. You are a reminder of God's love for me.

Dannette Bell Lund, for being a light in my world and for your enthusiasm that never fails to lift my spirits. I'm so glad you joined our family!

Tracey Victoria Bateman, who tirelessly and expertly critiqued every word. Thank you for panicking with me! You're a gift of joy and fun in my life.

Susan Downs, for your prayers and steadfast encouragement. What would I do without you?

Juanita Santiago, vivacious, on-fire Moody Bible Institute student. Thank you for giving me your time, your insights, your guidance. This book is a product of your testimony and courage. May the Lord bless you as you seek Him.

The Common Ground class, especially Kathy Kirchner, Lyn Lindberg, Laurie Stoltenberg, Kathy Tulberg, Wendy Cavness, Laura Miles, Karin Webster, and Carma Hayenga for your support and enthusiasm and for putting up with my endless jabber about what God was teaching me. Your friendship has helped me heal.

Karen Boberg and Pat Reycraft, for your faithful prayers and for being there to fill in the "grandparent" gap.

Eric Ericksen, for your generosity. Your kindness made this book possible.

Anne Goldsmith, for your limitless encouragement. Your laughter and warm notes kept me going. Thank you for believing in me.

Lorie Popp, for your patience and words of wisdom as I worked through this manuscript. As usual, you took a rough piece and made it shine!

Thanks to the incredibly talented Julie Chen—once again you've taken an idea, put color and beauty to it, and created a cover that is beyond my wildest dreams. Thank you for your dedication and imagination.

To Darlene Guinn, our very own Granny D. Thank you for taking us under your wing and loving us so well.

Finally, to our friends and supporters who continue to pray for the Warren family. We need those prayers! May the Lord bless you richly for your faithfulness and sacrifice.

I wait quietly
before God,
for my hope is
in Him.

Psalm 62:5

The crackle on the two-way radio gave EMT Anne Lundstrom a two-second warning that someone's life teetered on death's fine edge. The dispatch blared through the ambulance speaker and her stomach tightened, instinct telling her to brace herself.

"King One-Two, we have a fifty-two-year-old female complaining of chest pains. Respond to 2135 Franklin Avenue."

Anne made a wry face in response to the fire department dispatcher's voice. She tossed her half-eaten hamburger into its wrapper in her lap and reached for her seat belt as her partner, Gary Muller, popped the rig into drive.

"Try not to kill us," Anne said as she grabbed the dash. She didn't know what she hated more, lurching in the passenger seat or manning the wheel herself, as they careened through Minneapolis's congested inner city.

"Hey, gimme a break. Last time I only skimmed off one layer of paint." Gary grinned, but his hands whitened on the steering wheel.

Anne grimaced against the scream of the siren. More often than not, instead of parting traffic, the sound panicked drivers who slammed on their brakes, or worse, jerked into the empty lane. As the rig flew through a red light, Anne tensed, praying silently for the crosscurrent traffic to yield.

Her hamburger tumbled onto the floorboards. She kicked it aside and planted her foot. "Franklin. It had to be Franklin Avenue."

Mercifully, Gary stayed silent.

She didn't have to wonder what they'd find in Minneapolis's seedier part of town. Probably a dilapidated two-story Victorian, with paint peeling off once-beautiful columns, boarded-up windows, and a sagging, rotted porch. The front yard would be littered with battered furniture, rusty car parts, broken glass, cigarette butts, and even used syringes. Inside, amid the acrid smells of moldy food and the lingering smoke of illegal substances, she'd find a crying, dirty child or two. Of course, the grandmother, the only sane person in the dwelling, would be stretched out on the floor, stroked out or otherwise "fixin' to die."

Her pessimism had Anne kneading a pulsing vein in her temple.

"You've been on three days straight." Gary shot her a quick look. "You should take a sick day."

"It's not that."

Gary dodged a minivan full of children, whose driver apparently hadn't yet heard their siren. "I know."

Anne bristled as they barreled into the inner recesses of the city. Obviously her years spent walking this neighborhood hadn't dissolved from her system. She noted a few changes in the landscape—a new liquor store and the burned shell of a grocery store, plywood nailed to its windows. They passed Woodrow Wilson High. A few teens were playing hoops in the yard, adeptly skirting weeds that infiltrated the crumbling asphalt.

"We're at Twenty-second," Anne said without looking at the signs. "Next street up, take a right."

Gary slowed and took the corner on all four wheels. Despite the warning siren, they could be disrupting a game of street hockey. She wished that were the worst they were

disrupting. Summer calls made her instinctively wary. Too
many kids with empty time on their hands. More likely
they'd be upsetting a carjacking or a drug deal.

Anne winced again at her cynicism. She *did* need a break.
Unfortunately, she had bills to pay and a semester of school
to finish. Only then could she chuck this job and move
away—far, far away—from inner-city Minneapolis and its
ugliness. Maybe then she'd find a measure of peace and
safety, things she'd been praying for relentlessly for nearly
fifteen years.

She long ago stopped expecting God to answer.

"Three minutes, twenty-three seconds." Gary stated their
response time as he braked next to a quaint bungalow with
a fresh coat of baby blue paint. He parked behind a beat-up
green pickup with all its windows intact. "Go in. I'll get the
jump kit."

Anne blew out a breath, reined in her prejudice, and
leaped from the cab. A patient inside needed her help, and
she'd do well to focus on that.

The inner door of the bungalow hung open. Anne rapped
on the screen door. "Hello? Emergency medical personnel.
Anyone here?"

She waited three seconds, then jerked the door open. The
family room buzzed with an eerie silence. Two brown tweed
sofas, worn but clean, claimed much of the room, as did a
sprawling spider plant hanging from a green macramé
planter in the far corner. Anne called again, then stepped
onto the green shag carpet. Strange that no one had come to
meet them. Who had placed the call? Perhaps the woman
had called in her own symptoms.

Anne ventured farther, toward a short hallway. "Hello?"
No reply, save her own thundering heartbeat. The aroma of
supper cooking filled the house with an unusual hominess.
Her half-empty stomach twisted. She couldn't remember the
last time she'd eaten a home-cooked meal.

Gary pounded up the porch steps. "Where is she?"

"I'm not sure." Anne grasped a wobbly door handle

covered with several coats of paint and pushed the door open.

A large Native American woman, dressed elegantly in a lavender dress and cream-colored hose, lay on the bed. Her long gray hair fanned out over a floral pillow, but her pale face evidenced significant pain. Considering her size, she was primed for an angina attack. Anne's attention went to the linebacker-sized man holding a compress to the woman's forehead.

"I'm an emergency medical technician with the Minneapolis Fire Department." Anne directed her words to him, seeking consent. "Can I help?"

He stared at her, alarm glinting in his light brown eyes, a color unusual for someone of his Native American ancestry. A line of sweat dotted the man's forehead against his coal black hair pulled into a ponytail. Anne recognized the early signs of psychogenic shock and braced herself for refusal. It wasn't uncommon for family members to fear medical professionals or even faint at the sight of a loved one undergoing trauma. Especially in this part of town.

He raised his hand. "Stay back." His voice seemed pained.

Anne nodded and motioned for Gary to halt. Her partner's breath streamed over her neck. She couldn't place it, but something felt . . . wrong. Indeed, across from her, the man's broad chest under a gray army T-shirt rose and fell, as if fighting hidden emotions. The chiseled fierceness in his face and his bunched neck muscles told her he bridled a power that could easily explode from those tree-limb arms. Then he reached out to her with a piercing look, and she couldn't help but think he hoped to send her some sort of extrasensory message.

"My name's Anne. I just want to help." She took a step closer. "I'm not going to hurt her."

Then the woman's eyes shot open. The fear in their molasses brown depths froze Anne to the spot. The woman shook her head, her face twisted in panic. Or pain.

Anne unsnapped her belt kit and pulled out a pair of rubber gloves. "I want to check your heart, okay?"

Anne glanced at the man, who started to shake his head. She clenched her jaw. They didn't have time to coddle him. Judging by the patient's shallow, rapid breathing, the woman needed medical attention—now. Anne snapped on her gloves and removed her stethoscope from around her neck. Now that she'd identified herself, she had a legal responsibility to assist. Anne took another step, trying to communicate calm.

"No!" The man's deep cry made the flimsy walls shudder.

The woman started up on her elbows. Anne ignored the man and rushed to the patient, reeled in by her grimace of pain. But the woman's wretched gaze fixed past Anne, over her shoulder. Anne turned, and her heart caught in her throat.

"Anthony, no—," the old woman pleaded.

Anne couldn't wrench her stare off the scratched silver pistol nor the way it trembled in the teen's hand as he kicked shut the bedroom door. She fought her racing heartbeat. This wasn't the first handgun she'd faced.

"Calm down," Anne said, forcing her voice steady. She assessed his appearance and dread twisted her stomach at what she saw—fast breathing, sweat running over his wide cheekbones, and large, dark pupils in eyes that darted nervously around the room. She'd seen the signs of a drug user before, and this one was higher than the IDS building. She glanced at Gary, who stood frozen in the doorway. *Get out of here!* "This isn't about you," she whispered. "I'm just here to help this patient."

The teen twitched and fixed his weapon on Anne's chest, his eyes wide. Anne knew her words hadn't registered.

Although it happened in split seconds, a year later Anne remembered the next moments in glacier-flow slowness, in jerks and agonizing sensory bites.

"*No!*" A voice behind her thundered.

She froze. The teen cursed; the gun shook. A blur scraped across Anne's peripheral.

Gunshot. The sound shattered Anne's soul.

The man tackled the teen just as pain exploded through Anne's body, in crescendo with a heart-ripping scream.

Anne hit the floor.

Then the cold wash of darkness.

"'When peace like a river attendeth my way . . .'"

Singing wrestled Anne back to the living into the claws of searing agony. Her eyes burned under a bright light, and a blood-pressure cuff squeezed her arm. "What—?"

Gary's face came into view. "Stay still, Anne. You've been shot, and I'm taking your vitals before we transport you."

Her body felt on fire. "I hurt, Gary." She heard voices and the muffle of song and turned her head to search. Behind her, two uniforms subdued the teen, now cuffed and facedown on the carpet. His slurred curse words punched the air. She strained to focus on the undertone of the hymn, softly sung by a rich tenor.

"Ninety-five over sixty; we need to get her in—quickly." Gary muttered his assessment of her blood pressure, but Anne heard it and tensed.

"How badly am I hurt?"

Gary didn't answer. He opened her shirtsleeve and wrapped a tourniquet around her upper arm to establish an infusion line. Anne watched him work, recognizing the beads of perspiration over his pursed lips and the furrow in his brow as worry. His dark eyes occasionally went to hers, and she read in them everything she needed to know and more.

Panic pooled bitterness in her chest. *Oh, God, I'm not ready! There's so much more I wanted to do with my life!* If only her parents could see her now. She always knew, deep

in her heart, she'd die a gunshot victim in the Phillips neighborhood. The irony made her groan.

The singing seemed closer. "'. . . tho' trials should come, let this blest assurance control . . .'"

Gary held the drip bag over her head, and the cool liquid surged into her veins. The edge of pain softened. "Who's singing?"

Gary glanced over his shoulder. "Your hero."

Her eyelids bobbed. "Hero?"

"The man who tackled the shooter. The bullet nearly hit you chest high."

"Where am I hit?" It felt like her entire body had been shredded.

"Lower right. You'll never need an appendectomy." Gary attempted a smile but failed. She knew how he felt. If he'd entered the room first, she'd be the one administering the IV line and fighting guilt.

"She ready to move?" The gruff bass of fellow EMT David Nelson came from above her. "We're transporting Mrs. Peters right now."

"The woman with angina?" Her speech was thickening.

David squatted and touched her arm. "Someone wants to say hello."

He moved, and in his place appeared "her hero." His hand found hers and squeezed gently. But his eyes—honey brown, sweet with hope, and undulating with worry—fixed on her. She felt them reach out, along with his song, to comfort her. Ridiculous as that thought seemed, it made tears spring to her eyes. She smiled meekly. "You tried to warn me, didn't you?"

"You were awfully determined to help my mother." He brushed her hair from her forehead. His whisper-soft touch made her throat thick. "I'm sorry I didn't move quicker."

She must be drugged, Anne thought, for her eyes were glued to his face, taking in the stubble of dark whiskers along his jawline, his lustrous black hair, a small, intriguing round scar on his upper right cheekbone. Close up, a very masculine power radiated from him, mixing confusingly with the tender concern on his face. Topped off by a white smile, he'd turned . . . charmingly attractive.

She gulped. "You were singing?"

He rubbed her hand with his thumb. "It's a hymn. Can I sing it for you?"

She nodded as Gary moved into her line of vision. "No more talking." Her partner held up a non-rebreather oxygen mask and worked it over her head. The cold breath of 100 percent oxygen filled her nose and mouth. She closed her eyes.

She heard the tones of the low, melodic tenor, and though it was muffled under the hiss of the oxygen tank and the rattle of the stretcher, the effect seeped into her bones. It followed her as she was loaded onto the stretcher and toted out to the rig. She wasn't sure if he rode with her or if it was the memory of his voice, but even against the backdrop of the whining siren, she clung to his song, taking it with her as she sank into dark oblivion.

"For me be it Christ, be it Christ hence to live.
If Jordan above me shall roll.
No pang shall be mine, for in death as in life,
Thou shalt whisper Thy peace to my soul."

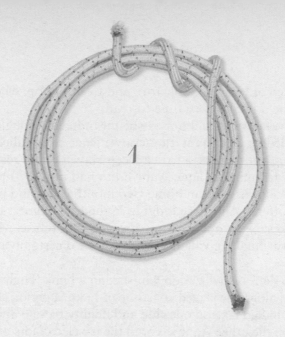

1

One Year Later

Anne Lundstrom turned down the opera music that swelled
through her Ford Explorer as she topped the hill overlook-
ing the town of Deep Haven. She'd waited half a lifetime
for this moment, and she'd start this new chapter in her life
listening to the waves of Lake Superior batter the shore and
the cries of complaining seagulls hanging on the breeze.

As she motored through the tourist town, she soaked in
the scenery. A donut stand, a dime store, and a rickety hotel
told her the town had advanced into the twenty-first century
with some reluctance. The log General Trading Store looked
like it might be worth checking out, and the Loon Café
reminded her of a 1950s soda fountain, with its specials
written on a sidewalk chalkboard. The rainbow-trout sign
dangling above Mack's Smoked Fish Stand made her
chuckle. Aunt Edith said her town had charm, and Anne
was beginning to believe her.

She made a mental note to stop in the bookstore. The
blooming peonies along the white porch and the cute little
tables on the veranda made her believe the sign on the door:

Footstep of Heaven Bookstore and Coffee Shop. Maybe here she'd finally have time to read.

Anne felt stress unknot as she meandered through town. She filled up at a gas station/convenience store called Mom and Pop's and was sad to see Deep Haven in her rearview mirror ten minutes later. Aunt Edith had moved "up the shore" into her dream home two months ago, and when she'd offered Anne free lodging in the vacant guest cabin on her lakeshore property, Anne just couldn't refuse. Maybe God was finally giving her a break. She'd certainly done her time.

The signs of civilization vanished in a blink. Highway 61 wound along the jagged coastline of Lake Superior, embraced by the indigo lake on one side and mighty balsam and birch trees on the other. Anne savored the jeweled colors of a sapphire lake, the turquoise sky, and emerald trees. Especially in this stretch of the world, God's master craftsmanship could never be denied.

Anne had healed remarkably since that terrifying afternoon a year ago, yet the scars remained on her body and her heart. The words of Spafford's hymn she'd heard that day still mocked and called to her in a way she couldn't comprehend. Perhaps her thirst for peace accounted for the way the hymn—and the singer—never strayed far from her thoughts.

Next to her, Bertha watched the gulls spiraling from the heavens in search of scraps. Anne rubbed the Saint Bernard's coarse hair. The brute cast her a sad, brown-eyed glance, as if to comment on her state of hunger. "I'm sorry, honey. We'll be there soon." Anne rubbed her behind the ears, grateful for the animal's company.

When she'd adopted the dog six months ago from the local shelter, Anne thought, Bertha's lumbering size and serious fang teeth gave her a measure of menace. Anne soon realized, with mixed emotions, that a juicy saliva bath was Bertha's only weapon. Still, having the animal around meant that Anne had someone waiting at home. Someone who would listen to her, love her unconditionally, keep her feet warm, and offer a sense of security. All the benefits of a husband and more. Bertha would never challenge her goals. Never require her to venture beyond her comfort zone and force her to abandon her own dreams. A dog would never ask Anne to make the sacrifices her father had asked of her mother.

Anne would relinquish the hold on her etched-out life for no man, regardless of her childish fantasies of romance and happily ever after. Yes, she had her dream hero—an unnamed tenor with golden brown eyes and long dark hair—but she had less than a one-percent chance he'd stumble back into her life. And, minus him, she felt pretty sure the man she wanted—a man of courage and strength with a burden to minister to the hurting—would suffocate in the safe cocoon she planned to build for herself in Deep Haven.

So, she had Bertha.

She checked her odometer and scanned the road for Aunt Edith's drive, 6.2 miles out of Deep Haven. As Anne moved up on four miles, she wondered if the hospital was close enough for a bicycle commute. She'd benefit from time inhaling the crisp, pine-scented air.

She'd just passed five clicks when the Explorer lurched, coughed, and sputtered out. It coasted noiselessly along the highway. Anne's pulse skipped a second before she thought to put the car into neutral. She tried to turn the engine over, but no life sparked from it. Anne groaned and turned the SUV onto the shoulder. *What now? C'mon, God. Gimme a break here.* She'd emptied her bank account to pay for gas for this trip and would survive on Club crackers until her first paycheck. All she needed were major car repairs.

After a moment of resting her forehead on the steering wheel, she trailed a hand through Bertha's fur, sighed, then popped the hood and got out. Thankfully, she'd chosen the right outfit for fixing her car—a pair of faded jeans and a University of Minnesota sweatshirt. However, although she could describe the human body down to the last corpuscle,

3

she had no idea how to unravel this mess under the open hood. *Now, where is the oil cap?*

The highway stretched out like a black ribbon east to west, completely void of vehicles save hers. Anne kicked a tire and threaded her hands into her newly cropped hair. Across the road, the wind combed the trees and reaped the fragrance of the June wildflowers. Behind her, the waves lapped the pearly shore. Well, at least it wasn't a horrible place to be stranded.

"Hello there! Need a hand?"

Anne whirled. Treading up the beach, spilling rocks under huge brown work boots, a man waved at her. From a distance, he looked large. Linebacker large.

"You broken down?"

Anne shoved her hands in her back pockets and took a deep breath, fighting the swell of her heartbeat. Every instinct screamed at her to dive into the car, lock it, and dial road service on her cell phone. If she were stuck on a lonely strip of I-94 outside Minneapolis, that would be a gut instinct, but out here, she doubted she'd find a signal on the Nokia in the glove compartment.

As the man walked along the ditch toward her, she measured him, watching the wind wrestle with a red baseball cap hitched backward on his head. He'd pushed the sleeves of his gray sweatshirt up past his elbows, revealing powerful tanned forearms, and his faded fatigues completed the look of unemployed mercenary out for a stroll. He held a bucket in one hand, as if he'd been hunting for clams. "What seems to be the trouble?"

She decided to chance it. After all, she'd left the city five hours ago and made a point of discarding her fears there also. Hadn't God given her this new beginning in Deep Haven? Even the town's name augmented the feeling of refuge and safety. "She coughed and died on me."

He joined her, set down the bucket, and placed one of his large hands on either side of the hood. Amazing how wide his reach was. Up close, he unnerved her with his size. Six

feet three with the stance of a fighter. She kept her distance and rubbed her arms, suddenly feeling cold.

"Spark-plug connections look okay." He jiggled a few wires. "This the only sign of trouble?" He looked at her over his shoulder.

She froze, gripped by his eyes. Golden brown, like sweet honey. She could only nod.

"Hmm." He turned back and her knees felt like cooked oatmeal. She'd seen those eyes before. They looked uncannily like the ones burned into her brain a year ago. She'd reenacted that day on Franklin Avenue a thousand times, trying to dissect her missteps, clinging to the memory of an unnamed tenor who'd spoken peace to her terrified heart. She'd memorized every nuance she'd seen in her hero's gaze, despite the brevity of the moment. Those deep liquid eyes had seen her deepest fears, had comforted in her darkest hour.

Certainly those same beautiful eyes couldn't belong to this muscled beachcomber. Anne shook away the comparison and focused on her wounded engine. "I filled up with gas in Deep Haven."

"At M&P's?" His playful grimace threw her and she nodded warily. "You're not from around here, are you?"

"Nope."

"That's it. Plugged fuel filter. Mom and Pop's have a . . . reputation. I'd steer clear of their gas near the end of the month. They sell great apple butter, however. It's homemade." He was already unscrewing a greasy cylinder.

"Is it fatal?" Anne couldn't believe something the size of a battery could render her Explorer helpless.

"The apple butter?" He tapped the filter against her fender, and she saw chips of grime break free. "No, I don't think the butter is near as fatal as the gas."

She stared at him, blinking. A smirk edged up his rugged face. She noticed how it wrinkled a small round scar high on his cheek. She swallowed hard, her thoughts racing ahead of her, pumping her heartbeat on high. He didn't seem to notice her white-knuckled grip on the hood as her world tilted crazily.

Her hero, the one who'd edged her dreams for over a year, couldn't possibly be this unkempt beach bum.

"If you pick up dirty gas, it'll plug your filter." He put the cylinder to his lips and blew. More grime flew out.

Anne made a face. No, definitely not. The man who had held her hand with such impossible tenderness couldn't be this rough-edged Joe Mechanic.

"That should do it." He wiped his lips on his shirt, then replaced the filter. "Fire her up."

Anne stood rooted, eyes on his black hair sneaking out from the baseball cap. And something in his voice resonated . . .

She climbed in the SUV. "Here goes!" The engine turned over on the first crank. She hopped out as he lowered the hood. "Thank you so much."

"I was just in the right place at the right time." He smiled, and it was so warm her stomach did a small, rebellious flip. "You just passing through?"

Anne shook her head, scrambling to find her voice. "I'm staying with my aunt for the summer while I finish my internship at the Deep Haven Hospital." And in the meantime she'd pray that God would find her a full-time position in this quaint, safe community. Someplace to bury her fears, her past, and live a life of peace.

"Doctor?"

"No." She toed the dirt, unable to meet his unsettling eyes. "Nurse. I'm getting my master's in community nursing."

"Like teaching young inner-city mothers how to take care of their babies?"

Anne scowled. "No, more like administering immunizations to families in remote locations. The last thing I want to do is dive back into the city and its problems. No way." A thousand wild horses, elephants, and dogs couldn't drag her back to the nightmares awaiting in Minneapolis. In fact,

she had doubts that even the three hundred miles between Deep Haven and the Twin Cities would be a safe enough distance for her.

He went silent, and when she chanced a look at him, the pained expression on his face jolted her. "I'm sorry to hear that."

She frowned. "Is that why you're here, combing the beach for—" she peered into his bucket—"rocks?"

He laughed, and light reentered his eyes. "It's a project I'm working on."

"Do you live here?"

"Sometimes." He picked up the bucket. "I hope you find what you're looking for here. Deep Haven isn't just a pretty place. It's more than it seems."

"Right." She patted the hood of her Explorer. "Full of all sorts of surprises. I'll stay clear of Mom and Pop's."

He backed away from her vehicle. "Maybe I'll see you around."

She opened her door. "Hopefully it won't be because I'm in the ditch. Thanks again . . ."

"Noah." He gripped the bucket with both hands.

The look on his face—tender concern, friendliness, and not a little naturally etched fierceness—glued her to the spot. Somehow she took his hand, and the gentleness in it threw her pulse into overdrive. She smiled at him, wrenching herself free of the memory that gripped her. Besides, although he was tan, with coal dark hair sneaking out from under his cap, this man didn't look like he had a touch of Native American blood in him.

"Noah Standing Bear."

Anne yanked her hand out of his grasp. Wide-eyed, she dove into the cab and, without another word, peeled away.

Noah scowled at the suspicion written across the lady's face as she drove away and disappeared around a curve.

Destroying fears was why he'd come to Deep Haven, why he'd begged and cajoled every little church from Minneapolis on north for funds, why he'd invested his life in reaching kids with the gospel. The hope of breaking stereotypes had him beachcombing for smooth, paintable rocks, praying with every step about tonight's meeting, that the missions committee might also embrace that hope.

Unfortunately, as a youth he'd deserved every one of those fearful glances. Growing up a foster child—and a Native American one at that—had molded his character quickly. He'd learned that life gave only what you took—by force. Noah cringed, remembering his years wasted with the Vice Lords, or "the People," fighting for gang turf, lying, and stealing. Somehow he'd steered clear of drugs, but he'd managed to rack up a list of sins that would make a convict flinch.

By the grace of God, those days were not only forgiven, they were obliterated. And every tomorrow God gave Noah would be used to fight for the lives of the next generation of gangbangers. This time, he battled with the power of God behind him. If only he could convince the church of the righteousness of this war. If he didn't fight for the discarded kids on the streets, who would?

Life in the city hardened people on the outside, creating a crust so deep that breaking through it took the patience of St. Francis and the force of a jackhammer. But Noah had had enough victories as a youth pastor to keep him dreaming the impossible. Hope kept him hanging in the hood, drove him to knock on church doors asking for donations. Most of all, it sent him to his knees until he'd worn out more than a few pairs of fatigues. God could change lives; he knew it from personal experience. He was this close to fulfilling his dream of taking these at-risk kids to his wilderness camp. And he dearly hoped that God had handpicked him as the right man for the job.

Noah was painfully aware that he still looked like a hoodlum, a fact confirmed by the fear written on the young lady's countenance. She was beautiful, with her cropped auburn hair and heart-shaped face. Too bad she had a chip the size of Alaska on her shoulder, a protective, stay-on-your-side-of-the-street wariness, and a formidable dog sitting in the passenger seat that gave her attitude bite and muscle.

Thankfully, looks of unmasked prejudice like the one she had just given him had forged a bullheadedness in him that God could use. Nevertheless, it hurt to have someone stare at him that way . . . especially someone with such paralyzingly beautiful hazel green eyes. When she gave him that wide-eyed look, as if she'd seen a ghost, he nearly forgot his own name, and it had ignited a ludicrous protective impulse to give her an encouraging hug.

A breeze lifted the hair sticking out of his baseball cap and chilled him. He swallowed hard. No doubt if he'd even hinted at approaching her, she'd have deployed a defensive maneuver and taken out his front teeth. She had the appearance of a tiger cat in pounce position.

He couldn't ignore the disappointment pinching his chest. He had dreams that one day God might drop into his life a woman with guts, strength, and a spiritual vision. But that would take a serious miracle, and such a woman certainly wouldn't resemble the lady who just floored it out of his life. A woman like that, clean and honest and untainted by a wicked past, would never see beyond his exterior to a redeemed man who loved God. In these moments, the reminder of who he'd been—and in many ways still strived to be for the sake of the gospel—stung.

Noah scrambled back down to the beach. Deep Haven Hospital, she'd said. He wondered if she'd be working for Doc Simpson.

He resumed his hunt for large smooth rocks. He doubted the city kids had ever thought to make sculptures with rocks before. Usually the stones were used as missiles. But that was what Wilderness Challenge was all about—confronting stereotypes about life, offering a vision beyond the kids' concrete boundaries to what God might have in store for them.

Hadn't God also challenged Noah's boundaries with this wild idea? Start a summer camp for inner-city kids, God had said to him through his quiet time three years ago. He'd been happy in his life as a youth pastor. Happy hanging out on Franklin Avenue, yanking kids off the street and into church. He'd dismissed the camp idea as a delusion.

Then he'd seen his drugged neighbor blow away an EMT. He'd personally led Anthony to Jesus a week before the attack. But the teen hadn't been able to escape the street's death clutch and see his potential. That potential now languished in adult lockup.

Grief had crystallized Noah's mission. A year later now, he was just shy of all the funding needed to take his former youth group out of the city for the summer and give them a fresh perspective through a wilderness challenge.

The enormity of the task—and the need—made Noah sink to his knees on the beach. *Oh, God, only You can pull this off. You put this vision in my heart. Please make it happen.*

He sat back onto the rocks and looked into the sky. A light wind played with a wispy scattering of cirrus clouds. On the waves, closer to the horizon, seagulls rode Superior like buoys. The air smelled wet, and the breeze washed through him like a cool breath. God embedded this place. Noah prayed that the kids could see Him. *Give them Your vision. Your hope. Change their lives. And please help Deep Haven Chapel see You through this former gang member with ancestors who happen to be Ojibwa.*

Three hours later Noah paced the annex of the church building, trying to focus on his prayer and not the muffled voices spilling out from under the library door. His hiking boots clunked on the floor, and he winced at a black streak they left across the white linoleum. Why didn't he think of buying a suit for the occasion? He'd thought he looked spiffy enough in black jeans, boots, and a brown suede jacket. He'd even unearthed an iron and pressed the white oxford he wore with a tie. Looking into his cracked bathroom mirror hanging in the dilapidated cabin he called home, he'd seemed suitable.

He combed his fingers through his hair. The shortest he'd worn it in years and *still* the two women on the missions committee scrutinized him the entire meeting as if he'd crawled out from under a Dumpster. He blew out a heated breath and deliberately peered out the foyer windows at Main Street. Tourist season had bloomed. A number of pickups loaded with nets and tackle lumbered by. It made him think he ought to learn to fish. A couple of lovebirds meandered hand in hand along the beach, kicking up stones. A trail of white smoke spiraled from Mack's Fish Stand.

"Noah?"

The friendly voice startled him. He turned and clasped Pastor Dan's outstretched hand. The man always wore a kind smile, and he'd donated an entire day at the camp, helping Noah pitch army tents. If anyone in Deep Haven cheered for him, it was Pastor Dan Matthews.

"So?" Noah studied Dan's face and braced himself.

Dan shook his head. "I'm sorry. The committee thinks it's a liability. Kids inherently possess their own set of troubles, but these kids . . ."

Noah clenched his jaw. "These kids need it more than any others."

"There's no disputing that—"

"I've got a great staff trained to work with these at-risk kids, plus junior counselors who know exactly the shenanigans they're liable to pull. I've sent them all through hours upon hours of counselor training, besides training each of them as a first responder." Noah shook his head. "Frankly, I think we're more than ready for what these kids will throw at us."

"I'm sure you are, Noah. No one believes in you and what you're trying to do more than I do. I've seen the hours you've put in, and I know you spent hours praying and handpicking your staff. But be honest, besides the everyday accidents that happen at camp, you want to take the kids backpacking and canoeing. What if you had a medical emergency while you're out on the trail?" Dan's tone turned grim. "What if somebody died?"

Noah cupped a hand behind his head and sighed. "You're my last bid, Dan. Without the church's additional funding, I gotta tell those kids to fend for themselves this summer." His throat burned. "I can't do that."

"I know." Dan clapped him on the shoulder. "And I couldn't be sorrier. But it's not my money. The church doesn't want to invest in something that might blow up in their faces."

"What if I got a camp nurse or a paramedic to serve on staff?"

Dan's silence stretched out until disappointment tightened Noah's heart. Noah looked away, unwilling to see the answer on his friend's face.

"That might work."

Noah gulped a spurt of hope.

"No promises, but I can ask." Dan crossed his arms. "This camp is a great idea, Noah. But I can only give a recommendation. It's the committee you have to convince. Get a paramedic or a nurse. Someone with serious emergency training. Then we'll talk." His eyes glinted, matching his sly smile. "Meanwhile, I'll go sand some grit off their tough hides."

"Thank you, Dan." Noah scrubbed his hands down his face and turned back to the window. Where was he going to unearth a nurse?

He walked outside and stood in the parking lot. The fragrant air bespoke hope and promise. Lake Superior glinted deep sapphire, and the setting sun ran a finger of gold along its choppy surface. A black Labrador barked from the back of a pickup truck, catching Noah's attention as it traveled down the street. The truck turned into Mom and Pop's and pulled up in front of a gas pump.

He looked heavenward and smiled.

2

Anne leaned against the rail of the guest-cabin porch and let the wind skimming off Lake Superior dry her freshly washed hair. The sun bled purple over a gray horizon and lit a bronze path across the giant lake. A lone seagull called overhead, in harmony with the waves pounding the shoreline rocks.

"Magnificent." Anne cupped her hands around her teacup. "You're right, Aunt Edith. I love the place."

"I knew you would, honey." Aunt Edith's voice came from inside the cabin, where she banged about in the galley kitchen. "I had you in mind when Bruce fixed up the cabin. I know it's a bit small—"

"It's perfect." The two-room cabin seemed palatial after her efficiency off-campus apartment. And if she caught cabin fever, with one step she could lose herself in the expanse of God's forested world. Anne sipped her tea— Constant Comment, with a touch of orange and cinnamon and a dab of milk. "My mother would love it."

Edith appeared at the door. "If I could ever get my sister up here. But she won't take time away from the mission."

"I know." Anne gave a wry smile. "After Dad's death,

it's become her entire life. I barely talked her into attending my graduation." She swirled her tea. "It felt surreal, anyway, since I have another quarter of internship left."

Edith opened the screen door. It squealed, bristling the hair on Anne's neck. She gazed at the sunset as Edith's arm wrapped around her shoulders and enveloped her with the smells of cookies and cotton and something Anne could only describe as love. She leaned into the hug.

"Your mother needs a break."

Anne harrumphed. "She can't escape Dad's 'unfinished work.'" She shook her head. "How hard can it be to shut the door to the church basement, sell the house, and head south to Arizona? If she really cared about me and Ellen, she'd ditch the inner city and let us sleep a night in peace."

Aunt Edith stayed silent. Anne knew her own words sounded harsh. But after her father's accidental death under the wheels of a drunk driver's car, she and her sister thought MaryAnn Lundstrom would have the good sense to throw in the ministry towel, cash her life insurance check, and buy a home somewhere that didn't host regular drive-by shootings. Maybe not Arizona, but perhaps in the Minneapolis suburbs or in Deep Haven near Aunt Edith.

Aunt Edith represented the gentle voice of reason and had spent countless summers harboring Anne and Ellen in her home in Minnetonka, a Minneapolis suburb located a satisfactory distance from the homeless shelter the Lundstroms operated. Now ten years after Aunt Edith and Uncle Maynard had moved to Deep Haven, she'd come through to rescue Anne again.

"When do you start at the hospital?"

"I have an appointment with Dr. Simpson Monday morning. He'll be supervising my internship. He didn't mention payment, but I'm hoping a stipend comes with the job." She didn't add that she also had her sights on the job of community nurse. Aunt Edith, her sensitive thumb on the pulse of the community, had told her that Jenny someone, current job holder, had supposedly entertained plans to retire—a timely event in Anne's opinion. Anne hoped that if she impressed the board with her internship skills, she could slide right into that position. It might not be the cutting-edge ministry her father had wished for her, but it felt close. One didn't need to live in the thick of crime and violence to bless the lives of one's fellowman.

"I'm sure Dr. Simpson will figure out something. He's a nice man. You'll like him."

Anne didn't doubt Aunt Edith's opinion even though the doctor had sounded brusque on the phone. Aunt Edith had a decade of Deep Haven experience in her corner. Anne hummed agreement.

"He attends our church," Aunt Edith continued, "and has a raspberry patch half the size of Lake Superior. His wife, Naomi, puts up hundreds of jars of jam and sells them at that new bookstore in town."

"The Something of Heaven place I saw on the way in? With the flowers along the porch?"

Edith smiled, the lines around her eyes wrinkling. "The Footstep of Heaven. You'd like the proprietor. She's a lot like you. Feisty and determined."

Anne playfully jabbed her aunt.

"Her name's Mona, and her husband is a best-selling author."

"Really? What does he write, books on how to smoke fish?" Anne chortled at her own humor.

"It's Reese Clark."

"Oh." Anne winced. "The Jonah series." The series about a drifter named Jonah was one of her bedtime favorites. "He lives here?"

Edith's eyes twinkled. "Yep. But his name's really Joe. And he has a brother who lives up the trail at a home for the mentally challenged. It's a strawberry farm."

Anne quirked an eyebrow. "What other secrets are hidden in Deep Haven?"

"I'll never tell." Edith patted her arm. "Why don't you come to church with us Sunday? Mona and Joe Michaels attend, and you'll get a chance to meet Dr. Simpson before your interview on Monday."

The wind rustled a nearby balsam. Anne shivered. She wasn't quite ready to dive into the social life of Deep Haven, even if corporate worship did speak to a lonely place in her soul. For the near future, she'd worship on the Lake Superior shore, thanking God for a time of rest.

Anne measured her aunt. Edith had aged so beautifully, with soft laugh lines around her eyes and mouth and a lush mane of gray. The elderly woman made a jade green leisure suit look like a fashion statement. Edith stared out toward the lake, a fresh breeze combing her hair from her face.

"This is a beautiful place to retire." Anne had to admire the house Aunt Edith and Uncle Maynard had built. The two-story, white-pine A-frame sat at the lot's pinnacle. One could survey the lake through its floor-to-ceiling windows. Anne stored away the effect in her dream files for future use. It was the type of place she could easily hide herself in—and planned to someday.

"After years of looking at the lake from this porch, it seemed time to build something bigger." Aunt Edith's smile faded. "Are you sure the cabin isn't too rustic?"

Anne settled into a folding lawn chair and pulled her legs up to her chest. "I love the guest cabin, and I love you, Aunt Edith."

Her aunt gave her a smile that made Anne blush. "I just hope you can find your footing and escape some of those demons."

Anne nodded. If she couldn't do it here, she never would.

The older woman waddled up the trail toward her home. Anne sipped her tea. The spicy liquid went straight to her bones. Oh, how she'd longed for just this moment. She'd clung to it like a bulldog during her three months in rehab, rebuilding her strength after the bullet had ripped out half her insides. She had one less kidney and a scar that meant she'd never wear a bikini. Skimpy swimwear had never been her attire of choice; nevertheless, it felt like one more thing the drugged-up punk had stolen from her. If it hadn't been for that fateful afternoon, she would have graduated with her nursing class in December. Bitterness filled her throat and she swallowed it back down to her chest, where it simmered. Yes, perhaps here she could escape the inner city and its painful tentacles.

I'm sorry to hear that. The words of a stranger came back to her like a cold splash. She narrowed her eyes. What would he know? Did he live with the scars of someone else's sins on his body? Anne shook so violently, she sloshed tea onto the cuff of her sweatshirt.

She put the cup on the rail of the porch and clenched her fists against the image of his piercing brown eyes. The look he gave her still made her tremble. She couldn't shake the familiarity of those eyes . . . and his name, Something Running Bear, had rattled her. Certainly he couldn't be the same man who'd sung a hymn of comfort to her as she descended into months of suffering?

She hated to admit how much that hymn had meant to her. The memory of the man who'd held her hand tugged her mouth up in a soft smile. Now there was a real hero. A man who could replace Bertha without a second's hesitation. A man brimming with faith, ready to risk his life for her. She felt a twist of sadness that she'd never been able to track him down. To thank him, of course.

Obviously not all strangers were drug-crazed murderers. Take her newest stranger, for example. The hero-mechanic with the mysterious eyes who had helped get her car back on the road with nary a rude remark or advance on her turf.

It had been ages since she'd lowered her guard with a man. She'd learned the hard way that men wanted one thing . . . something she wouldn't offer. Her chest tightened, and she fought a horde of bad memories. Perhaps it was only certain men, from certain walks of life. She cast another look at the horizon, appreciating the deep crimson separating day from night. She'd sorely missed perfect sunsets—those unblemished by a choppy metal-and-concrete skyline, smog, and the noise of rush-hour traffic.

Anne's tea had turned cold, and she made a face as she swallowed. Easing herself off the chair, she returned to the small kitchen and lit the burner under the teakettle. She leaned against the counter and flipped on her CD player. Andrea Bocelli's operatic tenor filled the cabin. She felt her pulse slow. Quiet moments with a cup of tea and serious music were what this move was all about. A new life, a new start with God. The chance to escape the specter of the past and finally make peace with the Almighty. She wouldn't deny she'd felt abandoned over the past year. God had seemed painfully absent in her tragedy—a grief of her own making. She couldn't get past the feeling of heavenly betrayal to turn into His embrace.

She feared she never would.

Obviously God wasn't keeping score because He had intervened, offered this job and this place of refuge. *Thanks, God.* She folded her arms across her chest. *I needed this, and You knew it.* Tears edged her eyes and she flicked them away.

If only she could hide inside this moment for eternity.

Noah parked his Suzuki 350 next to a gleaming silver Lexus and secured his helmet to the seat. He still wasn't accustomed to leaving the bike or the helmet unattended, but he'd been stretching his trust boundaries since arriving here. Moments like this reminded him that Deep Haven was worlds apart from the inner city of Minneapolis.

He pocketed the keys and swiped both hands through his hair. Common sense demanded he wear a helmet, but he cringed at his rumpled hair reflected in the glass entry doors. He tried in vain to smooth it down, to match it with the suit and tie and mask his biker guise. He hoped Doc

Simpson was a man of good humor. And compassion. And he prayed the man kept Saturday hours.

The ER lobby hosted a kid in a baseball shirt clutching an ice pack to his eye and an elderly gentleman with a bloody towel wrapped around his thumb. Noah grimaced at a fishhook poking from the appendage.

A redheaded duty nurse with curious blue eyes watched as he approached the desk. Noah tried a smile. "Hi. I'm looking for Dr. Simpson."

"Just a moment, please." Her gaze ran over him like a cop's as she picked up the phone. "Hello, Dr. Simpson, there's a . . ." She raised her eyebrows at Noah.

"Noah Standing Bear," he filled in.

"Mr. Standing Bear here to see you."

Noah kept the smile on his face as she nodded, then clipped out directions. He felt her eyes on his back as he strode down the hall.

The stew of antiseptic, cotton, and food baking in the cafeteria made his stomach clench. Something about hospitals always made him woozy. He nodded a greeting to a dark-haired man ambling toward the exit, toting a bulging duffel bag, as if leaving the hospital after a year. He guessed that feeling of freedom rivaled the one he'd experienced when he'd walked out of prison.

Noah followed a worn trail down brown carpet, noting the few aerial photographs depicting the growth of Deep Haven on the walls. The lighthouse on the point had obviously been one of the town's first buildings.

Dr. Simpson waited outside his office door and stretched out his hand in greeting two paces before Noah clasped it. His long face curved into a wrinkled smile, and the warmth of his green eyes immediately slowed Noah's pulse down a notch. "What brings you to Deep Haven Municipal Hospital, Noah?"

"My camp, sir." He followed Dr. Simpson into the office. The window was open and faced an empty, weedy field. An overhead fan mixed the office air with fragrant forest smells—pine, wildflowers, mossy dirt. Noah lowered himself into a wooden straight-back chair while Dr. Simpson settled into a creaky metal rolling chair from the sixties. Over the doctor's head, a trophy rainbow trout sprang from a mount, and Noah could almost feel the breath from the moose head hanging high behind his chair. He noticed a rough-hewn statue of a bear in the corner and recognized the work of a local wood-carver, a man talented with a chain saw.

Noah gulped, hard. "I need some help."

Simpson clasped his hands on a tattered blotter. "Wilderness Challenge, right?"

Noah blinked. "Right. How'd you know?"

"Dan and I have been praying about it for some time. Men's Bible study."

Noah kneaded a neck muscle. "We can sure use those prayers. I've got a place to stay, tents over our head, staff and a full roster, but I'm short funds to feed them."

"How can I help?"

Noah took a deep breath. "I need a nurse."

Dr. Simpson quirked a brow. "So, hire one."

Noah studied his weathered hands. "With what money? I need someone willing to work for free, someone who has emergency training."

Dr. Simpson pursed his lips. "I don't know how to help you, son."

Noah rested his hands on his thighs and let the silence stretch out.

"Unless . . ." Dr. Simpson leaned back and folded his arms across his white lab coat. "I have a young lady on her way here, due to finish her internship in community nursing. She has some EMT experience . . ."

Noah looked up and kept his voice even. "Yes?"

"Maybe I could assign her to you for the summer. If she wants to do rural nursing, a stint in the wilderness would only add to her resume." He narrowed his eyes at Noah. "But something tells me you already knew this."

Noah looked out the window. A deer had crept out from the clasp of forest. Noah stilled, watching it. "I think I met her yesterday on the road. Her car broke down."

"Anne Lundstrom."

"Pretty brunette, a dangerous amount of attitude. She mentioned she was doing an internship here this summer."

"And you saw an opportunity."

"No. I saw an open door and I'm walking through it."

Dr. Simpson nodded, his eyes hard on Noah. "I don't want her getting hurt."

"I'll take care of her."

The doctor's mouth tweaked into a smile. "She doesn't give the impression of one wanting to be taken care of."

Noah matched the doctor's grin. "I caught that." He edged forward in the seat. "Listen, she's perfect for the job. And if I can get her on board, I might be able to get the funding I need. It'll change these kids' lives; I guarantee it." He winced at the urgency in his voice, but he was willing to surrender a little pride for the sake of the kids.

The whir of the ceiling fan filled the silence. Noah met Dr. Simpson's gaze and read in it the compassion he'd prayed for.

"Go back to the board. Tell them you got your nurse."

The moonlight had turned the highway silver. Noah longed to pull off his helmet, let the wind sing in his ears and scrape cold fingers through his hair. Instead, it billowed through his leather jacket. His suit coat and tie were neatly rolled up in his saddlebag. He should have hightailed it back to camp after his meeting, but he'd let joy drive him straight to Pastor Dan's office. The price of strangulation in a monkey suit was worth it. He'd earned the probational camp funding.

He gunned the engine and popped a wheelie. Only God could have put together today's events. It was no small miracle that he'd met the answer to his problems while rock hunting and praying his way across the beach yesterday.

And an attractive answer at that. He easily conjured up her tentative smile and the needy, shocked look in her eyes when he offered to help. He had to admit, he was looking forward to the opportunity to erase the fear he'd seen on her face. *If* he could erase it. He'd avoided women long enough to have grown rusty in the charm area. Not that he'd ever had much, but there'd been a day, long ago, when he'd found it easy, perhaps *too* easy, to sweet-talk a lady. He cringed at the recollection. Anne Lundstrom wasn't that kind of woman, and he certainly wouldn't be sweet-talking her into anything.

But maybe he could change her opinion of inner-city kids. And he meant every syllable when he'd told Doc Simpson he'd take care of her. Nothing would happen to Miss Lundstrom on his watch.

He couldn't stop a bubble of pleasure from leaking out into a song. "'What a friend we have in Jesus . . .'" The motor and wind ate his words, but his soul danced to the music.

Noah rounded a bend just as a dark, hulking shape dashed across the road. Slamming on his brakes, he felt his bike skid. From somewhere in his periphery, he heard a scream, then throaty barks that thundered into his brain.

Fire ripped up his leg as the bike slid toward the shoulder. He gritted his teeth and held on to the machine, praying he wouldn't crush the figure paralyzed in the ditch. The bike turned and threw him off. He tumbled into the grassy gutter.

He lay in stunned silence under the canopy of stars, hearing only the labored gasps from his own body.

"Are you hurt?" A feminine voice, rushing toward him. Feet thumped down into the ditch. "Lie still."

He groaned and propped up on one elbow. Except for an agonizing burn on his calf, he seemed unbroken.

"I said, lie still. You might have a broken bone." She crouched next to him and ran a hand down his arm.

Noah shrugged her off. "I've been hurt worse than this, lady. Calm down."

"You almost killed me."

Noah's mouth hung open as he stared at Anne Lundstrom. Sweatshirt hood up and dressed for exercise, her gaze surveyed him, not yet registering recognition. He swallowed and dredged up his voice. "Something ran across the street." He worked off his helmet.

Anne sat back hard on her heels, mouth agape. Utter horror swept her expression. "You!"

In emphasis, a beast the size of a horse tackled him.

"Agh! Get away!" Noah pushed at hair—everywhere hair—and a slimy tongue licking his ear.

"Bertha, down. No!" Anne somehow hauled the animal off him.

Rescued, Noah sprawled in the grass, gathering his wits. When this lady invaded a man's life, she left no room to breathe.

"Sorry about that." She squatted beside him, restraining her brute. "Are you okay?"

He gave a small smile. "We meet again."

"Are you following me?" Anger edged her voice.

"Hardly." He couldn't bear to admit he'd not only tracked her down, but would be her quasi boss for the next two months. She'd probably deck him into the dirt. "I was driving home. What are you doing in the middle of the road?"

She glared at him. "I was on the shoulder, and you were speeding."

Irritation made the hazel in her eyes shine like gold. He tore his gaze away and examined the scrape on his leg. Luckily, his jeans had given first.

"You have a mild abrasion. You should get it cleaned and dressed."

He had to smile at the warm concern in her voice. The

hardened street kids would melt in a second. Never mind what it was doing to him. "How's my bike?"

Hopping up, he groaned at the surge of pain that spasmed his leg. She gripped his elbow, as if to help him. The Suzuki lay on its side ten feet away in the middle of the road. Noah hobbled over, hoisted the bike up, and wheeled it to the shoulder. "I think she'll live." He didn't mention the dozen or so dents the bike had acquired over the years.

"I live just down the road. Let me get my truck and drive you into town. A doctor should look at that, Mr. . . . um, Running Bear." The wind had yanked off her hood, and now her hair shone bronze in the moonlight, tiny wisps dancing about her face. She was short enough to tuck under his arm, but her presence—the way she stood with her hands on her hips, the jut of her chin, and the tenacity in her eyes—made him feel small.

He searched for his voice. "*Standing* Bear. But you can call me Noah."

"Well, *Noah*, you're certainly not going anywhere until you get bandaged up."

"I don't—," he started, then stopped at the cool arch of her brow. Obviously, arguing would only earn him more trouble. Besides, compliance might be a good way to let her in on their future association. He swung a leg over the bike and jump-started it. The motor churned the air and coughed up dirt.

She made a face.

"Hop on. I'll drive you home."

He couldn't help but wince at the fear that leapt into her eyes.

They'd not only found him; they'd sent a watchdog.

He'd sat in his car and watched the flesh-and-blood Doberman roar out of the parking lot on his terror machine. It sent a chill of pure fear dripping down his spine.

Here, of all places, he thought he'd be able to hide.

And finish his business.

But they'd found him and sent a thug to hound him. A pair of biceps and a mangy face to never let him forget that they owned him. At least until he scraped up what they wanted. What they'd already paid for.

Did they think he couldn't see through the man's facade? Camping director? He wasn't stupid. The guy looked like a recent escapee from the projects.

He blew out a breath and ran a hand through his short, sweaty hair. His stomach growled but it wasn't food he needed.

Not right now.

He'd survive for a year on pure freedom if he could find a way to get his hands on it. Permanently.

Trust wasn't a high value in this business, but he'd guaranteed them—especially when they pointed a Glock two inches from his nose—that he'd make good on their deal.

Then again, it had taken them nearly a month to find him. A month clear of shadows and death threats, four glorious weeks absent of panic in every footstep. He hoped to stay AWOL until he unraveled his mess and arranged his escape.

How was he supposed to finish the deal with a shadow nipping at him?

He tapped his manicured fingers against the steering wheel, watching the greedy gulls swoop out of the sky, screaming, fighting for scraps of meat. He knew how they felt. Desperate. Hungry.

Who would have thought fifteen years ago that he'd land in the exact pit from which he'd spent his childhood scrabbling to escape? He'd learned—back then at the gritty age of sixteen when he finally summoned the guts to swing back—that there was only one way to survive a sound beating from the bullies, the Dobermans of life.

Strike first.

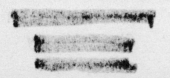

3

Anne paced the hospital corridor, wearing a trail through the brown carpet. She had memorized the pictures on the wall, finished off an orange juice, and even made friends with the duty nurse down the hall, Sandra. Anne liked her. Something about a woman in her mid-forties still wearing her blonde hair in braids and adding a pink chamois shirt over her uniform resonated a chord of kinship in Anne. Wanting to fit into the local dress code, she had briefly considered returning home to change out of the black suit pants and silk blouse, but she didn't want to miss Dr. Simpson when he actually showed up.

She returned to the small lobby and perched on a vinyl chair.

Sandra looked up from her desk. "I can't imagine what is keeping him." She glanced at the clock. "He knows you have an appointment."

Anne forced a smile. Perhaps in the backwoods time ran like cold syrup. She smoothed her hands over the manila folder she held on her lap. Of course he already had a copy of her transcripts, but the write-up she'd received from her last supervisor couldn't hurt his impression. Especially if she wanted to earn the freedom to stretch her wings and explore her new hometown.

Community nursing meant meeting needs, something she supposed she'd inherited from her parents. But unlike them, she wouldn't dive into the cesspool of the inner city, hoping to heal the homeless and the drug addicts. No, her sphere of influence would be tamer—the homebound elderly, educational services, perhaps humanitarian assistance on a local Indian reservation. She hoped the closest thing she'd come to a drug addict would be someone who overdosed on Peanut M&M's.

"I'm sorry, Sandra."

Anne looked up to see a tall man breeze past her. His blue windbreaker hung open, and he thumped down the hall in hiking boots.

Sandra rose and started to follow him but stopped when he reached the end office and slammed the door shut. She whirled, and silence hung from her open mouth. Anne frowned.

"That was Dr. Simpson." Sandra cleared her throat. "I'll inform him you're here."

Anne watched the nurse creep down the hall, knock on the door, and poke her head in.

"Go ahead, Anne," Sandra said when she returned. But her face had lost a shade of color.

Anne's heart hammered. She somehow made it to her feet. She fought to hear Aunt Edith's positive assessment of the good doctor above the cacophony of doubts. She shuffled down the hall and licked her lips as she stood outside the door. It was open a crack.

Inside, Dr. Simpson was talking on the phone. He motioned for her to enter. "I want to keep it under our hats for now," he said, "but you should know the situation, Sam."

Anne sat on the edge of a straight-backed chair, taking in her surroundings. She hid her revulsion at the sight of a fish, its jagged teeth bared, mounted on a block of wood. Books

had been crammed into a floor-to-ceiling bookshelf and piled atop a filing cabinet. A rickety coat tree laden with two sweaters, a white lab coat, a down jacket, and a compact umbrella looked dangerously near collapse, and a rather coarse carving of a bear inhabited the corner. She turned and nearly died of fright at the sight of a moose mounted above her, dripping fur onto the back of her neck. She scooted her chair forward.

"Thanks for your assistance, Sam. We'll be in touch." Dr. Simpson hung up the telephone and smiled at Anne. "Sorry to keep you waiting, Miss Lundstrom." He reached across the desk and offered his hand. She found it warm and gentle. "We had a hospital situation I had to deal with."

Anne felt her pulse slow. "No problem. I met Sandra."

"She's the glue that keeps this place together." Dr. Simpson pulled a manila file folder from a tall stack on his desk. "Dr. Meyers sent your transcripts and evaluation. She speaks highly of you."

"She's been a big support." Dr. Roberta Meyers was a prime reason Anne had stayed in the nursing program after her injury. It took a woman with experience fighting for a place in the medical society to pull Anne back to the land of the living. Anne would never forget the sight of Roberta's chocolate brown hand holding hers when she'd awoken from surgery.

"You've made a remarkable recovery, Miss Lundstrom." He put down the folder. "But I have to wonder why you chose to finish your internship here. Dr. Meyers expresses regret at losing you."

Anne folded her hands on her lap. "I'm just looking for a change. I did my time in the city, and I need some fresh air." She smiled. "I am hoping Deep Haven has some to share. And, frankly, I'm hoping to make my stay here . . . permanent." She hoped he could read between the lines to her desire for a full-time job.

Dr. Simpson quirked a brow. "I see." He looked out the

window. "How do you feel about spending some time at a camp?"

Anne blinked at him. Camp? She pictured ten-year-olds with scraped knees lining up for Band-Aids. She fought a swell of panic. "I thought I'd be visiting the elderly or teaching mothers how to care for their babies."

"You've been doing quite a bit of that these last few months. I think your time at the University of Minnesota Hospital gave you sufficient experience in community education. If you want to work in this community, a knowledge of the wilderness is a must." He reached for a pad of paper. "I'll assign you to visit members of the Granite River Indian Reservation. Meet with Jenny Olson. She runs the clinic on the reservation." He grabbed a pen.

Anne's voice caught in the back of her throat. She blinked, trying to comprehend Dr. Simpson's words. Spend her internship cooped up at a camp? How would she impress the board with her competence when all she did was pull out slivers? Still, the idea of nothing more traumatic than a bloody nose had its appeal.

"Where is the camp?"

Dr. Simpson looked up from his scribbles. "Up the Gunflint Trail about twenty miles. You'll be close enough to come home on the weekends."

"I have to sleep there?" Anne winced at her outburst and stared out the window. Her face grew hot as she felt the doctor's gaze on her. "I'm sorry. I pictured something different."

Silence, save for the whir of an overhead fan, filled the room. She watched the wind skim through the forest at the edge of a meadow. A squirrel ran down from a nearby poplar and stared at her, its jaw moving. Anne sighed. Perhaps she needed a summer of peace. She might even be willing to acknowledge God's involvement. Perhaps a positive attitude would also add to her marketability.

She turned back to Dr. Simpson. She was startled at the

sight of his head bowed, his hands clasped. Was he praying? Anne wondered what she'd done to elicit such concern.

He cleared his throat and looked at her. "Let's give it two weeks. If it doesn't work out, we'll revamp your course of study." He handed her the paper. "These are the directions to the camp and Ms. Olson's telephone number. I'll expect you in my office in two weeks for a report."

"You don't want to see me every day?"

"Why? You're ultimately accountable to yourself, and I'm going to trust you to do your best job."

Anne nodded. Another change from the city—no one looking over her shoulder. It made her feel oddly naked. "Um . . . I was wondering about pay. Usually the school covers my internship costs, but since I am working outside their usual sphere, they won't fund my internship." She swallowed the embarrassment thick in her throat. "I don't suppose . . ."

Dr. Simpson did have a kind face. She read it in his smile, the crinkles around his eyes. "I don't have anything worked out right now, but the camp should cover your expenses, and perhaps when your time there is complete, Deep Haven Municipal can offer you a compensation package."

At least in camp she wouldn't have to buy a uniform, and they would feed her. She stood and clasped the doctor's hand. "Thank you for accepting me."

"We're pleased to have you. You're not the only new face in town, by the way." He stood and gestured to the door. "Dr. Jefferies, please come in."

A slim man, slightly taller than herself, pushed the door open with two fingers. His smile seemed genuine, and he extended a hand to Anne. "Richard Jefferies. Family practice."

His wide hand held hers a moment longer than necessary. She pulled away but noticed his gaze linger.

"I see I arrived just in time." He smoothed down a teal-and-brown tie and buttoned his lab coat.

Anne frowned at a tremble in his hands.

"Dr. Jefferies is taking over for Dr. Holm while he is on summer sabbatical." Dr. Simpson came around the desk to clap the younger doctor on the shoulder. "He's fresh out of residency at St. Katherine's in Duluth."

"Good to meet you," Anne said quietly.

"Anne's here to finish her internship in community nursing." Dr. Simpson edged back toward his desk, perhaps to give her room to move past them in his cramped office.

Dr. Jefferies didn't budge. "Where are you from?" His brown eyes, muddy in color and depth, captured hers.

"Minneapolis," she heard herself say. What was it about him that sent her shivers?

"I've been there a few times." He backed away and shoved his hands into his pockets. "I love the Sculpture Garden." He folded his arms across his chest; his tone spoke of interest.

"Have you ever walked through the arboretum at night? It's gorgeous." Anne felt her tension dissipating. She was just a bad judge of character . . . always had been.

"No, but Nicollet Avenue on a snowy night is something magical."

His short blond hair and clean-shaven chin gave him a cultured look, and the way he leaned against the file cabinet invited her conversation. "Yes, it is," she agreed with a smile, giving him a second chance.

He smiled back, and she recognized something more than polite attention in his sweeping gaze. A blush started at her toes.

"Well, that's nothing compared to our night sky. You both ought to spend some time walking the beach while you're here." Dr. Simpson returned to his wobbly metal chair. "Thank you for coming in, Anne. Oh, by the way, please stop by human resources and get your security pass card and ID picture taken, okay?"

Anne nodded, clutching the folder to her chest, the one with her recommendation. "Nice meeting you, Dr. Jefferies." She walked out before she babbled further and

completely disgraced herself. Certainly Dr. Simpson wasn't suggesting she and Dr. Jefferies should spend time—together?

Then again, Deep Haven presumed an entirely different set of rules. Perhaps here men weren't to be feared.

She marched past Sandra, embarrassment fueling her steps. No, just *certain* men weren't to be feared. The memory of last night shuddered through her, and she shivered again, a reaction to Noah Standing Bear's suggestion that he drive her home.

He'd stood there, one leg hitched over his bike, acting like she would be thrilled to hop on his danger machine, throwing all caution and common sense to the wind. She knew firsthand what kind of damage a motorcycle could do to a rider, and beyond that, she wasn't going to let any man—let alone Mr. Standing Bear—within spitting distance of her safe haven. She'd come to Deep Haven specifically to avoid people like him. Noah Standing Bear profiled danger. The way he looked at her with his cocky grin, the wind tangling his black hair, those mysterious golden eyes kneading hers as if they held some sort of secret. No, she'd give him a wide berth if she ever saw him again.

No doubt he'd do the same after her reaction last night. She'd slapped him and scrambled up the road toward home.

She hadn't stopped running until she slammed and locked her cabin door.

Noah slung a stack of roofing material over his shoulder and climbed the ladder leaning against the lodge. Sweat carried chips of asphalt from the roofing tiles down his back and chest; his army fatigues were black and soggy. Still, the hard work kept his mind off a certain brunette that would skin him alive after she met with Dr. Simpson. He didn't relish their next conversation.

Not that the last one had gone well. He grunted as he

hauled up the fifty pounds of tiles. His aching back was nothing compared to the pain he'd felt when she'd walloped him, knowing that his innocent words had elicited such raw fear in her. He'd stood in stunned silence as she ran off and felt dread seep into his bones.

She hated him.

And he needed her. He groaned, set down the tiles, and sat on the roof, breathing hard. If only she knew of his profound gratefulness for her help. Pastor Dan and the missions committee had agreed to meet again in a week to finalize their funding, and if he didn't have Anne Lundstrom convinced by then, he'd have to shut down the camp before it even launched. He couldn't imprison her at Wilderness Challenge, even if a little time at camp facing the very people she was dodging might make her realize that city kids needed the same things as all kids . . . unconditional love and hope. Maybe she'd rethink that not-for-all-the-money-in-the-universe attitude about city living.

He wasn't a fool. He saw her hackles rise when he'd mentioned the city the first day they met by the beach, and something about his suggestion to drive her home had pushed that fear into action. Some sort of emotional night-mare had fueled the smack she'd given him. She was wounded, and judging by her reaction, it wasn't something she'd heal from quickly.

Unfortunately, Noah wasn't a doctor. And he seemed to be ripping open old scars every time they met. *God, I don't know what You're doing, but something is up with this lady, and I'd like to help. You brought her into my life, and I have to believe it's for good.*

A white-breasted nuthatch landed on the roof ten feet away and chipped at a piece of stripped wood. Noah watched its tiny black head as it bobbed and rooted for seeds; then he leaned back and let his face absorb the full blast of the noon sun, relishing this quiet moment.

Above him, towering oak rubbed shoulders with beech, basswood, birch, and a generous mix of balsam fir. The air, redolent with pine and a hint of lake water, spoke of peace, of escape. God had led him right into the lap of this forested luxury when an old pal from Bethel College mentioned the camp was for rent. Built as a private fishing retreat on tiny Mink Lake, it had been purchased by a denomination and remodeled into a camp, complete with lodge, a cook's shack, an outfitter's cabin, and cement pads for tents nestled at the end of overgrown footpaths.

From his perch on the roof, Noah could trace the layout of the fifteen-acre camp, including the waterfront and the campfire pit with its rough-hewn rows of benches in a semi-circle, to a field of purple violets and coneflowers, where they'd play capture the flag, soccer, and group-challenge games. The leaders at the church denomination had cut him a God-helmed deal. Hopefully, Noah could live up to the Almighty's expectations.

Noah's stomach growled, but he ignored it. He had a Snickers bar in the fridge downstairs. Any needs beyond that would require a trip into town. He was willing to starve in order to finish the roofing job today.

He heard gravel crunching from across the lake, where the road wound around the water, and he rolled over to track the vehicle. When he spied a black Explorer churning up dust, he grimaced. He made a mental note to keep Miss Lundstrom a good distance from the camp bus—she drove like a maniac.

He was climbing down the ladder when the SUV pulled in. Noah clambered under the porch roof for his shirt. Cleaning up would be futile. He already knew what she thought of him.

Since he had home-court advantage, he ducked inside the lodge and watched her exit her vehicle and wander around the weed-rutted courtyard. She looked so sleek in her black pants and crisp white blouse that it made him feel like roadkill. Noah grabbed his baseball cap and snuggled it down over his head to hide the grime. He hated to imagine what could be snagged in his two-day stubble.

She sauntered toward the porch. "Hello? Anyone here?"

"In here." Noah met her at the door.

Her shock glowed neon on her face. She went white.

Noah winced. "Hi again," he said softly.

"What are *you* doing here?" She backed away, as if she'd seen a ghost. He let her go, then followed a moment later. She stood in the sunlight, rubbing her arms and staring at the sky.

"I'm roofing the building." He grimaced at his cowardice. *Lord, give me the right words.*

She turned and surveyed his work. "You're a handyman?"

"Among other things."

"Rock collector and jack-of-all-trades." She regarded him with cool interest while she twirled her keys round and round her index finger. "So, how's your leg?"

He didn't miss the way she flinched slightly when she asked, and it bolstered his courage. Maybe the memory of his sacrificing his skin for her dog would mitigate her less-than-stellar opinion of him.

"I'm fine, thanks. I cleaned it and put ointment on it, like you suggested."

She nodded, but her wariness felt like a wall between them. "I'm here to see the director." She scanned the lodge, then stared at an army tent airing out over a makeshift clothesline. Its open flap shifted in the breeze. "What is this place called?"

"Wilderness Challenge. Would you like a tour?"

She glanced at him, and a tiny smile poked through the wall. "Yes."

His heart did a tiny jig. "It's a small camp. Only twenty kids, but we have a great program planned, and I hope it's really going to change lives." He motioned to a trail between two trees and she moved toward it. "We sleep in army tents, but someday maybe we'll build cabins."

"Was this always a camp?"

"Fishing lodge. I rented it cheap about six months ago and spent the winter weekends remodeling the inside."

She went silent. He saw her swallow—hard. "You're the camp director."

He shoved his hands into his pockets, fighting every impulse to drop to his knees and tell her that he hadn't meant to deceive her by omission last night. That he'd had every intention of confessing, but it had been forgotten between the attack of her mountain-sized dog and Anne's resounding slap. Most importantly, he wanted to assure her that he'd keep her safe.

Instead, he gave her his most apologetic smile and shrugged.

Instant fury clouded her eyes and she shook. "Did you plan this? Are you stalking me?"

He blew out a breath, feeling punched. "Of course not. I need help, and God provided you."

His confession didn't have the calming effect he'd hoped. Her face paled; she blinked. Then, in a pinched voice, "He provided me?"

"Without you, my camp loses its funds." He hated the desperation in his voice. "I need a full-time nurse on staff in order to get the church to back me." He turned away, embarrassed by his raw need and the fear that it was scribbled all over his face. "And when you . . . uh . . . sputtered to a halt right in front of my eyes, I had to believe it was divine intervention."

"Divine intervention?" Her tone made him cringe. "I think it's down-to-earth deception! Coercion. Try *slave labor.*" She shook her head and shot past him. "This has to be some sort of sick joke—"

"No joke. I talked to Doc. He okayed it."

Anne whirled, white with fury. "Okayed it? Sure. Fine." She shrugged, as if suddenly confused. "Why didn't you just knock me over the head last night and drag me up here by my hair? I mean, that's what a normal, red-blooded caveman would do." She put a hand to her forehead while Noah fought to close his open mouth.

"I can't believe it," she mumbled, as if he weren't standing there. "I've escaped the world of gangbangers and death by drive-bys into a world of Neanderthal chauvinists who've never heard of the—" she looked at him now and glared—"Emancipation Proclamation!"

"Now, c'mon, Anne." Noah had to admit that from her vantage point it did look very . . . ugly. "We didn't mean to—"

"Wait!" She stared at him with a look of pure horror. "You expected me to stay here with . . . with . . . *you?*"

He took a deep breath, kept his voice steady. "That's the general 'camp nurse' idea. Being on site in case the kids need you."

"Kids?" She raised her hands, palms up, as if waiting for him to produce them.

"They'll be here in a couple of weeks." He took a step toward her, a desperate feeling knotting in his gut. "Look, I didn't commit a felony. I mean, you *are* working for the doc, right?"

"That doesn't mean I can be loaned out like a lawn mower." She looked pointedly at the lodge. "I don't see any other staff."

"They arrive on Saturday."

She regarded him with a stare that could freeze a slug. "Saturday? So until then it's you and me, happy campers ten miles from the nearest telephone?" She clenched her teeth, then defied physics and spoke through them. "I. Don't. Think. So."

That crouching tiger–cat analogy was right on the money. He expected to see claws any second. "Listen—" he smiled ruefully—"I'm not Bigfoot. I won't hurt you."

She flinched, and for a desperate moment, he saw something vivid and painful flash in her eyes.

"I don't get it," he said. "I hardly know you, yet you're shaking like I'm Jack the Ripper." He closed his fists in his pockets, willing himself not to reach out to her. Her broken look told him she needed the comfort, but his gut said she'd flatten him faster than Joe Louis would.

"Well, just maybe it has something to do with the 'hardly know you' part."

Her sudden sarcasm felt like a knife in Noah's ribs. "Okay," he said, "so we'll get to know each other, be friends—"

"Not on this side of eternity." She whirled and stalked toward her SUV. "I'm sorry. I'm not doing this."

He was hot on her heels. "What do you mean? Okay, you don't have to show up until Saturday. It's not like I'm going to need a nurse between now and then." He didn't mention the fact that he felt like he was bleeding from a hundred tiny cuts. "After that, it gets easy. You don't even have to talk to me. All you have to do is hang out for the summer in this incredibly gorgeous place, patch up the kids when they fall, administer cold packs now and then. How hard can that be?"

"Not hard."

"Then what is it?" He braced his hand on the door of her Explorer as she tried to open it.

She looked up at him, and the smallest hint of pure terror entered her eyes. "Get away from me."

Anger bubbled into his chest as he recognized the expression on her face, the set of her jaw. This wasn't fear—it was prejudice. She didn't want to help him because she believed everything she saw on the outside and refused to see beyond her preconceptions. He fought the same disease with the kids on the street. Ignoring her dark look, he edged in. "You don't even care that the kids won't have a camp, do you?"

She narrowed her eyes. "I do care. But how can I work for—"

"Someone like me?" His voice raised in challenge.

Her eyes sparked. "Yes." She crossed her arms.

"You know only what you see. Not who I am."

"I see a man who nearly ran me down last night. That tells me all I need to know."

"You saw a man who wanted to introduce himself properly. A man who cared that you were going to be spending the summer with him. A man who saw in you potential and hope."

"A man who wanted to use me to get money."

He closed his eyes, looked away. "I'm sorry." He cupped a hand around his sweaty neck. "You're right. I didn't consider your feelings. I just assumed you'd want to help." He turned back and saw that she'd raised her chin, a give-me-a-big-stick expression in her simmering eyes. "Please forgive me."

She tightened her glare, but moisture glistened in her eyes. So, Miss Tough-as-Steel had a heart under that polished veneer.

Suddenly, she yanked open her SUV door and dove inside.

He remembered her cold stare long after she'd gunned the motor and raced down the gravel road.

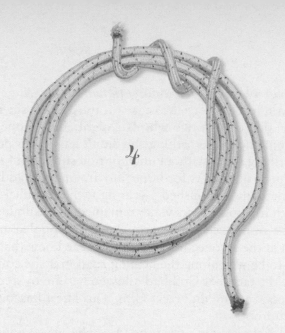

4

Anne's SUV spit gravel as she floored it around Mink Lake. What had the trauma counselor told her? Deep, calming breaths. Physical reaction to emotional invasion was typical.

Despite the fact that Noah had seemed . . . well . . . kind . . . even desperate in his attempts to keep her calm, her heart pounded out a staccato rhythm of pure fear. Slave labor. Someone was going to hear about his attempts to use her, and in about twenty minutes she planned to rip her resume out of Dr. Simpson's hands and head it for—

Where? Deep Haven had always conjured up feelings of peace and refuge. She needed that in her life more than she needed her self-respect.

But she wouldn't stay there with him. In a nightmarish, backwoods tangle of shadows and sounds ten miles from the nearest telephone? No way. His words rang in her ears: *A man who wanted to introduce himself properly. Who cared that you were going to be spending the summer with him.*

"Ha!" she slammed her fist against the steering wheel. She wouldn't spend a minute, let alone the summer, with prehistoric, chauvinistic Noah Grizzly Bear.

A man who saw in you potential and hope. Anne gritted her teeth, forcing herself to ease off the gas lest she take the bend in the road on two wheels. Potential and hope. Now how could he see something she didn't have? Her potential had nothing to do with a bunch of rich suburban kids needing a nurse nanny. As for hope, any fragments had been excruciatingly demolished a year ago when a bullet ripped through her body. In its wake remained a consuming fear.

Anne swallowed the bitterness that still pooled in her mouth at the recollection of that day. She knew that she ought to be well along the healing road, but she couldn't hurdle the fact that God had allowed her life to spiral into darkness. She couldn't trust Him. This latest fiasco was perfect proof.

And if she couldn't trust the One who was omnipotent, how could she possess anything remotely resembling potential or hope? Both, she guessed, entailed trusting in the unseen, having faith that God had the future safely in pocket and confidence that it was a good future at that.

No, Noah Standing Bear didn't see anything in her but sheer despair. The destruction of both potential and hope.

Anne sailed past Hedstrom's Lumber Mill, then slowed as she headed toward the hospital. Compared to the institutions in the Twin Cities, Deep Haven Municipal Hospital resembled some back-hills clinic out of the novel *Christy*— a whitewashed one-story building, a weed-sprouted parking lot, and an ambulance bay that housed one rusty unit. For a moment Anne smiled, remembering her hours spent as an EMT for the Minneapolis Fire Department. If Noah searched for hope, he'd find it in those heroes. They gave away a little chunk of their life every day in their desire to make a difference in the world. Anne's smile faded and she shook her head.

She pulled into the parking lot, turned off the vehicle, and drummed her fingers on the steering wheel. Now that she'd had a little time to calm down and think, she couldn't deny that inside her lurked the smallest longing to dive into

Noah's hopes. The idea of steering children toward Christ
and down a path that would help them say no to drugs,
crime, and the abuse of their bodies tugged at a latent
desire. Noah Standing Bear, for all his rough edges, had
righteous goals guiding him.

Too bad he resembled so many of the hoodlums she'd
grown up with, complete with roughshod manners and
callousness to a lady's feelings. He didn't smell like a dream
either, with all that roofing material coating his arms and
army pants.

Anne tried to ignore the notion that underneath his
uncouth coating, gentleness had reached out and intrigued
her. His ears had turned red from her accusation that he'd
stalked her, and his chagrined expression chipped at her
anger. In spite of what she'd said, she wasn't blind to the
fact that he'd put an ugly abrasion on his leg yesterday
trying to dodge Bertha. Without his quick reflexes, she
wouldn't have her Saint Bernard waiting at home right
now, chewing on her aunt's futon.

I'm not Bigfoot. The echo of his words tugged at the
corners of her mouth. She could argue that point, with his
hair spiking around his cap, a smattering of whiskers on his
chin, and his towering height. Magnetic honey brown eyes
made her wonder at his ancestry. Native American obviously, but the color hinted at a genealogical story. She had a
good working knowledge of the plight of Native Americans
in Minnesota and guessed his history might not be pretty.
Had he grown up on the Indian reservation? or in a foster
home in some ghetto?

A tap on her window nearly sent her heart arrowing out
of her chest.

"Anne, are you okay?" Sandra smiled as Anne rolled
down the window. "I saw you sitting here and was worried.
Something about the way you leaned your forehead into
your steering wheel told me you might need a friend."

Anne made a face. "I'm that transparent, huh?"

Sandra shrugged. "You haven't been in town long. Today

was a doozy, right?" She tucked her purse, a woven Indian-patterned bag, over her shoulder. "I'm headed to the Footstep of Heaven for some coffee and book browsing. Wanna tag along? I'll introduce you to the locals."

With a swell of warmth, Anne nodded.

"Leave your SUV here. I'll drive you back later."

Sandra owned a very old, very intriguing, red, restored '67 International Scout. "I guess seat belts weren't invented yet?" Anne asked as she slid in.

"I had them installed." Sandra dug in between the seat and found Anne's strap. "Haven't had guests for a while." Laugh lines crinkled around her blue eyes, inviting Anne's friendship.

Anne fought the urge to blurt out a stream of frustration and instead measured her thoughts. Wisdom dictated that she determine what team Sandra played on before she started bemoaning Dr. Simpson's managerial practices. For all Anne knew, Sandra was in cahoots with the doctor and Mr. Grizzly. The woman looked the type to have a soft spot for kids.

Sandra drove out of the hospital parking lot. Along Main Street, seagulls waddled like regal old men, and the smell of fish tinted the cold breeze. The sun had begun to gather the day on the horizon, preparing for departure. Along the shoreline, the lake had piled up driftwood, foam, and debris.

"A storm is brewing," Sandra commented. The stiff breeze tangled her braids out behind her.

Anne nodded, not adding that her life felt as if the storm had already hit shore. "I noticed that lighthouse in a picture in Dr. Simpson's office." She gestured to the white lighthouse on the point. "It's pretty old."

"Only about one hundred years. It's been restored more times than I can count. It's still in use, you know. She's guided many a ship home by her light." Sandra found a parking spot along the street behind a white Lincoln Navi-

gator. Her pickup looked like the wreck of the *Hesperus* next to it, but somehow it fit better with the rugged scenery.

"The lighthouse has had only one real hiccup," Sandra continued as she wrestled the stick shift into first. "There's a wreck offshore, about a century old. The story goes that the lighthouse drew the ship in, giving her hope in the middle of an October gale, and then suddenly, *poof!* The light vanished. The schooner sank just yards from the harbor."

Bitterness filled Anne's chest again. Wasn't that how life worked? When she thought she was safe in the middle of God's hand, He dropped her. Her warm knitted world unraveled, the guiding light snuffed. "That's a terrible story."

Sandra pointed at a white bungalow beside the lighthouse. "Yes, but that's not the end. The lighthouse keeper saw the light blow out and knew the ship was in trouble. He took his own whaler out in the middle of the gale, risking his life. Moments after the *Elgin* went down, he rescued the survivors. Not a soul perished." Sandra touched Anne's hand. "In the darkest moment, God's always there."

Anne glanced at her. "You sound like my mother."

"I talked to your aunt in church yesterday." Sandra offered an apologetic smile. "You can't keep many secrets in a small town. I'm sorry to hear about your trauma last year." She squeezed Anne's hand. "I'm glad you moved here."

The kindness of the gesture pushed tears into Anne's eyes. "Thank you." Her gaze tracked back to the lighthouse, imagining the light that it would broadcast when the sky blackened. She saw a man picking his way along the rocky base of the structure, a bag banging against his hips. Propped up some twenty feet away, a photographer's tripod explained his puzzling movements. Evidently she wasn't the only one affected by the mystique of the lighthouse.

Sandra didn't say another word as they climbed out and strolled toward a two-story Victorian. Peonies in bloom edged the stone walk, up to a railed front porch. "I saw this bookstore on my way into town."

"It's also a pottery shop. Liza Beaumont is our resident potter, and Mona Michaels runs the bookstore. You'll like them, Anne. They know all about moving to Deep Haven to build a new life."

Anne's mouth slacked open. "How much did my aunt tell you?"

Sandra shrugged, but her eyes twinkled. "Let me just say that you're not the first person to find refuge here. You have a sort of . . . edginess. As if you are waiting for the bomb to explode."

Anne laughed. "Oh no, I left all my bombs behind. Deep Haven may have lobbed a few grenades at me, but I'm smarter and wiser now. Besides, I seriously doubt there are ticking bombs in my backyard."

Sandra raised her eyebrows. "Deep Haven isn't a war-free zone." She tucked her arm through Anne's. "Just ask Mona. One of our locals once tried to burn this place down."

Anne climbed the porch stairs and took in the row of round tables dressed in bright yellow tablecloths fluttering in the breeze. Planters overflowing with red, white, and pink impatiens hung between the porch columns. A lush lilac tree perfumed the yard with serenity. "Looks like Mona came out on top. She must be a hard worker."

"Well, yes. And God is a giver of good things. She has a wonderful faith-building story if you ever have time to listen. He not only put this shop on the map, but He also brought her husband, an author, right to her doorstep. She calls Joe her 'flesh-and-blood hero, right off the pages,' whatever that means."

Sandra called out Mona's name as they swung open the screen door. Anne stood a few paces behind, mesmerized by the entryway, the luminous shine of the oak railing spiraling upstairs, the wrought-iron light fixture sending a warm

glow along the floor. The smell of something baking coaxed her inside, toward the bookstore on her right.

Sandra made a trail toward a young blonde seated at a gleaming walnut table. The woman looked up and greeted her, a warm smile on her pretty face. Anne wondered at Sandra's words: *God, giver of good things.* She had to admit, that hadn't been her experience of late. In fact, although she knew God had given her the grit to climb back to her feet and finish her degree, He certainly hadn't made it easy. And where was He that hot summer day when she'd been blindsided by a gangbanger? More than that, why did God keep plunking her right in the middle of her worst nightmares? Why couldn't He, just once, arrange for her a safe, easy life?

Anne sighed, wishing she could escape the residue of Noah's words tugging at her heart. *I just assumed you'd want to help.* She *did* want to help. She simply wanted to have a choice. It would be easier to write Noah off as a gorilla if he hadn't looked so genuinely sorry when she'd left, staring at her until she churned up a good cloud of dust, his hands in his pockets, his heart bleeding on his sleeve.

But the man was dangerous. Everything about him screamed "warning!"—from the grimy work attire, to his waiting-for-someone-to-pounce posture, to the secrets prowling behind those intense brown eyes. He reminded her of what she'd left behind, and the last thing she wanted to do was return to the life she'd escaped from. So Mr. Bear had a sort of rough-hewn appeal, an attractiveness that could paralyze an unsuspecting woman. But she wasn't that woman. Even if his soft tenor, as if spoken over velvet, did do painful, confusing things to her pulse rate. She would belt him and run for the hills before giving in to his humble words.

"Mona, I'd like you to meet Anne." Sandra grabbed Anne's elbow. "She's new in town. A nurse. She's working for Dr. Simpson."

Mona's green eyes sparkled with sincere warmth when she shook Anne's hand. "Glad to meet you. We transplants need to stick together or the locals will gang up on us." She winked at Sandra, who rolled her eyes. "Will you be here long?"

Noah surfaced into the twilight-soaked air and hoisted himself from the lake onto the dock. The crisp June breeze turned his skin to gooseflesh but soothed the frustration threatening to boil him alive. He'd felt ill watching his hopes flee with Anne's desperate escape three hours earlier. Instead, he'd stood there, fists bunched at his sides, listening to a thousand voices tell him he'd failed . . . again.

What was a guy with his past trying to achieve by this do-gooder impersonation, anyway? Didn't he know he couldn't escape the generational tug into a life of misery and sin? Noah sat down, squeezed out his wet hair, and scrubbed a towel over his face. He didn't mind the chill seeping into his bones. Maybe it would snap him into reality, out of the dream he'd been living for too long. Maybe it hadn't been a godly vision he'd seen three years ago but desperation.

It had obviously been sheer desperation that made him believe that Anne Lundstrom would join his team. From her expression when she'd peeled away, only whips and chains could drag her back to Wilderness Challenge.

He didn't blame her; he didn't feel one ounce of reproach toward her. Noah dug his hands into his hair and hung his head. No, he alone owned all indictment. Her accusation had ripped a hole right through his chest: *A man who wanted to use me to get money.*

He let out a groan that echoed across the lake. *Oh, God, I'm sorry.* His throat burned. Guilty. He had been thinking only of his camp, his wants. He hadn't given a solitary consideration to how Anne wanted to spend her summer,

nor had he given her a chance to choose. So his intentions
were honorable, even righteous. But he'd trampled over her
feelings with the sensitivity of a stock horse. The realization
made him sick.

If only Anne could see the despair in the kids he'd left in
Minneapolis. If only she could watch what drugs and pros-
titution did to their innocence, count the times he'd buried
teens next to their brothers and sisters. If only she could
peek inside his own life and see the scars buried in his past.
Then maybe . . .

He cupped his hand over his left arm, hiding beneath his
grip a gray blue, tiny five-point star. He still battled the urge
to have it removed, wanting to erase all remnants of that
former life. But something inside him—he couldn't pinpoint
what—kept him from obliterating the last piece of concrete
evidence. His fingers dug into his flesh, remembering the
day he'd been branded, body and heart, for life.

Rock Man, they'd called him. He figured it had something to do with his bullheadedness when they'd tried to
beat him senseless the night of initiation. His jaw hadn't
closed right for a month, but he'd stayed standing and
earned the right to be a Vice Lord. He'd belonged. Forever.

His fingers formed the three-finger homeboy salute and
gang lingo flooded his memory. To this day, every time
he heard *all is well,* "the People's" typical expression, he
bristled.

All was never well when he'd run with the Lords. He
should have figured that out the last night of initiation.
Noah shuddered and lowered his forehead onto his knees.
What an idiot he'd been—over a bag of tortilla chips.

Shorty Mac had shoved a 9mm Glock into his hand as
they crouched in the shadows. Cold and heavy, the weapon
sent a thrill of fear through him as they watched the Tom
Thumb Convenience Store, waiting for L'il Lee's sister to
emerge. "She's unlocking the back door," Shorty Mac said,
a devious glint in his eye.

Noah hadn't seen the deceit, even then. Shorty Mac,

childhood friend turned homeboy, had learned well in a month's time how to lie with the best. But Noah had believed him and inched toward the back door, the October wind whistling under his Chicago Bulls jacket. He counted it a triumph when he'd five-finger discounted it from a local mall, despite the fact that he'd yet to wear it home. Mother Peters would have skinned him alive if she suspected gang colors in her foster home. Noah's heart panged, thinking of the Native American woman who'd given him over a decade of 110 percent mothering, complete with anguished prayer and tough love.

The night had been black, only a few streetlights pushing back the darkness. Noah hooked his hands in his belt loops, then bumped his Bulls cap to the left. He knew that more than Mac's eyes trailed him, keeping tabs on his progress. But tonight he'd be in. He'd have family. Sisters and brothers and someplace to belong. No matter where the CPS—Child Protective Services—threw him, he'd still have home turf.

He scuttled behind a Dumpster. Security lit up the place like high noon, but he didn't care, believing foolishly that the other VLs would be on his six to bail him out. He flashed his sign, then ran for the back door.

Locked. Noah's blood froze in his veins. He tried again. Kicked the door, then shot a look at Mac. The kid was doubled over, clutching his gut, laughing.

He remembered the fury. It exploded like a living thing, took possession of him. Even today the power of it still shook Noah. His brothers had set him up. He reacted poorly, flashing Mac sign language, making sure the entire unseen audience in the street saw it.

Rock Man. Right then, he'd put skin on his name. Rock Man—someone who had the stone-cold guts to get the job done. He saw himself tugging out the pistol, stepping back, aiming just above the knob, and pulling the trigger.

The shot ripped through the door. The gun bucked in his hands and metal screamed. He aimed and shot again. This

time the door jerked, jumped on its hinges. Noah grabbed
the knob and yanked the mutilated mass open.

A terrified store clerk, her eyes white against her dark
skin, met him in the stockroom. "Get out!"

Noah laughed. He waved the gun. "Zip it."

Fear clamped her mouth shut. She whirled, raced through
the store and out the front door.

Although time blurred some of the sounds and smells, he
recalled stalking to the front, his pulse racing. He slammed
the butt of his weapon into the cash register, but it didn't
open.

Then sound blared through Noah's memory—sirens
whining in the padding of night.

He'd driven his shoulder into the register, kicked it, shot
it twice. It dinged like a bell, and he heard the sweet sound
of coins rattling around inside. But the stubborn thing still
wouldn't open.

Sirens . . . closer. His assignment had been to rob the
place clean. Yeah, right. He hadn't even been able to open
the register, not to mention clean out the safe.

Noah dug his hands into his hair, remembering now the
women—one with an infant, crouched near the ice-cream
freezer—and a man sprawled on the floor by the counter,
hands clutched over his head. "Stay down and keep your
mouths shut or you're going to die—and fast," he had said.
Had those words really spurted out of his mouth? He felt
sick now, elated then. His absolute power had emboldened
him.

What could he steal?

The sirens rattled the windows.

Then he'd made his eternal mark of stupidity. He grabbed
a bag of groceries sitting on the counter, obviously the
purchases of the patron facedown on the floor. Shoving it
under his arm, he dove for the back.

Thirty seconds later he sprinted through the well-known
back alleys of his neighborhood, feeling giddy, indestructible. He ran the entire way to L'il Lee's house, where the

VLs waited. Ten guys loitered on the porch, including three Vice Lord lieutenants and two foot soldiers Noah had beaten to a pulp two days earlier.

He collapsed on the back steps, gasping, his breath burning in his lungs. He ached everywhere—it felt delicious. "You. Guys. Set. Me. Up."

"Yeah. And pow! You take out the door?" L'il Lee slapped him on the back, laughing. "Gimme that piece, boy." He shot a grin at Mo-Jo, VL minister. "Don't get Rock mad. He'll fire first and never ask forgiveness!" He punched Noah on the shoulder. Noah had relished the pain that spiked down his arm.

"So, what's the take?" Shorty Mac huffed up, looking like a proud father.

Noah handed over his spoils.

Shorty Mac opened the bag, dropped it, and burst out laughing. "Boys, we have a regular felon here. A real Billy the Kid. He goes in guns ablazin' and comes out with—" he reached into the sack—"Doritos!"

Noah gasped, his stomach twisting at the memory. The lives he'd endangered for a bag of chips. Tears coursed down his face as he sat on the dock. He gazed heavenward and traced the first hint of stars in the bruised sky. His throat tightened, but he forced his words out. "Lord, I know I'm the worst candidate to be leading kids to You. You've seen my life and sometimes Your grace is simply overwhelming. But, God, these kids need Your salvation. Only You can wrench them out of death, drugs, and despair." He swallowed, and regret lodged in his throat. "I handled it badly with Anne, Lord. She deserved better. Please forgive me."

The memory of her slight smile when he'd offered to show her around camp hinted that maybe—just maybe—if he went crawling on his knees, she'd hear him out. Allow him to draw her a picture of the despair etched on the kids' grimy faces and let him plead his case. She'd nearly ripped him to shreds with her cutting words, but the shred of pride

that remained wouldn't keep him from approaching her with his hat in his hands. He needed her. The kids needed her. And for their sake, she needed to know why. Then he'd cut her free and let her take the reins.

He smiled. *Lord, You choose. If You want this camp to be a go, please change Anne's heart. Please convince her to stay.*

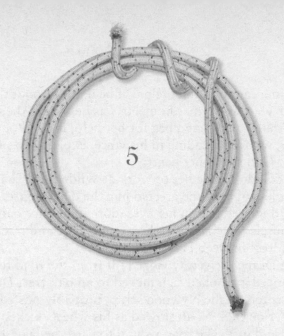

5

$\mathcal{N}$oah gunned his motorcycle along Highway 61, one eye on his speedometer, looking for the gravel drive Edith Draper had described on the telephone.

If Anne Lundstrom hoped to hide from society, she'd picked the perfect place. Noah had hunted down Dr. Simpson at Pierre's Pizza to find Anne's address, and he'd spent several more minutes watching Sally Williams's toddler drive toys around her sandbox while the Grace Church secretary dug up Edith Draper's new telephone number.

He'd caught the elderly woman just as she was leaving for a dinner out at the Granite River Resort. "She's staying on our property, Mr. Bear, but she doesn't have a telephone."

"Can I come by and wait on her porch?"

For some reason he pictured Edith pulling her chin as she thought that over. "I suppose so, but I don't keep her schedule. She might be long."

Had he scared her all the way back to wherever she hailed from?

The wind plowed through his hair. The air smelled of storm. Black clouds obscured the moon in a gloomy nighttime canopy. Noah felt as if he'd gone about three rounds with his former homeboys as he fought the urge to grab Anne's ankles and beg for her help, instead of simply, calmly, without pleading in his voice, explain the situation and let God tug at her heart.

He couldn't force her to work at Wilderness Challenge. Regardless of how she greeted him, he'd apologize. Knowing he'd ignited fear in her eyes more than once had helped him muscle the courage to hop on his bike and track down her address in Deep Haven.

The Draper driveway jagged off from the road to the left. He noticed a crooked sign tacked to an oak tree. *Draper* was written on the plywood scrap, probably posted for the plumber or UPS. Noah slowed as his wheels kicked up stones and dirt. The road wound toward the lake, between balsam and birch, the foliage providing a natural sound barrier to the highway. The forest closed over him briefly before he emerged into a cleared parking area. He parked the bike next to an outbuilding and considered the two trails—one leading toward a beautiful log A-frame with a wraparound porch. The other cut through more forest.

Noah chose the road less traveled and emerged at a tiny box cabin. Although it had seen better days, obvious by the saggy front porch and peeling paint, the cabin looked cozy, even comforting. Noah hopped up the stairs and knocked on the door, in hopes Anne had returned.

Something slammed into the door on the inside. Then barking, low and somewhat desperate, with a lilt of whine at the end of the dispatch. Anne's dog. No, Anne's furry horse. "Anne, are you home?"

Again barking, but this time, more whine attached— enough to make Noah frown. Had something happened to Anne? Was she lying inside injured or ill? Maybe her reaction to him had triggered some sort of psychosomatic episode. "Anne?"

More barking, then the whines tumbled on top of each other, frantic, afraid. Noah flung open the screen and

wiggled the doorknob. Locked. "Anne!" He pounded on the wood, hard enough that anyone reasonably near consciousness would hear him.

He thumped his shoulder into the door. Pain shot into his neck. The wood shuddered but held. He swallowed an expletive and let the screen door slam.

The dog howled.

An image of Anne in the throes of an epileptic seizure or a diabetic coma pitched his heart into his throat. He was going in.

Noah tried the window next to the door. Closed. But locked? Not likely, in this part of America. Noah flicked open his Leatherman, something much more useful than the switchblade he once carried, and jammed the screwdriver into the frame. The window argued as he jimmied it up six inches, the century-old frame reluctant to be manhandled. He pressed his hand in and found a screen. "Anne!" he yelled into the gap.

The dog nearly took his hand off. Giant paws slammed into the screen, then a tongue, snuffling. "Okay, okay, I'm coming. Back off." Noah yanked the window up to waist height and again felt the screen. Old-fashioned tabs held it in place, and it took about thirty-five seconds for his child-hood talents to pop them off. He pushed the screen open at the bottom and slid into the cabin, feetfirst.

Anne's giant beast attacked him like a long-lost friend. Noah dug both hands into the dog's hair, pulling him off while the animal bathed his face. "Where's Anne?"

The Saint Bernard jumped back, sat on the floor, and swished her tail. Noah fumbled for the light, found it by the door, and flipped it on.

He gasped. "What happened here?" An antique, milk-glass table lamp lay shattered in a thousand bumpy pieces on the wooden floor. Intermingled with the white shards were the fragmented remains of a hickory log, perhaps used as an appetizer right before the animal dove into the main course—a lime green foam macramé pillow. The pillow's shredded remains littered the room, along with what looked like a rejected portion out of the dog's stomach. The stench, mingled with dog saliva and a very suspicious-looking puddle next to the woodstove in the corner, nearly knocked Noah to his knees.

A war zone, and no sign of Anne. Noah beelined to the bedroom, praying she wasn't injured or worse. He popped on the bedroom light.

The pink knitted bedspread webbed the room, now an unraveled dog toy connecting the overturned lamp to a gooey pile of hand lotion. The bottle looked like it had waged a decent fight and spilled its contents in a final act of defiance.

"Oh, dog, you're in big trouble."

Noah knelt and finally accepted the dog's welcome, his heart rate settling into a reasonable thump. Anne wasn't here, she wasn't dead, and hopefully he'd have time to clean the place up before she walked in the—

A scream nearly made him leap out of his skin. Anne stood in the bedroom doorway, her face ashen, eyes wide with terror and fixed on Noah. She dropped her bag of groceries, took a breath, and belted out another scream.

Noah jumped to his feet. "Anne, stop. It's okay." He glanced at the mess. "I'll help you clean it up."

When he turned back to her, the panic on her face halted him. She shook, on the thin edge of control, as if seeing an apparition. "Anne, calm down."

He grabbed her arm as she whirled to escape. "Let go of me!" she shrieked. She hit at his arm, and he instantly released her.

For a second he felt sure she was going to race out the door, just like she'd floored it away from the camp. He froze, frustration and helplessness tying him into knots.

"You! What are you doing here?" Fury sizzled in her eyes. As her glare pinned him, words clogged in his throat.

She didn't wait for a response. She hauled back and slapped him. The sting didn't hurt nearly as much as seeing

tears spring into her eyes and watching her crumple to the floor, sobbing.

He knelt beside her, his chest throbbing with each wretched sob. Had he done this? What fear prowled under her skin that roared to life every time she saw him? He longed to draw her into his circle of protection, to smooth her hair and comfort her despite the fact she thought him a close relative to a street rat. The lady was afraid and crying.

He wasn't about to let pride stand between him and chivalry. Even if she was bound to slug him. Again. He braced himself, reached out. His hand grazed her arm.

She jerked away. "Don't touch me!" When she looked up, her agonized expression made him cringe. The emotions in her eyes told him that she'd seen things and held secrets that put substance to her fearful behavior. He felt sick to his soul when she whispered, "What kind of criminal are you?"

Anne had never seen someone turn white so fast. She knew it; she just knew it. The guy in front of her, despite the worry on his face, probably had a case file at police head-quarters so thick they used it as a footstool. She gritted her teeth, not caring that he looked like he'd been hit in the gut, pale, slack-jawed. She wondered how soon she could charge him with breaking and entering. And if she did, wouldn't that erase her camp problem?

Then he clamped his mouth shut, as if coming to his senses, and backed away from her. Way away. As if he couldn't put enough distance between them. He even stood and stalked across the room, standing with his back to her as he faced the woodstove. It unnerved her the way he shook.

She wondered how fast she could get to Edith's tele-phone. First item on Anne's to-do list tomorrow was to order her own service. She would even pump bad gas at Mom and Pop's to pay for it.

Something about Noah's demeanor made her throat raw. His shoulders were hunched and he'd cupped his hands over his face. Even eight feet away, she could see his neck muscles tense.

Then Bertha tackled her. Slobbering and smelling of— hand lotion? "Get off me!" She ran her hands over Bertha's thick hair, thankful beyond words for her giant companion. Just think what the hoodlum would have done to her place had Bertha not been here. He'd probably locked the poor thing in her bedroom while he ransacked Anne's tiny home.

Ransacked—why? Anne pushed the dog away and surveyed the carnage. The chaos nearly sent a wave of fresh tears. "What, taking me prisoner wasn't enough? You had to demolish my cabin too?"

He shook his head, his back still to her. "I found it this way. Your dog—"

"My dog did this? I highly doubt that."

She watched his broad shoulders rise and fall, as if breathing in calm. When he turned toward her, the moisture in the corner of his eyes shocked her silent. "Yes, your dog did it. I don't have a habit of chewing up pillows, even when I'm near starvation. And maybe if you came home a littler earlier and took her out for a walk, she might not resort to eating logs!" A tiny muscle twitched in his bronze cheek, right below that intriguing round scar.

She blinked at him, fixed for a moment. Then she dismissed the spark of familiarity and registered his accusation. "Excuse me, but I was out trying to recover from your attempt to sell me into slavery. Edith promised to take Bertha out for a run, not that it's any of your business."

"She was whining."

"What?" He had this annoying habit of shaking his head while he talked, as if he were patronizing a small child, and when he forked his hand through his luxurious black hair and looked up to the heavens, her fury boiled over. "Get out! Get out this second or I'll call the police and have you arrested for breaking and entering." Milliseconds away

from snapping, the last thing she wanted to do was confront the fact that she'd left Bertha at home without a bladder break and starving since breakfast. Or the fact that, for a hideous split second, she'd been paralyzed in the past, watching her life explode in slow motion.

"No. I'm not leaving."

"You *are* leaving. Right now."

"No, not until I help you clean up this mess and apologize for hurting you today." His eyes, a breath-stealing brown, held her like glue, and for a moment, her focus zeroed in on his expression, awash with a raw desperation that made her heart bang hard against her ribs. He had an unrefined charisma about him that suddenly tangled her fury into confusing knots. She fumbled for a response and watched in dismay as Bertha, Saint Benedict Arnold, ran over to him and pawed his chest.

Noah scrubbed the dog behind both ears and even leaned down so the animal could lick his chin.

Anne clenched her teeth. "Some guard dog you are."

"Let me help you, Anne." The voice, softly toned, soothed the ragged edge of her nerves. "And then let me tell you why I wanted you to spend the summer with me."

When he smiled at her, her traitorous mouth said, "Okay."

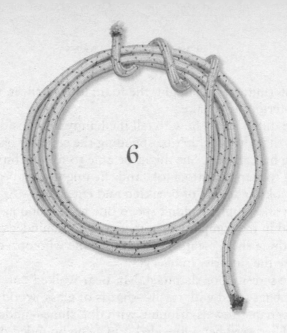

6

Anne sat on the porch, watching the stars shift among approaching storm clouds, beacons of hope against the blackness. The smell of rain layered the air, and the breeze carried with it the moist breath of the lake. Anne tugged the sleeves of her sweatshirt over her knuckles and wrapped her arms around her waist. At least she'd stopped shaking.

It had taken a mere hour to subdue her terror after she'd discovered Mr. Standing Bear in her house. She winced, remembering how she'd completely unraveled in front of him. The last thing she wanted was him peeking at her vulnerabilities. Especially when he had turned out to be so . . . so . . . infuriatingly gentlemanly. It would be a thousand times easier to hold a grudge and brand him the local menace if he hadn't just swept up debris, untangled her bedspread, and washed her bedroom floor with the finesse of a cleaning team. And he'd hummed a hymn—"O, How I Love Jesus"—while he'd done it, something that made her want to burst into idiotic tears.

She got up and leaned on the porch rail, gazing out over the cliff a few yards away and onto the shoreline below. In the intermittent moonlight, the foam looked silver, ringing a mysterious opal lake.

She didn't know how to tell the handy hero inside her cabin that she wouldn't be spending the summer baby-sitting his campers. She might be able to forgive him for trying to trap her into a job, and she might even be able to overlook the felony of breaking and entering.

But she simply couldn't spend one hour, minute, or second in the company of someone who reminded her of everything she'd escaped from. Someone who oozed danger, despite the sincerity in his eyes.

The screen door slammed. Mr. Bear walked out, two paper bags filled with trash—shards of glass, wood fragments, paper towels dripping with dog slime—under his arm. He tossed her a lopsided grin as he bounded down the steps and shoved the bags into the metal garbage can. The lid scraped as he replaced it. She braced herself as he hopped back up the stairs.

"Are you okay?" Something about the tenderness, the concern in his musical voice made her tingle to her toes.

She couldn't look at him as she nodded. She couldn't deny the possibility that despite his rough exterior, inside lurked a man of honor.

Then again, he did break into her home.

She watched as he knelt beside Bertha and rubbed her behind the ears. The dog licked him on the chin, and he laughed. It sounded so rich and enticing Anne had to smile. "Thank you for cleaning up my house."

"Would you like to go for a walk?" He indicated the shoreline below. "I'd like to talk to you."

"Mr. Bear—"

"Noah, please. Call me Noah."

"Okay, Noah, listen. I know what you're going to say. I forgive you for breaking into my house, although how you did it freaks me out. But it was for a good cause." She glanced at Bertha, feeling a twinge of guilt. Even if she did ask Edith to walk the animal, Bertha needed more than a

fifteen-minute prison break, especially with the June air calling to her like a hot steak.

"Anne—"

"No, hear me out. I'm pretty sure you came here to convince me to work at your camp, but you can save your breath. I've already made up my mind." She stared at his worn work boots, the ones he'd worn earlier that day while roofing the lodge. The wind chose that moment to reap his scent—fresh soap, the smell of clean cotton, and authentic male aroma that made her feel strangely safe. "I'm sorry but I can't work for you. I'm going to ask Dr. Simpson for another assignment, and if he can't give me one, then . . . well . . ."

Actually, she hadn't worked out anything beyond that. In the first scenario she'd conjured up, she marched into Dr. Simpson's office at the crack of dawn and unleashed both barrels of indignation. Later images, birthed sometime after Mona Michaels had mixed her a soothing cup of tea, contained elements of sanity, including a constructive discourse on the ethics of assigning a young, single woman to live in the backwoods with a male stranger.

"That's okay, Anne. I understand. I wanted to trust the Lord to work it out, but my faith took a nosedive and I handled it poorly. I'm going to talk to Dr. Simpson in the morning and tell him to let you off the hook. But I wanted to apologize to you." His voice dropped to nearly a whisper. "I treated you with disrespect. Will you forgive me?"

The sincerity in his voice made her search his face—the hard jawline, a smattering of whiskers, and a small scar that insinuated a suspicious past. But those gorgeous eyes drew her in and his chagrined half smile, full of remorse, made her insides tumble. The Noah Standing Bear package might have an intimidating wrapper, but she suspected that inside lurked a man who might be worth knowing. A man of character.

Anne looked away. Learning whether or not her hunches were correct wasn't worth the risk. "Of course I forgive you." It didn't come out at all the way she wanted, but perhaps he'd take the hint and exit before she collapsed into her deck chair and began to weep. Why did she feel like she was the hoodlum here? "What will you do about your funding?"

Noah was so tall that when he turned away from her and leaned on the railing, she suddenly felt the breeze lift her hair, as if he'd been protecting her from its invasive touch. She shivered.

"Well, I guess I need to exercise a little faith. I can't see God's plans, but I know that He's there, even in the dark moments, waiting to rescue me. I have full confidence that if He wants this camp to work, He'll provide."

"What if He lets the entire thing crumble? What if all your hard work is for nothing?" Her voice sounded tight, and it wouldn't take a genius to sift through her question to see her own searching, her own lack of faith. Thankfully, Noah didn't even glance at her, leaving her unscathed by those probing, way-too-sensitive eyes.

"Well, that's a pretty universal question, isn't it?" He folded his work-worn hands and stared toward the lake. His profile, bold and noble and suddenly overwhelmingly Native American, made her heart thump hard. In the soft glow of the starry luminaries, Noah Standing Bear was impossibly, undeniably handsome.

"Where is God in the dark moments, when our dreams crumble, when the worst happens?" His voice became so soft, she leaned closer to hear him. "Where is God when children die, when disease racks a parent . . . or when a woman is attacked?"

He looked at her, and she could barely breathe. She managed a nod.

"He's there. He's there in the darkness, saying, 'Look up! I'll hold you. Look up!' His grace is sufficient for even the worst moments."

Anne flinched, wanting to refute those words. Where was God when she awoke in the hospital, unable to breathe,

minus a kidney, morphine flooding her veins? Her throat burned and she looked away. "It might be for you."

She felt his gaze on her, hot on the back of her neck. Tears bit her eyes. "I'm a Christian, Noah. But I'm not so sure about the sufficiency of God's grace. What does that mean, anyway? What part of pain and sorrow and grief does God's grace eliminate?"

"None, Anne. And all."

She fought a crest of fury. A man like him, tall and capable and oozing strength, couldn't possibly understand what it was like to feel vulnerable, afraid, alone. The gunshot had been only the topping on a lifetime of fear, a lifetime of seeing God fumble. No, God's grace wasn't sufficient. It was a Band-Aid, a placebo the Christian community used to cover the agony of suffering. No one wanted to look grief full in the face or admit its ruthlessness. So they dodged it and called it "God's sufficient grace." But she knew from firsthand experience that God checked out of people's lives when the going got tough. At least, that's what it felt like.

Anne folded her hands across her chest, battling the grief of spiritual betrayal. "It's late, and I have to go to bed."

He didn't move.

She gritted her teeth. "I'm not debating this with you. I don't care what you believe." She thumped her hand on her chest and felt her heart hammering. "I know that God's grace isn't enough. Frankly, I don't have the faintest inkling what God's grace in the dark moments might look like because I've never seen it. I've never felt His arms around me, never noticed the bright light that is supposed to calm my fears. I know the truth, and it doesn't resemble your religious platitudes."

Noah nodded. "I guess you do."

What did he mean by that? "Just leave, Noah. I'm sorry I can't help you."

He made a small noise in the back of his throat that sounded suspiciously like a groan. "Lord, give me a little grace here!"

"Ha!" Anne jutted out her chin. "See?"

He blinked at her, opened his mouth, and gave a huff that sounded suspiciously like . . . laughter?

Anne nearly punched him. "What's so funny?"

He shook his head. "You are." He gave her a tender look. "Anne, you are delightful. There's no denying it. I wish you could see your face, all screwed up and angry. You're ready to run from God's grace." He smiled, and it hinted at a kindness that made her bite her trembling lip. "I don't know why you are in Deep Haven, but I know that whatever lessons God wants to teach you, He can do it here or anywhere. It doesn't matter to Him. And that's also a part of God's grace. You can't escape it. You simply can't run from His love in your life."

She swallowed, feeling like the insensitive brute had slapped her. "Right. Oh yes, God is just brimming with love for me. What a gift to be . . ." Tears clogged her throat. No, she wasn't going to return to that moment. The last thing she wanted from the man before her was his pity.

"What?" His voice was so soft it hurt.

She clenched her jaw and turned away. "Nothing. Nothing at all. I don't see God's love as easily as you do, I guess."

He sighed, as if longing to respond. Then he started to leave, and she closed her eyes, immensely thankful that he wasn't going to chase her down the road of grief to her most private sorrows. A man like him, packed with muscle and menace and immune to vulnerability, wouldn't have the foggiest idea how to respond to her horrors.

Then, as if unable to let her troubles linger between them without comment, he spoke into the wind. The words chilled her to her bones. "Whatever darkness you've walked through, Anne, God was there. You just don't want to open your eyes and see Him. Don't run from your fears. Face them."

She recoiled, unable to believe the audacity of his words. She was struck with the sudden impulse to haul up the edge

of her shirt to just below her ribs and show him how she
hadn't run from her fears. How she'd planted herself long
enough to get a jagged scar that shattered not only her
body, but her faith in a good and protective God. She
ought to show him exactly where God wasn't at that ugly
moment. *Yeah, sure, God's love surrounded me, didn't it?*
She didn't want to open her eyes to see God? She'd begged
for His almighty presence as she tumbled into a pit of
despair, of blinding darkness. Anne balled her fists at
her sides, wanting to barrel them into Mr. I-Have-the-
Sensitivity-of-a-Grizzly's face.

Instead, she said tightly, "My darkness is my business.
You couldn't possibly understand what kind of darkness
I've lived in." She folded her arms, pressing against the
hollowness in her chest. "I came here to find peace. Please
leave."

He stared at her, his smile erased, his eyes piercing. She
clenched her jaw, refusing tears. Then he left without a
word. His motorcycle's roar drowned out the scream of her
racing pulse, the only recognizable sign of life in her bereft
heart.

Noah paced the shoreline, his heart still lodged squarely
in his throat, choking off any words of sympathy he might
have said to Anne. At least it had silenced his pat answers.

He couldn't fault her for wondering if God had dropped
her. He'd fought that faith battle more times than he wanted
to remember.

Like when he'd seen a boy he'd led to the Lord, a
boy with promise and hope, flush his future away with
a scrum—intravenous drugs. Or when he'd seen the
woman who had raised him, the closest thing Noah had to
a mother, die of a heart attack a week later. He even remembered the first time he felt as if he'd been drop-kicked by
God—at the age of five when his newly widowed father,

stupefied by drink, had thrown him out of the house and told Noah how he'd murder him if he returned. Yes, Noah knew all about dark moments and the paralyzing fear that God had fumbled.

But he also knew how it felt to be rescued. To see God's love in a smile, to hear it in a song, to feel it in the embrace of strangers. Strangers who found a hungry shivering boy in a Dumpster, huddled in a soggy apple box. Strangers who took him to a shelter and finally found him a home. God's grace meant they delivered an orphaned boy to Mother Peters, a new mother with a heart as wide as the Pacific.

God's grace didn't mean life skipped over the hard parts. Grace meant that when life threatened to drown him, in those catastrophic moments, God enclosed him in the pocket of His embrace. Noah had learned that the only way to discover God's sufficient grace was to let the storm buffet, then cling to God, like David said in Psalm 62:5, Noah's favorite: "I wait quietly before God, for my hope is in Him."

Noah dug his hands into his hair, feeling grubby and small in the face of what he'd seen in Anne's eyes and the avalanche of pain storming her words. How was he supposed to comfort that kind of emotional wreckage?

"O my people, trust in Him at all times. Pour out your heart to Him, for God is our refuge." The verse pulsed in his heart, something that he wished he'd said to Anne in place of his shocked silence.

Where did a beautiful woman like Anne get emotional scars that shattered her faith in the God who had made this wondrous landscape around her? Noah sat on the beach under the glow of the Deep Haven lighthouse and listened to the storm gather, wishing he'd been there to stop the one who had assaulted Anne's soul.

"Noah? What are you doing out here?" Pastor Dan crunched in the rocks down the shore, holding a flashlight. Dressed in a rain slicker, he looked prepared, as usual, for the daily unpredictabilities. "I was at the nursing home and

saw your bike." He sat down, digging a place in the stony beach to hold the light. The beam flashed skyward and was devoured by the night.

"I'm just wishing I was a different man. Wishing I had the right words."

Dan frowned at him.

Noah picked up a fistful of tiny pebbles, shaking them. "I blew it tonight. That nurse I got for the camp, well . . . I sort of trapped her."

"What?"

Noah grimaced. "I know it wasn't the right thing to do, so I went to apologize to her and managed to not only scare her to death, but I also stomped all over her feelings."

"That doesn't sound like you."

"You don't know me that well, Dan. I've been accused of having the sensitivity of a porcupine." He gave a wry smile. "She's been . . . emotionally injured. And I—" he could barely pry the words out of his constricting chest— "laughed."

Dan stayed mercifully silent.

"She was so . . . cute and frustrated, and I had no idea her issues ran bone deep." Noah buried his face in his hands. "I don't know what to do."

The waves washed on shore, growing violent. The spray landed on their boots.

"Noah, you'll figure out a way to make it right."

"No, I think I really blew it this time." He stared at his hands, at the scar across his right palm. "I'm not sure why God picked me to do this job. I'm so unqualified. How am I supposed to reach kids' hearts with the gospel when I can't even encourage Anne?"

Dan threw a handful of stones into the surf. They crackled as they hit the beach. "Well, that's where you forget that you're just the vessel. Remember Galatians 2:20: 'I myself no longer live, but Christ lives in me. So I live my life in this earthly body by trusting in the Son of God, who loved me and gave Himself for me.' It's God who has to reach the kids. It's God who will encourage Anne. God made you the way you are, and you'll have to trust Him to mold you into the person He wants you to be. Trust Him to give you the right words for this woman."

Noah blew out a long, unsteady breath. "I can't help feeling like I'm in way over my head, treading water for all I'm worth but going under fast."

"Hmm." Dan reached for the flashlight, flicked it erratically toward the sky, then straight out across the lake. The beam lit the frothy peaks of waves. "It seems to me that a man who is drowning has no choice but to reach up for help."

Noah closed his eyes, letting Dan's words settle deep into his soul.

"You know," Dan said softly, "I wonder if over your head and drowning might be exactly where God wants you to be."

Noah opened his eyes and pitched a rock into the swell of waves. "Perhaps. But if Anne Lundstrom doesn't change her mind, I won't even get a chance to get my feet wet."

The night toyed with his emotions. Sliding over him like a snake, slithering through his pores.

Infecting his bones.

He itched, shifted, struggled against the claw of the past. Voices—loud, drunk, angry. Fear, cold and thick, icing his veins.

No! Father!

He flinched, reeling from the blow of the memory. Fought to open his eyes. The room spun with the smell of anger—sweat, beer, iron-ore shavings.

Then the shadows lurched over him, and the icy sting of a gun barrel screwed into his jaw.

"Where is it?" a voice growled, and he came fully awake.

Three shadows, accented by the spark of moonlight on silver gun barrels.

"I don't have it. Yet." He sounded pitiful and adolescent. Fear rose and clogged his throat. "But I will."

Breath, thick with booze, streamed across him. "You have one week. One."

Relief melted every muscle. He lay down, a soggy, trembling mass on his double bed as they filed out and closed the door with a soft click.

7

The sunlight woke him, a kiss of hope after the onslaught of the night. Noah sprawled on the ratty sofa of the Wilderness Challenge lodge and closed his eyes, feeling as if he'd been beaten and left for dead. He'd chased his worst fears around in his sleep, and somewhere in the wee hours he knew he had no choice but to surrender. Wilderness Challenge would have to wait another season to open.

His heart felt like cement in his chest. *God, I am sorry I'm not the man to make this happen. Please forgive me for being less than who You needed.* He sat up and swung his legs onto the floor, the chill somehow a balm to his knotted nerves.

The idea of calling the mothers and aunts of the campers and having to tell them the kids would be spending the summer on the streets pitched his empty stomach.

He needed coffee. He staggered into the kitchen, newly outfitted and sparkly with a new industrial refrigerator and stove. The bag of coffee lay crumpled and empty next to the Mr. Coffee. He made a face at the two-day-old sludge crusting the bottom of the pot. Closing his eyes, he held the bag up to his nose and inhaled deeply. The aroma would have to do until he made it into town and grabbed a cup at the Footstep of Heaven.

He enjoyed his occasional mornings there, chatting with Joe, the owner's husband. Evidently, the guy knew something about being judged by external appearances, although Noah wasn't sure how. Joe Michaels seemed to have life in the palm of his hand—a beautiful and charming wife, a life goal that didn't need the approval of three committees to attain, and a very definite niche in the community. Everyone loved Joe, and it wasn't rare to find the guy hosting a small crowd, like he was some sort of celebrity.

Noah grabbed a towel and headed out to the men's washhouse, a building with nothing more than a trough and a few faucets, half open to the sky. He'd built a private shower on one end, but Noah counted on the attraction of a clear Boundary Waters lake to entice his campers to cleanliness.

The icy water, pumped up from the lake, made him gasp. He dunked his head into the trough, washed his hair, and felt frozen when he toweled dry.

The sun blinked through the sodden trees, turning droplets into diamonds against a jade background. The storm had littered twigs and leaves across the yard, and Noah counted at least two big branches across the trails. He'd have to do some cleanup before he tackled assembling cots.

No. He stopped and shook his head. There he went, thinking like a guy with a mission instead of a soggy failure with nothing but expenses piling up around his ears. It was so easy to fall into the plans, skipping ahead on the hope set before him, the grace already granted to him. He took a deep breath and trudged back to the lodge.

He bent into the fridge, scrounging up some sort of sandwich—pickles and mayonnaise, maybe—when he heard the gravel crunch of wheels on the drive. He paused, riffling through his mental files. Staffers? Not until Saturday. Inspectors? His stomach knotted.

He closed the fridge and plodded outside. He was half-

way out the door and across the porch when he saw her standing with her hands on her hips, surveying his freshly tiled roof.

The wind toyed with her hair, the delicious color of copper. Dressed in a pair of track pants and a sweatshirt, she looked suspiciously ready to . . . work?

Then she looked at him and smiled, and for a moment, he thought he would never move again.

"Good morning!"

Where was his voice? He managed to nod.

"I thought, well . . ." She wrinkled her nose, as if trying to conjure up the right words. Then she took a breath and shrugged. "You helped me last night. I thought I could repay the favor."

His heart took a flying leap right out of his chest and landed at her feet. "Swell," he croaked, trying not to sound like a besotted idiot. He had the sudden urge to race over to her, shake this alien being hard, and demand that the Anne he knew, the one with inborn spitfire, be immediately returned to her human body.

Or maybe not. Perhaps he liked this new version better.

He must have missed a few days here, a few episodes of their rocky relationship, because to save his life, he had no idea why Anne Lundstrom was standing in his yard, rolling up her sleeves.

"Don't make any assumptions. It's just for one day." But the way she smiled, well, he didn't believe her for a second. No, not for one second. Because he'd make this day the best of her entire life.

Shame had driven Anne up the Gunflint Trail to Wilderness Challenge. Noah had helped her clean her house and sat with her on the porch, listening to her spew out spiritual bitterness. Yes, she felt orphaned by God, but the pastor's kid in her couldn't leave that last ugly impression on Noah's brain.

And when he grinned at her, his expression turning to pure delight when she offered to help him, her heart did a tiny flip. With his wet hair, a shag of dark whiskers on his chin, his rumpled black T-shirt and army fatigues, he looked like a confusing, way-too-attractive mix of gangster and hobo. She shook off the impression and opened her car door. "Hope you don't mind, but Bertha begged to come along."

The dog jumped off the driver's seat and into Noah's arms. He laughed and fell on his backside, saturated by Bertha's sloppy affection. Anne shook her head, oddly warmed by the sight of him wrestling with her dog. "I guess she likes you."

"Well, you know, we're partners in crime." He winked at Anne, and she decided that . . . well . . . maybe . . . she could try and like him too. If he didn't sneak up on her or tread into her spiritual wasteland.

"So, where do we start?" The camp looked . . . rustic. The Lincoln Logs lodge, with its sagging porch and weathered steps, looked about a century old. She couldn't imagine spending any significant amount of time here. She liked the North Shore scenery, but Anne had been a city girl most of her life, and she appreciated the benefits of, say, indoor plumbing and electricity.

Noah pushed Bertha off. The dog bounded in a circle, tongue flapping, then bolted up the trail. "She'll be okay," he said, ESPing Anne's sudden flare of worry. He stood, brushed off his pants. "I have to build a new outhouse, put up that army tent over there, chop and stack firewood, and rebuild the fire pit."

"Is that all?" She still wasn't used to his size, which probably accounted for the way her pulse had rocketed off the charts when she'd seen his shadow lurking in her bedroom last night. When he strolled over to her, panic rippled down her spine. Perhaps this was a bad idea. . . .

"Well, no, actually, but that's today's list." He made a wry face. "I never seem to catch up."

"You're doing all this by yourself?" She tried to keep the wariness from her voice.

He nodded. "Well, until today, that is." His bright smile melted her fear into a hot puddle. "It's just been me and the squirrels." He leaned closer to her, lowering his voice. The fresh smell of soap and toothpaste made her reconsider the hobo impression. "But between you and me, the squirrels are a loud and lazy bunch. Always running off to play or napping on the job. And they snore something terrible."

She smiled, and he rewarded her with another wink. "Well, I'm better with a stethoscope than a hammer," she admitted, "but I'll give it my best shot."

They started on the outhouse, something Anne, in her twenty-seven years, never thought she would build. The sun escaped the reach of the oaks and basswoods, drying the sodden ground and heating the day.

Two hours into the morning, Anne had shed her sweatshirt, and her skin began to bake. She noticed a V of sweat down the back of Noah's shirt, but he didn't remove it.

He had a simple grace about him, adeptly measuring twice, cutting once, his strong arms working the circular saw like he'd been born a carpenter. Anne held nails, chatted about the weather, and listened to him hum. While he worked, he managed to exhaust a repertoire of hymns. She recognized most of them—"How Great Thou Art," "Fairest Lord Jesus," and "Amazing Grace." She even hummed along to "Blessed Assurance."

"Why do you sing hymns?" She asked during a water break down at the dock. Ten o'clock by her watch, and her stomach had already growled once. She could go for a cup of tea and a bran muffin from the Footstep of Heaven Bookstore and Coffee Shop, but Noah didn't hint at slowing.

"I love hymns. They're like mini-sermons set to a tune. Whenever I am at a loss for a Bible verse, I go right to a hymn." He poured a sierra cup of lake water over his head, letting it drip down his back. Another quick drenching, then he scraped his hair back from his face, looking dangerously like a Wild West warrior. He didn't bother to towel off the water on his face; it dripped through his dark whiskers. "I learned them when I went to college, and they stuck. I prefer hymns to all other Christian music, although Michael Card's ballads run a close second."

Anne felt like a heathen. "I like opera."

He nodded, as if that was the type of music he'd expect her to like. Frankly, she'd developed a taste for it only in the last year. Something about the tones of a rich tenor, regardless of the language of the lyrics, ministered to her battered soul.

By lunchtime, he'd placed the new seat, with attached ceramic lid, over a hole he'd dug inside the outhouse back in the woods. Anne never felt so proud of a toilet in her entire life. She broke into giggles when Noah closed the new door and wrote *Ladies* on it.

"At least I'll know where to find the place when it's pitch-dark," she commented. Her words hovered in the warm air as Noah's smile faded. He stared at her. The sunlight drew out the gold in his widened eyes. She dug up quick words to fill her glaring lack of good judgment. "I'm starved. How about some lunch?"

Mercifully, he didn't leap on her first comment. He shoved his hammer into his leather work belt. "I think I have some pickles in the fridge."

"Pickles?"

He shrugged. "Food hasn't been a high priority yet."

That was an understatement, Anne decided as she stared into his empty refrigerator. Pickles, yes. Mayonnaise, a wrinkled apple, a crusty hunk of Swiss cheese, and a smoky-smelling, foul brown fish head in Saran Wrap. "Quite the selection here, Noah."

He stood before a large pantry, as if waiting for something to materialize. "A half bag of Doritos and a can of tuna."

Anne closed the fridge. "How about if I run into town and get us something decent?"

"Wait. I think I have hot dogs in the freezer in the outfitter's shack."

"Do you have a microwave?" She'd been profoundly grateful to see the camp had electricity when he'd offered her—thanks, but no—the last sludge from the coffeemaker.

"Negative on the microwave. We'll have to let them thaw. Maybe tonight we could have a cookout, roast marshmallows?" He sounded like a ten-year-old, charming and unpretentious, and she couldn't help but nod, his enthusiasm catchy like a song. She hadn't roasted a marshmallow in her entire life, but she had no doubts Mr. Outdoors could teach her. "I can offer you the rest of the pickles to tide you over."

"I suppose I could carve up that wrinkled apple." Anne reached into the fridge.

"I'm sorry. I didn't really expect . . . company." Noah made a wry face, then said, "I mean, I'm glad you're here . . . really glad. I didn't expect . . . um . . . well, especially after last night . . ." He had turned red, a charming touch to his earthy appearance. Anne couldn't help but smile at his chagrin. "Anne," he said, his expression so solemn she stopped tossing the apple in her hand, "I am so sorry I laughed at you last night."

Oh no, tears sprang into her eyes. Where had they come from? She thought she'd cried herself dry last night into Bertha's fur. Anne blinked them back. *Noah, don't go down that path.* "No problem," she said too quickly.

He closed his eyes, giving her space to gather her suddenly fraying emotions. "No, it's not okay. But we'll talk about it later."

Oh, that made her feel better. No, sorry, but they'd never discuss it again if she had her druthers. "Okay," she said, ducking the issue.

They made a sorry picnic on the porch, sitting in the sun, eating pickles, a mealy apple, stale Doritos, and tuna straight from the can. But Noah told her a story of his dorm life, and Anne had to admit the company made up for the meal.

"So, have you been a Christian all your life?" she asked as she picked through Doritos crumbs.

"Nope."

When he didn't offer any more, she glanced at him. He stared out over the yard as though caught in time, wrestling with unseen phantoms. Her heartbeat filled the silence, as she wondered what he wasn't saying.

"How about you?"

"Yes." Anne slapped the crumbs off her fingers. "My dad was a pastor. I grew up watching my father evangelize our neighbors and minister to our community. I have to say there's never been a time I can remember that I didn't know God." *Know* Him, yes, but *trust* Him—now that was a different answer, but she didn't particularly want to revisit that topic. Not with the sun warming her heart and Noah sitting beside her like a real friend. Her bitterness was sure to hang a cloud over the rest of the day and send a cold shudder into their fragile friendship.

"That's wonderful. What a treasure." His comment intrigued her. But he didn't allow her a rebuttal. "Ready to stack wood?"

A pile of unsplit logs had been dumped next to the camp's woodshed. Noah grabbed the ax, and Anne watched with a tight breath as he set the log up on the block, then chopped it neatly through. He handled the ax as if he'd been born with it in his hands. Relief flushed through her that she wasn't going to have to sew his leg or foot back to his body.

How did a man who looked like a gangster learn to survive in the wilderness? She rephrased her question as she picked up the split logs and piled them neatly against the back of the shed. "Did you grow up around here?"

He swung the ax in a graceful swoop, his arm muscles tight. The movement hitched up his shirtsleeves, and she

noticed a layer of Band-Aids on his upper arm. Obviously the man wasn't indestructible.

"Nope," he answered, catching his breath. He repositioned the logs. Chopped.

O-kay. So he wasn't a fount of information. She knew he'd attended an upscale Christian college . . . he must have had a somewhat decent upbringing. "Where did you learn to run a camp?"

He swung the ax again. She'd never seen someone chop wood. The rhythm amazed her. "I attended wilderness training classes in Duluth. It's been a passion of mine for a number of years."

Swing, chop, wood tumbled off the block. "How about you? Where did you grow up?" Sweat beaded his brow, tangled in his dark hair.

"Nowhere I want to remember, that's for sure."

He stopped his swing and looked at her, concern in his expression. "Ouch."

She brushed her hair back with her wrists. "I'm here now. That's what matters."

He finished his swing. The wood cracked. "Where did you get your nurse's training?"

Hadn't he read a personnel file on her? She picked up the fallen wood. "The University of Minnesota. I worked my way through school as a part-time EMT."

She threw the wood on the stack. "I think the nursing career came from my father's influence. I've always had an urge to be a part of some kind of ministry, and the nursing profession seemed in that realm. I can't preach, but I can bandage hurts, help heal wounds. It feels like I'm working for the kingdom." She didn't add that since that day last summer, she'd barely had time to think, let alone figure out, where those lofty goals fit in with her sudden abandonment by the God she'd wanted to serve.

"Absolutely." Noah's smile seemed warmer than the sun's rays, and suddenly Anne felt grimy, with sweat glistening on her face and bark and woodchips sticking to her forearms. She hated to imagine the current state of her rebellious mop.

He took a red bandana out of his back pocket and tied it around his head. Now he looked like Geronimo, wild and fierce. She couldn't help asking, "So, where did you get the name Noah? It's so . . ."

"Unusual for a fella with my ancestry?" He cracked a lopsided smile when he finished her sentence, and it loosened the grip of embarrassment in her chest.

She nodded, thankful he hadn't been offended.

"My grandmother. She was as saintly as they come. She persuaded my parents to name me after a man of faith, hoping perhaps that I would turn out better than they did."

"You're not . . . ?"

"One hundred percent Native American?" He gave a sharp laugh. "Nope. I'm pure mixed breed, from mongrel parents. Somehow I inherited most of the Ojibwa traits floating in the Standing Bear gene pool, but I've even got a touch of authentic Minnesotan Swede in me."

When he winked at her again, the third time now, she realized that the shiver that shimmied down her spine had nothing to do with fear. His hardworking presence felt so comfortable, so much like a budding friendship, she couldn't help but wonder what other misconceptions she had created about Noah Standing Bear.

They split wood and stacked it until the sun hovered half-mast over the horizon. They spent the hours before twilight staking out the army tent and rebuilding the campfire pit, repositioning stones or adding new ones they lugged from the lakeshore. By the time long shadows scraped the lake and Noah constructed a textbook Boy Scout campfire, Anne felt as ravenous as a bear in March.

Bertha had finished her explorations of camp and found a place in the shade on the lodge porch, sides heaving. Poor lady, she wasn't dressed for summer, with her white-and-brown shag coat. The setting sun took the heat with it and

unleashed a hint of breeze. Anne lifted her face, intoxicated by the outdoorsy fragrances of pine, lake, and wildflowers.

Noah had disappeared with a towel around his neck, leaving her to sit in front of the fire pit to finish her blackened hot dog. Three rows of rough logs set in a semicircle hinted that Noah had plans for this area beyond roasting dinner.

She'd come to the semi-reluctant conclusion that perhaps Mr. Break-and-Enter wasn't who she'd carved him out to be in her mind. Maybe—and this thought had riddled her for the past two hours—Noah had a character worth exploring. Bertha liked him. That upped his reputation in Anne's mind. Then again, the dog's qualifications were minimal—a guy who rubbed behind her ears, could take a slopping tongue-lashing on the choppers, and remembered to save the soup bones. Noah had endeared himself to the brute forever when he tossed her the remnants of the smoked cisco carcass he'd had buried in his refrigerator.

Anne couldn't remember the last time she'd felt so deliciously tired. So completely and contentedly worn to the bone. She heard footsteps behind her and turned. Noah trotted down the path, grinning at her, a bag of marshmallows in his hands. She noticed he'd washed up and changed into a gray army T-shirt, looking every inch a modern-day warrior in his fatigues and slicked-backed hair.

He climbed over the logs and settled next to her, smelling fresh and masculine. "Dessert," he said and handed her the bag.

Anne opened it and dug out a marshmallow. "I've never done this before." She poked it onto the willow stick Noah had cut and dangled the marshmallow over the embers, sizzling red against the creeping twilight. Overhead a smattering of stars competed with the moon for brilliance.

"You're going to burn it." Noah reached for her roasting stick. "May I?"

Now he wanted to teach her to cook? It didn't surprise

her in the least that he'd know how to toast a marshmallow to perfection.

"Aim for the red coals, the ones that haven't turned white but don't have a flame. And turn the stick slowly, as if on a spit. She'll turn golden brown and melt in your mouth."

When he returned her roasting stick, Anne mimicked his movements. "I guess you're an old pro at this, huh?"

He shrugged, but his smile went straight to her heart and turned it to pudding.

He had a noble purpose here in Wilderness Challenge. She'd fallen into his dream, swallowed by his enthusiasm as he explained his plans to immerse the kids in the wild. "They'll see God's handiwork firsthand and know He is big enough for their problems at home."

Anne had no trouble envisioning the campers' chubby grins, the delight in their innocent eyes, and their gleeful laughter coming from the beach. "Are you sure it's wise to have both boys and girls here at the same time?" she had asked earlier, as she swept out the cement pad for the tent. She hadn't missed the fact that the tents were well-distanced from each other, located on both sides of the wide center path that acted like the Jordan River.

"Well, part of our goal is to teach the fellas to treat ladies with respect. They need the practice. Besides, we'll keep eagle eyes on them. We have one counselor and a junior counselor for every five campers, so I think we'll be able to keep them in line."

She had to admit that the camper-counselor ratio seemed a bit intense, especially for church kids who should know how to behave themselves. But Noah seemed to know what he was doing, and she couldn't ignore the anticipation budding in her chest. Whatever happened here this summer, it would be magical.

A whippoorwill called out over the dark water, and occa-sionally against the crackle of hot coals, she heard a gentle

plop as a fish slapped the surface. Beside her Noah had
folded his hands and was staring into the landscape.

"I'm impressed with your camp, Noah." A small lump
formed in her throat. She had made it clear that she
wouldn't be staying, hadn't she? One day. She'd said that
out loud. Twice. Now that she thought about it, the second
time it might have been a dying echo in her mind.

"Be impressed with God. He did this."

She looked heavenward, at the streak of the Milky Way
in the velvet night. "Yes, He did."

"God has a history of impressive acts. I try to remember
them when I'm feeling like life has hit the skids." Noah
picked up a log and set it in the fire. Sparks showered the
night. "The only way to survive the dark moments is to
remember the ones in the light."

"But what if the dark moments make no sense?" Anne
watched as flames flickered around the log in a blistering
embrace. "What if they just seem . . . harsh?" Here they
went again, wandering into the no-man's-land of her
wounded spirit. Only now, somehow, it didn't seem like
such an invasion.

"You mean like when God let Satan wipe out Job's live-
stock and family, and then let Satan attack the man with
boils?"

Anne had to smile. She liked a man who knew his Bible.
"Yes. Now doesn't that seem a bit harsh to you? Or take
Moses. There he was, leading a bunch of ungrateful, thirsty
Israelites across the desert. He loses his temper and instead
of speaking to a stone wall like God commanded, he
whacks it. I would too. And for that felony, Moses doesn't
enter the Promised Land. Harsh."

Noah chuckled. "Well, you're certainly a woman who's
thought it through."

"C'mon, I told you my father was a pastor. We were fed
Bible stories for supper." Anne moved her marshmallow
away from the flames and found a new nesting place. The
marshmallow had begun to bubble brown at the tip.

"I think whenever we encounter something that God does that doesn't mesh with our view of Him, we need to take a closer look. Why did He do it? Confusion is a perfect opportunity to understand God better." Noah stood up, slapped his hands. "Stick around one more second?"

How could she say no to the texture of pleading in those sweet brown eyes?

Noah ran toward the lodge and returned moments later with a guitar. Anne just about fell off her log when he sat down and began to strum. Noah Standing Bear certainly knew how to tangle her stereotypes.

And his voice, like warm syrup, went right to her bones. A soft, sweet tenor that had obviously done time in a choir. He closed his eyes, and the sight of a man, vulnerable before God, nearly brought tears to her eyes.

Who was this man?

"'Seek ye first, the kingdom of God, and His righteousness. And all these things will be added unto you. . . .'"

She closed her eyes, listening, wanting to join in the familiar tune, fighting the sudden constriction in her chest. Tears burned the back of her eyes. Seek His kingdom. Seek Him. She had sought Him . . . at one time. But since that fateful day, she'd barely looked at God. Didn't want to face the One who had turned her life inside out.

Noah's song ended without her making a blubbering fool of herself. She gave him an insincere smile, wondering if disappointment ringed his eyes.

"Thank you for your help today, Anne." Noah strummed the guitar, the tune haunting but melodic as it filtered into the mosaic of other night songs. "I don't know what pain you've gone through, but I know you confronted it to help me today."

The lump returned and with it an annoying glaze of tears. Then her marshmallow flamed. Anne waved the torch and screamed, spraying pieces of marshmallow into the campfire.

Noah grabbed the stick. "Stop!" He blew it out, laugh-

ing. "I see you need another lesson in proper marshmallow management."

"Listen, Mr. Eagle Scout," Anne said, fighting giggles, thankful she had a distraction for her tears, "there's more to life than roasting marshmallows."

"Doubtful. Roasting marshmallows is key in developing character. You have to be patient. Seek the perfect embers. Learn to stay out of the blaze." He looked down at her, stern. "And most importantly, you have to be willing to eat the burned part."

"I happen to love burnt marshmallows." She reached for the stick, hiding a grimace.

He crouched in front of her, a smile on his face, his eyes warm. He lowered his voice. "I'll let you in on a little secret, Anne." He blew softly on the charred mallow. The flaky black skin puffed away, leaving only soft cream. "Sometimes the things that look the most ruined are really hiding the prize underneath."

He handed her the treat, but his gaze, twinkling with some sort of magic, held hers. She heard only the beating of her heart, smelled only the fragrance of his masculine woodsy charm.

No, Noah wasn't such a big, scary hoodlum after all.

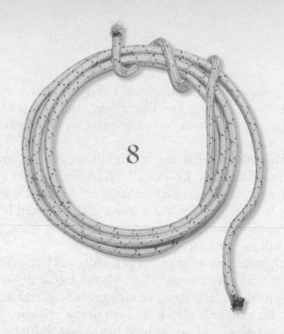

8

Noah knew it was a dream. The voice of sanity in the back of his brain chanted softly, but the smells, sounds, and tastes of that night still constricted his chest.

In his sleep, the Southern Comfort burned his throat and pitched his stomach. The world tilted around him. He smelled the enticing mix of perfume and hair gel and felt the soft-as-a-whisper touch of lips. "This homeboy's putty," a voice cooed. A smattering of laughter, then it mixed into the clamor of voices and music. The world spun again, a menagerie of bright, vibrant colors. Impressions, none of them distinct. Senses melded together until he couldn't extract reality from reverie.

Noah woke up hard, his heart pounding, feeling sick to his pores. The darkness filling the room felt thick and oppressive. He kicked back his blanket, thankful for the cold night air that snapped him to consciousness. Still the past filled his brain.

He'd never forget, no matter how he tried to erase that moment, when he'd awoken in a strange bed, feeling and smelling like he'd been run over by a garbage truck. And to complete the sensation, his mouth had tasted like he'd licked the inside of a Dumpster. Then he saw the girl next to him and horror hit him like a fist. One of the VL homegirls had her arm curled around his body as if she owned it.

Noah sank his head into his hands, hearing again the laughter, seeing it on L'il Lee's face, in Shorty Mac's eyes. Lecherous, victorious laughter, as if he'd passed some sort of test. It embedded his heart like a stain, burned him like acid. Pursued him like a wolf.

He still hadn't outrun that night.

Noah trembled, cold sweat prickling his body. The nightmares always tore a swath through the fabric of his heart, ripping to shreds the sheen of cleanness he'd created in Christ. He groaned, then rolled off the couch onto all fours. The wood-planked floor cooled his hands. A hint of dawn invaded the room, golden light seeping across the wood. The things he'd done and the person he'd been sometimes threatened to consume him.

He had no business cultivating a relationship with Anne Lundstrom. She was clean, pure, light, and joy. Despite his new-creation-in-Christ status, he still had scars etched in his heart, scars that he'd never erase.

Pastor Dan's voice echoed in his brain. *You have to trust Him to make you into the person He wants you to be.* How he wished he could be someone without blemish, someone worthy of Anne's heart.

He wanted to tell himself that his only desire yesterday had been to give Anne a vision for what could happen here. But once she'd arrived, bringing the sunshine with her smile, his tongue glued to his mouth. He'd resorted to praying that perhaps, just by inhaling the fresh breeze, by seeing the crucible of God's fabulous creation, Anne would dive into his project.

But by evening he'd moved past hoping that she'd stay for the summer to dreaming she might stay . . . forever. He'd been wildly jigging into the realms of fantasy, wanting to believe she smiled for him, laughed at his jokes. That the

shine in her eyes was generated by her own budding dreams, and that she'd spent the day at Wilderness Challenge not because of guilt or obligation but because she wanted to be with him, a man who wanted to know her more.

Noah touched his forehead to the floor, fighting a swell of nausea. Anne was light-years out of his universe. Yes, he'd prayed and dreamed for a woman, a partner who would be everything he wasn't and more, a woman who lived to change lives, to love the unlovable. It did dangerous things to his heart to hope that person could be a lady with hazel green eyes and rich chestnut hair. Anne had made it unequivocally clear that her future was here in Deep Haven.

And his was in Minneapolis.

But she was so beautiful, with an innocence written on her face that made all his protective instincts spring to life. He didn't know what kind of demons she had roaming about her past, but he wanted to grab each one by the throat and free her. She'd probably never even envisioned the life he'd lived, hadn't the slightest clue what it felt like to be so deep in sin you started your day gasping. If she harbored even one inkling about the type of man he'd been, well, she'd turn and peel out of his life so fast the breeze in her wake would turn him cold.

No, he was treading dangerous territory hoping she'd return today. He'd enjoyed the way she laughed, the texture of her beautiful smile, tentative yet fascinated. And something about the fragrance of a woman who spent the day not caring what she looked like but rather about what she did tugged at his heart. He wanted to believe trust finally hued her incredible eyes. And a man worthy of trust ran from temptation and the appearance of evil.

Anne shouldn't be here. Not alone. Not with him. That realization felt like a sledgehammer in his chest. He groaned, then rolled over on his back and stared at the beamed ceiling. He liked her way too much for a man who was supposed to be her boss, way too much to invite her back for another round of roasted hot dogs and marshmallows in front of a romantic campfire. If he didn't watch himself, he'd be offering her his heart instead of a job. Even if in his wildest dreams she would cater to that thought, he knew better. He might be a saved and cleansed member of the body of Christ, but next to Anne, he felt like a tattered refugee straight out of some war-torn country.

Anne Lundstrom shouldn't be within ten miles of Noah Standing Bear alone.

One more night sitting under the canopy of the heavens, listening to a loon call skip across the lake, watching the moon turn her hair to copper might make him lose his mind.

He might take her into his arms.

And wouldn't that kindle trust in her eyes? Just when he might have convinced her he wasn't the local thug.

Why couldn't God supply a hairy, muscular, rough-edged paramedic for his camp nurse? No, the Almighty had to provide a pretty, petite woman, with an attitude that packed a punch and a smile that could turn a man inside out.

Then again, Anne's smile, her tenderness were exactly what the street kids needed. Especially if they got hurt. Noah had more raw toughness than Wilderness Challenge ever needed. Obviously God knew his staffing needs better than he did.

Still, a smart man would look his weakness straight in the face, ignore the pang in his chest, and tell her not to come back.

At least not until Saturday.

Anne sat in the hospital parking lot feeling giddy. How odd that one day with a near stranger could send her heart skipping like a teenager's before prom. She ran her hand through Bertha's thick fur. "You liked him too, didn't you?" She rubbed her nose on the dog's wet snout. Bertha sniffed her, then responded with a sloppy kiss. Noah evidently had a positive effect on all women.

Anne had barely slept the night through, replaying the way he stood in the yard, hands in his jeans pockets, watching her drive away. The wind had mussed his dark hair, and the return-to-me look in his eyes had her promising the summer to him.

She admitted that her fledgling decision to commit to Wilderness Challenge for the summer wasn't completely altruistic. Was it so terrible to surrender to his warm friendship or his honorable project? She'd been numb for so long, it frightened her to know that a man she'd barely met made her feel so alive, so wildly hopeful. She hadn't come to Deep Haven looking for romance.

She laughed aloud. Bertha looked at her, blinking those glassy brown eyes. *Romance?* She shook her head. She'd obviously let fancy have its way with her. For a moment she had wondered what it would feel like to hold Noah's wide hand. To be caught in his strong arms. The idea made her giggle. So maybe romance could be in her future. Noah surely had romance in his eyes.

She hoped she hadn't dreamed that part.

She watched Sandra drive up in her Scout, get out, and stride up to the hospital entrance. Anne lifted her hand in a wave, but Sandra didn't see her. A surge of thankfulness swept through Anne for her new friend. Only two days ago, Sandra had let her rant and rave without comment, and her only word of wisdom had been *pray.* Anne glanced at heaven, at the wispy cirrus clouds, the golden sunlight as radiant and warm as Noah's eyes.

Thanks, God. The words tightened her chest. She'd been avoiding heaven for a good while, but this turn of events felt pretty heaven sent. Maybe God had decided to cut her some slack, add abundance to her dreary world. Maybe the Almighty still cared about Anne Lundstrom. It didn't mean she could trust Him, but certainly He had kindled an ember of hope. Perhaps that spark would ignite her faith.

If Anne were to be honest, she had to admit to a regular inferno of hope raging in her chest.

"Stay here, Bertha. I'll be right back." Anne cracked the windows and exited her SUV, shutting the door before the dog could barrel out. Bertha let out a whine. "Sorry, honey; it'll just be a second." A short stop in Dr. Simpson's office, and then she'd floor it up to Gunflint Trail. She couldn't wait to see the look in Noah's beautiful eyes when she appeared on his doorstep, sleeves rolled up, ready to sign on the dotted line.

The roar of a motorcycle made her pause, turn, and freeze as she watched the man in her thoughts pull into the lot. The sight of Noah dressed in a leather jacket, black jeans, and work boots, handling his bike as if he were astride a galloping stallion, made her heart stand up and jig.

She stayed beside her vehicle, forcing herself not to run out to him. Her mother's voice twanged in the back of her brain: *Don't appear too anxious, honey. Let the boys do the courting.* Anne rolled her eyes at the practical advice.

But she obeyed. As she watched Noah park the bike, she wondered what element about him always sent a thrill through her. Yes, his eyes turned her weak and he had arms sturdy enough to hold back her fears. It wasn't his hair, although that begged for a woman's touch. It had to be his bearing. Noah Standing Bear exuded a very intoxicating mix of danger and protection. Like a lion pacing around his pride. She wondered, for a rebellious, giddy, idiotic moment, how it would feel to be the woman in his care.

He turned toward the hospital. His face looked grim, and something about the way he strode across the parking lot, his fists clenched at his sides, sent a streak of fear through her. "Noah?"

He stopped and looked her way. For a second, she wondered if he had actually paled. He didn't smile, and that omission made her feel oddly ill, as if she'd eaten the smoked fish head in his fridge. "Hi."

"Hi, back." She fought the wild impulse to dive in the car and floor it, but some sort of desperation rooted her to the spot as he trudged over to her.

"I was hoping to catch you."

The way he said it told her he wasn't intending to ask her out for breakfast. She swallowed a swelling lump in her throat. "Yes?"

He looked away, and she thought she saw him wince. Then his jaw hardened, and when he faced her again, the coldness in his eyes made her hurt to her toes. "I'm sorry. I don't want you to return to Wilderness Challenge. You did a great job yesterday, and I'm very thankful for your help. But please, don't come back."

She felt as if she'd been punched in the chest. Her breath vanished. "Don't come back?"

"Not until Saturday—that's when the rest of the staff arrives. Staff training starts on Monday, if you want to wait until then."

She wanted to turn and flee, to escape this raw moment before she burst into betraying tears and he saw clear to her wounded heart. Pride kept her feet in place. She forced herself to nod, totally confused. "Okay."

But it wasn't okay. Did he think he could just use her— which he was so obviously doing—to get the funding for the summer? Noah didn't want her; he wanted her skills, her diploma. Her eyes began to burn.

He didn't look at her. "Great. So, I'll see you Monday?"

Total shock made her agree before she realized she'd even spoken. Sure, she'd love to spend the summer letting him twist her heart right out of her chest.

"Thanks again for your help yesterday." The words sounded wooden, to match his expression.

Anne shrugged, unable to comprehend how her golden future had turned completely black.

Then he turned and walked—no, ran—back to his motorcycle. Anne clenched her jaw, but she couldn't stave off the flood of tears as she watched him drive away, his back straight and proud like a warrior who'd just shot his prey.

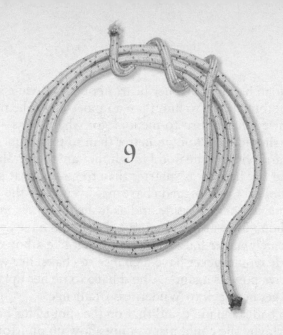

9

The air smelled of Lake Superior, fresh and cleansing—exactly what Anne needed after three days of rain and gloom. She hung her elbow out of Dr. Jefferies' silver Lexus, thankful he'd chosen to drive to the reservation clinic today. The silence on her lonely trek north up Highway 61 the past three days, through a gray sheet of fog and surprising June chill, had left her raw and barren. Solitude—something she'd once craved—seemed like honorable mention after Noah's vibrant company.

She'd been instantly grateful for Dr. Simpson's meddling and bossiness when he commanded her to assist Jenny Olson at the Granite River Indian Reservation medical clinic. These last couple of days in the nurse's capable and cheerful presence had kept Anne's mind from wandering back to Wilderness Challenge and diving into a heart-wrenching daydream of Noah chopping wood or rigging the tents. It nearly made her cry the few times she thought of him with his hands in his pockets, watching the lake, eyes filled with some exotic mystery she would have longed to solve.

Anne groaned and closed her eyes. It felt totally unfair

that Noah had invaded her heart in one day, while she had been nothing more to him than a money cow. She now recognized that return-to-me look for what it was—greed.

She should have known better than to trust him. Hadn't her years living in the hood taught her anything? She thought her heart was smarter than to go soggy at a pair of beautiful eyes and rugged charisma. Even if for the briefest of moments she'd felt safe and as if she'd found someone who didn't look at her like prey, she should have kept her heart safely under lock and key. She felt like a boy-crazy dolt. He would never have a chance to charm her with his deceptive powers again . . . he'd have to tie her up and gag her to get her back to Wilderness Challenge.

Too bad she hadn't said that on the spot to his handsome face. Maybe she could just . . . not show up on Monday morning? The thought of him tracking her down, fire in his eyes, made her wince. The last thing she needed was his disturbing the peace at Edith's. She moaned, wishing she had been quicker with her tongue so she could have scraped up the words to tell Mr. Noah Standing Bear exactly what she thought of him and his employment techniques.

Dr. Jefferies smiled at her. "Glad to have you along with me today. I hear you've had a good week."

Anne nodded as she glanced at the doctor. Now here was a man worthy of her attention. Clean-cut, blond hair, kind brown eyes, groomed hands firmly on the steering wheel. She'd been a fool to fall so easily for tall, dark, and handsome. She'd let her idiotic heart whisk her off to never-never land, making it apparent she'd left her brain in Minneapolis when she moved to Deep Haven. Thankfully, it had tracked her down in time to settle her into her job. She was here to learn, and today she was under the tutelage of handsome, normal, proper family doctor Richard Jefferies, the latest and best catch from the pool of eligible bachelors. Not that she was fishing, but it was important to be in the right company.

"It's been nice to be busy," Anne said in answer to his

comment. "Jenny brought me out on Wednesday, introduced me to the tribal council, and showed me around the reservation. She mentioned the clinic needed some work."

"That's an understatement." Dr. Jefferies turned down the swell of hip-hop on the radio, to Anne's silent gratitude. "With the new casino opening, I know the reservation has plans to sink some profits into the community." He shrugged and gave her a bleak look. "About half these folks live below the poverty level, even with the casino profits. The other half send cash down to the cities to help their families."

Anne had no problem picturing those folks. Half of them lived in her former neighborhood. Many of them escaped the reservation to find jobs or attend the university. The others had simply exchanged rural poverty for urban hopelessness. There was a good reason why alcoholism skyrocketed among the elderly Native Americans. Many still had difficulty finding their footing, regardless of where they lived.

"I met some wonderful young mothers," Anne offered, "and according to the reservation statistics, about half are double-parent homes."

"Granite River Reservation has a better percentage than many. Over 75 percent of the population is gainfully employed, between the state parks, the federal jobs, the casino, and the border jobs in Thunder Bay. That's not typical, however." Dr. Jefferies passed a crawling minivan, piled high with luggage. Anne waved at a little girl who had pushed her nose up against her grimy window.

"Most Native Americans struggle with a place to call home," Dr. Jefferies continued, his foot stomping on the accelerator as he passed a slow-moving car. "The reservation is no picnic. Jobs are hard to find. Poverty, broken marriages, and alcoholism are the norm. And the city offers no escape. Without a decent education, they find themselves on the street or crammed in with their distant relatives."

"What about drugs? I've heard they're on the rise." The

memory of one punk, high on some sort of uppers—snow or perhaps black beauties—raced through her mind. She blinked it away.

Dr. Jefferies paused, pursed his lips. "It's always an issue."

"And gangs? In the cities, they play no favorites. Native Americans are sucked in along with the rest of the kids."

"I don't know about the gang activity in Granite River, but I wouldn't be surprised." He drummed his fingers on the steering wheel, brow furrowed, as if wrestling with his thoughts. "By the way, if you haven't already heard, there's a burglar afoot in Deep Haven. Gloria Miller—she works in the PT department—had her house vandalized while she was on vacation. And one of the local nurses claims she was followed while coming off late shift last week. She called the cops on the way home, and they were waiting for her at her house. It scared the mugger off. But he's out there, so, well . . . just be careful, okay?"

He glanced at her, and she saw concern in his eyes, reaching out to her. "If you are ever afraid, you know you can call me. I'd be glad to help . . . walk you home or whatever."

She imagined Dr. Jefferies standing in front of some mugger, and while his slight form didn't inspire the confidence that, say, Noah the Thug would have, the kind offer warmed her heart. "Thank you."

They passed the sprawling Granite River Casino, crafted to resemble a cozy 1800s lodge in the tradition of the fur traders who once blazed a trail from Canada down to Lake Superior. Anne was under no illusions that this new enterprise held the latest in blackjack, bingo, and video slots designed to suck up a person's hard-earned paycheck.

"You know, the dining room serves excellent apple dumplings." Dr. Jefferies smiled at her, and she couldn't help but notice a twinkle in his eye. "If we're late driving back, maybe we can stop in."

Anne nodded, debating how to respond wisely. Sharing dessert with a coworker wasn't a date, was it?

"Okay, maybe," she said. Perhaps Dr. Jefferies, with his safe, calm demeanor and a nicely constructed future, was just the medicine she needed to heal her wounded heart. "That would be nice."

Granite River itself couldn't be defined as a boomtown. The main street resembled something out of a Hollywood mock-up with a convenience store/gas station, a grocery store, a postal office/federal building, and the shabby clinic comprising the hub. A collection of micro single family homes, with peeling siding and weed-rooted yards, spiraled out from the main drag on half-paved, half-dirt streets. Rusty bikes, broken yard toys, and fraying furniture littered the streets and occasional saggy porches. A few children sat on the cement front steps of a trailer, one playfully fighting with a dirty mutt for a rag.

Even the medical clinic had seen better days, judging by its weathered clapboard siding and the once-neon, green-and-white light over the door. The reservation felt as miserable as it looked, evident, for instance, from the empty eyes and drawn faces of two elderly men holding long-neck bottles as they lounged in front of the grocery store. Anne hoped it was root beer. She tried not to look at the old-timers but felt their probing gaze on her as she followed Dr. Jefferies into the clinic.

Jenny waited inside, wearing a pink nurse's jacket over her jeans and T-shirt. Anne donned a similar jacket and tried to feel comfortable. Hard to do with twenty pairs of eyes on her. Three young mothers holding sniffling babies, an elderly couple, and two chubby middle-aged women sat in the cracked vinyl chairs. A handful of teenagers clumped in the corner. The tension felt oily and thick as she slipped into the supply room behind Jenny.

"Is it always this full?"

"Only once a month." Jenny readied a tray of vials,

swabs, alcohol swipes, and gloves. "Most are here for HIV tests. First Friday of every month, they're free."

She shoved the tray into Anne's hands and trotted out of the room. While Anne stood there, openmouthed, her courage careening to her toes, Jenny called the first name.

To Anne's dismay, one of the teenage girls stepped forward, hugging her skinny waist. Eyes downcast, her shiny black hair obscuring her face, she scuffed across the dirty linoleum floor in her clogs.

Anne glanced at the group, hoping the rest were here for moral support. The three other girls turned away and stared out the window, watching traffic.

Anne directed the girl into the lab. "What is your name?"

"Ella." It sounded more like a grunt. She sat, but her gaze stayed glued to the floor.

"Well, Ella, can I ask you a few questions?" Anne stared at the form, hoping to find some sort of solace on the blank page. She held no delusions that the reservation somehow protected the inhabitants from the evil of the cities, but this girl couldn't be more than fourteen. Anne felt sick.

Ella shrugged, but her hands shook. She stilled them by folding them together, then tucking them between her knees.

"Ella, have you been . . . um . . . active recently?"

Ella looked away.

"Within the last year?"

She saw the girl's jaw tighten.

"Okay then, let's take a sample." Anne glanced at the form. "You know, you don't have to give me your name. I can do this anonymously."

"It don't matter. If I'm dying, I'm dying."

Anne knelt before her patient. "What is done is done. You can't change the past. But you might not be HIV positive, and if you aren't, this is a great time to think about your future. Even if you are, AIDS research is extending life expectancy. This isn't the end of your life, Ella. It's just a dark moment."

The girl said nothing, but tears welled in her eyes. Anne fought the urge to take Ella into her arms. She knew Ella's fear. As a health professional, she'd been tested every year for the fatal virus. She'd never tested positive, but she understood the dread and knew more than she wanted to about bleak moments. "It's going to be okay, honey."

"If I have it, who would ever marry me?" The pitiful words, spoken so softly, almost ripped out Anne's heart.

Anne smoothed Ella's silky hair. "Someone who loves you very much. To the right man, it won't matter. All the scars on your body and soul won't matter."

"I hope so," Ella said.

Anne silently agreed with her. She had her own scars, body and soul, and while she felt pretty sure she'd never let a man within shooting distance of her heart again, if one ever did make a direct hit and meet her at the altar, he would eventually see the destruction to her body. Seventeen stitches in her stomach and a spiderweb scar in her back weren't something she ached to reveal. She shuddered against the thought.

To Anne's dismay, she tested all seven teenagers milling about the waiting room. None of them seemed as young as Ella, but all had eyes ringed with fear. Anne prayed that the tests would return negative and that this scare might reap a change in their lives. The need for a camp like Wilderness Challenge to change young lives nagged at her all day.

Jenny had assisted Dr. Jefferies in attending to the other patients. Anne noticed how one elderly couple hung on to Jenny as if she were their own child. She wondered briefly, if she were to fill Jenny's position, would the locals adopt her, or would she even want them to? These people weren't so different from the ones she'd escaped . . . lonely, desperate, on the brittle edge of poverty, filling their time with seedy pursuits. Did she think that moving north would obliterate the human sin nature?

When the last of Anne's teenagers left, she stood at the window, watching the entire group climb into a pickup—

four in the bed—and roar through town. Dust fogged their wake and churned up despair in Anne's heart. What would it take to touch these teens? She recognized in their eyes the same emptiness that plagued the kids in Minneapolis. A black hole of despair.

Perhaps that was why her father had chucked a comfortable pastorate in the Minneapolis suburbs for a home next to a drug lair. Maybe that was why Anne and her sister were yanked out of their safe junior high and plunged into a world of security checks and language that had curdled their ears. It certainly wasn't a lifestyle Anne wished for her own kids, if she ever had any.

But as Anne gathered the vials of blood, making sure each was labeled correctly, she acknowledged that her father's work had changed lives. He'd dragged homeless kids off the streets and restored light to their grungy faces. He'd taught young mothers how to parent their out-of-wedlock babies and even convinced a few to offer their children a new life through adoption. And he'd taught his own daughters how to say no, how to think on their feet, and how to live a life of holiness in a world of filth.

Noah had a worthy idea—so worthy that a decent person, one with EMT training and no other job prospects, wouldn't hesitate to reconsider his offer and invest her summer in it. If she could change one life, keep one young lady from the grip of drugs and disease, wouldn't it be worth letting her heart get a little trampled? Her father would have nearly exploded with pride. And he, in surrendering his life, had found peace. So Anne would have to surrender her summer. Wasn't peace why she'd moved to Deep Haven?

The thought of Ella's tear-glistened eyes convinced her. At least at a camp, Anne wouldn't find herself staring down a gun barrel. Dr. Jefferies' warning flickered through her mind. Maybe by the end of the summer they'd nab their burglar, and Deep Haven would become the safe "haven" she needed to start her new life.

She'd have to don that tough-as-nails shell her father had helped create and face Noah. Well, maybe she'd hide behind the other staffers, but she would be there, bright and early Monday morning, making sure Wilderness Challenge changed lives. At least until Dr. Simpson could find a decent replacement. The last thing she wanted to cultivate in her new hometown was the reputation of shutting down dreams. Just because Noah had demolished any fragment of trust she had for him, it didn't mean these kids had to pay the price. She'd simply remind herself not to fall for his dangerous, break-her-heart charisma.

Anne packed the blood samples into a padded case and set it next to her bag of notes and files. She'd noticed a number of rusted Fords tucked behind houses, and she wondered how many of them had seeped unused fuel into the ground. She had a sick feeling there might be a few kids in Granite River battling lead poisoning and wanted to sleuth through the files to confirm her hunch. The first thing she needed to do, if she landed Jenny's job, was requisition a computer.

Dusk threw dirty shadows across the linoleum in the waiting area. Jenny had hauled out a mop and bucket and had swabbed down the entryway. "Can you stack those magazines?" she asked.

Anne heard a door click in the back of the clinic and turned to see Dr. Jefferies entering. Where had he been? Carrying a white paper bag, probably containing supper, he hustled into his back office and shut the door.

So much for apple dumplings at the casino.

Anne piled the magazines on the table, picked up a few crushed candy wrappers, and had just tied the garbage bag when a cry rent the air. "Help me, somebody, please!"

Anne swallowed her heart back into place and ran to the door. A young woman clutched a small boy to her chest. His red color made Anne's mouth run dry. "Bring him in here." Anne pointed to the examining room. "How old is he?"

"Three. Please. I found him like this on the floor of our

family room." Panic pitched the young mother's voice high. "He seemed tired today, but now he won't wake up."

Anne felt the boy's face—dry, warm skin. His pulse seemed thready, rapid. She tipped his head back to clear his airway, then checked for breathing sounds. He seemed to struggle.

"Jenny, get Dr. Jefferies, quick." Anne checked his nose and ears. They indicated no head trauma, but she checked for bumps to confirm. She unbuttoned the boy's shirt, ignoring the stains of ketchup and Kool-Aid. "What's his name, ma'am?"

"Justin. He's my only son; please help him."

Anne glanced up at the woman.

Tears streaked down her pretty face. "He's all I have."

"Justin, can you hear me?" Anne grabbed a stethoscope from the wall. Where was Dr. Jefferies? Justin's heart raced. She ran her knuckles along his sternum. He didn't flinch. She opened his sunken eyes. Pupils weren't dilated.

"Are there any medicines missing? or poison? Could he have gotten into detergent, perhaps?" The child seemed deprived of air. He sucked in deep, sighing respirations.

The mother rubbed her skinny arms, backing away. "No, I don't think so. No."

Justin stiffened. Anne's heart dropped when she saw the child soil himself. She scooped him up off the table and set him on the floor.

"What are you doing?" the mother shrieked. Anne's EMT training kicked in, and she ripped open his shirt lest it ride up and choke him.

"Turn around!" she ordered. The last thing the woman needed was to watch her son enter the next phase of his seizure. "Jenny!"

Justin jerked. The mother screamed as Anne made sure the child didn't slam his arms and legs against the wall. "Are you sure he didn't eat any poison? Maybe rat poison? Do you have any houseplants or mushrooms in your yard?"

The child's seizure lasted two agonizing minutes as his mother wailed and Anne filed through her brain for clues.

Jenny appeared at the door, looking white. "Dr. Jefferies won't answer."

Anne swallowed that bit of information and turned to the mother. "Has Justin vomited recently?"

She shook her head, her hands over her mouth, horrified as she stared at her son. The boy stopped convulsing and Anne immediately checked his eyes. Pupils responded slightly to her penlight.

She checked his respiration. "Tell me what you did today, ma'am. Everything."

"Nothing. We did nothing. We slept in a little late because we were at a birthday party last night. Justin seemed so tired, I hated to wake him."

Jenny had the woman in a tight embrace. "It's okay, Mary," she soothed. The mother clung to Jenny as if she might collapse.

"A birthday party? Was there cake?"

"And ice cream and cookies. Justin had a ball." Mary buried her face in Jenny's shoulder.

Anne leaned over the boy, smelled his breath. She nearly gagged at the sickly sweet, acetone odor. "Jenny, get me some sugar."

"What?"

"Just get me some sugar!" Anne wound a blood-pressure cuff around his arm and pumped it up. One hundred ten over fifty. She needed help—and fast.

"He did vomit . . . a few days ago," Mary hiccupped.

"How many days? Has he been confused? lethargic?"

The mother knelt beside Anne and touched her son's leg. "I thought he had the flu. He said he had a stomachache. And he seemed extremely thirsty, but he always is, especially when his stomach is hurting."

Anne prodded Justin's stomach. There seemed to be no distention. "Has he ever been tested for diabetes?"

The woman went white. "No. He's always been normal. A happy, active child. No, nothing like that."

Anne put her hand on Mary's shoulder, holding it tight. "I don't know what's wrong with your son. I'm just trying to help him."

The woman nodded. Tears dripped off her chin.

Jenny ran in with a bag of sugar. Behind her trailed the grocery-story clerk, still clad in a green apron, and the two old park-bench sentries. But no Dr. Jefferies. "Thank you, Jenny." She took the bag and ripped it open. "Go try to rouse Dr. Jefferies, please."

Lifting the child's head, Anne pinched out a small amount of sugar and gently sprinkled it under his tongue. *Please, O God, let me guess correctly!* With Justin unconscious, she couldn't administer liquid glucose, and pure sucrose, table sugar, was the quickest remedy. Whether he was in a diabetic coma or insulin shock, the sugar would keep his system from totally shutting down.

"Get a blanket," she said, and heard someone running to the supply room. The exam room had a full oxygen tank, one she had personally inspected only two days ago. She set it for eight LMP, then unwrapped a non-rebreather oxygen mask, filled it with oxygen, and snapped it over Justin's head.

His chest rose and fell with the rhythm of 85 percent oxygen.

"C'mon," she said to his mother as she tucked the blanket around him and scooped him up. "We're taking him to Deep Haven."

Anne muscled through the door and stopped. She didn't have a car. Jenny's SUV was at Mom and Pop's for a tune-up, and her substitute pickup didn't look like it would max 30 mph without perishing.

Jenny remained inside and kept pounding on Dr. Jefferies's door. "Open up, Doctor!"

Anne looked at the two old bench warmers. They suddenly reminded her of the man who'd barreled his way

into her home and rescued her dog. They stood there, exuding the same fierce demeanor she'd seen in Noah, complete with wide shoulders and clenched fists. Perhaps it had been root beer they'd been drinking. "Can you break down a door?"

10

𝒩oah made a face in the mirror, disgusted with the tie
he'd just knotted around his neck. The double Windsor
took up half his chin and made him look like a hippie reject
from the seventies. He'd brushed his hair back from his
face, but it had dried into a shaggy mess, and he'd nicked
himself shaving in at least two places.

Who was he trying to fool? After his rude behavior
toward Anne last Wednesday, it would take more than
spit and polish and a dash of cologne to convince her he
wasn't Attila the Hun. Not that she should think any more
of him than he thought of himself. No matter how he'd
tried to drive Anne from his thoughts this week, the hurt
written on her beautiful face haunted him. He'd never felt
more like the felon he was trying to forget he was than
when he'd looked her straight in the eye and kicked her out
of his life.

Even if he had done it for her own good. Noah was the
last person Anne should get involved with, and that resolve
had crystallized over the past four days. He didn't deserve
her, and the sooner he accepted that and the fact that he had
no hope of repairing their friendship after the way he'd

treated her, the sooner he'd stop spiffing up in hopes of seeing her in town.

Obviously, he was far from getting that thought through his thick noggin. Noah tugged off the tie and threw it on a growing pile of clothing at the end of his army cot. Now that the senior staff had arrived, he'd moved his gear into a dusty cabin he'd share with two other male staffers. It once housed fishing supplies, and the smell of bait embedded the walls. Noah still didn't have the guts to walk around barefoot. He had no desire to lodge a discarded hook into his toe.

Thankfully, his male staffers—especially the lead counselors, Ross and Bucko—were good sports. The two college students had histories working with kids, and Bucko, in particular, hailed from such a rough home life, Noah had flinched when he'd heard the big man's testimony. Noah and Bucko Jones were walking proof that Jesus Christ saved not only their eternal souls but their existence on earth. Only the Savior's grace could pull a couple of former homeboys out of depravity and give them purpose and hope. Bucko and kids like him were the reason Noah dove back into that darkness. The joy written on their faces was worth the wave of memories and the frustration of seeing so many lost.

Ross Springer sprawled on his cot, his hands laced behind his head, earphones pumping out P.O.D. The kid, raised in a suburban upper-class slice of Minneapolis, had his heart in the right place. When interviewed, Ross unveiled a history of white-collar drug use that made Noah realize the problem wasn't isolated to the inner city. Despite his high, tight crew cut and prom-king smile, Ross knew the fears that churned in the hearts of today's youth.

Both new staffers had come straight out of Bethel College's child psychology program. Noah knew God had delivered them into his hands. They had to be God-sent . . . they were working for free.

The two female head staffers, along with Noah's favorite

cook, had also arrived, hauling twice as much gear as the fellas. Noah had billeted them in the cook's shack, a winterized building with a stove and five bunks. He hoped the bats he'd chased out earlier in the week hadn't returned to roost or he'd have mutiny on his hands.

He knew the shack had some rough edges, but he hadn't expected the ladies to toss out the lumpy mattresses that he'd dug up from the Salvation Army and demand cots. Admittedly, the prison-striped mattresses smelled like they'd been infested with mice, but he had been thinking of their comfort. And he thought it had been totally unnecessary for them to fling open all the windows, sweep down the walls, and spray the place with Lysol, as if it would kill the decades of bacon grease and fish oil saturating the walls. But who could explain women?

He counted his blessings, however. His cook, Granny Darlene, had surfaced from his home church congregation, volunteering her summer to scramble eggs, boil hot dogs, nd bake cookies. Fifty years young, with her own grand - children already out of diapers, she had a burden for the kids Noah hoped to reach. She'd lost two sons to the scourge of the gangs, and Noah knew that if anyone even hinted at trouble, Granny D. would scalp them alive. He had stopped short of calling her their resident bouncer, but with her dark, solid hands that had held her own family together for two decades and grit that would stop a train, Granny D. was not to be messed with or the kid would be sorry.

Noah's female head staffers, Katie and Melinda, had warrior spirits dedicated to diving into the wasteland of desecrated lives and cultivating hope. He'd been grateful they had seen through his ragged exterior to the vision he'd painted for them. It also helped that they studied with Ross and Bucko.

Although Noah felt he had more enthusiasm than brains, God had seen his fears and equipped him with a staff that knew how to minister to hurting kids. And in another week, the junior counselors—teenagers who'd proven they could outmaneuver the pull of the streets by the grace of God— would arrive with the campers. Two pairs of eyes for every five bodies. Noah had planned for every contingency. Now he prayed that Anne would show up and give Wilderness Challenge a fighting chance to save lives.

"Going to church, Noah?" Bucko thumped into the cabin, a soggy towel around his neck. He'd shaved his hair down to the scalp and was carrying the red bandana he'd been wearing when he arrived at camp.

Noah had nixed the bandana right off—the last thing he needed was Vice Lord gang colors fanning the flames of turf possession in the backwoods. So poor Bucko had to wear a dish towel Noah had scrounged up from the kitchen, but the way Bucko tied it into four knots and slopped it on his head like a candy wrapper, Noah had no doubt the guy would turn the rag into a fashion statement by the end of the summer. Besides, the stained white rag made Bucko's smile glitter against his dark skin and added an element of "wicked cool" that Noah knew Bucko would work to his advantage.

"Yep. I'm heading down to Grace Church," Noah answered.

It hurt too much to speculate if Anne would be attending. In hopes of expunging that thought from his mind, he unbuttoned the dress shirt and reached for a clean white oxford. He'd dress for the Lord today, not to impress the congregation. Regardless of how the other believers, and especially Anne, saw him, Noah knew he was a signed, sealed, and delivered member of the family of God and he'd show up dressed to appear for his Savior.

He tied his work boots, now considerably scuffed, and grabbed his leather coat. "Ross, you want a ride into town?"

Ross lifted one side of his earphones. "Nope. Gonna sit here and read a bit of Romans today. Thanks though, boss."

Bucko toweled off his head, then pulled on a T-shirt. He looked every inch the fitness addict, another small bonus for Noah—campers would think twice about going a round if they knew Bucko and his biceps were there to enforce camp rules.

Yes, God had equipped Wilderness Challenge for the task. At least He'd equipped the staffers. Noah squelched a spurt of inadequacy. He glanced again in the mirror, as if it would reflect a better image the second time around.

He grimaced at the crooked nose, a souvenir of L'il Lee's right hook; a tiny nick on his chin, a brush-with-death reminder; and the round scar high on his cheekbone. If anything reminded him of his youthful stupidity, it was the memory of diving headfirst into a hedgerow while escaping a gang of angry Gangster Disciples. It probably served him right for trying to boost a pair of wheels from under the Disciples' noses. In truth, he'd deserved worse.

But the late-night memory of Shorty Mac's screams seemed punishment enough. The Disciples had cornered Shorty and him at the end of an alley, and without L'il Lee's diving tackle, which drove Rock Man into the bushes, he'd have joined Shorty for eternity. But God had spared him. Spared his life and later saved his soul. Despite Rock Man's attempts to avenge his fallen VL brother.

Noah closed his eyes and fought the voices from the past.

Surely, if God could use a fisherman to build a church, the Almighty could use an ex-con to touch the lives of a few teenagers.

At least Noah hoped so.

He drove down Gunflint Trail, listening to his fears dissipate in the sound of the motor, in the rush of the wind through the fingers of pine and birch trees. Lake Superior sprawled like a sapphire before him, and the smell of fish and froth drew him into town. It wasn't hard to lose himself and everything he'd been in the lush serenity of Deep Haven.

He arrived at Grace Church and noticed a row of

Lincolns, a Lexus, and two Mercedes in the parking lot—most likely snowbirds up from their Florida condos to spend the summer in deep-woods elegance. He tucked his jacket and his dark glasses inside the seat, grabbed his Bible, and headed for the church. The chords of "Holy, Holy, Holy" strained out, drawing him in like an embrace.

The fragrance of a spring lilac bouquet perfumed the lobby. He received a bulletin from Bruce Schultz and snuck into the back. The tiny paneled sanctuary brimmed with worshipers singing with gusto. Noah crept up the aisle, seeking an open space.

He felt a pinch on his elbow—Joe Michaels had him by the shirtsleeve. The guy grinned, his smile welcoming, and nodded toward his row. Noah slipped in beside him and smiled at Joe's wife, Mona. What a lucky guy. Noah felt a spurt of jealousy that Joe didn't have a past to push at him, keeping him from feeling firmly rooted in grace. Joe handed Noah his hymnal, then tucked his arm around his wife. The gesture erased the twinge in Noah's chest and settled upon him a feeling of fellowship. Deep Haven had healing potential, not only for the kids at Wilderness Challenge.

The congregation finished the hymn and sat. Pastor Dan climbed the platform and began greetings, but his words suddenly blurred in Noah's ears.

Anne Lundstrom had made it to church. She sat two rows in front of Noah, hair groomed to perfection, neck straight and slender. Noah imagined he could even smell that subtle floral fragrance she'd worn on Wednesday, the day he'd stomped all over her feelings.

She'd apparently recovered. She sat safely ensconced in the possessive embrace of a well-groomed and obviously smitten Dr. Jefferies.

"I still can't believe I slept through the emergency, Anne." Dr. Jefferies turned to her the second Pastor Dan finished

the benediction and repeated the litany of apologies he'd started on Friday. He'd scooted in next to her before the service and made a point of apologizing for nearly costing a child his life. He'd leaned over and whispered during the offertory, "I hope you've forgiven me."

"Of course." If there had been more room in the pew, perhaps she could have put some distance between him and his overkill penitence. He certainly didn't have to put his arm around her. The last thing she needed was to have the entire congregation think she and the new town doctor were on more than acquaintance terms.

She was trying hard to forgive him for being slouched on his desk, zonked out like he'd run a marathon. She supposed she owed him mercy, especially after she had helped the two old men decimate his office door trying to get to his car keys. And Dr. Jefferies did work horrific hours—most doctors in small towns put in shifts that turned their eyes bloodshot. He looked worse for wear this morning, despite his tidy blue suit, woven silk, geometric tie, and shiny wing tips, as if he was at the Ordway Concert Hall in Minneapolis rather than a country church service.

But the way he smiled at her, genuinely, with contrition in those dark eyes . . . well, yes, perhaps she could pardon him for being pushed to exhaustion. It wasn't so awful to be seen in the company of the most eligible bachelor in town either. He did cut a dashing pose, and he smelled like riches and elegance. Just the kind of man she wanted beside her, right?

"Anne, so glad to see you!" Sandra reached over from a pew in back of her. The ER nurse looked delightfully casual today in a seventies top with puffy sleeves and a peasant skirt. Anne had a feeling the woman had ferreted the shirt out of her teenage collection and probably had no idea the look had returned to the height of fashion. "Would you like to join Mona and me for lunch?" She nodded to Mona Michaels and her gorgeous husband chatting with . . .

Noah. Anne stared at him, unable to wrench her eyes off

the man, furious that her heart had started a full-fledged gallop in her chest. She gritted her teeth. He appeared heartbreakingly handsome this morning—his hair tousled, his smile as bright as it had been the morning she'd shown up for work at Wilderness Challenge. Her stomach had done a small flip that morning, and now it betrayed her in another wild somersault. He had cleaned up—the white oxford and black jeans didn't do him justice, but they made him seem just on this edge of refined. Antonio Banderas with honey eyes.

"Anne? Lunch?" Sandra studied her, eyebrows raised. She tracked Anne's gaze and smiled. "You know Noah?"

Anne wondered later if she had nodded. She might have, because Sandra's smile turned sly. "I'll ask them to invite him too."

"No, please. Thanks, though." Anne gathered up her Bible, her bulletin. "I actually have plans. Sorry, Sandra." Hadn't Edith invited her over? Certainly Bertha would need her company after a morning cooped up in the cabin.

"Yes, she's having lunch with me." Dr. Jefferies' arm looped through hers. "I owe her after she saved my skin on Friday." His gesture turned Anne's mouth to cotton. "She's quite the trauma nurse. Spotted a diabetic coma right off."

He obviously had no idea how thankful she'd been to have her guess confirmed at Deep Haven Municipal. Justin and his mother had been sent by ambulance to Duluth hours later.

"I'm not surprised, Doctor." Sandra's face betrayed surprise, however, and her smile had disappeared. "I hear Anne was an EMT in Minneapolis. So I'm sure she knows how to keep her wits about her." She looked at Anne as if sending her some sort of cryptic message.

Anne opened her mouth, but no words emerged. Dr. Jefferies had her by the elbow. "Good to see you, Sandra." He fairly pulled Anne out of the pew. "By the way," he said softly, "you were amazing, you know. I'm hoping we can keep you."

A blush started at her toes, and she couldn't speak, even if she could have found the words. By the time she gathered her thoughts, Dr. Jefferies had guided her to the back of the sanctuary and into the line to meet Pastor Dan.

"You must be an old pro at emergencies if you were an EMT in Minneapolis. Things can get pretty dicey down there, I heard." Dr. Jefferies settled his hand territorially on the small of her back.

Anne nodded, not wanting to relive those dicey moments.

"I did an ER shift during my internship in Duluth. Rough stuff." He shook his head. "Can't help but think that if more people went to church, we wouldn't see them in the ER."

"How's that?"

Dr. Jefferies shrugged. "Simple cause and effect. You obey God, He protects you. You run from His law, you get what you deserve."

Unexpected tears pricked her eyes. "Yeah, I guess so."

"Have you met our new addition to the local scenery, Pastor?" Dr. Jefferies asked as they approached Pastor Dan. He nudged Anne forward. "Anne Lundstrom, EMT, nurse extraordinaire."

Anne managed a mortified smile.

"Glad to meet you, Anne," Dan said. His warm grip told her his friendly smile was genuine. Up close, he seemed young for a head pastor. "You aren't by any chance the nurse who's going to work up at Wilderness Challenge?"

Was she? She swallowed, digging up an answer. As if he'd been snagged by her unspoken answer, Noah appeared behind the pastor. His eyes found hers, latched on hard, and held that devastating, come-back-to-me look. His power to render her weak kicked into high gear, and she fought the memory of the way he'd trampled her feelings with the finesse of a wild boar.

She tried instead to focus on reasons why Wilderness Challenge was a good idea. Reasons like Ella and her gang of friends living on the edge of disease. Reasons like hiding out in the woods while the Deep Haven police department tracked down a cat burglar. Reasons that had nothing to do with a man who could sway her traitorous heart with a smile.

Without breaking Noah's gaze, she nodded.

The amazed, heart-stopping, completely delighted grin he gave her made her idiotically giddy all afternoon.

When would her foolish heart ever learn?

11

𝔐onday morning the clouds vanished, leaving a glorious
canopy of azure. The breeze blew in a fragrant perfume of
lilac and water lily, and the essence of summer, complete
with levity and joy, filled Noah's chest. He climbed out of
Mink Lake, deliciously cold, alive, and ready to congregate
with his staff. He felt like a boy on his first day of grammar
school, anticipation expanding his lungs, swelling his heart.

Or maybe his joy had to do with that incredible shy smile
Anne had offered him over Pastor Dan's shoulder yesterday.
She'd said yes. Yes! And in about one hour he expected her
to cruise into Wilderness Challenge.

And then what? She wasn't about to give him a second
chance. He should count his abundant blessings that she
would consider being in the same country with him, let
alone the same fifteen acres. But it was a start. A good start.
And maybe, if he put on his best behavior and acted like the
gentleman he desperately wanted to be, she'd develop X-ray
vision and see past his rough exterior to a man who wanted
to be her friend. He wasn't foolish enough to hope for
more, to believe she might be able to trust him. He would
be happy for mere civility after the way he'd treated her.

Still, he could barely keep to a walk as he toweled off and headed toward the lodge.

Granny D. had already roosted in the kitchen, and the smell of flapjacks and sausage links reached out to snag him. Noah ducked his head into the kitchen. "You're already spoiling us."

Granny D. waggled her wooden spoon, delight in her gray eyes. "That's why I'm here, young man. Now git dressed and don't show up in my kitchen late." She winked at him.

Noah felt a pinch of grief. If only Mother Peters were alive, she'd be working right alongside Granny D. But Noah had failed her, right along with Anthony and a young EMT who might be lying in her grave right now. The thought wiped the smile off Noah's face.

It would do him well to remember exactly why he'd needed Anne to join his staff. So that kids might not repeat the crimes of their big brothers. So that hope and life might sweep through the streets of the Phillips neighborhood.

In the cabin, Ross and Bucko had risen. Noah noticed both young men had their Bibles open. Ross mouthed the words to some hard-rappin' beat pulsing out of his headphones. Bucko had a highlighter out. Noah dumped his shampoo on his shelf and tossed his towel on a hook. He had a few priceless minutes before breakfast so he grabbed his Bible and headed out to the campfire pit.

He recalled sitting in the way-too-romantic shadows of the pines with Anne. With the sun winking overhead, Noah couldn't keep a swell of hope reined in his chest. Maybe, just maybe . . .

Friends. Only friends. He had to stay centered on that thought.

Sitting on one of the benches, he opened his Bible. He'd been studying Paul's letter to the Philippians, sharing a like-minded happiness with the apostle for those who had joined him in the overwhelming task of Wilderness Challenge.

"For I live in eager expectation and hope that I will never

do anything that causes me shame, but that I will always be bold for Christ, as I have been in the past, and that my life will always honor Christ, whether I live or I die. For to me, living is for Christ, and dying is even better. Yet if I live, that means fruitful service for Christ. I really don't know which is better. I'm torn between two desires: Sometimes I want to live, and sometimes I long to go and be with Christ. That would be far better for me."

Knowing the man Noah had been, it wasn't a giant leap to see that any success he saw in the ministry department depended solely on God's ability, not his. As he'd drawn closer to God, seen salvation transform junkies, prostitutes, and narc dealers into the creations of heaven, Noah had fallen five million percent in love with the Almighty. God in heaven had his heart, and there were times—many, in fact—when he longed for eternity. Yet he understood intimately Paul's dilemma in verse twenty-two. "Fruitful service for Christ," the heartbeat and joy of the Christian life, done for and by the Savior.

Noah closed his eyes. *See my heart, Lord. Fill me with Yourself, and let Noah and his desires die. Take this man and use me how You will, for Your glory.*

He heard a sparrow chirping in a nearby basswood. The smell of the morning, the warmth of the sun, and the hope that lay before him because of this great commission thickened his throat. *I am unworthy of Your grace, Lord.*

Tires spit gravel and he looked up as Anne drove in. He smiled and blinked away the tears. *So unworthy, Lord.*

Gulping in a deep breath, he gathered his composure and sauntered out to the SUV, hoping Anne could see past the jerk who'd battered her feelings to the Savior dwelling inside him.

Where was the man who had confronted her with the sensitivity of a piranha and treated her like a contagious disease?

Gone, and in his place, Sir Gallant, complete with jokes and compliments. "You're looking nice today," had actually come out of his mouth with believable sincerity. She'd stifled a frown. She was a regular beauty queen in her faded jeans and university sweatshirt. Still, her heart bought it and did a wild dance in her chest. Then he'd hugged Bertha like a lost friend, took the medical bag out of Anne's hand, and thanked her for showing up.

It didn't help that he'd shed his slicked-up disguise of yesterday and donned his backwoods soldier-of-fortune costume—a pair of ripped army fatigues that looked comfortable enough to spend a Saturday in, a black T-shirt, work boots, and a smile that could light up a room.

And just when she'd talked herself out of noticing. In fact, she'd spent half the night reminding herself that his smile represented nothing more than triumph. That he saw her as nothing more than a bargaining chip with the local church. That he was more interested in her medical skills than her company.

The charming sneak. Anne sat across from him at breakfast, watching as he spelled out the plans for the day. His gaze kept alighting on her, eliciting a spurt of delight. He had a crooked smile, and he talked with his hands, something she'd noticed before but didn't enjoy nearly as much as now. The guy had energy streaming out of his ears, and his enthusiasm was as catchy as a flu bug in a preschool. She couldn't wait to meet the kids, to take them canoeing, rock climbing, and share the gospel with them.

She was turning into her father right before her very eyes.

No, not quite her father. Her father had a saint's heart. These kids were different. For one thing, they weren't going to be armed to the teeth, and they certainly wouldn't have the vocabulary of convicts. Even so, Noah's passion to reach his kids certainly put a smile on her face.

Even her co-laborers seemed to brim with his fervor. She met Melinda and Katie, who spent most of the meal coercing her to move up to camp immediately. She'd nearly given in to Melinda's bright smile, sunshine against her dark, beautiful face. And Katie had the charm of her Irish ancestors, complete with a stubborn streak to match her red hair and green eyes. Ross oozed charisma and, judging by his straight teeth and Ralph Lauren polo shirt, braces and a college scholarship had been part of his background. Even Bucko, despite the screwball hat he wore on his head—was that a kitchen rag?—grinned at her, swallowing her whole with his friendly demeanor.

So maybe she'd live through this summer, even if Noah turned out to be exactly the heartbreaker she suspected him to be. Suspected? Anne grimaced inwardly at the way her pulse galloped, the short-term memory connection to her heart obviously on the fritz.

An African-American woman, nearly six feet of grin and opinion called Granny, waddled out of the kitchen, thrilled that they were stuffed to the gills and couldn't move another inch. Granny's pancakes had tasted like heaven. Anne certainly wouldn't starve this summer.

Noah left them halfway through breakfast. Anne breathed finally and discovered that all the staffers hailed from Bethel College in the Twin Cities. *Small world,* she thought, keeping her own previous address in pocket. She wanted to think of herself as a Deep Havener, and she'd start right now.

She helped Granny with the dishes, ladled scraps into a dog bowl for Bertha—where was she?—then assembled on the lodge porch with the rest of the crew. The sun wove golden fingers between the elms and maples surrounding the camp and lit the courtyard aglow. Anne couldn't help but conjure up the day she'd spent here with Noah, the sound of his laughter like a song in her heart.

Out of some clasp of trees, the subject of her errant thoughts ran up holding a wad of rags. "First day of training, I want us to learn to act like a team." Noah passed out the long strips of cotton. "This is a trust test. Melinda and Ross work in one pair, Bucko and Katie the other."

Anne's heart did a rebellious flutter as she did the simple math. As if reading her mind, Noah looked at her and winked. Her knees turned to jelly.

"I have directions," Noah continued, oblivious to the fact that his EMT was about to fall into a heap. "The object of this exercise is to communicate clearly and learn to trust your partner. One of you will be blindfolded, and the other will give instructions and, if needed, support toward the points listed. When you reach the halfway point, you'll find an envelope and instructions to switch. The guider will then be blindfolded and follow directions back to camp." He handed the directions to each team.

His smirk had tease in it. "Remember, what goes around comes around." He waggled his eyebrows and sent Katie into a fit of laughter. Anne, however, fought a wave of fear. Blindfolded? At Noah's mercy? What if his charm turned sour when they got alone? She stared at the rag in her hands.

And then Noah was beside her. "Do you want to be blindfolded first? or do the guiding?" His eyes sparkled, but all mischief had vanished, as if he had seen her turmoil. His expression turned somber. "I know you don't have any reason to trust me, but I promise I'll take good care of you."

Oh, his gentle words and soft voice balmed her bruised heart. She could hardly dredge up her voice. "I'll guide first."

"Perfect." He took the cotton strip from her hands and tied it around his eyes, looking like a bandit. "I am at your mercy."

While the other teams moved off in different directions, Anne consulted her directions. "Uh . . . go forward."

He nearly fell off the porch, but he had enough kindness not to mention that she'd botched the first instruction.

"Sorry."

Why did his goofy grin, misaimed by his blindness, make her mind muddle? And of course he had to smell woodsy

and masculine. Anne took a deep breath and touched his shoulder. "Go right ten paces."

He obeyed like a soldier. She had to admire the way he strutted out boldly, investing in her words like she would never steer him wrong. "Veer left, about . . . um . . . eight steps."

In fact, he'd poured out his dreams into her hands. She realized, as he marched straight for the men's outhouse, that she had the power to crush his dreams. She could close this camp down with one word. One negative report, one mishandled event. The thought made her shudder. A woman who could barely take care of her dog shouldn't be allowed that much power. Noah had no business trusting her, and yet there he was, nearly plowing into the—

"Stop!" Anne stifled a giggle. "Sorry."

"I guess payback is good medicine, huh?" He turned, and a smile graced his face.

But she couldn't ignore the fact that he knew he'd hurt her. And good. For a second, her lungs wouldn't work. In a shaky voice she said, "Turn around and walk toward me."

He wore a quirky smile. "I thought you'd never ask."

Was he . . . flirting with her? She fought to steady her voice before reading the next direction. "Now stop and pick up the ribbon at your feet."

He obeyed and stuffed the marker in his pocket. "Now what?"

"Go forward until I say stop. But go slowly. There are a few dips in the yard that may trip you up. Just keep one foot in front of the other and you'll get to the other side. If you start to trip, reach out and I'll steady you."

He paused, and the slight smile, full of tease, on his blind-folded face made her blush.

"Sweeter words were never spoken," he said softly.

12

Anne didn't know whether to laugh or cry. She sat before the campfire, stirring a blackened-end stick through the embers, trying to sort out a stew of feelings.

Was Noah truly after her heart or was she just a smitten fool? She tottered dangerously close to falling for his charm, and if she didn't find her footing soon, she'd fall hard for a guy who could rip out her heart.

Had she learned nothing last week or during her entire childhood? Guys who looked dangerous *probably were*.

Anne pushed over a smoldering log, and sparks spiraled into the velvet night. The stars blinked at her, and the moon split the lake into two dark, ominous halves. She couldn't deny the swell of joy that had gathered over her the past three days, and it scared her more than she wanted to admit. Had she dreamed his rude rebuff a week ago? Perhaps that had been a nightmare, a residue from her own fears, imagined by a heart that assumed the worst about a man who looked like a phantom from her past.

Yes, Noah had danger on the fringes of his exuberant personality. His zest for life suggested he wasn't afraid to face it head-on, something she couldn't seem to embrace.

She'd learned quickly in her graffiti-scrawled school halls that evasion had its merits. Noah had once accused her of trying to run from her fears, but she considered it tactical survival. Why fan the fires of terror when you can hold on to dignity and live in peace?

She had to admire, however, the way Noah dove into each situation, unafraid of the problems under the surface. He lived with a passion that made her want to hang on for the ride. She could admit that she moved like molasses into the unknown . . . but didn't she have good reasons? A bullet scar the size of a fist was the first one.

Then again, there weren't any gun-wielding drug addicts in Deep Haven, and she should stop evoking villains. Especially when they fit the description of uncanny hero.

She chuckled to herself. She hadn't dredged up the heart-stopping hero of that hot June day over a week ago when she met Noah. That unnamed tenor who had held her hand and carried her through the darkness on a song had set the bar for her standards. But that man—whoever he was, wherever he was—was history, and Noah, the resident hero in camouflage, was present, seemingly available . . . and if she read his emotional signals correctly, enjoying her company.

Or she could be imagining his flirting, or worse, misinterpreting it for something else. Like bribery to keep her on his good side. To keep his dreams alive.

At the cost of her heart.

She drew a deep breath of night air, battling a voice inside that fed on her fears.

Now that made perfect sense. Mr. Mercenary Bear had shifted the charm into overdrive for one reason—self-preservation. If she walked, his camp was finished. Anne closed her eyes.

Why, oh why, couldn't God give her a break? She seemed to be continually walking into ambush—physically, emotionally, spiritually. A loving God might put up a few road signs like Warning: Steep Grade, Beware of Tumble

into Heartache, Blind Intersection Ahead, or Duck the
Gun-Wielding Druggies.

She hugged her waist, feeling again the burn of a bullet
tearing through her body. Tears pricked her eyes. *Please,
God, guard my heart.* The feeble prayer felt hollow as she
mouthed it. Who was she kidding? God had betrayed her,
and she'd have to possess more than a few loose screws to
ever fling herself in His hands again. Bitterness welled in her
chest. Wasn't the Christian life about His love, His protection? She didn't want to feel this way. She loved God, at
least she wanted to. It wasn't her fault she'd been shot, but
her faith didn't need to come crashing in around her.

In truth, she longed to have the naive trust that surrounded her mother and her sister. They'd never had life
bludgeon them and certainly had never seen their beliefs in
a safe God blow up in their faces. All their platitudes about
God's grace being sufficient made her ill inside.

Like they knew what it felt like to be drop-kicked by
God.

Anne tightened her jaw, tears washing down her cheeks.
To add horror to the moment, she heard Bertha trot down
the hill from the lodge, her dog collar clinking in warning.
And ten steps behind her came the thump of boots. It would
have to be Noah. Bertha worshiped the man.

The big dog ran up to Anne. She dropped her stick and
buried her face in Bertha's fur, wiping the betraying tears.
The last thing she needed was for Noah to see her scars. She
wrapped her arms around herself, a physical barrier to the
wounds inside.

"Beautiful night." Noah's voice always sounded like a
melody sung in a rich tenor.

Anne swallowed her emotions, still raw and dangerously
close to the surface. Noah stood beside her for a moment.
When she looked up at him, he wasn't staring at the sky but
down at her. She smiled, hoping to deflect his curiosity.

He was a devastatingly gorgeous addition to the night-
scape. The moonlight softened his unruly hair and silhouetted

his stature, a formidable presence against the darkness. She couldn't help but be drawn in by his raw strength and dependable smile. By his wide hands that had felt like velvet on her arms as he led her around camp the first day. The memory suddenly made her wince. *He was using her.* Why did she lose her grip on that thought the second he entered her airspace?

"Can I sit beside you?"

She nodded, furious at her weakness. An intelligent woman with a master's in community nursing would jump to her feet and flee.

"I think it might be better if you moved up here so you can be with the campers 24/7. Besides, I worry about you driving home in the dark every night."

He tucked his hands between his knees and stretched his long legs in front of him. She noticed the rip in his fatigues and their fraying gathered hem. He'd obviously taken a dip in the lake after dinner, for his hair smelled of soap, and his redolence of soft leather and strong masculinity softened her raw nerves. How she longed to surrender to his larger-than-life personality.

And now he was worried about her? Against her will, his words embraced her.

"Bertha would like to stay here. She's smitten with you." Anne watched the dog, settled at Noah's feet. As if in response, the Saint Bernard raised her head.

Noah rubbed her behind one ear. "Of course. She loves me for my depth and understanding."

"And because you give her table scraps."

"I could give you table scraps . . ." When he looked at her like that, she could barely remember to breathe let alone stay angry at him.

"I don't know. I think my stomach would rot on your diet. Snickers bars for breakfast? Fried pork rinds for lunch?" She made a face.

He put on a shocked expression. "Listen Miss Fruit-and-Nuts, one can't live on rabbit food entirely. A real man

needs protein, calcium, and carbohydrates. A Snickers bar is the perfect meal." He nudged her, waggled those eyebrows, and she knew she was a goner.

So maybe she'd let irrational fear manhandle her. Hadn't Noah, only a week ago, told her that he didn't want her here? Even before that, he'd let her off the hook, told her to make her own decisions. That didn't sound like a man who was using her as live bait.

"Maybe I could move tomorrow. I have a meeting with Dr. Simpson in the morning; then I'll haul up some gear in the afternoon. How does that sound?"

Noah looked over at her with a grin that turned her heart to mush. "Wonderful."

Across the lake, the loons began their nightly serenade. Anne sat in silence, arms wrapped around her knees, cementing the idea that she'd been inventing suspicion. Noah had given her choices, and she'd embraced them without extortion. His recent attention had to be based on pure attraction. She let that thought push a giddy smile onto her face.

He turned toward her and his gaze roamed her face. "I'm so glad you've joined our staff. We couldn't do it without you."

Anne felt sucker punched. Her stupid smile froze, and she pinched back a howl, wanting to curl into the fetal position and hide. Her suspicions had been dead-on. He wasn't interested in her but in her presence on staff, her ability to bring in the bucks. She broke his look. *Don't cry!*

A loon called, the sound forlorn as it echoed across the water.

"The kids arrive on Friday afternoon," he said, totally unaware that he had the power to break her heart with a single comment. "Are you ready?"

Anne struggled to brace herself, to wind her emotions back into her constricting chest. She had to toughen up. Hadn't past experience told her that men only used the women in their lives? Noah may have a few manners and a heart-stopping tenor voice, but at his core he was a hood-lum. She took a deep breath and dredged up small talk. "Sure." *C'mon, Noah, how hard could a bunch of church kids be?*

"It's going to be a great summer. God gave us an incredi-ble staff—all of them have such a heart for kids. And with your medical expertise, I'm sure everyone will be safe and healthy. You're really a godsend, Anne."

With each word, she winced. But she couldn't blame heaven. She'd walked into this one herself. She'd pledged to avoid Noah and his heartbreaking magic like the plague, but inside she'd run full speed ahead, arms outstretched like a kid at Christmas. She ached from her own stupidity.

Noah went silent, his face to the sky, as if counting stars. Anne wanted to bolt for the hills. She was scraping up the courage to grab her dog and run when he turned to her again.

His eyes glistened. "You know, I'm not a great man. I just have great dreams. God put those dreams in my heart. Whenever I am overwhelmed by them and the magnitude of the task, He gently reminds me that He is supplying everything I need." His voice turned thick. "But you are definitely more than I expected."

Moisture caught in his dark lashes, and the look in his sweet eyes made her chin tremble. Suddenly, idiotic tears filled her eyes. "I am?"

His tender smile eliminated her every accusation as a tear ran down her cheek. He cupped her face and rubbed the tear away with his thumb. "You're a gift that reminds me that I'm loved by God."

She opened her mouth, but no words came out, knitted as they were in a wild mesh of foolish hopes.

Then his gaze studied her face, touching her eyes, her nose and landing on her lips. "Anne . . . I . . ." His voice had turned . . . strangely hoarse. "Can I . . . ?"

She nodded before he could finish speaking. If she had any doubts about his question, they were gloriously erased

as he kissed her sweetly, with impossible tenderness. It lasted only a moment, but she felt her heart sprout wings and soar.

"Anne," he whispered as he pulled away, his forehead against hers, "I know I coerced you into working here, but I'm so glad you agreed."

This time, she took no offense at his words. "Me too."

Bertha sighed at his feet—a long, contented benediction to her thoughts.

"I'd better go," Anne said.

Noah nodded and took her hand. "You'll be back tomorrow."

It was more a statement than a question, a resolution that shored up their fledgling relationship.

"Absolutely."

Noah remained at the edge of the fire pit, watching the embers die, staring occasionally at the sky as if in silent hallelujah. The wind shifted, carrying with it the last chilly fragment of air and the voices of the night. A cricket spun a melody not far from shore, and even his heart seemed to beat a rhythm that sounded like a ballad.

He couldn't wipe the euphoric grin off his face.

And he was definitely going to ignore the monster inside him that demanded to know why he was kissing Anne Lundstrom as if they had tomorrows on their horizon.

Then his euphoria took a nosedive. He knew better. Noah had no business cultivating their hopes and dreams. Even if his camp turned out to be a success, come August he was heading south. Back home to Minneapolis.

Anne made it abundantly clear that she intended to plant roots in Deep Haven. Theirs was far from a match made in heaven. He'd been drawn in by her smile, those luminous eyes shimmering with tears, those tentative soft lips. He'd wanted to pull her close, deepen his kiss, show her she already had his heart.

But what was he doing, giving away something that didn't belong to him? God had his heart first. And He would have to give Noah permission to share it. So far, the only way that would happen was if Anne Lundstrom about-faced and followed him back home. To the Phillips neighborhood.

To her fears. Something about the city ignited in her eyes a terror so real it made him ache. He longed to draw it out of her and slay her dragons. But to do that she'd have to trust him.

Perhaps . . . there he went, dreaming about a future with a woman whose laughter sounded like a song, who smelled like a field of fresh wildflowers—a sober dilemma if he wanted to stay sane around her.

Thankfully, if her current expression told the truth, she might be renaming his "local terrorist" label to something a little more . . . safe. At least he hoped the way she'd trembled at his touch had nothing to do with fear.

If God could change her opinion of him, then perhaps—just maybe—she could learn to trust him. And then, maybe . . .

As he sat under the stars looking at the potential of his living God, he wanted to burst. *Lord, I know I don't deserve any of this. But if You are willing, please use me to bless Anne. To heal her heart, to calm her fears. Please help me be the man she needs me to be.*

13

Bertha hung her head out the window, her tongue flapping in the breeze, as Anne drove into Deep Haven. Anne had to laugh at her roommate . . . the dog seemed as delirious as her human and had spent the morning trampling on clothes and knocking over furniture with her hairy bullwhip tail.

Anne tried to convince herself that Bertha's excitement had to do with the fresh air and abundant squirrel supply at Wilderness Challenge, but she suspected that her dog, like her, had a serious crush on the camp's director.

Well, Bertha had great taste.

Anne swallowed back a wave of delight that seemed to consume her entire body. Noah had kissed her. The man had touched her with gentleness, as if she might break, and it had sent tingles to her toes. When he'd whispered her name, as soft as a dream, she'd turned right into jelly.

This summer was turning out to be so much more than she'd ever hoped. A carefree job at a camp tucked away inside a fortress of Norway pine—not even the demons of the inner city could find her there. She could be sure she wouldn't walk into a drug-high murderer's gun sights, and nothing more dangerous than a sunburn or a bad case of poison ivy loomed ahead.

Anne began to hum, and with a start, she recognized the song as the hymn her mysterious stranger had sung over a year ago: "It Is Well with My Soul." She certainly felt well as the wind tousled her hair and she motored along the jeweled shoreline. Lately, God had reached right out of heaven to bless her, and hope never felt so palpable. She smiled at the sky, an awning of puff and azure. *Thank You, God.*

She supposed, if she paid attention, she might be able to count a trail of blessings all the way to Minneapolis. Anne made a wry face. Somehow it wasn't until arriving at Deep Haven, however, that the fog of darkness had cleared enough for her to see them. Regret pinched her throat. Perhaps, if she had turned around long enough to thank God for bringing her this far, she would have seen His footprints beside her path. Perhaps.

She continued along Main Street, past World's Best Donuts, which had a line of people jagging outside the door, past Mom and Pop's and the memory of Noah's laughter, and finally stopped at the Footstep of Heaven Bookstore and Coffee Shop. She could use a cup of tea to rein in her runaway dreams. It didn't help that she'd spent half the night reliving Noah's kiss and the smell of him mingling with the night campfire air.

It hadn't escaped her that when she looked at him, she no longer saw the trappings of the hood she'd escaped. In fact, she wondered how she'd even equated him with the bullies that ran the street. From the first moment she'd met him, he'd been nothing but a complete gentleman. Even when she'd accused him of slave trade and prowling her home, he hadn't raised his voice or made a move to protect himself— even when she slugged him on the road. That didn't sound like any of the bad boys from her childhood.

She'd been horribly prejudiced to believe that he had even one gangbanger bone in his body. Frankly, now that she

knew him, she had a hard time picturing Noah surviving the Phillips neighborhood. He'd get rolled in about three seconds and smile while they did it. He was simply too . . . nice.

Anne had a sneaking suspicion that he'd shopped at a local Salvation Army store and dug up a costume that would appeal to the campers—something visual to add to his size that would make them respect him. It certainly didn't seem his style to bully them into obedience, so maybe the clothes were both the tool and part of the secret she saw in his eyes. But she'd seen right through him. The guy couldn't produce enough menace to intimidate even his helpful squirrels, and she shouldn't have let her fears take possession of her brain.

"Stay," she said to Bertha, who licked her soundly and whined. Anne took the steps two at a time and beamed at a local who sat on the porch enjoying a cup of brew and the local *Superior Times*. He nodded to her, a bright smile adding to his chubby jolliness. Yes, Deep Haven certainly had its share of exotic flora and fauna.

The door jingled as Anne entered. The bookstore had few patrons—an elderly vacationer with a "Welcome to Deep Haven" bag over her arm and a tall, dark-haired man. He rang a chord of familiarity in Anne when she noticed a black bag slung over his shoulder.

Mona greeted her from the coffee bar, where she was filling muffin orders and chatting with her husband, that author fellow—what was his name? Anne stopped short, staring at a poster of an upcoming hardcover. The incredibly handsome author on the poster couldn't be—the echo of Edith's words clicked into place. "Reese Clark?"

Mona's husband looked up at her, grinned, then nodded. His blue eyes danced. He shrugged. "That's me. Sorta. Around here, I'm just Joe, Mona's lucky husband."

Anne stared at the picture. Reese Clark appeared significantly more slicked-up than the local now perched on the tall barstool. Joe wore a pair of rumpled jeans and a thermal shirt. Reese was sharp and handsome in a pair of cowboy boots, black jeans, and a black Stetson.

"You clean up pretty well." Anne picked up one of the books on the display. *Disaster in Deep Haven.* Is this about our town?"

Mona laughed. "Sit down, Anne. What's your pleasure this morning?"

"How about a cup of tea?" She flipped through the pages of the book. "Wow. A bookstore owner married to an author. Guess that's convenient." Anne slid onto the bench. "Will you sign it if I buy it?"

Joe reached over and took the book. "It's a gift." He grabbed a pen from over the countertop and opened the front cover. "And yes, it is convenient." She didn't miss the wink he gave his wife. Mona blushed a beautiful pink. "Unfortunately, the poor woman didn't know I was an author when we fell in love."

"Really?" Anne took the tea and sipped it. The spicy blend went right to her marrow. "Why is that?"

Joe grimaced as he wrote. Only the scratch of his pen filled the silence. "Let's just say I was less than completely honest."

Mona ran her fingers along his cheek. "He turned out to be one of the many wonderful surprises awaiting me in Deep Haven."

Joe returned his wife's gesture with a look of such devotion, Anne felt a curl of pleasure in her chest.

What surprises were waiting for her here? What had Noah said the day he'd met her, when he repaired her car? *I hope you find what you're looking for here. Deep Haven isn't just a pretty place. It's more than it seems.*

Noah had certainly turned out to be more than he seemed. His carefree passion for life made her feel decidedly alive and giddy, and all that raw protectiveness had loosened her death grip on fear. Without a doubt, his warm friendship had soothed the raw edges of her ragged heart. But had she found what she'd been looking for?

And what was that again, exactly?

Anne sipped her tea, listening to Mona bustle about the coffee nook. The dark-haired shopper stepped up to the bar and ordered a mocha cappuccino. Anne glimpsed his choice of reading material and suddenly everything clicked. "You're a photographer!"

She realized she'd voiced her brilliant deduction when he turned, surprise etched on his angular face. He had a goatee of mink dark hair, and the curly mass on his head showed some scalp. When he gave her a friendly grin, the lines around his dark eyes crinkled. "Garth Peterson. Freelance photographer." When he shook her hand, she noted how soft his grip felt against the memory of Noah's.

"Have you been in town long?" Anne asked.

He shrugged, but his smile dimmed. "I've been traveling up the shore for about a month, shooting anything that looks promising. Just looking for the perfect opportunity." He winked, as if including her in some secret club. She forced a smile, all of her inner-city instincts jumping to attention. "Right now, I'm taking some new pictures of your lighthouse for the hospital." More clicking went through Anne's head, and she turned her suspicion monitor to low voltage.

The jangle of the bell over the door made her turn. A grinning Sandra sauntered in, a twinkle in her eye. "How's our local EMT?"

Sandra looked like she'd just stepped out of an L.L. Bean catalog, complete with a turquoise crewneck T-shirt, khaki shorts, and blue leather moccasins. Her blonde hair hung in a long rope down her back, and despite the wrinkles around her eyes, she didn't look a day over twenty-five. She slid onto the bench beside Anne and gave her a one-armed hug.

"Dr. Jefferies can't stop talking about you. Seems you made an indelible impression on him last week." Sandra waggled her brows at Anne. "I don't think you'd have to do more than smile in his general direction and you'd have an eligible bachelor knocking at your door."

Anne blushed. She hadn't had this much male attention since high school and never for reasons she wanted to embrace. "He's very nice."

"Nice! Girlfriend, you're not going to find a more eligible man than Dr. Jefferies. Handsome, clean-cut, churchgoer, and rich to boot."

Anne fingered her cup. Yes, Dr. Jefferies certainly had the veneer of a saint, and a girl using all her brain cells would jump at the chance to attract his eye.

If she hadn't already given away a scary hunk of her heart to Mr. Tall, Dark, and Dangerous hiding in the backwoods. She shrugged away Sandra's comment as the woman ordered a cup of cappuccino from Mona.

"Hey, by the way, Dr. Simpson is trying to track you down. He's issuing new ID tags and keys to all the nurses, and I guess you're on the list since you load up supplies for the Granite River Clinic."

"New keys . . . why?"

Sandra looked at Mona and Joe, then around the room. She spotted Mr. Pickle settled on the plaid sofa, engrossed in the pages of a Boundary Waters coffee-table book. Sandra lowered her voice when she continued. "There are some drugs missing. Vicodin and Soma . . . painkillers and muscle relaxants. Also, there is some Percocet missing and a supply of Ritalin."

"Ritalin has street value." Anne traveled back to the days when she'd seen two grown adults balancing along the edge of the Hyatt Hotel roof, high on the ADD drug. She always thought it curious that the very thing that depressed a child's system, helping them concentrate, pumped an adult's brain into high gear and beyond. "Ritalin is a controlled substance. The prescriptions can't be refilled without a checkup."

"Which means that someone either miscounted or someone pocketed it," said Sandra.

Anne ran her finger down the side of her mug. "Tell Dr. Simpson I'll stop by as soon as I can." The thought of some-

one stealing drugs for personal abuse or to sell on the Deep Haven streets tightened her jaw. Hopefully they'd track down the thief before Anne started her regular shift at the hospital.

"Hey, I noticed gear in your car, along with your very loud dog. Are you taking off?" Sandra asked as she sipped her cappuccino.

"Sort of. I've decided to work at Wilderness Challenge for the summer, and I thought it would be easier if I lived there." She offered an innocent shrug to accompany her explanation. This little congregation didn't need to know that it would also be easier to enjoy time with Noah without having to run back and forth to Deep Haven when the moon was casting a warm glow on their evening.

Sandra smiled and lifted one blonde eyebrow. "So Dr. Jefferies isn't the only attraction in town."

Anne gaped at her, then clamped her mouth shut lest she reveal an embarrassed smile.

Mona laughed. "I like Noah. He's a charmer, and he certainly has zeal to fuel his dreams." She set a chocolate-chip muffin in front of Sandra. "Where is he from, anyway?"

"He's not from here?" Anne frowned. For some reason she'd settled on the thought that he hailed from the Granite River Reservation. Maybe it was his finesse as a Boy Scout. He hadn't been exactly forthcoming about his background. . . .

"I don't think so," Joe offered. "He's been pretty tight-lipped about it, but he seems to be a little bit more big-city savvy than the lumberjacks from this area. I do know he's bringing in kids from his hometown for the summer." He handed Anne her book. "I hope I spelled your name right."

"Yes, Anne with an *e,*" she said, touched that he'd guessed correctly.

"You just seemed like the *e* type," he said, shrugging, but his warm smile told her she'd made a friend.

"Well, wherever Noah is from, he's certainly made a

mark on our fair town," Sandra said. She looked pointedly at Anne, then at Joe and Mona, and winked.

Deep Haven wasn't the only thing on which Noah had made an impression. So much for tea to harness her daydreams. Anne gave in to the impulse and let herself enjoy the mark he'd already made on her heart.

Anne arrived after lunch, dragging a sleeping bag, a dog bowl, and her pillow. "Can you carry my suitcase, Noah?"

He could carry the entire SUV if she wanted, to Siberia and back. "Sure."

His heart skipped out ahead of him as he hauled her suitcase, bulging with clothes and whatever else women needed, from the back hatch. He ran to the outfitter's shack for another cot. When he returned, Melinda, Katie, and Granny D. were already giving Anne the deluxe tour. He stood outside the door, feeling like a fox in a henhouse, listening to the ladies giggle. Obviously he wasn't the only one overjoyed by their newest arrival.

He knocked on the door, and all went silent. Frowning, he opened it. Melinda and Katie flanked Anne like ladies-in-waiting. "Well," Melinda barked, "put it down and back out!" She shooed him away with a gleam in her eye.

Noah had the oddest feeling that the camp program had just begun to spiral out of his control.

Thirty minutes later, he attempted to scrape up a modicum of authority by gathering the staff on the lodge steps and announcing the afternoon's activity.

"Ropes course? What's that?" Anne's eyes widened with a look of sheer panic.

"Calm down, Anne," Ross said. "It's fun. It's something Bucko and I rigged up to help the kids prepare for rock climbing. They'll work on knots and get the hang of being on belay."

"Not to mention confront their fear of heights." Bucko had a decidedly wicked smile when he wanted one.

Noah grimaced. "Anne, if you want to beg out—"

"No way." She had a delicious jut to her jaw when she acted tough. "I'm on this staff. I'm doing the ropes course."

Noah nearly hugged her. Perhaps that would wait until tonight, around a flickering campfire, with the loons serenading and the breeze . . .

He felt his face flame at the look Bucko gave him. He gulped and shouldered a coil of climbing rope. "Grab your gear. We have a little hike ahead."

He didn't miss the murmur and chuckles that trailed him as he marched off into the brush. So much for respect from the masses.

Surely Noah had lost his marbles. Anne stared over the fifty-foot perch at the ground below and shook her head. "Nope. Not going down that thing. Not for a zillion dollars. No way."

Beside her, Ross laughed. Easy for him. He'd already been tied into the metal contraption they called a zip line and rocketed down, doing some sort of acrobatic dance meant to make her feel like a klutz. Anne heard Noah calling encouragement to her from the bottom. Ropes course . . . more like death trap in the sky.

First they had her climb a rope ladder to a perch in a towering elm. Then she'd traversed a rope bridge that nearly sent her into the fetal position and had the rest of them in hysterics. Sure, she was trussed up in a webbing diaper they called a harness, meant to catch her if she fell. But she had named it "the tourniquet," and she was 110 percent sure that the stringy diaper linking the rescue rope to the zip line with a flimsy hook wasn't going to do anything more than unravel like a badly knit sweater.

And wouldn't the ugly splotch in the dirt be an attractive way to inspire confidence in their new camp nurse?

Now they wanted her to dangle from a T-contraption and whiz down to the ground into Noah's waiting arms. She had to admit that reward was almost worth the terror . . . almost. But she'd watched Melinda's speed-of-light journey, accompanied by her shrieks and the whine of metal on metal. And short of lighting her backside on fire, she wasn't taking that death-wish trolley down to the ground.

Then again, the other option, as Ross had suggested, was to swing herself over the edge and rappel down. As in fall. Anne peered over the edge and knew she'd turned into a full-fledged, yellow-bellied coward. "Nope," she repeated just in case no one heard her the first time.

Ross sat on the perch, looking smug, a grin on his clean-shaven face. "Anne, trust me; it's safe. Noah checked your harness. I checked your belay. It's fun." A lilt tipped his voice, as if he were talking to a ten-year-old.

She glared at him.

"Grab the pulley and jump."

Right into midair and sure death. She made a face at Ross that she hoped communicated exactly how she felt about his suicide suggestion.

He laughed and called out, "Noah, she's not going! I told you."

Anne gaped at him. "You told him what?"

Ross lost the teasing look. "I just said, well . . ."

"What?"

He shrugged, looking fairly chagrined for a cocky college kid.

"What?"

"It's just that, well . . . okay, you don't look like the adventurous type."

Anne narrowed her eyes. Smart aleck. "I'll have you know that I grew up in the inner city and have jumped between buildings higher than this tree, pal. I have more

adventure in my little finger than you have in your entire
puffed-up, empty head!"

Ross's eyes widened, and he raised one blond eyebrow as
if in disbelief. "Okay, so, prove it." He grabbed the pulley.
"Hop on."

Anne swallowed and looked down at the ground. Noah
did await her at the bottom, arms open, a solid rock wall of
safety waiting to catch her. And she had . . . well, okay . . .
once jumped between two buildings. It had been a stupid
dare and she'd broken her leg, but still . . .

Truth be told, she simply wasn't that gusto gal anymore.
Anne the Adventurous had died an apropos death when she
started working her EMT shifts. It had only taken scraping
up a couple of unfortunate losers in a drag race for her to
realize that safe living had its merits. Safe driving, no drinking, no drugs, and especially no high diving.

Then again, where had living safely landed her? Shot and
in six months of rehab.

And this time Noah waited to catch her. He stood there
like some mighty prince awaiting his Rapunzel. A swell of
idiotic rapture made her bounce to her feet and grab the
pulley.

The metal felt cold in her sweaty hands. Suddenly, all she
could hear was the thunder of her pulse. Ross spoke, but his
directions became a blur in the panic that swelled in her
chest. Her legs shook. Her grip turned slick, loose. No! She
was going to slip and fall and—

Ross gave her a push.

Anne screamed.

The ground rushed toward her. Her body flailed, yanked
down by gravity. Her grip fought the slippery metal.
Weakened . . .

She fell, lurched, and screamed again. The pulley
screeched. The diaper pinched her thighs. The sickly sweet
smell of burning.

She fixed on Noah. His face paled. He started to run.

The pulley jerked to a stop.

149

She hung dangling twenty feet from the ground. In a white-hot moment of sheer terror, she saw fear flash across Noah's face.

Then the belay line ripped free of the pulley.

Anne's heart leapt from her throat as she plunged to the ground.

Noah, catch me!

14

Anne fell in gut-wrenching slow motion. Her arms flailed. Her scream ripped Noah to shreds as he dove for her. *Please, God—!*

He missed completely. She landed with a breath-stealing oomph.

Noah skidded to his knees a gulp behind her and scooped her up. "Anne, are you okay? Anne!" Her beautiful eyes were closed. *Oh, please, Lord, let her be okay.*

Then her chin began to tremble, and she opened her eyes.

"Oh, Anne, I'm so sorry."

She shook her head, as if unable to latch on to words.

"Is anything broken? Where are you hurt?"

She managed a tremulous breath. "I think I'm fine." Noah heard Ross hollering and Melinda and Katie were rappelling down from their roosts.

"I'm so sorry," he gasped, his words on a hiccup of horror. "I checked the gear. I did, but I must have missed—"

Her wide eyes, drinking in his apology with acceptance, made him stop. He couldn't help himself. Relief poured through him as he pulled her close, tucking her head under his chin. "I'm sorry. I'm so sorry."

She curled her fingers into his T-shirt and for a moment tensed within his embrace, as if still paralyzed by the fear flooding her veins. But then, with a glorious sigh that he felt to his bones, she relaxed and began to sob into his chest. He held her tight, knowing he could stay here forever, eyes closed, drinking in the intoxicating feeling of her trust.

"Is she okay?" Bucko ran up behind Noah and nearly knocked him over. "Any broken bones?"

Reluctantly, Noah let her go. Tears had etched grimy lines down her face and turned her eyes into pure, rich, gold-flecked jade. He used his thumb to wipe the moisture away and was rewarded with a heart-stopping smile. "Let's get her back to camp," Noah said, not wanting to let her go. He wrapped his arm around Anne's waist and helped her to her feet. "Can you walk?"

Anne nodded, her gaze never leaving his.

She might be okay, but he knew she'd taken his heart with her in that fall.

Two hours later Noah stood on the trail to the cook's cabin, waging World War III with his guilt. How had her belay line ripped? After he'd helped Anne back to camp, he, Ross, and Bucko had hiked back to the ropes course, the gavel of indictment slamming with each step.

Anne had nearly been killed.

What if it had been one of the campers?

Noah knew they'd been lucky—and perhaps negligent—when he examined the trolley on the zip line. When she'd taken off, the belay rope attached to the metal line got tangled in the pulley. The combination of heat and pressure on the hemp rope had frayed the belay line. A freak accident, but preventable. He should have used a nylon climbing rope. He should have attached the carabiner to the trolley.

He should never have forced Anne to jump off a five-

story perch. He'd seen the terror on her face, and instead
of pressuring her into something he thought she needed, he
could have been a hero—the protector he'd promised he'd
be. He should have climbed up and rescued her.

Instead he'd pushed her right into danger. He felt sick.

He already had serious fears that catastrophe loomed like
a guillotine, and accidents like Anne's told him he flirted
with fire. In twenty-four hours Wilderness Challenge would
be filled with twenty teenagers with a legacy of crime and
pain. Adding physical danger to that mix was a sure powder
keg.

If he didn't stay on his toes, this entire ministry would
blow sky-high.

Noah scraped both hands through his hair. They came
away slick with sweat. The sun had turned selfish and spent
most of the afternoon sequestered behind slate gray
thunderheads. The smell of storm laden the air, and even the
breeze sounded angry.

What was he thinking? He'd done it again—rushed out
without a nod at good judgment. And, again, he'd landed
smack into folly.

It seemed to be a response he couldn't shake, even though
he knew the cost. He'd nearly cost lives and paid dearly for
his impulsiveness. He heard the past rise like a phantom and
mock him.

He was in over his head, and he was going to get someone killed. Again. He would have thought five years in
lockup and the horror of his sins would have taught him to
tread with caution.

Tears fell as Noah looked up to heaven. His fears threatened to swallow him whole. *God, I've made so many
mistakes in this life. So many wrong choices. Please, help
me to stay alert. To save lives, not cost them.*

Unbelievably, he'd been saved from those past sins by
the grace of Jesus Christ, and despite the tug toward
despair, he'd cling to that reality now. He wasn't Rock Man
any longer. He was Noah Saved-by-Grace Standing Bear,

standing on the Rock of his salvation. Even today, Anne had forgiven him. In the middle of his relentless barrage of "I'm sorrys," as they trekked back to camp, she finally touched his lips with her hand and shook her head. Forgiveness, when shining in Anne's incredible eyes, never looked so overwhelming.

Noah summoned his courage and marched toward the cook's shack. Certainly by now the ladies had determined Anne's injuries. At the least, he could say good-bye before he left in the camp bus to pick up the kids in the city.

He heard a gasp as he approached the cabin. A glow from a kerosene lamp hanging on the porch pushed back the gloom shrouding the forest and beckoned. Noah stepped up to the screen door. The inner door hung open. He heard Anne's voice and instantly brightened. She was alive and obviously in the middle of a story.

"So I walked into the room, and there was this fella standing there. He sorta looked at me as if sending off signals."

"What kind of signals?" From the tone of Melinda's voice, Anne had her wrapped in suspense. Probably a tale of love from her high school years. Curiosity pulled at him, but Noah fought it and lifted his hand to knock.

"He had these incredible brown eyes . . . and he looked at me as if saying, stop."

"Did you stop?" Katie asked. Noah could picture her sitting on the end of her bed, green eyes wide with intrigue.

"I had to." Something in Anne's voice made Noah pause, and a sick feeling welled up in his stomach. "Standing behind the door was this punk, totally freaked-out on drugs and waving a pistol."

Noah's breath clogged in his chest.

"I must have scared him because the kid looked at me and *pow!* He pulled the trigger."

"He *shot* you?" Melinda's voice betrayed the horror that thundered in Noah's ears.

No, it couldn't be.

"Right in the stomach."

Noah didn't have to close his eyes to conjure up the picture of the pretty EMT sprawled in a pool of blood, an ugly wound gurgling life out of her abdomen.

Noah braced his hand on the doorframe, unable to swallow the avalanche of pain. Anne was that EMT, the lady he'd seen blown away. By his own failure. By a boy he'd tried to save.

His legs gave way, and Noah sat down hard on the edge of the stoop. No wonder Anne looked spooked when he'd first met her. She didn't recognize him, of that he felt sure. But she'd turned white, as if she'd seen a ghost and he had no trouble pinning down the reasons why. Seeing him had transported Anne back to her stumble through the shadow of the valley of death. Seeing him reminded her of pain, fear, and danger.

And he'd forced her to work for him. Forced her to stick around and tend the scrapes of the very hoodlums she feared. He should tell Anne to leave. Pack her suitcase and head for the hills.

But he needed her.

He sank his head into his hands.

"Noah, what are you doing out here?"

Anne had opened the door and leaned out, looking down at him with a smile that said she hadn't the faintest idea that he was the man who'd seen her at death's door—who had, in fact, opened it for her.

He swallowed, found his voice in the pit of his stomach. "I . . . uh . . . ." He tried to smile, but all he could manage was a weak grimace.

She looked so trusting, so pure and honest, with eyes that drew him in and made him feel like a snake. *Why, O Lord, did You bring her here? It's not fair to either one of us!* "I'm just here to say good-bye." Noah scrabbled to his feet and immediately glued his eyes to his boots, wrestling to find the guts to finish the sentence. "I have to go get the campers."

"Oh," Anne said, as she let the door close behind her. "Where's that?"

He cleared his throat and half turned so he could make his escape without seeing her expression. "Minneapolis."

15

Anne lay on her cot watching the moonbeams sweep the floor, wondering about Noah's warp-speed exit. As if suddenly, by breathing her air, he'd catch leprosy or the plague.

She clenched her jaw against the only explanation that filled her brain. Maybe she'd embarrassed him. She'd clung to him, weeping unashamedly, this afternoon after her near-death plummet. Perhaps whatever fledgling feelings that might have germinated toward her had been weeded clean by her cheap display of cowardice. Of blinding, needy emotion.

Yes, he'd practically carried her home, and she thought she'd read worry in those sweet eyes. But the man who'd flirted with her for a week now was not the man she said good-bye to this afternoon. The morphed persona on the steps of the cabin had told her, in no uncertain terms, that something about her made him edgy. From the look on his face, it wasn't due to a wild desire to pull her into his arms.

This particular brand of agitation made him want to run. All the way to Minneapolis.

Her eyes filled, recalling their conversation. The wind

had smacked out of her when he announced he was headed to Minneapolis. "What?" she'd rasped in a croak.

The look he gave her felt so raw, so vulnerable that she could barely make out his words. "I'm headed down to the Twin Cities to pick up the campers." He swallowed and ducked his head, as if somehow dreading the impact those words might have on her.

And then, with those words, right there before her eyes Noah morphed back into the gangster she'd been dodging. Suddenly the scar on his cheek, the motorcycle, even his swagger screamed drug lord, or worse, murderer. She froze. No. It had to be her fears, her past scrambling her vision. Noah may look dangerous, but over the past week she'd realized it was an act for the benefit of the campers. Identification. A youth-director gimmick.

But he'd never contradicted her when she accused him of being a convict the night he broke into her cabin . . . but truth be told, she'd been . . . well . . . exaggerating. The Noah that was her friend, the one who taught her how to roast marshmallows and who chopped wood like Paul Bunyan couldn't be from Minneapolis. Well, maybe the suburbs. But not the inner city. He was simply too nice. Pure hero. Besides, God wouldn't do that to her. Not after what she'd been through.

Anne had forced a smile, shaking away her idiocy. "When will you be back?"

"Tomorrow afternoon."

Why didn't he look at her? After he'd nearly carried her home, concern ringing his eyes and tightening his arm around her, she felt sure he . . . she nearly choked on the confusing emotions knotting her throat. He'd shot her a half smile, but it spoke more of chagrin. "Try and get some rest while I'm gone, okay?"

Then he'd turned, hands balled at his sides, and strode away. Anne watched him go, wanting to call after him, yearning to ask the questions just now forming in her heart.

Who were these kids he was picking up and why did Noah Standing Bear look like he'd seen a ghost?

Anne wiped a pool of disloyal tears, turned onto her side, and smacked her pillow. Well, she wasn't here for him, was she? She was here to serve the kids in the camp. Even if they were from Minneapolis didn't mean she had to instantly assume the worst. The picture made perfect sense. City kids, probably from a nice suburban church, needed a wilderness experience, a camping atmosphere outside their manicured lives to test their faith. If living in army tents, battling mosquitoes, and bathing in icy water didn't push them to the edge, the five-story vault off the ropes course would certainly encourage them to wrap their fingers around their faith.

Anne battled the recurring image of Noah as drug lord, gangbanger, hustler. Yes, with a nylon hat, a tattoo, and baggy pants, Noah might fit the Phillips profile. But his gentle smile, his patience, even his wisdom belied the truth. She had more street experience in her little finger than he had in his entire muscle-bound body, even if he did look the part.

That street history told her that Noah Standing Bear harbored secrets behind his grimace. She couldn't be imagining the feelings budding between them—no, not after the kiss he'd given her last night. Sweet and gentle, and she'd felt a tremble that told her it meant as much to him as it had to her.

The memory of his touch curled her insides in a swirl of pleasure. She wasn't imagining the way he looked at her or the stirring of her own feelings. When Noah returned, she was going to look him straight in the eye and ask him what he was hiding.

Because—she couldn't deny it any longer—she was here for Noah. And this time she wasn't going to run from the fears lurking behind the doorway of her heart.

Noah vise-gripped the steering wheel of the ancient bus, trying not to be unsettled by the potholes and dips in the

logging road that ran the final five miles to Wilderness
Challenge. Behind him the twenty tired kids had quieted
after five hours of sweltering, uncomfortable travel under
the relentless commands of Noah's capable bouncers, Bucko
and Ross.

The kids had been patted down for weapons, had their
gang colors confiscated, been deloused, and now, as the
birch arms enclosed them, each mile they drew closer to the
edge of the world, fear tightened its stranglehold on Noah.
These urban warriors were no match for the real jungle
wiles.

Three years ago, when Noah had first trekked into these
woods with his motley youth group, he'd watched a sixteen-
year-old Vice Lord minister reduced to tears at the hoot of
an owl and knew he'd found the golden ticket. Noah smiled
at the perfection of God's plan. He never ceased to marvel
at the effect the wilderness had on kids—especially street
kids. Kids who had never seen the beauty of a loon, never
heard the song of the night absent sirens, traffic, and the
scream of neighbors. These kids didn't know the world
wasn't painted entirely in gang symbols, rutted cars, and
broken homes. Surrounded by mosquitoes, the sounds of
the wind lashing the trees and forest animals lurking about
their tents, these junior highers in the back would be hanging on Noah's every word in less than twenty-four hours.

"Hey, Noah! Where ya taking us? The dark side of the
moon? I mean, man, do you even got electricity up here?"
Darrin Marlow hung his arm over the rail separating the
bus driver and the passenger seat. "I thought you said we
were going to camp. I don't see nothin' but trees."

"Calm down." Noah flicked the kid a look in the overhead mirror. "I promise you'll have a good time."

"Yeah, sure." Darrin flopped back in his seat, arms
folded across his chest, in the throes of a deep pout, looking
every inch a thirteen-year-old homeboy with a rugged
history. His size alone had made him a fine catch for the
Vice Lords, and it was only Noah's shadow standing sentry

every night after school that had kept the kid out of the gang's lasso. For now.

Darrin's father, a man who'd loved his kids, had been found facedown in the Mississippi two years ago, a gang-related murder statistic. The man, the owner of an electronics store, had said no too many times. It hadn't taken Darrin's mother long to shop other options. Noah didn't blame her—she needed a father for her kids, but Darrin wasn't having any part of the replacement, a man from Noah's church. Tricia had called Noah twice last year to drag Darrin home after he'd shown up drunk at Casey's, the local pinball/pizza hangout. Noah counted his blessings that the kid wasn't hanging out in darker playgrounds.

Darrin slipped on his headphones. His CD player was probably on the last of its juice because he fiddled with the toggle and made a face.

"You're gonna lose it in about ten minutes anyway, big D," Noah said. He didn't wait for Darrin's response. He knew the entire assembly would take off his head when he confiscated their electronics. But gangster rap and hip-hop were the last things these kids needed. He wasn't a great singer, but he had a few new tunes that might catch their interest. These kids weren't ready for Michael Card, but Christian rap might turn their ears.

Noah steered over a rut and heard a trio of ten-year-olds in the back give a screech of delight as they bounced. He couldn't hide a smile. These kids weren't so hardened that they didn't break free of their cool-as-ice shells and enjoy childhood. Junior high or even younger was the optimum age for moral and spiritual change. At ten to fourteen, kids were still searching, still available, still fueled by a remnant of hope. High school punks had a firmly gelled worldview and an outer layer so thick it took a sledgehammer to break through.

Maybe someday, if this summer didn't crumble, he'd begin to dream bigger, into that demographic also. Right now, just thinking about the next month turned him cold.

He had no illusions that this little party could turn into a brawl with one serious dissing between campers. With kids from all over the Phillips neighborhood crammed into this rusty 1974 school bus, he couldn't count the different gang affiliations on one hand. These kids might be decloaked, disarmed, and displaced, but it would only take a few negative hand gestures for battle lines to be drawn.

God and all His heavenly armies had better be in shape because this summer might see a battle to rival the L.A. riots.

Or it might succeed. He glanced at Darrin, then at his little sister, Latisha, sitting behind him, singing softly to herself, her dark fingers weaving a friendship bracelet. Wilderness Challenge might force these kids to the end of themselves where they'd find nowhere to fall but into the arms of their Savior.

Noah muscled the bus through an embrace of foliage, brush screeching as it scraped the sides. He could see the sign ahead, rough cut by his own jackknife into a piece of stained oak: "Wilderness Challenge: Psalm 62:8." The verse came readily to mind: *"O my people, trust in Him at all times. Pour out your heart to Him, for God is our refuge."*

Gratefulness welled up inside him. Without a doubt, God had been his refuge, and only pure trust in God's goodness had brought Noah to this moment. He had so many people to thank, starting with God and going down through supporting churches, his own staff at the Christian Fellowship Center, and finally Ross, Bucko, Melinda, Granny D., Katie, the rest of the counselors, and not in the least Anne. Without her, he wouldn't even have the gas money to yank these kids off the streets for the summer. God had certainly surprised him with Anne. A lady who laughed at his stupid jokes, who was as tenacious as a badger, and who had more guts in that petite body than he'd first given her credit for.

Being near her sent his heart into overdrive and turned his legs weak. It didn't help that she'd let him kiss her. Surrendering, tender, offering him a piece of herself he knew, deep in his gut, he didn't deserve. But he'd held her soft face in his work-weary hands and touched those beautiful lips, and he'd never be the same for it. He had begun to cultivate serious hopes that Anne would consider joining the Wilderness Challenge team for the long haul—as in a partnership of the permanent kind.

He winced at that thought. He wanted to deny it, but the anticipation churning in his chest told him he was halfway too far in love with Anne to pull back now. His heart-ripping fear as he'd watched her fall hadn't escaped his notice. In ten seconds of utter agony he'd realized that Anne was embedded in the fabric of his heart, and the delirious feeling had him singing one second and poised to bolt the next.

Bolt was exactly what he'd done, struck nearly dumb by the fact that he'd met her a year ago. It had taken him ten-plus hours in the driver's seat of this rattletrap bus to really shake his brain free of the shock. He'd spent most of the trip wincing as he thought of the way he'd scared the life out of her—more than once. No wonder she looked at him as if he'd sprouted horns the first time she saw him and nearly fainted when she'd caught him in her house acting like a stalker.

Or a drug-high killer.

That night came back to him in shuddering clarity. Her fear, her tears, her whispered voice when she told him she hadn't seen God's grace, couldn't fathom His love for her. He cringed, remembering how he'd challenged her not to run from her fears. His words felt even more hollow as he grasped the depth of her wounds now. Her scars went faith deep.

She didn't need a hoodlum reminding her of the split second of terror that had nearly ended her life and shattered her belief in a good and present God.

His chest tightened, that moment searing his brain. What did she remember? He recalled everything in unadulterated, agonizing detail, down to the odor of Anthony's fear on his sweaty face and Anne's calm, precise courage, to the way she'd clung to Noah's hand while bleeding into the threadbare carpet. Sweat beaded the back of his neck as he drove. Perhaps she didn't remember him at all—amnesia in trauma victims wasn't rare. Or, and he guessed this from the permanent etching of fear in her eyes, she too relived every horrific second in surround sound and Technicolor.

If so, *did* she remember him? Noah licked his dry lips. Would she remember him as friend . . . or foe?

Suddenly the idea of her spending the summer with him, a man who represented the darkest moment of her life, made him hurt, bone deep. He scanned the campers in the rearview mirror—their pierced faces, the defiant slump of their bodies, the emotional baggage they wore like tattoos— and cringed.

Anne had run from her pain, her past.

And Noah had brought it right back to her front door.

He felt like a weasel.

No, worse.

He felt like he'd assaulted her himself.

Anne stood on the porch of the lodge, watching the bus bounce along the road. Noah manned the wheel, and she instantly ached at the exhaustion written on his face. It couldn't be easy to travel ten hours in two days, hauling a bus full of rowdy kids. His nerves must be nearly in shreds.

She tugged at her T-shirt and smoothed her hands over her jeans. So she'd put on makeup and a touch of perfume. It didn't mean he would notice.

Katie and Melinda lined up beside her. Katie had cornrowed Melinda's hair into tight, functional braids, and both girls had moved out of the cook shack and into the army tents. Excitement lined their faces, complete with beaming smiles that had sprouted after their prayer time this

morning. Noah had chosen his staff well—these girls were already praying for their campers by name.

The bus wheezed to a stop and Anne braced herself. She'd be spending the next six weeks looking after these kids, and they needed to see her as disciplinarian as well as housemother if she expected them to obey her. The door opened, and Bucko emerged with more energy than she thought she possessed in her entire body. Well, she supposed that might be apropos for a guy the size of Texas. He waved to the group on the porch, his white teeth gleaming. So the ladies weren't the only ones oozing excitement.

Anne heard Noah on the bus, his words muffled but his voice strong as he no doubt laid down the camp rules. The tone of his voice shocked her. Not gentle. Not quiet. Mr. Grizzly possessed exactly the stern voice required to keep these kids in line. So why did he need the mercenary biker getup?

When the first kid thumped out of the bus, Anne's heart stalled in her chest. Wearing a long, red Chicago Bulls T-shirt, he had his pants hitched below his backside, and one pant leg had been neatly rolled up higher than the other. Gang signals were hard to spot unless you'd grown up in the hood and knew what to look for. This kid couldn't be any older than fifteen, but he was pushing six feet, and from the body piercing, his swagger, and his arranged attire, she knew in the pit of her stomach he was a gangbanger.

She watched in horrified silence as a string of gang wanna-bes, or, as in her nightmares, full-fledged homeboys and girls lined up outside the bus, doing their best to broadcast to the critters peering at them from the forest that they were taking this turf. Backs stiff, arms folded, twenty street-hardened kids—no, criminals—glared at the small assembly on the porch and dared them to change their lives.

Anne wanted to flee, but fear held her body rigid. Her throat tightened, nearly cutting off her air supply. God couldn't be this cruel. Not after all she'd been through, not after the scars speared into her body. She crossed her arms and held in a scream.

Beside her, Melinda and Katie dashed off the porch to greet the newcomers.

Obviously, she was the only one without a clue as to the biographies of their campers. She had been left in the dark, deceived, betrayed. Anger spiraled through every vein, every muscle until she felt she could take out Mr. Standing Bear with a death-ray glare.

Then Noah emerged. Before he plastered that ever-present, melt-her-heart-in-an-instant smile on his face, he glanced at her. In his face she saw the guilt that told her he knew exactly how he'd trapped her.

No wonder he'd slunk away from her like a rat.

16

"Anne! Please talk to me!" For a woman with short legs, she could hustle. Of course, he'd seen the glares she'd been sending him the past hour, and he had no doubt that fury coursed through her veins that could fuel the space shuttle for a few thousand millennia. As if to prove it, she'd taken off like a rocket the second he'd dismissed the campers to their tents.

There might not be steam spiraling from her ears, but the wake she stirred up made him want to duck.

He'd seen the way she'd turned ashen and he felt heartsick. Why hadn't he talked to her about the kids before they arrived? or at least warned her?

Because, until last night, he hadn't realized it mattered. Kids were kids, regardless of their economics or race, and each one needed God as much as the next. God didn't choose demographics. Just sinners. And the platoon of street soldiers unpacking their gear in the army tents certainly qualified. Noah lengthened his stride. "Anne! C'mon, talk to me!"

She whirled, and he shuddered at the red outlining her eyes. Her mouth opened. Closed. She trembled as if fighting emotions so deep she couldn't churn them out of her chest to be vocalized. Then she buried her face in her hands and shook her head again and again, her body starting to rack.

Noah felt a groan deep inside his body. He stepped toward her—how could he not take her into his arms? Her hair flung over her face; her shoulders trembled. Every fiber of his body longed to hold her. He reached out, touched her shoulder—

She flinched. "Stay away from me."

Noah froze. *No, Anne, please. Don't do this.* He swallowed his hurt and strengthened his voice. "Anne, what's wrong?" He couldn't tell her what he knew. The last thing she needed right now was a phantom from the past. "Is it the kids?"

She raised her head, and a wild look entered her beautiful face. She shivered so hard he thought she might shatter right there before his eyes. But her voice emerged steady. "I know this sounds so incredibly prejudiced, Noah. But, yes. Yes! Excuse me, but don't you think you might have informed me that you were dragging up a bunch of street punks for the summer? that you planned on infecting the wilderness— and my life—with kids who don't care a whit about what you might say to them as long as they can trash this camp? These kids have hearts of stone, and they'd just as soon throw them at you than let you soften them." Her eyes sizzled with achingly raw pain.

"I'm sorry they upset you—"

"Upset me?" She narrowed her eyes at him. "Noah, do you have any idea what you are walking into? These kids will steal you blind while they smile at you and raise their hands to be baptized." She had more color now, and the heat in her voice tamed his ferocious desire to fall to his knees and beg her forgiveness.

"You're a real thundercloud, aren't you?" Noah answered. "Can't you see beyond the fog to the potential? to all that could happen here this summer? These kids need

to escape their turfs and find God's world. They need to be pushed beyond themselves until they fall—"

"And kill us all. Noah, I'm not a thundercloud. I'm your voice of sanity." Her voice shrilled. "I won't be spending the summer doctoring cuts—I'll be trying to keep these kids from murdering each other!" She shook her head again, hands up in surrender. "Sorry, pal. I didn't sign up for a war." She took a step back. "I'm sorry."

Noah felt as if he'd been belly punched. "What?"

She had already turned. "I can't do this. I can't do this." Her words became a mutter as she trod down the path, stumbling. "I can't do this."

Noah couldn't watch the future of twenty children disintegrate. "Anne, please!" He ran after her and grabbed her by the arm. It felt as limp as rubber, and even as she turned, her eyes didn't focus on him. He resisted the urge to shake her and turned his voice soft. "Listen to me, honey. I know you're afraid. But I believe God sent you here. These kids need you." Her expression looked so fearful it nearly ripped out his heart. "*I* need you."

Fresh tears welled in her eyes, and this time, when she began to tremble, he pulled her against his chest, wrapped his arms around her. The impulse rose to tell her that he knew, understood with gut-wrenching clarity the sacrifice she'd made and the pain that drummed in the background when she looked at these kids.

She stiffened and pulled away. "Yes, I know how much you need me, Mr. Standing Bear." The ice in her eyes hurt. "Don't worry. I won't destroy your little program." She lifted her chin. "But you mark my words. I give you one week before you have an all-out war here." She lifted one elegant finger. "One week."

She stepped away from him, and her expression told him not to follow. "I'll stay, but you keep away from me."

Then she lowered her gaze and rubbed her hands on her arms. "And don't ever call me honey again."

Anne sat against a giant basswood tree and stared through its gnarled arms toward the heavens. At her feet, Bertha sniffed, as if disgusted at the recent play of events, and Anne found solace in the innocent empathy.

She felt like the heavens were laughing—all the stars, the moon, and the Milky Way—the entire cosmos awash in hilarity. Her eyes stung. How could God be so cruel? Hadn't she learned her lessons? Hadn't she done her time ministering to kids who would rather laugh at her than listen?

Anne bowed her head until her forehead touched her drawn-up knees. Tears that burned her eyes trailed down her cheeks. The thought of her duffel bag, already packed and shoved into her SUV, pushed a bitter taste into her mouth. She should leave right now. Forever. Forget Deep Haven and its tricks and floor it south, past Minneapolis, maybe to Iowa. That was a nice state, wasn't it? Corn and cows?

She wanted to sink her fist into Noah Standing Bear's handsome face for what he'd done, the lying, manipulative jerk. She balled her hands, desperate to cry out, strangled by the betrayal that knotted her throat. She couldn't even pray.

So she groaned.

She groaned for all the years that she hadn't escaped, fifteen years of personal grief reflected this afternoon in the glares from forty hard, suspicious eyes.

Why, Father, why?

The question took her back in time to a twelve-year-old voice, inconsolable and filled with fury.

"Why, Father, why?" she'd asked as she leaned over the oak kitchen table around which her family had spent hours praying. The late-autumn sun glazed the table pure gold as her father sat across from her, his features as calm and gentle as they were on Sunday mornings in the pulpit. "Why?" she repeated, and this time, tears broke her words.

"Sit down, Anne." Her mother, always pragmatic, spoke with a hint of warning in her voice. Anne reined in a glare and sat, not mannerly, on her chair. She made sure everyone—Mother, Father, and Ellen—knew that this decision would not be received with grace by the way she folded her arms across her chest and harrumphed.

Her father didn't even stop smiling. "God wants us to move, that's why. He doesn't want us to simply reach in from the outside, but to be His hands, His feet inside the battleground." Her father had a way of explaining things, even from the pulpit in his small rural church, that made everyone nod.

Anne would do almost anything for her father—sing at the nursing home, teach a Sunday school class, even clean pews, but this—

"But why us? Why didn't He choose someone else?" Anne blinked back a fresh wash of tears. Spend the rest of her life in a drug-ridden neighborhood, dodging drive-by shootings? Had her father completely lost his marbles?

"Because we're willing." He continued to smile but closed the Bible, from which he'd read Matthew 28, like she didn't know that chapter by memory in three versions.

"No, we're not!" She had him there and smiled a little back. No *we* involved here. She glanced at Ellen, sure she would take her side. Three years her senior, certainly her fair-haired sister would join forces and help her father see logic. They weren't willing.

Ellen smiled, like of course she would be happy to sacrifice her high school years on the altar of service. Sure. No problem. It'll be fun.

Anne felt the air puff out of her. Outmanned, triple-teamed. She resorted to pleading. "Please, Father. I've read about the Phillips neighborhood in the paper. I know what kind of people—"

"And don't they deserve a chance to know that there is a different way? that God can change their lives?" For the first time, her father's smile dimmed.

171

Anne gulped.

"Anne, Jesus died for these people also. They're broken and alone. They feel hopeless, and we are called to show them His love. His grace."

She managed a whisper. "Why us?"

"If we don't, who will?"

Anne had buried her head in her folded arms, listening to the roar of pain in her heart, the resounding crunch of the great commission stomping on her hopes and dreams. Then she felt her father's hand, soft yet firm on her arm. She took his hand in hers and let the tears flow. When she opened her eyes, tears sheeted his.

"Philippians 1:20-25. Say it with me, honey. Say it with me."

"'For I live in eager expectation and hope that I will never do anything that causes me shame, but that I will always be bold for Christ, as I have been in the past, and that my life will always honor Christ, whether I live or I die. For to me, living is for Christ, and dying is even better. Yet if I live, that means fruitful service for Christ. I really don't know which is better. I'm torn between two desires: Sometimes I want to live, and sometimes I long to go and be with Christ. That would be far better for me, but it is better for you that I live. I am convinced of this, so I will continue with you so that you will grow and experience the joy of your faith.'"

Anne could still hear her father, his gentle voice an echo in the barren cavern of her heart. She wrapped her arms around her knees, folding herself into a ball, and sobbed until her cries punctuated the sounds of the twilight. She didn't care. No one but the loons and night owls, her faithful dog, and the Almighty would hear. Only God knew the battles she'd waged, inside and out, as her father had moved their family to a ramshackle bungalow in the inner city of Minneapolis, with a drug lair on one side and a family of warring immigrants on the other. Only God in heaven knew the abuse she weathered in high school—words she'd never,

ever heard in her school in Waconia. She'd entered a new world, a dangerous, dark world, and had survived.

Survived and escaped. Or so she thought. Anne let her tears chap her cheeks, not caring that she felt puffy and bloated and raw. The wind rustled through her windbreaker, bringing with it the smell of dirt, leaves, and lake. A loon called, and the sound echoed off the slivers of twilight bobbing at her feet.

Finally, in the still of the moment, she heard the voice of the One at whom she wanted to shake a fist: *"I will continue with you so that you will grow and experience the joy of your faith."*

Joy of your faith. Anne touched her lips, willing her heartbeat to slow. It had been years since she'd experienced real joy of her faith. Perhaps since that agonizing day in her family kitchen when God had reached in with the sunshine and turned the altar where they'd made their commitment to pure gold. What did she have to be joyful about? The fear that stalked her like a shadow? The scars on her body? The anger that made her shove the one man she'd wanted to trust out of her life?

No, faith and joy didn't occupy the same place, at least not in her heart.

In fact, at this moment, as she stretched out her legs and ran a hand through Bertha's fur, she knew exactly what her faith gave her. A guilty conscience and bitterness that embedded her bones.

Perhaps she'd turned into the very person her father had spoken of when he'd used the words *hopeless, broken,* and *alone.*

Perhaps she had become like one of Noah's campers—an inner-city kid with a heart of stone.

The dark swatch of pine made him invisible as she, his prey, stepped from her SUV. She opened the door to let her dog out, something he hadn't counted on. The animal didn't sense him, at least he hoped it didn't, for it ran in frenetic circles around her legs. She opened the back hatch and pulled out a bag, locked her arms around it.

Perfect.

He'd been waiting for days, stalking, planning. Fighting the wrong moments, the heady thrust of desperation.

Until now.

Yes, now.

She turned her back to him so that the night outlined her frame. The dog ran out ahead, away from her. Leaving her undefended.

His heartbeat roared and filled his ears. His system finally absorbed the synthetic boost and kicked in pure adrenaline. He relished the way the world seemed sharper, choppy, the angles and colors severe.

It deadened his feelings, focused him on a singular moment, one task. His fists clenched, manic to be unleashed.

He lunged. Felt no pain when he took her down and shoved his knee into her spine. She screamed but it kindled his strength. Cleansed his soul. Filled him with triumph.

He pinned her to the ground. Ran his hands over her, searching. She writhed, rolled, clawed at his arms and hands.

Fantasy and reality mixed and he wouldn't stop it if he could.

He'd waited for her and won.

Strike first.

Noah leaned against the railing of the lodge porch, stretching his calf muscles after his morning run, trying not to look too winded in front of twenty winded campers who glared at him as if they wanted to shoot out his knees. Some of them still wore their pajamas or what looked like them.

Cutoff shirts, fraying gym shorts. The kids littered the yard in various stages of recovery after their 6 A.M. jaunt along the shore.

He wanted them challenged, tired, and even sore. He wanted them to reach beyond their borders and find potential waiting there. "Everyone who wants to take a dip in the lake, run to your tents, change, and I'll meet you back here in ten minutes!" He saw very little movement. Obviously they didn't hate the stench of sweat on their bodies enough to dive into an ice-cold lake.

He, for one, couldn't wait. After a restless night of listening to Anne's words haunting his brain, he felt wrung out and groggy at best. He'd risen early, greeted the dawn in prayer, and dug into God's Word, hoping for wisdom. The verses that he'd meditated upon, Philippians 2:3-4, seared into his brain, offering indictment: "Don't be selfish; don't live to make a good impression on others. Be humble, thinking of others as better than yourself. Don't think only about your own affairs, but be interested in others, too, and what they are doing."

He hadn't missed Anne's barb, her not-so-hooded sarcasm that reminded him of how he'd stiff-armed her into working for him. *Yes, I know how much you need me, Mr. Standing Bear.*

Now that he had his campers here, he had even more to lose. If Anne changed her mind . . . after seeing the death hue on her face last night, he knew without a doubt that his selfishness had landed her in the middle of a nightmare.

He let the door of the cabin bang behind him. *Trust Me, Noah. My grace is sufficient.* Noah listened to the soft voice in his heart, wondering which direction trust should take him. He'd been in this place two weeks ago and surrendered Anne to God.

And God had returned her.

He slicked off his track pants and dragged his shirt over his head. Perhaps God had plans in mind for Anne bigger than Noah's camp. Bigger than Noah's vision. Hadn't he once accused Anne of running from her fears? Little Miss Thundercloud. She not only ran from her nightmares; she saw others looming on the horizon.

He refused to think her forecast might be on the money.

Noah tugged on his swimsuit and threw a towel over his shoulder. God had certainly brought Anne's storms right back to buffet her in the face. Noah winced at that thought. Sometimes God's ways could seem so harsh, especially in light of Anne's history. But personal history of God's character told Noah that mercy permeated the Almighty's actions. Somewhere, despite Noah's crude bobbling of Anne's feelings, God meant it for good. For everyone.

He heard the kids assembling, a few hearty souls who esteemed cleanliness above comfort. Noah paused a moment inside the cabin door. Trust meant he had to pursue communion with God to conquer this fear, and the next . . .

He turned and knelt beside his bed. *Lord, I am sorry I pushed Anne into this, but I know You are at the helm and have good purposes for all of us. Please help me to trust You. Help Anne to trust You. And please, use me somehow, not to hurt but to bless.*

The year-old memory of his own voice singing a hymn of faith and the way Anne had stared at him, her gaze filled with pain, riveted into his thoughts. She'd needed him in that moment. He wanted her to need him again. His eyes burned. *Lord, Your ways are higher than mine. Thank You that when I don't understand why, I can understand who. I can trust in You. And what You are capable of.*

Noah might have coerced Anne to Wilderness Challenge, but God wanted her to stay. If that meant keeping a distance from the woman who made him want to dance and sing just by walking into the room, well, then he would.

For his sake and for hers.

He groaned at the despair that pinged his heart. Anne had turned him inside out, and his very breath hinged on her smile. He put a hand to his chest. How was he supposed

to work beside her for the next month and keep his distance? When all he wanted to do was make her grin?

Trust.

Noah rose and headed for the door. He froze, watching Anne stride down the road, backpack over her shoulder, Bertha at her heels. Gorgeous in a pair of jeans and an orange windbreaker, the sun turning her hair copper. His heart did a rebellious jig. He wanted to call out, run to her, but the sight of her straight shoulders, her jerky movements as she walked to her car, opened it, and climbed in, rooted him to the spot.

She was leaving.

He didn't blame her.

Trust Me.

17

The wind tangled Anne's hair through the open window of her SUV as she drove down to Deep Haven. Lake Superior spread out like an indigo carpet, dotted with bobbing white gulls. Rimming the carpet stood a lush line of evergreens. The town—quaint shops and antique houses—was tucked into a fir-lined pocket like window dressing, an afterthought of landscaping.

Riding in the backseat like the queen of Sheba, Bertha shoved her snout in between Anne and the window, battling for air. The dog licked Anne's neck and she laughed, feeling her tension begin to loosen. She'd done the right thing dragging her duffel bag back to the cook's shack last night. Somehow sitting by the dark lake listening to a lonely loon seemed wiser than searching for Edith's dirt road in a dark clasp of trees, stumbling through a rutted path to her cabin, and crying herself to sleep in an unmade, cold bed.

She could do that just fine in her cot, to the sound of trees scratching the rafters.

But in the light of day, she knew she needed supplies—and perspective. She hoped a firm chat with Dr. Simpson about her definite future at the hospital would give her reason to turn the SUV toward camp at the end of the day.

A reason beyond Noah Standing Bear and his deceitfully winsome grin.

She couldn't deny that Noah had a God-honoring idea. Thoughts of her father's faith, the way he risked it all—even his family—for the sake of the gospel, made her both hate and admire him. But she couldn't be called to do the same thing. She didn't have a heart for these lost kids—they made her jumpy, tense, and downright hostile.

Noah had called her a thundercloud—but she'd become a tree-whipping, hail-and-pelting-rain, finger-of-God tornado if that's what it took to shake Noah loose from this insanity.

She relaxed her grip on the steering wheel and realized she was gritting her teeth. Anne reached over and popped in a CD of Vanessa-Mae. Her violin magic swelled through the vehicle and drowned Anne's turbulent thoughts.

Deep Haven Municipal Hospital hosted three cars in the parking lot—Sandra's, Dr. Simpson's, and one unknown. She should have guessed that they would be on call this weekend. Anne wondered if Dr. Jefferies was on shift today as she lowered the windows and left Bertha in the car. He might not have Noah's charisma, but the doctor certainly had a smile at which most girls would look twice. Perhaps when the summer was over, she would have recovered her footing enough after the Standing Bear disaster to consider the Dr. Jefferies option. If she survived the next six weeks without getting knifed, shot, or beat up, that is. As she trotted into the hospital, her own cynicism made her grimace.

Sandra was manning the admitting desk, and she glanced up when she heard the scuff of Anne's shoes. The woman's welcoming smile told Anne she'd been missed. "Emerged from fighting the mosquitoes, huh? Any battle wounds?"

Anne couldn't even begin to explain. She answered with a smile. "Is Dr. Simpson in?"

Sandra nodded. "Go on back. I'll tell him you're here."

Anne heard Sandra's voice announce her as she treaded back to the office. Dr. Simpson had risen from his desk by the time she reached the door. Her heart jolted at the strain on his gaunt face. Bags of sleeplessness hung under his eyes, and he looked like he hadn't eaten in a week.

He greeted her, but his smile was forced. "Glad to see you, Anne. I'm sorry I wasn't here when you stopped in earlier. Did you get your key?"

Anne fingered her key chain containing the addition of a new key to the pharmaceutical closet. Last week when she'd stopped in, Judy, the human resources rottweiler, had issued her a new key, along with instructions to guard it with her final breath. "Yes, thank you."

"Please be extra careful. Report it if it's lost."

"Of course." Anne nodded. "Why?"

Dr. Simpson paused, and in the brevity of silence, she heard him sigh, as if measuring his burden and her faithfulness. "Jenny Olson was attacked last night."

Anne blinked, braced herself on his desk. "What happened?" Her stomach clenched at the sudden image of Nurse Jenny, her gray hair pulled back into a sturdy braid, her blue eyes brimming with compassion as she tended elderly patients. "Did it happen on the reservation?"

Dr. Simpson's lined face betrayed grief. "No, outside her house. Someone was waiting for her and ambushed her when she came home."

A split-second image of a stranger with dark eyes flashed through her mind. *Garth Peterson, freelance photographer . . . just looking for the perfect opportunity*. What opportunities, exactly? Anne fought a shiver and forced her next question. "How badly is she . . . is she . . . ?"

"No, thank the Lord. Her neighbor heard her dog barking, then Jenny's screams." Dr. Simpson sat back down and covered his face with his aged, elegant hands. "She'll be okay. But she's pretty rattled."

Anne understood how it felt to wake in a hospital,

disoriented and grasping for comprehension. "Did they catch the person?"

Dr. Simpson shook his head, and his face twisted. "I don't know how to tell you this . . ."

Anne had the oddest impulse to reach across the desk and squeeze the doctor's hand. "What is it?"

He looked away from her, his shoulders rising and falling with a sigh that clawed at Anne's heart. She sank into the chair under the gaping jaws of the moose head and braced herself.

"Jenny is the third nurse who has been attacked this month."

Anne swallowed hard. Shakily, she said, "Here in Deep Haven?" As if they would be from somewhere else. Panic tightened her throat at the notion of crime afflicting the shores of this town.

"Chief Sam suggests that no one gets keys to the hospital unless they are checked in and on duty, but since you'll be off campus, hang tight to yours."

Anne frowned. "Does he think the attacks have to do with the hospital?"

Dr. Simpson met her eyes, and his face hardened. "Maybe. We have a shortage of a few prescription medicines. Drugs that have street value."

Percocet, Ritalin . . . her conversation with Sandra raced back into Anne's head.

Dr. Simpson folded his hands on his desk, as if stopping short of reaching across the messy top and holding her hand like a father. "Jenny is going to be okay, but I'm shutting down the Granite River Clinic for now. I want you to spend the summer at camp. You'll fulfill my requirements of your internship and when the summer is over, we'll talk about your future."

Anne blinked at him. A confusing ball of regret and hope lumped in her chest. "Jenny's position?"

"We'll see. But I promised your aunt that I'd keep an eye

on you, and I'd prefer if you'd spend the summer at camp, out of the reaches of some drug-crazed mugger."

Anne nearly rolled her eyes. Obviously the naive doctor had no idea the type of people she'd be spending her summer with. She managed a nod. "Are you sure you don't want me visiting Jenny's patients while she's recovering?"

"No. I'll be looking in on them myself. You concentrate on finishing well. I know you expected more experience following on Jenny's heels, but I think your time as an EMT prepared you better than six weeks in her shadow." He stood and grinned. "And after this summer, you'll have backwoods experience."

Anne folded her arms across her chest and steadied her voice. The last thing she wanted to do was jeopardize Noah's camp, but really, someone should be warned . . . "Did you know that, uh . . . Noah's campers are from Minneapolis?"

Dr. Simpson raised one eyebrow, waiting for her to continue.

"As in inner-city Minneapolis. The urban jungle?" No response. "Gangbangers?" Her voice rose. "Thieves, criminals, hoodlums?"

His smile dimmed. "Didn't you know?"

Anne's words vanished and her chest felt strangely vacant. "I . . . uh . . . no."

"I see." He rubbed his chin. "Noah didn't tell you?"

She grimaced. "He was pretty vague."

"Hmm. Well, I'm sorry it came as a shock. I thought you'd be a perfect fit for the job, with your EMT experience."

Aunt Edith obviously had kept Anne's secrets, from Dr. Simpson, at least. Anne sighed. "Yes, I suppose I am."

"In fact, Noah's told me more than once that you are a real answer to prayer. A gift from the Lord."

She fought to exorcise her sarcasm. "Yes, I know." Obviously Dr. Simpson had no idea that those words felt like a knife through her heart. She dredged up a smile. "Can I see Jenny?"

Dr. Simpson didn't move. "I was against Noah's idea, you know. The first time he suggested it, I hated it. But God reminded me that it's not the healthy who darken my door who need my help. It's the sickly. The blind, the deaf, the wounded. These kids are wounded, and they need all we have to give."

Anne clenched her jaw, but his words squeezed past her folded arms and tugged on the edge of her heart. "I already told Noah I'd stay and help him."

Dr. Simpson's expression told her he hadn't even considered otherwise. "I'm glad to hear that."

She gulped. What kind of wishy-washy, flimsy-hearted woman was she to walk out on a commitment, even if it pushed her to the edge of her courage? Sure, her boundaries felt invaded . . . but she'd walked into the mess of her own accord. She hadn't needed a push to pack up her dog and her belongings and hightail it to camp after Noah had smiled in her direction. Just because life didn't turn out the way she'd dreamed didn't mean that she was allowed to cut and run. Besides, the little girl who'd been dragged into the inner city as a budding teen had learned a few savvy lessons. She lifted her chin.

Perhaps God *had* sent her.

Perhaps she *was* the person Noah needed.

At least the person he needed to run his camp and keep his hoodlum campers alive. She tried to ignore the voices inside that told her Noah Standing Bear had unloaded both barrels of his charisma to hook her. To keep her on staff and make all his dreams come true. Her throat felt raw as she shook Dr. Simpson's hand and went in search of Jenny.

Noah stood at the edge of the dock, stopwatch in hand, timing the kids as they treaded water. They all wore life

jackets, and their skinny bodies trembled as they practiced staying afloat. "Five more minutes!"

A collective groan, punctuated by a few colorful adjectives, rose from the shivering tadpoles. Few of the boys and girls knew how to swim and they needed to learn how to stay upright in a life jacket in case the canoes capsized.

Ross and Bucko were in the water treading alongside them, instant assistance should fear rise from the depths and cramp muscles. Katie and Melinda, both lifeguards, stood on the dock, and junior counselors Megan, Juanita, Carmen, and Elijah paddled in nearby canoes, poised to reel in the weary.

On the shore, looking graceful in a pair of shorts and a T-shirt, Anne watched the swimmers like a hawk, searching for panicked faces and possible cramping. A veritable human iceberg for the last three days, she'd yet to look at Noah, let alone warm him with a smile in his general direction. Just being close to her sent chills up his spine . . . unfortunately it wasn't the type of chills he was hoping for. He'd done his best to keep clear of her. Making sure they were never alone, never in talking-close proximity, even in the chow line. But he felt like he'd taken out his heart and pinned it to his sleeve, and she took a good whack at it every time she passed him and didn't even glance in his direction.

He grieved for what they'd lost. Even if she could never love him, never again surrender in his arms—and that thought made him ache—he longed for her friendship. Her laughter made him feel new and whole. And the sunlight in her eyes reflected an image of himself that didn't resemble a seedy hoodlum but a man she'd trusted. He'd never had a lady as a friend, and now he knew why. Losing Anne felt as if he'd been scraped out from the inside. He put his hand on his chest and pushed against an ache that went so deep he wondered how he was still standing.

"Okay!" he yelled, incredibly grateful for these real-life distractions that kept him partially sane. "Time's up! Haul yourselves to shore, get changed, and meet me in the mess hall for snacks!"

The campers were too tired to whoop for joy. Some of them made a dramatic show of crawling onto shore and landing in a heap.

Darrin had made a pal, George, a kid with dark eyes and Native American ancestry who took great pride in the braid he wore to his waist. The two snapped towels at each other, following Bucko and Elijah toward their tents.

Katie and Melinda rounded up their girls, wrapped in towels and shivering like wet cats, and scooted them off to change. The sounds of laughter and screaming peppered the air.

Three days and no mishaps. Noah hadn't stopped thanking God for the holy intervention. He'd outlined the dress code both before and after the kids arrived, just in case it didn't sink in. The last thing he wanted at Wilderness Challenge was gang borders being drawn. He'd told them, accompanied by gentle threats, that gang identifiers would send them into the red zone and solitary confinement. Signs included "representing," or flashing gang hand signals, hats being bumped or tilted to indicate gang affiliation, pants worn rolled up, or pockets pulled out. Earrings had been confiscated, and tattoos covered with Band-Aids.

He had no doubts, however, that gang pride hadn't been surrendered. Bucko and Ross patrolled their cabins like alpha wolves looking for dissent.

It pained him that he had to police ten-year-olds with the vigilance of a sheriff, but he'd made promises—to parents, to churches . . . to Dr. Simpson.

Noah watched Anne as she followed the children. He had to admit that regardless of her fears, she had true-grit spirit. She knew how to dish out exactly what these kids gave in a way that told him it wasn't an act. She understood kids and how to deal with them. Unfortunately, they had yet to see her soft side, the side that laughed and teased. The side that nurtured.

Noah gathered the life jackets and hung them on the post near the beach.

Movement on the trail leading behind the lodge caught his attention. He stilled, watching as George emerged from some clasp of forest where he'd hidden. Before Noah could bark at him, the boy started toward the outfitter's shack, which housed the canoeing and backpacking supplies.

Noah quietly stole after him. He hadn't cultivated his stealth skills in the hood for nothing.

George crept up the path at a speed that told Noah the kid had felonious plans in his boyish heart. Noah stopped where George had hidden and watched through the trees as George snuck up to the porch and swung himself over and out of view.

Noah narrowed his eyes. Was the kid after food? Noah had a strict rule—no goodies in the tents. Granny D. offered plenty of snacks . . . Noah picked up his pace and edged along the shack.

He heard voices, then a giggle and his heart sank. He peeked around the corner and saw George working male magic on a brunette named Shelly. She had her arms over his shoulders. Noah recognized the moves of a boy who had been introduced to girls way too soon. George moved close, whispered something into her ear, and she laughed again.

Noah felt sick and he fought his roiling temper. Not so many years ago he'd been this kid, enthralled with the intoxicating amphetamine of girls, amazed that they even noticed him let alone melted at his fumbling charm. He dug up a measure of mercy and approached slowly.

Shelly saw him first. Her eyes widened, and she dropped her arms and cleared her throat. When George turned, shock was replaced much too quickly with a chip the size of an iceberg.

Cold silence spoke Noah's reprimand.

George glared at him.

Noah shook his head. "You know the rules, George." He stepped aside, and George stalked past him, muttering

187

beneath his breath. Noah grabbed him by the arm, stopping him in midstride. He leaned close to the kid, smelling on him lake water, sweat, and not a little defiance. "Watch yourself, George. I'm not stupid."

Every muscle in George's young body stiffened, and he yanked his arm from Noah's grip.

Noah watched him walk away, a swagger to his step that told Noah that he hadn't won the war. Noah sighed and turned to Shelly. The young lady rubbed her arms, embarrassment pinking her skin.

"Shelly, you know George is after one thing. Please, don't be a fool." *And please, don't tell me he loves you.*

She raised her chin. "George isn't like that. He cares about me. We're together."

Noah shook his head. "Not here, you're not."

Shelly harrumphed and marched past him, spiking him a glare that could peel skin, a look inherent in women's genes. With a heavy heart, he watched her stomp back to her tent.

Noah turned to return to the beach and halted at the sight of Anne, paused in the path. Miss Doom-and-Gloom stood with her hands on her hips, eyes hard on his, her mouth a muted line. His throat thickened at the sorrowful look she gave him. Then she held up one finger and moved her lips, no sound.

One week.

18

Anne sat three seats away from Noah at the dinner table, and she could still feel him gloating. He'd honored her request and hadn't said two unnecessary words to her in a week, but after seven days without a major shakedown at camp, he didn't have to actually speak for her to hear him shouting for joy.

She could see it in his eyes. His beautiful soul-piercing eyes. For the first time in a week, she wanted to chance looking at them, to suppose that she'd been wrong. In fact, she wanted him to be right. Wanted to believe that plucking these kids out of their concrete dungeons and letting the forest work its magic had freed them from the despair that hovered like Big Brother. Perhaps she'd been overreacting, listening to her fears instead of hope. Whatever the case, Noah Standing Bear knew how to tame their wild hearts with a smile, crazy games, and a slew of nutty songs he taught them at the campfire each night.

Whoever heard of rapping "To God Be the Glory"? Noah had pulled it off so well the kids rapped the chorus in their free time.

Noah had certainly done a number on her calloused heart

in the three weeks since she'd known him. She couldn't even breathe the same air as the man without feeling his presence as a sweetness to her soul. The delicious ache told her that Noah wasn't going to be exorcised out of her life by pure will. Even now, his laughter drifted down the table and tugged at her. Wherever he went, Noah's charm, patience, and gentleness paved a road before him into the souls of the campers. Even George, the local Don Juan, had stopped trying to woo the girls, leaving Anne to wonder what power Noah wielded.

Either that or God had begun to soften their hearts, including hers. The dramas and talks at the campfire each night drew her in and soothed her wounded soul. Only God's Word, His truth spoken plainly under a brilliant night sky, with the wind reaping the blossoms from the forest, and crickets and bullfrogs singing the melody of twilight, could minister to her ragged spirit. If God had been trying to wrap His divine arms about her and remind her of His love, He couldn't have picked a better place. Never once in the past ten years, and especially through the trauma, had she doubted God's existence.

It was His love with which she struggled. Why did it feel so rough and prickly while others had a God who filled their lives with cotton? She'd met other Christians who seemed to live in a puff of soft marshmallow, troubles only glancing off them. Like Noah. Didn't he ever struggle with his faith?

She wondered if he'd grown up in Minneapolis—hadn't Joe mentioned that Noah had gone to his hometown to pick up the kids? But Noah simply didn't fit the image of inner-city gangbanger, at least not on the *inside*. She couldn't deny it—Noah was morphing back into a real-life hero. Maybe it was time to actually talk to him. As in words, cordially spoken. It was getting nearly impossible to hang on to her fury. Especially when the man looked like he'd drop to his knees in apology if she ever gave him a second of attention.

The awful truth was that she missed him. Missed his
kooky jokes, the way he wrestled with Bertha and teased
her about his junk-food habits. He'd reached down with his
kindness into her frigid, wounded heart and wrapped his
strong arms around her. With Noah and his friendship, she
felt . . . safe. Even if he had connived and deceived her to get
her to stay, he'd gone out of his way to make sure she felt
appreciated and welcome.

Lately, he'd been going out of his way to stay out of hers.
It cut like a switchblade to see him hanging out with Katie
or Melinda, watching their eyes light up when he made
them laugh.

But Noah did that to people. Made them feel alive.

Made *her* feel alive.

She ached for his friendship like she'd ache for a missing
chunk of her heart.

"Anne, could you pass those fries?" Latisha, the cutest
little girl Anne had ever seen, with smooth ebony skin and
long dark lashes, pointed down the table.

The young ladies in Katie's tent—Latisha, Shelly, Akeia,
Chantee, and Jasmine—had begun to worm their way into
Anne's heart. She'd given herself license to enjoy their girlish
banter as she checked on the kids each night. She found
them oddly charming and waging the same battles she'd
fought as a twelve-year-old—parents, boys, and makeup.

Anne reached for the plate of French fries as Noah
grabbed it. Without giving her heart warning, she connected
with his gaze and her insides stumbled. He still had that
knee-rubbering effect on her, even more so after a week of
trying to dodge him.

He smiled sadly, one side of his mouth turning up, and
she knew without a doubt she'd made a terrible mistake.
Why had she ever thought she might avoid Noah and
survive infection? repel his charming guerilla ambush on
her emotions? A blush filled her entire body as she handed
Latisha the plate.

Around her, gabbing boys and girls were oblivious to the

fact that her heart lay flopping and bleeding in the middle of the table, waiting for Noah to scoop it up and forgive her.

Noah pulled a nylon mask made from a pair of panty hose over his head, intending to appear evil. After all, tonight he was Satan.

He'd been planning the salvation drama for months, even tried it once during a youth event at church before Easter. Few plays could compare with this symbolic enactment of Satan prowling a kid's soul. Ross made an excellent sinner, with a backpack of rocks hanging from his shoulders, despair written across his unshaven face. Bucko, glorious in head-to-toe white, was just the man to represent Christ. Katie and Melinda looked devastatingly seductive as "drugs" and "worldly love." As they applied makeup, the girls discussed their campers in low tones.

He could hardly believe they'd managed seven days without a problem. And the campers' souls seemed as fertile as a Nebraska cornfield. Tired, dirty, and not a little afraid, they'd finally started to respond. A day on the ropes course had pushed them to their last nerves, and Katie reported that two of her girls had begun to respond with curiosity to their nightly Bible reading.

Hope felt like the breath of the Almighty drawing through him. Tonight, Lord willing, the hearts of these street kids would break for their sins, and in the shattering of those formidable walls, God's love would pour through. Noah expected to see a great divine work before the sparking campfire tonight.

He'd already seen a hint of it earlier today when Anne met his gaze. He'd nearly heard fireworks bursting inside his head, and when she looked away and blushed, he knew that, indeed, she'd missed him too. She had pushed her fries through her ketchup, attempting nonchalance, but twice after that, he felt her eyes on him. Only his commitment to her wishes had kept him from running to her after supper.

Noah was banking on the fact that he had four more weeks to capture her heart and show her she meant more to him than a lunch ticket. He didn't know what she thought his motives were, but he had a heart-wrenching suspicion that she'd ranked him a little lower than a toadstool.

A ranking he intended to improve.

"How do I look?" Bucko flexed his muscular arms in the white turtleneck.

Noah liked the image of a powerful Savior that the guy presented. Yes, these kids would respond to an African-American with a serious physique representing God Almighty. "I'm glad you're on my side."

Bucko frowned. "Man, I am so not on your side. Look at you! You're evil incarnate."

Noah didn't have to look in the mirror to picture himself. He knew perfectly well how easily he could don the part of dark and sinister. He smiled wryly. "Let's go. Granny D. and Anne have their hands full."

Twilight had blanketed the lake, turned the water platinum, and calmed the forest air. These nightly campfires, with their smell of burning wood spicing the air and sparks shooting to the heavens as a backdrop, made the perfect setting for Noah's Soul Talks. He used a mix of Christian rap—with Bucko and Ross keeping beat—army chants, and monologues to get these kids' attention. Afterward, the counselors fertilized his talks with the truth of God's Word.

Now, as Noah tromped down to the campfire dressed completely in black, he marveled at how God took a man with darkness in his heart, wiped him clean, and set him in a beautiful place with a ministry that made him feel alive. Noah certainly regretted his wicked former life, but remembering those moments lived on the edge made him ever more grateful for his salvation.

Granny D. was barking at the kids to sit down, her no-nonsense voice making a superb dent in the murmuring.

Anne tended the campfire. She'd turned into a regular Girl Scout over the past week, and it wasn't lost on Noah that she'd grabbed his camping dream with both hands, diving in with guts and gusto. She'd even begun to warm to the campers, and according to Katie, spent more time each night hanging around after devotions.

He couldn't deny the swelling hope in his heart that God had bigger plans for her here. Hadn't the Almighty told him to trust? As he approached the campfire, it warmed him to the core to see Anne laugh, the firelight illuminating her face in a precious glow. When she glanced his way, his stomach dropped right to his knees. He grinned at her, but her smile dimmed, and for a moment he thought he saw terror flicker across her face.

He was dressed like a terrorist.

Just when he was hoping to crush that unfortunate impression. Before he could shake his head, she looked away and joined Katie's campers, wary eyes on the approaching troupe. Noah and the players paused outside the light of the fire and waited.

The campers quieted as Ross stepped forward. Street kids responded to drama. Their lives were so full of soap-opera emotions, drama was often the most effective way to communicate, especially to children inundated with words.

Ross lugged the backpack and turned so the kids could read the label *Sin* on the back. Sinner Ross stumbled under the heavy and oppressive weight of the rocks. Brow sweating, desperate, he looked out into the audience for relief.

Enter Noah. He felt the role move through him, taking possession as he stalked around Ross, grinning, motioning his sympathies. When Noah snapped his fingers, Katie rushed in. Dressed to the nines as an immoral lady of the night in a low-cut, sequined dress that Noah had to talk her into, she raised her eyebrows and pantomimed suggestions to Ross. She intimated that she might remove his backpack of sin, even help lift it from his shoulders. Ross dove for her, clung to her.

As relief crested Ross's face, Ladylove opened the sack and dropped in another boulder. And laughed. The singular sound echoed across the lake and through Noah's soul. Katie yanked her leg from Ross's clutches and danced away.

Noah entered again, this time empathizing with his prey. Ross threw himself at his feet and begged. Noah motioned in Melinda. She'd decorated her cornrows with rolled-up paper, representing marijuana cigarettes. Dressed in suede and swinging a set of keys, she shimmied up to Ross and dragged a roach clip holding a fake butt across his nose.

Noah watched the reaction of his audience and saw a number of kids narrow their eyes, swallow, or fold their arms across their chests. A precious few leaned forward, enraptured. For these, Noah prayed.

Ross threw himself into the grasp of Duchess Drugs. When she added a boulder to his backpack, she also deposited a mock kick to his stomach that made Noah wince. Ross acted broken and slumped in the dirt. With zero options before him, he raised his hands to the crowd and groaned.

A lump lodged in Noah's throat. It might be a play, but he knew what it felt like to be pushed to the edge of desperation. He forced himself to laugh, to dance about his prey, even as his insides churned. *Please, oh, God, reach even one!*

Wonder reflected in the eyes of the audience when Bucko appeared. He made an imposing savior, and the big guy milked his part. He strode up to Noah, grabbed him by his black leather vest, and pulled him away from crumpled, fearful Ross. Then, in a move that brought tears to Noah's eyes, Bucko reached down and tugged the lethal backpack from Ross and shouldered it himself. Kneeling, he cradled Ross in his arms, wiping Ross's face and smiling.

Ross's expression betrayed the feelings he had about his own salvation. Before Noah's stunned eyes, Ross transformed from a broken creature to a living man, burgeoning with hope. He stood, and tears streaked down his cheeks.

Then, in an unscripted move, he threw his arms around Bucko. Thankfully, Bucko stayed in character and hugged him back, embracing the one he'd saved.

Noah's face mask was wet, and when he looked around, he saw tears on several faces. Latisha, Shelly . . . and Anne. She glanced at him. For a moment their eyes met, a thousand unspoken emotions pulsing between them. *Thank You, God, for this camp. This salvation.*

Bucko let Ross go, and together they walked stage left, arms clasped about each other's shoulders.

Silence filled their wake. A log fell in the fire and the colorful sparks spiraled toward heaven as if in divine applause.

Noah tugged off his mask and faced his campers. "Satan has your hearts and minds, and only one person can break you free. Jesus Christ. He's your Savior. Drugs and illicit sex are only counterfeits. They'll only crush you. They'll tear you apart. Then they'll laugh."

He scanned the audience. Every gaze riveted on him. "And I know you don't like to be laughed at." He fisted the nylon mask in his hands. "You have a choice tonight. You can get busy with your lives, letting your friends dictate your choices. Or you can get busy with God and let a real friend lead you. Tonight you can change your future forever, if you have the guts."

He zeroed in on George and saw his own youthful defiance. But even George had softened, and in those dark eyes Noah noticed a hint of despair, a hint of longing. He rushed in to grab it. "You don't have to live the lives of your parents or your big brothers and sisters. You have your own life, and God wants you to live it free. But freedom doesn't come from following the crowd. That's the devil's lie. Freedom comes from letting go and letting Jesus, the one who loves you, forgive you for your sins."

Noah's voice filled with emotion. "You see, God doesn't care about your yesterdays. About what you did and who you did it with before you came to this camp or even to this moment. He cares about your future. He wants to wipe away your history and give you more than you can even dream." He fought the desire to look at Anne.

"My friends, God loves you and has good tomorrows for you. But you've got to hook up with Him, and do it His way. And I promise you, He's not going to let you go. Once you belong to God, you have a Father who won't take off. Ever." He glanced at Darrin, and his heart wrung at the sight of tears glistening in the kid's eyes.

"Tonight, if any of you want to start over, to break free from the load you're carrying and the cords pulling you into death, talk to your counselor. They have the answer and they'll help you cut that cord. You're dismissed to your tents."

Noah watched the group go, praying he'd made an impact. Anne rose, frowned at him for a long time, then climbed over the benches and started up the trail. He longed to run after her, to explore the expression on her beautiful face. But a lone camper sitting on the benches, shoulders racking, rooted Noah to his spot.

Darrin.

The big kid tried to hold in his tears, but they glistened off his dark face like crystal in the moonlight. Noah shot a prayer heavenward and sat next to him. The fire crackled, and Noah waited until the din of voices vanished and the boy gathered his composure. His throat thickened to see the youngster cry, but hadn't he brought them here for that very reason? To push them to the end of themselves so they might find God waiting?

"You want to talk about it, pal?"

Darrin snuffled and wiped his nose on his arm. "No."

"Hmm." Noah tucked his hands between his knees.

Darrin took a deep breath. "You just don't get it, Noah." He didn't look at him. "I ain't got no one. And Jesus ain't gonna swoop out of heaven and hang with me. Where's He gonna be when the guys dog me in school?"

"What, you think Jesus doesn't know about being alone?

Try forty days in a desert without food. That's lonely. And
the temptation to do drugs? You know, while He was on the
cross, someone offered Him a painkiller."

Darrin faced him, eyes wide.

"Yep. Wine mixed with gall. Kind of a Roman Vicoden.
He turned it down. So, my friend, when the Bible talks
about Jesus being intimately acquainted with our tempta-
tions, it's not lyin'."

Darrin looked away.

"And as for hangin' with you, why do you think I keep
coming around? God sends us His people to close us in and
watch our backs. It's called fellowship. Sort of 'holy hanging
around.' And Jesus also hangs with us through His Holy
Spirit. He's here, man. Right now."

"Hovering? Like a ghost?" Darrin's voice held rich awe.

Noah smiled. How he liked the logic of children. "No.
He doesn't haunt us. He comforts and guides. He's inside us
and all around. I promise, Darrin, if you ask Him to forgive
your sins and lead your life, you'll know exactly what I'm
talkin' about. Your eyes will open and you'll see Him everywhere, all the time."

Darrin fixed his gaze on Noah. He squinted, and for the
first time, defense dropped from his voice. "How do you
know? You did this, right?"

Noah wanted to hug the kid. "Absolutely. I was fresh out
of prison with nowhere to go. God picked me up, cleaned
the mess I'd made of my life, and put me on a new path."

"You did time?"

Noah didn't want the kid to focus on that piece of information. He grimaced and nodded.

"Why?"

Maybe this could be a good thing. "I ran with the Vice
Lords and right into trouble." He held his breath, watching
the reaction on Darrin's face.

To his surprise, Darrin's face tightened. "You're just
saying that. No way a Holy Roller like you ran with the

Tying the Knot

Lords." He shook his head. "Man, and I thought you were for real."

oah's mouth opened. Couldn't this kid see the scars written on his heart? Had he changed so much he was unrecognizable to the generation behind him? Noah fought the shock rushing through him, thrilled that God could make such a transformation, struck by the changes in himself. Now why couldn't Anne see what this kid saw? Noah swallowed hard, then reached up and dragged his left shirtsleeve up.

"What're you doing?" Darrin scooted away from him, his eyes dark.

"Showing you something." Noah turned toward Darrin. He'd covered his tattoo with three strips of Band-Aids during the afternoon swim. Now he grabbed the edges and ripped them off, wincing slightly. "Can you see it?"

Darrin's eyes glued to the Vice Lord tattoo, the one Shorty Mac had chiseled into Noah's left arm over fifteen years ago. Noah fought memory—the wave of shame and the stupid flint of pride he'd felt when he'd first received it. "You got it, kiddo. I was a Vice Lord minister."

Darrin looked at Noah with an inscrutable expression. "Huh."

Noah's chest clinched. *Please don't let him be impressed. Please let him see the violence in that scar and a man redeemed by Christ.* "Darrin, it's not cool. It's death."

Darrin backed away, disgust on his thirteen-year-old face, disbelief in his eyes. "I can't believe you've been hounding me for a year, keeping me out of the very gang you were in! What a hypocrite."

Noah rolled his sleeve down, his throat tight. "You don't get it, do you? I did that because I know what it's like. Gangs are death."

"Gangs are life, man. You just got caught." Darrin stood. "I don't want to hear your voice in my ear again, got it?"

Darrin whirled, and Noah fought to breathe against the emotional blow to the solar plexus. He watched Darrin strut up the path, a young man with balled fists, headed into darkness.

Then he noticed Anne standing at the edge of the firelight, a stricken look on her face.

Before he could wrestle out words, she turned and fled.

19

Anne ran from Noah's voice screaming in her head: *"I was a Vice Lord minister."* Dread boiled in her throat, pushing against her control, nearly beating her to the cook's shack. She slammed the door, slid down to a crouch in the darkness, and wailed, an eruption of anguish that shook her entire body.

No! She should have clung to her gut instinct that he was just what he appeared—a street-toughened thug. Instead she'd bought his charm and let him steal her heart. Her idiocy made her stomach churn.

In the dusty embrace of darkness, Anne clamped her arms around her waist and fought the bitter irony. Not only had God infiltrated her life with the very street scum she'd tried to escape, but now she'd let a man who personified her every demon inside her heart.

She felt duped and betrayed. Her throat stung as she began to pray. "God, I don't understand. The one thing I asked You for is safety. Peace. Instead You bombard me with the very elements of my darkest nightmares. Every time I look into Darrin's or George's eyes, I see that punk who shot me." She dug her fists into her closed eyes. "I want to forget, Lord. To heal. To feel safe, just once. Can't You please ease up?"

Her voice sounded tinny and hollow in the expanse of darkness.

"*So we have stopped evaluating others by what the world thinks about them.*" She stilled as 2 Corinthians 5:16-17 filled her mind in the strident tones of her father, flinging out hope as he filled bowls of soup in the shelter: "*. . . those who become Christians become new persons. They are not the same anymore, for the old life is gone. A new life has begun!*"

To reach people like Noah Standing Bear was the reason her father had taken her out of her safe rural life. Her childhood had been sacrificed so her father could run after the souls of Vice Lords and Gangster Disciples and hoodlums that vandalized her home.

Her innocence.

Noah Standing Bear embodied every vile comment, every crude grope, every invasion of her privacy in her past. His type was the reason she had run home from school every day, taunts ringing in her ears, misery in her wake. For all she knew, Noah had been one of the many who'd pushed her to tears. She'd let her guard down for the very person she'd hated as a child. So much for finding her hero.

And God had saved his soul.

She tightened her jaw against the raw truth. Mr. Mercenary with the heart-melting eyes might be the fruit of her father's and her sacrifice. She covered her head with her arms and wept.

Why couldn't God be gentle, just once?

A new person. A new life. The words thumped in her head as her heartbeat slowed. *A new person.*

People like Noah Standing Bear were exactly the type God fought for, the souls of the unloved, the unwanted . . . the hated. God took people and changed them so completely they were unrecognizable. New. As in, start over. And God's power wasn't halfway. God didn't need work-

able material to change a person. In fact, God was most glorified when He redeemed the dregs of society.

She'd watched Noah laugh with the camp girls, wrestle with the boys, challenge, comfort, and stand beside these kids who needed a role model. Despite the fatigues, the tattoo, the etched hardness in his face, she couldn't find one hint of the gangbanger he'd been in his transformed heart. No wonder she had come to overlook his attire, his obvious street scars. Noah's insides, Christ in him, made him a new creation. Noah was a child of grace, not the gutter.

Anne gulped heavily, aware for the first time that God might have brought her right into the sights of a man who could truly understand her pain. Only Noah, a man who had lived in the battlefield of the streets, could comprehend her wounds . . . and her fears.

Only Noah, perhaps, would know how to hold her, to soothe her demons, to whisper comfort.

To be the arms of God around her.

Warmth started at her toes and swelled through her entire body. Could it be that God would use the very object of her fears, her scorn, her bitterness, to remind her of His love, to reach out and heal her scarred heart?

Oh, God, You do know me. You do love me. Anne's chest filled with a whirlwind of tears as she gasped at the magnitude of God's grace. Only the Almighty, the one who knew her heart better than she did, could deliver her perfect—her only—hero.

She raised a hand to her lips, felt again the toe-curling touch of Noah's lips, and a wall inside her broke open. She recalled their conversations, the many times she'd asked him about his childhood. Noah had taken serious pains to hide his history . . . something she totally understood. Was it for her? Did he fear her rejection, her scorn? She suddenly hurt for the part of him he'd held inside for her benefit.

But if he had been trying to conceal his past, why had he bared his soul to a kid?

Because, indeed, Noah was a soldier of the kids' souls.

A man of courage, strength, and with a burden to minister to the hurting. Right here in Deep Haven. Regardless of the cost.

The thought made her weak. In the silence of the dark, she heard her heartbeat, thumping out possibility.

"Anne?"

The soft voice on the other side of the door nearly made her jump through her skin. She could barely mouth his name. "Noah?"

Wariness laced his tone. "Are you okay? I saw you . . . I mean . . . did you hear what I told Darrin?"

Guilty. She shouldn't have been eavesdropping. Something about the way Noah sat beside the sobbing child had tugged at her heart, and she'd been rooted at the image of his gentleness. "Yes."

He was silent. She pictured him scrunching his scary nylon mask in his strong grip, his eyes on the door, as if trying to see past wood and screen right into her soul. Tonight during the drama, he'd looked every inch a street punk out for trouble, and she'd even felt chills watching him stalk his prey as Satan.

She stood and opened the door. He looked broken. Something raw and vulnerable permeated his gaze.

"Hi."

She stepped out, knowing she looked a mess—swollen eyes, hair mussed—but her attention fixed on his appearance . . . the gangbanger transformed by God.

He'd rolled down his sleeve, hiding the tattoo, but she knew what it looked like. A gray five-pointed star on his left arm, probably homemade, lopsided, and black against his skin. She gently touched his arm.

He flinched.

"You were a Vice Lord," she said.

He took a deep breath and nodded. His expression told her that he still wrestled with that fact, and suddenly she wanted to fling herself into his arms and apologize. *Forgive me, Noah, for not believing in you. You're so much more than I expected, than I was ever prepared for. . . .*

But the words lodged in her throat, caught by the look of agony on his face.

He reached out, cupped her cheek. "I'm not that person anymore."

"I know." How sweet it felt to say that. To mean that. *"I know."*

"Anne, I . . ." He stopped and let his hand fall. "I owe you an apology. I should have told you about myself . . . about the campers, long before I dragged you in."

"I wouldn't have returned." She knew it in her bones. Had he not somehow coerced her—first with her job, and then with his affection—she wouldn't be here confronting her prejudices. Confronting and defeating.

She certainly didn't long to join forces with him and wage war against the elements of street life, but certainly she could see God's wisdom in putting her here—for now. This summer. With Noah.

"I'm glad I'm here." Her eyes filled. "More than you know."

"Really?" His eyes sparkled, deep and rich, and kneaded a place in her heart that she'd tried to harden.

She nodded, and the smile that followed felt cathartic. She'd been struggling to frown for a week and somehow letting loose the grin she'd so wanted to give him made tears spring to her eyes.

His mouth tugged up on one side, and he raised one dark eyebrow. "So, you're talking to me again?"

She shrugged, but it was meant to tease. "Maybe."

"Huh." He wrapped a hand around the back of his neck. "Well, I don't suppose you'd take a motorcycle ride with a former gangbanger to his favorite place in northern Minnesota, would you?"

She looked him up and down. Dressed in a black shirt, a black leather vest that did nothing to soften the outline of his wide shoulders, and matching black jeans, he looked right off the cover of *Dark and Dangerous* magazine. A scent of masculinity emanated from him, setting her head to spinning. Oh yeah . . . Mr. Soldier of Fortune was back in force and completely disarming her.

She tried to act coy but failed miserably. "I suppose. If we don't go too fast."

He laughed, then held out his hand. "C'mon. I want to show you something."

The wind raked through Noah's hair, the hum of the motorcycle filled his ears, and with Anne's arms locked around his waist for safety, he knew he'd found heaven on earth. The shoreline carved out a haunting beauty in the horizon, fuzzy, yet dark and foreboding. Noah revved the motor and found the dirt road tucked just north of town. The forest thickened—ageless maple, elm, birch, and evergreen hovering as if in sentry. All at once, the forest thinned and on either side of the road grass, smooth as silk, stretched out like wings.

"Is this a golf course?" Anne yelled in his ear. He liked her breath close, even if the smell of her did destructive things to his concentration.

"Yep!" He slowed the cycle to a roll, wanting to talk instead of scream. "A few years ago, they logged this place and left a field of ugly stumps. The city passed a referendum and turned it into a municipal golf course. Beautiful, huh?" The moon had groomed the lawn into a shimmering pool of silver, the flags on the greens whipping like masts above the sea. "I think I should learn to golf."

She laughed. The sound of it sent his heart soaring out before him. "How much farther?"

"Why? Are you cold?" She wore her windbreaker, but even the summertime air on a motorcycle could be nippy. *Hold on tighter; snuggle closer.* "We're almost there."

They passed the clubhouse, a parking lot of golf carts,

and motored farther, into another huddle of forest. Noah felt Anne pressed closer as the shadows approached. His headlight pushed ahead a trail of light, and soon the road turned rutted and choppy.

Noah slowed the bike to a stop. "Hop off and I'll park."

"Where are we?" Anne swung her leg over the motorcycle, and a chill rushed in where she'd let go around his waist.

Noah pulled the bike back on its kickstand and climbed off. "Pastor Dan's property. He's going to build a cabin here someday." He took her hand. Soft and warm, it fit perfectly. "It's got the best view in town."

He led her deeper into the forest along a narrow footpath. Twigs crunched beneath his boots, and he held his arm stiff, hoping to steady Anne. His destination lay ahead, in a milky stream of light parting the copse of brush and trees.

When they emerged, the scene snagged the breath in his throat as it always did. Below, Deep Haven glittered like a Christmas display. Pastor Dan owned just about the best property in the county, and it overlooked Grace Church and the community. Beyond the town, Lake Superior stretched to the limitless horizon, a black, ominous expanse. On the point, standing guard over the harbor, the Deep Haven lighthouse, proud and steady, beamed a stream of pure white light.

Anne drew up beside him. "Wow."

"Yep." Noah couldn't decide what was more beautiful in that moment . . . the Deep Haven display or Anne, her chestnut hair tangled by the wind, her face, clean and void of makeup, her eyes sparkling as they beheld his surprise.

He forced words through his thickening throat, before he had no voice at all. "They've restored the lighthouse five times over the years. There are bigger and better lighthouses, like the one on Split Rock, but this one is constant. Deep Haven doesn't want it to go out."

"It's beautiful. The light disappears into the night."

"Like it's searching for lost ships." He rubbed his fingers on her cheek. "And sometimes it bellows out a foghorn, the sound so resonant you can feel it in your bones. As if reminding the sailors caught in the storm that they aren't forgotten."

She turned to him. Her eyes were wide, brimming with emotion he'd thought he'd never see again. He felt as if he could take flight and soar like one of the Superior seagulls.

"Sandra told me this story of the one time it went out. About the lightkeeper going after the victims of a shipwreck."

"Did he find them?"

She nodded. "Even in the darkness, he saved them." She gazed at him with a look that told him it was okay, that he could pull her close . . .

Noah stalked away, afraid of the emotions that nearly overtook him. He wanted to kiss her. More than anything else in that moment, he wanted to wrap his arms around her, inhale the freshness of her skin, and kiss her as if it was the first time.

Yes, he'd kissed her before. But somehow, that delicate moment didn't begin to match the intensity of the feelings surging through him now. He was more frightened than he could remember ever being before, even when he'd run from a pack of cops, his future dissolving with each step. Even when he'd faced a judge and been sentenced to five years of lockup.

Even when his future turned so bleak, he'd had no choice but to turn to God.

And here he was again—desperate, fearful. Needing God to save him. Needing God to help him keep his heart in pocket when, with every aching breath, he wanted to hand it out to this woman with a smile that made him forget his very name.

Oh, she had power over him. Power that convinced him it didn't matter that he'd been a convicted felon, a near-murderer, a gangster. Power that made him hope and

dream. Power that made him forget exactly why he'd driven them to this moon-kissed scenic overlook.

He wanted to spill the truth. To tell her that he knew her better than she thought, and why fear etched her eyes.

Confess that it was all his fault.

He sucked a deep, calming breath. In. Out. In.

When Anne touched him on the shoulder, he nearly jumped off the cliff. "What's the matter, Noah?"

He somehow found his voice in his constricting chest. "I . . . uh . . ." He ran his hands through his hair. "There's a lot you don't know about me." That was an understatement. Aside from his ugly history, she also had no idea that he knew why she'd fled for her life from the campfire pit, as if she'd seen a ghost.

Because he was her phantom.

Anne deserved to know that his stupidity had sparked the explosion of pain in her life. He'd made the 911 call that brought the EMTs to death's abyss; he'd been the one who couldn't pull Anthony Debries from the clasp of drugs and death. Couldn't stop him from shooting—

He wanted to sink to his knees with the injustice of the situation. God had given him a second chance with this beautiful woman, and the last thing Noah wanted to do was risk frightening her away. Telling her his secrets—all of them—would only shatter this fragile moment with the land mines of the past. What would she think of him, knowing he'd set her up, albeit against his knowledge, to fall hard, right into the dark night of the soul? Terrorist with a capital T. Just the image he'd been trying to obliterate. But if Noah wanted any future with her, any hope of spending every day working side by side with take-my-breath-away Anne, he'd have to tell her. Everything. He stifled a groan.

"There's a lot you don't know about me also." Anne's soft voice felt like a caress.

He turned, and she was close enough to take in his arms. His hands lifted of their own accord and cupped her face. She stared at him, and the compassion in her eyes played havoc with his gallant defenses. He pressed his forehead to hers. "Oh, Anne, what am I doing here with you?"

Her breath came out in a tremulous shudder, as if she too felt the depths of his question. She brushed his cheek with her hand, and he leaned into it. "I don't know," she whispered, "but I'm glad you brought me here. It's a beautiful place. And you, Noah, are a beautiful person. I'm sorry it took me so long to figure that out."

His eyes burned, and he couldn't stop himself from brushing his lips with hers. She trembled at his touch, and it reeled him in. He held his breath and kissed her. Gently, but with a passion that told her how her words touched him. She tasted sweet, with a hint of salt on her lips, as if she'd been crying. Oh, how he wanted to wrap his arms around her, to deepen his kiss. But as much as his emotions wanted to lead, honor told him no. When he pulled away, he stared into her heart-stopping, very, very green eyes. *Lord, help me. You know the desires I've committed to You. Help me run from my past and walk in purity with this lady.*

He held her gaze. "Should I apologize?"

Her eyes glowed, and even in the darkness, he saw a blush creep up her face. "No. I've been wanting you to kiss me all week." She smiled, and he heard music in his soul.

He couldn't manage words, so he took her hand. Could she feel him shake? Did she know she'd touched a part of his heart so hidden he himself barely acknowledged it? She'd called him a beautiful person.

He hoped for a lifetime to hear those words.

They walked to the edge of Dan's property, gazing out over the beauty of Deep Haven. The wind nestled the trees behind them, reaping the night sounds, the fragrance of fir. Anne shivered again, and Noah drew her into the nook of his arm. She wrapped her arms around his waist, unafraid, trusting.

"I've been waiting a lifetime to find a man like you, Noah," Anne said softly, and his breath skipped in his chest.

Tying the Knot

*Is she the one, Lord, the partner I've prayed for? Please,
oh, please . . .*

"What a lovely town to build a life in," Anne mumbled
in his embrace.

She'd disappeared off the face of the earth. He stood outside
her cabin, the sound of waves pummeling the shore, the hint
of storm in the air. He'd seen her in town only three days
ago—and then, *whoosh,* she'd been abducted by aliens.

Which, at this moment, didn't sound so utterly awful.
Disappear. Forever.

His throat tightened. This is what happened when he
let himself think instead of simply moving, dodging his
demons. His living and breathing, leather jacketed, pistol-
toting demons.

He needed her. They were watching, and if he had any
prayer of squeezing free, he needed her. And what she could
give him.

He glanced at the house nestled on the end of the point,
at the yellow glow in the upper window, like a lighthouse
against the clutch of night. Certainly they would know where
she'd hidden. The maddening urge to stomp up the path,
knock on the door, and push this nightmare to its inevitable
conclusion pulsed through him.

No, he'd wait. He was the one with the control, the
power. He wouldn't let the fine edge of desperation push
him into the abyss of craziness.

She'd return, and when she did, he'd be there, waiting
like a father for the wayward prodigal.

He hoped she showed her pretty face in time to save his
skin.

20

Anne stood in the middle of the outfitter's cabin, surrounded by climbing ropes, floppy Duluth backpacks, paddles, garbage bags, life jackets, sleeping bags, and MREs—dried packets of army rations. The smell of dust, leather, and canvas clinched the camping ambience and confirmed that, indeed, Noah had lost his mind.

Ten days in the wilderness with these kids sounded like a surefire death sentence. And the man was actually giddy about it. The late-afternoon sun slid like molten gold along the rough-hewn floor and cast her shadow over Mr. Happy, who was shoving a sleeping bag into a stuff sack.

"There are two things you need to know about me right now," she said, still trying to drive home a point that he seemed determined to ignore.

He looked up at her with a cockeyed grin. "Is this a make-or-break our relationship type of thing?" He waggled his eyebrows, and she just about melted into a heap. Now that they were on talking . . . and occasional kissing . . . terms, he'd spent the last three days charming her silly. She'd relished every second, knowing she'd completely lost her heart to this rascal in leather.

"I don't know . . . could be."

"I'm all ears." He tied the sack closed.

"Okay. Listen well. I don't sleep on the ground, and I don't tolerate bugs."

Noah tossed her the sleeping bag. "Honey, you're about to do both, in spades."

She made a face at him, loving the way he teased her. Disarming in his full warrior regalia—a pair of army fatigues and a black T-shirt that looked about two sizes too small the way it pulled across his wide, muscular back—she could barely focus on packing the backpack at her feet. She pawed through her items, checking them off verbally. "Mosquito repellent, Bible, tennis shoes, three pair of socks, brush, comb, toothpaste, jeans—"

"Whoa, nix the jeans." Noah crouched before her and hauled out her new Gap boot-cut jeans. "They'll feel like two million pounds when they get wet."

"Wet? You didn't say anything about getting wet." When he'd announced the ten-day canoe trip though the Boundary Waters Canoe Area, Anne conjured up mental pictures of paddling gently through a wind-combed lake, listening to the melody of loons or the strident rattle of kingfishers, feeling the kiss of the sun on her face. Nothing in that dreamy scenario suggested moisture, other than the water on the paddle. "Make that three things—I'm not getting wet."

"Right." He laughed. "Just trust me on this one. Track pants and hiking boots. Three pairs of wool socks, two T-shirts, a flannel shirt, and rain gear. That's it."

"For ten days? You've got to be kidding. I won't need the bug juice—I'll repel the mosquitoes with my smell."

He brushed a strand of hair from her face. "No you won't because you'll bathe in the lake." He handed her a bar of Ivory soap. "It's biodegradable. Does wonders for your hair."

"No thank you. I'll bathe when I get back."

His expression told her how he felt about that.

She tossed the Ivory into her bag. How had she gone

from dispensing medicines at the local public clinic to trekking the backwoods with a bunch of street punks . . . well, slightly adorable street punks?

She couldn't deny that underneath the body piercings and the spiked, filthy hair lurked children who might be worth knowing. She'd been drawn in by their occasional eager questions that burst from their sullen postures like explosions of hope. And their smiles amid the grime on their faces could turn an iceberg into a molten puddle. Even so, she reserved the right to change her mind. Trouble festered . . . she felt it in the air. Like a rubber band tensing to snap. This camping trip, this trek through the wilderness, a zillion miles from medical care, was most definitely the worst idea Noah had ever dreamed up.

She closed the Duluth pack, sitting on it to get the leather straps into the buckles. "What about a pillow? Certainly—"

"Here's your pillow." He tossed her a life preserver. "Welcome to the wilderness."

She stuck out her tongue.

He laughed. "Grab those bags, please. I need to fill them with gorp."

She handed over a box of Ziploc bags. "I'm almost afraid to ask. What is gorp?"

"Granola, raisins, peanuts. A sort of trail-mix munchie. You'll like it." He opened a plastic container the size of a garbage can, grabbed a tin can, and began to fill a bag. "It's healthy."

She rolled her eyes. "Listen, pal, have you ever heard the phrase 'you are what you eat'?"

"Yeah. I'm proud to be a chocolate marshmallow Frito."

Hardly. Chocolate maybe, with that dark run-your-hands-through-me hair and tough-as-a-Frito shell . . . but marshmallow? When he put his arms around her, she knew without hesitation that he wasn't a marshmallow. Still . . . he looked at her with such a sweet, lopsided grin, and here he was, getting ready to drag twenty unruly teens out on a camping trip that might change their lives. Because inside that hard and crispy exterior, he was a softie for their souls.

Okay, maybe Noah was exactly the definition of a chocolate marshmallow Frito.

She bit her lip to stifle a giggle, grabbed the pack straps, and hauled the pack up to her shoulders. "Ugh. This feels like a ten-ton boulder. You can't be serious."

"As a heart attack. Duluth packs are the best canoe luggage. They're easy to handle, can be tossed into the bottom of the boat, and they're sturdy as Sunday." He sealed a gorp bag and set it on the worktable. "And they make you look like Happy, one of the seven dwarfs." He winked at her.

"Oh, very funny." She let the pack plop to the ground. "Just for the record, I feel I need to say it again. Clearly, in English." She leaned over, trying not to let his wild grin and delightful mock exasperation rabbit-trail her words. "This trip is a Bad idea—capital *b*, little *a*, little *d*. Bad. Trouble lurks in the forest, Noah, and these kids are going to find it."

He grabbed her hand and pulled her close. The smell of soap and leather sweeping over her as she fell into his embrace turned her pliable. "Have a little faith, my sweet thundercloud. I'm not going to let anything happen to you. I promise."

He kissed her on the nose, and she disentangled herself before she abandoned her reputation—one that didn't involve gossip about her and the resident, tough-and-tender camp director.

"So, I gotta know," she said, sitting on the Duluth pack-slash-Rock of Gibraltar. "How did a Vice Lord transform into the crunchy granola Boy Scout I see before me?" She shook her head. "You seem so . . . so born for the backwoods. It hurts me to think of you hanging with the Vice Lords I knew in high school, so I've decided to conjure up a different life for you."

"Oh, really?" She had his attention. "Tell me more."

"Okay. You grew up in a cabin in the woods, not far from here, learning to fish with your dad and cook with your mom—"

"Cook?"

"I told you this is an alternate reality. Now hush."

He rolled his eyes but smiled, his eyes twinkling dangerously.

"You ran track and played football through high school. In fact, that's how you got your scar on your cheek. State play-offs against the Moorhead Spuds. You were decked while making the game-winning touchdown."

"Okay, I can dig this alternate reality. How about girls? I'll bet I was popular—"

"Oh no!" She laughed. "You were much too shy and polite. You spent all your free time chopping wood—"

"And roasting marshmallows?"

"Absolutely. In fact you won a 4-H prize for excellence in roasting."

He nodded, like that fit perfectly into his resume.

"Then when you graduated, you went to a nice Bible college and decided to run a youth camp."

"Now that part isn't so far from fact."

She shrugged. "I'm good. What can I say?"

He came close and crouched before her, his hands on her knees. "Let me finish. I start this camp. One day this beautiful, knock-my-breath-away brunette shows up with Bigfoot the dog and begs to work as a camp nurse, just to be close to me and my charisma."

"Oh sure, back to fantasy," she said, but her throat threatened to close at how accurate his last words were.

"Shh. This is my version. She, of course, can't help but fall for the handsome hometown hero—"

"And they live happily ever after in Deep Haven."

He smiled. "I like that ending." His eyes were on hers, piercing, probing, as if the answers to some unspoken question could be found in their depths. She felt herself redden, and her heart pounded like a drumroll in her chest.

Then suddenly he broke her gaze, swallowed, and blew out a breath. "You know how to tell a good story." His smile turned wry. Abruptly he stood and stepped away. "I'd like to keep it."

She somehow dug her voice out of her constricting chest. For the briefest of moments he'd reminded her of someone she'd met a year ago. A man she finally happily freed into the recesses of distant memory. It wasn't as if the dream of meeting her split-second singing hero from the past ever held any element of reality. "Well, you haven't really told me much about your past. . . ."

She thought he might give a puff of agreement, but a dark shadow crossed Noah's face. His smile dimmed. He looked away, grabbed another plastic bag, began to fill it with gorp.

"Noah?" Oh no, now what had she done?

He shook his head and paused. "Anne, like I mentioned before, there are a lot of things you don't know about me." The way he said it, soft and not a little mournful, made her insides clench.

Anne hugged herself as her own omissions rammed into her brain. He might have a tattoo, a very permanent reminder of the man he'd been before salvation, but she had scars—ugly, pitiful scars that screamed out the fears she still dodged. Today. In spite of her salvation. If she hoped that Noah could ever, ever be God's embrace around her, a flesh-and-blood embodiment of unconditional love, she would have to let him see the real Anne Lundstrom, complete with pain and heartache and gunshot wound. She swallowed a choking lump.

It was one thing to tell her story to Granny D., Katie, and Melinda. After all, they'd seen the reddened starburst on her back and the pucker of stitch marks on her abdomen while hunting for broken ribs after her fall. Then telling her story had seemed, well . . . natural. But the idea of telling Noah and bringing him into her dark yearlong floundering . . . she exhaled hard. Perhaps she could just omit it. Did he have to know *everything* about her? Couldn't some things be kept private? The thought of facing the moment when her world and her faith had caved in made her shudder.

Besides, what if her scars and her story repulsed him? made her seem . . . ugly? pitiful? She fought the dark pull of shame and raised her chin.

The look on Noah's face made her wonder if he'd been reading her mind. Horrified, guilty. A perfect mix of rejection. Anne stiffened.

"Anne, listen. Obviously you know that I haven't been the stellar example of holiness. But there are some things about my past that are . . . buried. If I bring them into this relationship, I am afraid . . ." He tightened his jaw and ducked his head, and suddenly Anne sprang to her feet.

She wasn't the only one hiding scars.

She hopped over the backpack and touched him on his shoulder.

Noah closed his eyes. "I don't want to tell you."

Anne's heart twisted, moved by his wretched expression that so mirrored her own. Gently she rubbed the light stubble of late-afternoon whiskers. "Don't be afraid. I don't have to know. But if you want to tell me . . ." Whatever he had to tell her, it couldn't be that bad, could it? "I'll understand." She wondered, if the roles were reversed, would he be saying the same thing to her?

"Let's sit down." His tight voice made her frown.

He led her to the backpack, motioned for her to sit, then sat on the floor beside her. He opened his mouth twice before the words finally emerged. "I . . . when I was in the gang, I had a friend, a good friend named Shorty Mac." His chest rose and fell, and he didn't look at her. "He was killed—beaten to death—by the Gangster Disciples after he and I tried to boost a car from their turf."

She fought the horror that rose in her chest. "I'm sorry, Noah."

He shook his head and stared at his dusty boots. "It was devastating. His mother, she . . . blamed me." He closed his eyes. "I can still hear her screaming. Telling me I'd killed him."

She touched his arm. His muscles were bunched, as if he were holding his emotions together.

"I um . . . well, when you join a gang, you become . . . family. Especially for a foster kid, which I was, the gang meant everything to me. I had to avenge his death." His voice changed, as if he was reliving the moment, the rationale behind his actions. "I didn't even think twice. I just . . . I was so angry. It fueled me like a drug." He dug his hands into his hair. "We came up with this plan to take out the Disciples minister and his foot soldiers—"

"Take out?" she whispered.

"Kill." His jaw clenched. "I had murder in my heart."

Tears burned her eyes, but she said nothing.

"We . . . uh . . . snuck into their turf. It was supposed to be a drive-by, but I hid out across the street with another Vice Lord soldier. We waited until they came out on the porch and—" his voice stumbled—"well, I was young and stupid and by the grace of God no one was killed."

"You didn't shoot." She heard the relief in her voice.

"Oh no," he said harshly. "I aimed and shot. And missed." He groaned. "I shudder every time I hear the screams of fear that filled the night."

"But you missed."

He raised his face. His eyes were red. "But I *wanted* to kill them. And that's just as awful."

Words left her. She knew how it felt to want to kill someone. She'd wrestled with those very emotions while her attacker's trial filled the newspapers, every time she saw his face on the news.

"What happened?"

He looked away again, and she saw him flinch. "I froze. The Vice Lords hit the gas, and Jay-Jay, the other shooter, had to grab me, haul me into the car."

"You got away?"

He shrugged. "No. I mean, yes, in a way. I was so

shocked by what I'd done, I felt sick. But an hour later I wanted to return and finish the job . . . so I snuck back."

"You went back?"

Noah stiffened. "Yeah. Well, the police had swarmed the place. I hadn't made as clean a getaway as I thought. The Disciple minister saw me, and when the cops noticed me prowling the block, they picked me up. I was carrying."

"You had a gun on you."

He nodded. "Stupid. I know. I had five years in prison to come to that conclusion."

He looked so utterly broken she barely stopped herself from throwing her arms around him. Instead, she took his face in her hands, forcing him to look at her. "So you're an ex-con."

The sorrow she saw on his face sent tears down her cheeks. "Amazing what God can do, isn't it?" Anne smiled when she said it, and then, before he could protest, she leaned close and kissed him. "I would have never guessed. But thanks for trusting me."

He blinked at her, as if in disbelief. Then he smiled, small and tentative. It made her want to sing. Yes, Noah was exactly the hero she'd asked God for . . . vulnerable and gentle, wounded, yes, but healed. And noble. So noble he'd wanted to spare her the darkest parts of himself.

He put his arms around her and drew her down to the floor next to him. She could feel his heart beating as quickly as hers. He slowly tangled his hand into her hair and leaned his chin on the top of her head. "Never once, as I was doing time, did I imagine this life God had for me. I always thought I'd be nothing more than a street punk, surviving from job to job, hoping to live till my twenty-first birthday. But God has given me this, you—" his voice grew thick— "I know I don't deserve it."

Anne didn't comment. She'd asked God for one thing— safety. Sitting within Noah's embrace, she knew He'd answered. Not only had He given her this haven of rest but also a man to hold her. A man to keep her safe. A man to make her forget her past and offer her a future.

So what did that mean? That she'd solved an argument with the Almighty? *Where were You, God?* Had He simply bypassed her questions and moved on to healing?

Perhaps. Perhaps her battles were behind her, and peace was ahead. It didn't seem like enough to simply ignore her ugly history and go forward, but maybe that was exactly how she'd find joy in her faith. Not dwelling on the absence of God in the past, but His obvious presence now. Loving her through the tender, miraculous touch of Noah Standing Bear.

Noah lifted her chin with one gentle finger. A smile, full and joyous, graced his face and lit his gorgeous eyes. "I knew as soon as God got ahold of my heart that I had to spend my life telling the kids on the street about salvation. This camp is a small part of that vision."

Just sitting near him, seeing the joy of his salvation, made her tingle. Yes, this was the man she'd waited for. A man with a heart, with passion, with a desire to love the lost. She could see herself with him, running this camp. Tucked safely in this nook in the woods, creating a world away from the inner city, a place where kids could escape for the summer. She bought into his dream without him even selling it.

Perhaps she didn't need to make peace with God over her tragedies in order to enjoy His blessings. She could simply skip over the sordid, painful details and start now.

Wasn't that exactly why she'd moved to Deep Haven?

"Do you have bigger plans? Do you want to extend the camp, make it year-round?" The thought of cozying up beside him in the lodge before a flickering fire while snow blanketed the lake and pushed drifts against the window-panes made her warm to her toes. No past . . . only tomorrows. Yes.

"Oh yes, Anne. This is just the beginning. When I take these kids home, I'll be able to walk with them, to encour-

age them toward the commitments they made here at camp. I'll know them, and I'll stand in the gap between their street life and their new life."

Anne blinked at him. "Um . . ." An uneasy feeling rippled down her spine.

He touched her cheek with his fingertips, and they felt cool against her warm face. "You have a way with the girls. They like you. They respect you."

She stiffened, pulled away. "I'm sorry, but I don't understand. What exactly are you saying?"

His eyes darkened, shadowed by a frown. "I want you to come with me. Work beside me. You'd be great at the job."

She held up her hand as if to stop the flow of words, the way he was looking at her with such bewilderment. Dread wrapped cold fingers around her chest. "Come with you where?"

"To the Phillips neighborhood." He held out his hands, as if the answer lay in his palms. "I live in Minneapolis, 2135 Franklin Avenue." He looked at her, and this time a streak of fear lined his eyes. "I'm a youth pastor. Didn't you know that? This is only a summertime gig. My full-time ministry is with Christian Fellowship Center in downtown Minneapolis."

21

Noah watched Anne at dinner with deepening foreboding. A chilly wave had swept over the woman he'd held in his arms earlier this afternoon, turning her frosty and distant.

And it had happened right before his eyes. Anne had pulled away, finished packing her backpack in rigid silence.

He felt as if a part of his chest had been ripped open. He didn't—couldn't bear to—think that she'd backed away because of his confession. His history. Hadn't she said she'd understood? He'd believed the compassion in her eyes.

Perhaps too easily.

He managed to choke down a bite of garlic bread before his throat thickened. Of course his past mattered. An ex-con. Any decent woman in her right mind would run for the hills. He couldn't blame her for being human. Or smart. But she'd left a gaping, ragged wound right in the center of his chest.

"My tent is packed and raring to go." Ross sat beside him, his plate piled with spaghetti. "The guys can't wait."

"And I guess you're loading up?" Noah nodded toward Ross's mountain of food.

"Hey, man, I know what you're feeding us on the trail—

army MREs. Those things are made for prisoners of war, at best."

"I got a deal. Besides, they're light to carry and they'll fill your stomach."

"Yeah—fill us with gut-rot." Ross grinned at Katie, who winked at him from across the table.

Noah wondered suddenly, if he'd missed something.

"What route did the park service approve for us?" Katie pushed away her spaghetti and poked her spoon into the cherry Jell-O, grimacing slightly.

"The Rose Lake–Pigeon River route. We'll have to travel in two groups . . . the guys in one party and the ladies in another, but we'll take the same course. Up through Bear-skin Lake, overnight on Rose, a day climbing and hanging out in Partridge Falls, then over the long portage to Rove, through Waptap and along the border lakes to the Pigeon River."

Ross had put down his fork. He stared at Noah as if he'd just told them they were about to scale Kilimanjaro. "Noah, I know we mapped this all out months ago, but now that it's here, I wonder if that's way too much for these kids. They can barely paddle. Do you think they're ready for a sixty-mile trip?"

"We have ten days. That's six miles a day."

"With kids who freak every time they hear a mosquito buzz by their ear." Katie leaned forward and purposely kept her voice low. "Are you sure we're not jumping in over our heads?"

Anne's warning rang through his skull: *Bad idea. Trouble lurks in the forest, Noah, and these kids are going to find it.* Getting these kids into God's creation to face their mortality might be exactly what they needed to push them over the edge and help them see their need for a Savior. But was he pushing too hard, too fast? Just because immersion in the wilderness had worked on him didn't mean it was a sure remedy.

"I think we'll be fine." He twirled his fork into his

spaghetti, round and round. Katie's silence amid the chatter of twenty campers spoke volumes. "If we have to, we'll pull out at South Fowl. I'll have my cell phone and Dan said he'd pick us up anytime. We'll be fine."

Ross raised his eyebrows. "Okay, boss, you know best."

Noah tried to agree with a smile, but a flint of panic rose and pierced his confidence. Maybe Katie's and Anne's words were right on target. He shoved his plate of food away. He looked down the table at Darrin, verbally sparring with George, who sat across from him. Both had rolled up the right arm of their T-shirts. . . .

Anger flared in Noah's chest. Gang signals . . . People signals. Vice Lord signals. Obviously Darrin had taken Noah's revelation to heart and given himself permission to follow in Noah's treacherous footsteps. The food soured in Noah's stomach. Yeah, he'd been a great leader. Obviously making a gigantic impact in these kids' lives.

"Excuse me," he said to Katie, Ross, or whoever cared as they shoveled food into their mouths. "I have to get ready for Soul Talk." He grabbed his plate and climbed off the bench before his face could betray his gut-wrenching sense of failure. Sliding his plate across the counter to Granny D., he barely heard her offer him a cookie. No, he couldn't eat another thing. Not with his stomach roiling.

He didn't even look at Anne as he passed her table. The death of their brief, glorious romance was another wretched testament to his pathetic attempts to escape his upbringing.

He'd been the utmost of fools to believe a man of his background could not only change the hearts and minds of desperate kids, but also win the heart of a lady like Anne. Thankfully, he'd never confessed that they'd met before, that he'd been the catalyst of her nightmares. Never confessed the way he felt about her, the way he couldn't get through a minute without her fringing his mind. That somehow she'd taken up occupancy in his heart.

This afternoon, as she'd looked him in the eyes and thanked him for pouring out his ugly history, he'd put definition to his feelings that seemed to overwhelm him. He loved her. He loved her for her smile and her laughter. For her courage and her commitment to dreams that weren't hers. He'd wanted to dive into the fairy tale she'd created for them this afternoon. Wanted to sweep his feisty beauty into his arms and tell her he loved her. And then, as if realization had a thirty-second delay, he saw her eyes change and in them he'd become not Prince Charming . . . but a beast.

He should have known that he hadn't a prayer of burying his heritage. That reality made him weak with grief.

Down . . . down . . . down he went, in way over his head. And drowning fast.

Anne watched Noah stride out of the lodge, saw the sickly hue on his face, and fought a wave of heartache. She wanted to bounce off her bench and run after him, to take him in her arms and tell him that whatever the problem, they'd face it together.

Where? Here in Deep Haven? The horrific news that his future awaited him in Minneapolis made her want to crawl under the table and sob.

A team of wild elephants couldn't drag her south. Never. Her peace was in Deep Haven, not in Minneapolis, and nothing short of hog-tying and gagging her would get her to return to her old stomping—no, running—ground.

Besides, she hadn't come to Deep Haven looking for love. She'd been content to dream about the mystery man who fringed her memories. She'd choose peace over love any day, month, or year. Hadn't her mother's experience taught her that much? MaryAnn Lundstrom had loved her husband so much she'd given up her home, her teaching career, her life to follow him into ministry. She remained there three years after his death, spooning out chicken soup to the homeless.

Not Anne. She didn't care if it ripped her heart right out of her chest and left her cold and hollow for eternity. She would not let a man drag her back into that prison. Anne clenched her jaw and forced herself to finish her spaghetti.

She spent the next hour helping Granny D. in the kitchen, then wandered down to the campfire to catch the tail end of Soul Talk. Noah had morphed from the slump-shouldered man she'd seen shuffle out of the lodge into camp director with a passion. She steeled her heart against the way Noah explained the story of the Prodigal Son. Why did he have to be so charismatic, compassion and verve lighting his eyes, his strong hands drawing the story? Even the way he moved, with energy and excitement, barraged the emotional walls she'd spent the past hour trying to fortify.

She avoided him like poison ivy when the group headed back to their tents. Memories of the campfire pit called to her—a sultry voice reminding her of sitting in its magical embrace with the woods perfuming the air, a gorgeous man beside her, sometimes holding her hand. She fought the emotional ambush as she did her rounds.

Stopping at Melinda's tent, she checked on the girls, then made a cursory check outside Ross's and then Bucko's tent before heading over to Katie's group for the night. She'd begun to relish the evening chats with Katie's group.

Shelly, the young lady who'd been sucked into George's charisma, had turned out to be a delightful teenager with luminous brown eyes, a smile that lit up a room, and a feisty spirit hungering after truth. When Anne pulled up the flap and entered the musty tent, alive with flashlights striping the canvas walls, Shelly was quizzing Katie about God's goodness in the face of evil.

The question brought Anne back to the night Bertha had eaten her cabin to smithereens and she'd walked in on Noah the prowler. He'd frightened her, but in the sincerity of his apology, she'd seen the first hint of a man of honor beneath the garb of danger. And their conversation that night, as they'd stared into the sky, betrayed a man who walked in faith. *Where is God in the dark moments, when our dreams crumble, when the worst happens?*

Katie's answer seemed apropos for Noah's question. "His grace is sufficient, even for those dark moments." Katie's green eyes reflected a light not her own as she spoke softly to her group. Anne sat on the cot next to Shelly.

"But doesn't God care when we suffer? Why doesn't He stop it or protect us?" Shelly's questions echoed Anne's.

Anne quirked one eyebrow, held her breath.

"That is an excellent question," Katie said. "Consider with me Jesus' answer in John chapter 9. Jesus was walking along with His disciples, and they see this blind man. Of course, it's the nature of people to want to know why something happens, so the disciples asked, 'Teacher, why was this man born blind? Was it a result of his own sins or those of his parents?'" Katie leaned over and touched Shelly's knee, then scanned the group with a searching gaze. "And Jesus said, 'It was not because of his sins or his parents' sins. He was born blind so the power of God could be seen in him.'

"Then Jesus healed the man. I think the important thing here is that we can't always pin down reasons for tragedy. Life is tough—you know that. But every hard moment can be met by God, used by God. That's the glory of it. We can ask why, but we may never find the answer. But we will find God if we turn to Him. In that surrender, He'll turn the tragedy into something for His glory and your eternal good, according to His will."

Anne hugged herself, blinking at Katie's words.

Katie flipped through the Bible lying open in the pocket of her crossed legs. "'O my people, trust in Him at all times. Pour out your heart to Him, for God is our refuge.' That psalm was written by David, a king who was surrounded by his enemies. He knew where to turn for help, and he wasn't afraid to cry out to God." She closed her Bible and her gentle eyes found Shelly. "That's your answer. Life is cruel, but God's comfort is near, if you call out to Him. I don't know why He allows horror, but I do know that He sends Himself, like a light in the darkness, searching to save us when life assaults us."

Anne's mind tracked back to three nights ago, when Noah had driven her out to the cliff to watch the lighthouse. The beam arched through the night, searching . . .

Suddenly, the analogy fit. And it hurt.

Where had His light been the night she'd been attacked? The cry of her bereft soul swelled through her, and she fought the primal urge to flee and hide from the fears stalking her.

Fears that denied her the pleasure of fully enjoying God's blessings—now. Fears that meant she'd have to shove Noah out of her life if she wanted to survive.

Because if she couldn't find peace in her past and see God's hand in the darkness, how could she ever trust the Almighty for the shadowed future? Especially a future that meant joining Noah in his work among the riffraff of life. Outside her Deep Haven.

"Do you remember the prayer I taught you this morning?" Katie reached out her hands, locked them with the girls on either side of her. "Let's say it together."

Anne held Shelly's hand, her raw emotions soothed by the soft, vibrant voices reciting a childhood prayer: "Now I lay me down to sleep. I pray the Lord my soul to keep. If I should die before I wake, I pray the Lord my soul to take."

Tears gathered in the back of Anne's throat. How long had it been since she felt that safe, soul-keeping embrace of her Savior?

Anne pushed to her feet, bid the girls good night, and wandered down to the campfire. The dim glow of the cinders barely pushed back the night, and it wasn't until she neared the conclave that she saw Noah sitting just outside the ring of light. His head-bowed, hands-folded posture made her freeze.

He was praying. The sight of this street-raised man bent in petition before the Lord brought tears to her eyes. Noah loved God. Hadn't she longed for a man who loved God above all else? But not if he dragged her right back into danger.

Anne steeled herself against a wave of heartache. Oh, she loved him. Loved him. As she watched him, saw him wipe his eyes, listened to him hum a faint melody, the realization burrowed deep. She knew it as well as she knew her own name. She'd fallen hopelessly, devastatingly, gloriously in love with Noah. She loved his zeal for life, his laughter, his teasing, his soul-deep eyes. She loved his wind-tangled black hair that made him look like a Wild West warrior.

She loved Noah Standing Bear more with each breath.

But she couldn't be with him. Not when loving him meant facing her demons, abandoning her plans for a safe future.

She shouldn't have let her heart get so far off its leash. She should have gritted her teeth and stuck to dreaming about the only perfect hero—the one who knew her darkest moments and carried her through them.

Yeah, right. The utter hopelessness of ever meeting that hero of a year ago nearly made her huff in incredulous despair. The worst part followed and hit her hard—even if she ever, by some stupendous miracle of the Almighty, met the man who'd saved her life, her heart was already taken. Noah had full, universal occupancy.

How utterly heart-wrenching was that?

She turned, desperate to sneak away . . . and stepped on a twig. It snapped like a security alarm reverberating through the halls of guilt. She stopped.

"Anne?"

She slowly turned back. He had raised his head, and the raw vulnerability in his eyes, as if he knew she'd seen him crying, shook her. "Sorry to disturb you."

"It's okay. I . . . uh . . . was praying." He stood, shoved both hands into his pockets, and came near the fire. The glow barely dented the shadow around his face. "How are you? I mean . . . with us?"

How was she? How did she explain the despair blowing through her heart? How did she tell him that she loved him, that he seemed the fulfillment of all her wildest dreams?

And nightmares.

She wasn't going back to the Phillips neighborhood, and Noah couldn't guilt her, charm her, or bamboozle her into it. Even if she did feel utterly safe in his embrace.

She simply could not be with a man whose life's ambition was to get tough and dirty with the elements of the inner city, who walked into the night . . . and asked her to follow.

Why did Noah have to commit his heart to the street? Couldn't he stay here with her? Deep Haven had lost youth, didn't it? Unless . . . he didn't love her back. He had asked her to work for him—not to marry him. Big difference.

She backed away from him, nearly as afraid as when she'd faced her shooter. She wasn't going to hang around to get wounded a second time.

"I have to go to bed. Early morning, you know." She couldn't look at his face, at those oh-so-soft eyes. She would simply reel in her heart and tuck it safely, bruised and battered, back in her chest. He would never know that, for the smallest blip of time, she'd found pure happiness in his arms.

He opened his mouth as if to protest, his face tight in a frown, but she held up a hand. "I don't know, Noah. Just . . . stay away from me."

Then she turned, and like she had so many times in the face of her nightmares, she fled.

22

It would be a glorious, God-breathed day if Anne allowed herself to look at the sky—a perfect azure, accessorized with fat cumulus bullied by a slight breeze. The sun fought for space and, when it won, it rained down a blast of pure, glorious warmth. It went right through Anne's rain gear and warmed the cold places inside.

In Anne's canoe, Latisha lay sprawled in the middle, on "duffing" duty for this lake, her cornrowed head against a Duluth pack as she soaked in the sun. Her dark skin shone like priceless topaz. Shelly, working the paddle in the bow, had her brown hair pulled back in an inverted ponytail, and Anne wondered how the girl couldn't be freezing in a tank top and shorts. Anne felt chilled from the inside out, a phenomenon that had to do with the fact she was surrounded on all sides by water.

Still, it made her feel fresh and alive in a wild nature sort of way. Of course, it could be the aftereffects of sleeping while dangling between two trees—Noah's brilliant solution to her "no bugs" and "no ground." Swinging under the stars bundled in her sleeping bag, she had slept better the last two nights than she had in years. Even though she had yet to brave the morning plunge, she felt new and bright and whole when the dawn woke her with a warm kiss.

Perhaps, indeed, she'd found the peace she'd been searching for. Even the weight of doom had eased. She longed to be terribly wrong about her premonition of brewing trouble.

Noah sure seemed to be heading off disasters. He was militant about wearing life jackets and had made everyone put on enough mosquito repellent to kill a record infestation. Last night he'd paddled over from the guys' campsite down the shore to check on the ladies.

She wouldn't let him find a soft place in her heart to work his charm. Poor guy. He didn't deserve the cold shoulder she'd given him. Her resolve almost crumbled when he'd handed her a nylon hammock, those gorgeous eyes saying so much more. *What's wrong, Anne?*

She refused to walk away from the girls—busy roasting marshmallows in the dying campfire—toward the moonlit shore with him. One too-kind word from him and she'd jump into his arms, and what would that do to her already tattered heart?

She shuddered to know. If God were merciful, He'd send in her replacement before she felt totally wrung out. At first glance, it seemed God hadn't been generous with mercy, but if she were honest, she'd admit to seeing some merciful moments.

Like God surrounding her with a jeweled display of His majesty—the lush emerald evergreens hugging the shoreline, the sapphire blue of the Boundary Water lakes, and the golden sunshine in a perfect sky. Wildflowers perfumed the air. Even the absence of noise, the immense still that blanketed the night, ministered to her battered soul. Yes, God deserved the credit for bringing her here, and she owed Him that, even if He did play games with her heart.

In fact, escaping the city had begun to give her a measure of perspective. Perhaps the hard moments in her life had been tempered by God's touch more than she realized. Shelly, for example. The girl had nearly scared the socks off

Anne when she'd first arrived, with her pierced eyebrow, her sullen pout, and the dark eyes that followed Anne like a wolf's. But Anne had found a young woman with hope, dreams . . . potential beneath the dark accessories of her culture.

And Noah. He'd certainly proved that first appearances deceived. Anne half smiled, remembering the beachcomber who'd fixed her car. God had been merciful in helping her realize that her first-glance hoodlum could be Prince Charming in disguise.

A Prince Charming she couldn't have.

She swallowed a lump of misery and concentrated on keeping her canoe straight in the water. With her outstanding paddling skills, they were jagging all over Hungry Jack Lake, making a mockery of Noah's ambitious plan. They'd spent over three hours yesterday, sorting paddles, lacing life jackets, and teaching the kids—and her—how to climb into a canoe without dumping.

So much for not being wet. Her feet felt pruned and frozen in her soggy wool socks. She couldn't wait to peel them off and dive into her clean, warm pair. Only three pairs of socks? What was Noah thinking?

"Anne, hurry up!" Katie waved with her paddle from fifty feet away.

Anne grimaced and picked up her pace. "Sorry, Shelly," she said as she splashed water on her bow woman. So she had some north-shore skills to cultivate. She enjoyed this more than dispensing medication and giving AIDs tests.

Anne fell silent, the muscles in her back beginning to tire. The soft thump of the canoe dipping between the waves and the occasional scrape of paddle against aluminum hull accompanied Anne's and Shelly's labor. They drew alongside Chantee and Katie, who hooked their gunwale with a paddle and pulled them close. Juanita and Jasmine bumped against the other side. Anne noticed that Melinda and her group of girls were similarly hooked, bobbing ten feet away in a small island of canoes, packs, and people.

"Have a drink." Katie opened her water bottle and plunged it deep into the water.

Anne gaped at her. "You've got to be kidding. Have you ever heard of bacteria? amoebas? disease?"

"Relax, Anne. Hop off your medical horse for a moment. Look." Katie opened a packet of pills and dropped one into her bottle. It dissolved in a second. "Purification tablets. They'll kill the bad stuff." She handed the bottle over.

Anne peered inside and made a face at the littering of paramecia floating in their watery abode. "Uh, no thanks."

"Drink it. Trust me; you'll be fine."

"There's a big difference between trust and foolishness!"

Katie laughed. "Sometimes trust is foolishness. I know it looks yucky, but it's truly safe. Pure. Besides, you're thirsty and this is all we've got, so get tough and drink it."

Anne closed her eyes and gulped down the water. It felt refreshingly delicious, wild, pure. "Hmm . . . not bad."

Katie reached for the bottle, her eyes twinkling. "God doesn't make yucky stuff."

There was power in her words as her gaze tracked to Latisha and Shelly, to Chantee, Juanita, and Jasmine, then back to Anne. Anne couldn't squelch her sudden admiration for this woman who loved these teenagers. The thought of investing her life into these rough-hewn treasures tugged at a place deep in Anne's heart, and she had to take a deep breath to escape it. She smiled back at Katie and nodded, wishing she didn't agree so much.

Shelly had leaned back in her seat against a pack, soaking in the sun, and Katie's paddlers were munching on their ration of gorp. The canoes bobbed, hooked together like rafts in the sea. "So, what's with you and Noah?" Katie asked.

Anne glanced at Shelly, Latisha, then back at Katie and frowned.

Katie laughed. "C'mon. It's not like we haven't all noticed. The guy gets this sappy puppy-dog smile on his face when you walk into the room. He can barely sit still.

And I saw you two looking cozy down by the campfire on more than one occasion." Katie arched her eyebrows like a gossip queen. "Don't tell me he isn't your dream come true, either, because I've seen the way you watch him." She frowned. "Except last night. You barely looked at him. What's with that?"

Anne glanced away. "I didn't know we were such a subject of interest."

"Are you kidding? In a camp of budding hormones? You're better than a soap opera!" She laughed; then her voice fell to a whisper. "For these kids, you're setting an example."

Anne gulped. Super. She couldn't bear to think she'd made him a laughingstock, especially in front of kids who had a warped concept of love and honor. More than anything, they needed to see that a man and a woman could be friends, treat each other with respect . . . even if they couldn't be "together."

She fought the pinch of guilt. Noah had been trying so hard to treat her with kindness . . . she owed him honesty and a measure of warmth. At least until camp ended.

When he would turn his back on her and exit her life.

Anne managed a deep breath. If her life growing up amid drug pushers and gangbangers had taught her anything, it was to hold her head high and live above the current of her feelings. If she had to cede a small piece of her heart to honor Noah and his reputation, then she'd consider it a small price to pay for the gift of knowing a man who destroyed her prejudices and made her reach beyond her fears. At least for the summer.

"Noah and I are just friends," Anne said.

Katie nodded, her eyes glowing, a smile playing on her lips. "Yeah, sure."

"No, really. He's . . . a great guy . . ."

Katie chuckled and shook her head. "Girlfriend, you've got it bad."

Anne wrinkled her nose at Katie in argument, but she

couldn't help but surrender to the younger woman's words. Yes, she had it bad for the commando in the far-off canoe, so bad it felt like her heart took a nosedive into gravel every time he paddled by. She shrugged and smiled, agreeing.

Katie held up her hand to high-five her. "I knew it. I just knew it!"

Anne rolled her eyes, bouyed by Katie's friendship. The girl reminded her of Sandra, and Anne suddenly missed the warmth of the hospital nurse. She'd have to drive into Deep Haven Municipal when they returned to remind herself of everything she gained by surrendering Noah. "Don't get excited. It's not going to go anywhere."

Katie scowled. "Why not? He's loony over you, or haven't you noticed the way his chin drags on the ground whenever you're near?"

Anne shook her head, suddenly somber. "No, really, Katie. It's not going to work. It's over." She gave another shrug and fought the sudden sting of tears. "So, where are we going, anyway?" she asked, desperate to change the subject. She stretched her arms. Never had she felt so deliciously tired, so gloriously achy.

Katie, obviously as sensitive as she was biblically astute, caught Anne's deflection and played along. "See where the tree line vees over there?" Katie used her paddle as a giant pointer. "We'll camp there tonight, then tomorrow climb the Stairway portage into Rose Lake. On the other side are some great climbing cliffs. I think Noah's planning on making us climb the 'wall of death.'" She winked at Anne.

Anne smiled wearily.

Oh, joy.

Noah had set up a net of ropes, a belay system to rival Barnum and Bailey Circus. He surveyed his work in the late-afternoon sun, thrilled to be three days into the canoe trip without a major catastrophe. He thanked God every

minute that He had seen fit to equip him with a caliber
staff. Katie's gentle words of caution had made him realize
his folly. Overwhelming these kids might push them to the
end of themselves . . . or it might get them killed.

Let go and let God. That phrase drummed through his
skull three days ago as he watched his boys drag the expen-
sive canoes across the landing and listened to their
comments—not necessarily enthusiastic—as they tottered
into the boats and grabbed paddles.

"No motors?"

"Just hard work, pal." Noah had grinned at Darrin as
he checked his life preserver.

Darrin responded with a grimace.

They'd zigzagged across the lake and by nightfall had
covered half a mile. Noah scrapped the last hope for a
boundary-route canoe trip and decided to be thankful they
made it across Bearskin Lake.

Now, two lakes later, he had to admit that being overwhelmed and unscheduled might be a good place for him to
be. Clutching faith like a lifeline, he had nothing but faith
and his good equipment to keep him from plunging into the
rocks below, as these campers would do tomorrow with the
ropes that dangled over the cliffs. But faith was enough.
God was enough. Knowing that put a song of joy in Noah's
weary heart.

He checked his bowline knots one last time, then curled
the ropes up to the tree and went in search of his soap and
towel. Ten minutes down the trail, Partridge Falls called
to him like a melody. He'd left Ross and Bucko with the
troops at the campsite beneath the cliffs. Just up shore, a
five-minute jog along the border hiking trail, Katie,
Melinda, and Anne were setting up camp.

He fought the sudden urge to trot down there and watch
Anne tie her hammock to the trees. Something about the
expanse of sky had begun to unleash the tension in their
relationship. Perhaps simply being away from the woman
he couldn't stop thinking about, letting himself deny the

fact that it was over, had duped him into believing he hadn't fallen so terribly short of her expectations. That he might somehow be able to resurrect their wounded relationship. There was a God, after all. A big one, with the power to change lives . . . and hearts.

Obviously the distance had buoyed Anne's spirit as well, for the cold front from her general direction had blown north. She'd grinned at him this morning, a genuine here-comes-the-sun type of smile.

Noah tossed his towel around his neck, hearing the falls ahead, already feeling the water splashing over his shoulders. He crunched along the path, stress swirling out of him with every step, every breath of fragranced air. Yes, this was God's country, and anything could happen.

He veered off the trail, which merged with the Stairway portage, and rounded the falls. He'd been anticipating swimming in Partridge Falls all summer. The tucked-away falls were deep enough for him to submerge to his chest, strong enough for him to revel in the rush of being pelted by a force greater than himself.

He threw down his towel, stripped off his sweatshirt, and grabbed his soap. Stage one would be laundry—his T-shirt could use a good lathering, and backwoods fun meant he could do two tasks in one sitting. He climbed over the rocks and inched toward the falls.

He was just dipping his foot into the water when he saw Anne sitting on a ledge behind the falls like a water nymph. Eyes closed, water running over her face, down her black T-shirt, and across her shorts, she reclined as if in a spa, oblivious to the world.

He froze and started to back away. Despite her recent warming trend, she certainly wasn't going to do a jig if he disturbed her shower . . . even if she bathed fully clothed in the middle of a very public wilderness.

He started to climb out, slipped on the rock, and landed, backside first, with a splash. Water crested up his chest and stole his breath.

"Noah?"

He winced. "I was just leaving."

"No, that's okay. I'm done."

He watched as she moved through the falls. Her hair hung in thick auburn strands around her face, her hazel green eyes huge and gathering the sun, droplets of water hanging on her eyelashes and running off her chin. She stumbled near, one hand on the rock for balance. "You'll love it," she said, breathless.

I already do. "How did you find this place?"

"Katie told me about it, and . . . well, since I've been avoiding the morning-swim elective, I thought it was time for a shower."

When she smiled, his heart took flight. Did she have any idea that being near her made him want to burst into a song, to whoop and dance and unleash the bubble of joy building in his chest?

He refused to pass the clear, do-not-cross line she'd drawn in her demeanor, however. Somehow, he kept his voice normal. "You're doing great, by the way. A real trooper. I don't know about the bugs, but I do know you've been wet and cold, and I appreciate your chutzpah. I just thought you should know."

Her smile faded and she looked away. "Thank you."

She appeared tiny and waiflike in those sopping wet clothes, so fragile the wind could knock her flat with a puff. "Are you doing laundry?"

"What?" Her eyes were huge in her face, suddenly very, very green and swallowing him whole.

"Your clothes. Didn't you bring a swimsuit?"

She looked at herself, as if for the first time she realized she was fully clothed. She paled. "No, I . . . uh . . ."

"It's okay. Actually, seriously, it's a good idea. I'm going to do it too. Wash while you wear." He laughed, a chuckle that she didn't mimic. He felt like an idiot standing there, laughing at her attire as if she didn't look delightfully bedraggled and beautiful.

Mercifully, she smiled, but the grin didn't touch her eyes. "Oh, that's funny."

Regret as big as Texas lodged in his throat as he realized he could never, ever win the woman he wanted.

No, not just wanted, needed.

She turned to climb out of the water. Taking with her the sunshine, the warmth—

She slipped. With a cry Anne fell back, toward the pool.

Noah reacted in a second and reached out for her. She landed in the net of his embrace. Instinctively, he tightened his grip. The cold water swirled around them, but he could stay in this place forever, turning into a prune, if only she would let him hold her. "Got ya," he said softy.

Then she began to cry. *Oh, Lord, now what have I done?* She turned around and curled into a ball right there in his arms, buried her beautiful soggy head into his chest, and sobbed her heart out.

Noah was stone silent. He held her, as she totally unraveled. Was being near him so horrible it reduced her to tears? "Anne, honey. What's the matter? Please." He released her, tried to meet her eyes, but she refused to look up at him. "I'm sorry. Did I do something?"

She shook her head. Then nodded, then shook her head again. She looked so wretched he couldn't help but smile.

"Please. You can trust me." He cupped her chin in his hands and lifted her face to his. "Am I that scary?"

Her eyes widened, and to his horror she nodded. His breath stilled. She was serious. She was afraid of him. His ex-con status not only repulsed her—it *terrified* her. He felt as if she'd kicked him—hard—right in the heart.

As he let her go, he took her hand and helped her up to the shore. As she stood shivering, he wrapped his towel around her. She clutched it to her chest, looking bereft, dripping river water onto the ground.

Twilight encircled them, sending droplets of lavender into the fine spray. The music of the evening had started a symphony.

Her teeth began to chatter. He fought the impulse to envelop her in his arms.

Because . . . she was afraid of him.

Then she looked at him, her gorgeous eyes full of misery. She traced his face with her gaze, glanced at the tattoo on his arm, then bit her lip. He felt sick and wanted to race for his sweatshirt. At least then he could pretend he was someone else.

"Noah, I owe you an explanation."

He blinked at her, managed to shake his head. "You don't owe me anything. I'm the one who owes you. I dragged you into this mess—"

"No, that's not what this is about." She propped precariously onto a boulder and motioned for him to join her. He gulped, reached for his sweatshirt, and wrestled it over his head. It pasted to his wet skin as he sat next to her, feeling somewhat less naked . . . as least on the outside. Their shoulders and knees bumped together, but he resisted the desire to put his arm around her.

Because . . . she was afraid of him.

"Noah, I'm so in love with you it hurts." She blurted it, hard and fast.

He opened his mouth, but no words came out. What? He didn't know whether to gather her in his arms and dance or weep. "Huh?" With that intelligent reply he wanted to crawl under the rock from where he hailed.

"I am." Her voice turned soft. She looked at him, her eyes brimming with everything she'd just said, and he believed her to the marrow of his soul. She loved him.

And she was afraid of him?

He couldn't get past the knot of confusion in his chest to reply. He managed another endearing, "Huh?" *Way to charm her, Noah.*

She smiled, as if touched by his oh-so-witty charisma. "I've been fighting it since the day I met you. You are everything I hoped for and more, Noah. The man I wanted to build a life with."

Hoped. Wanted. His heart felt like it had been tossed in the air, then speared. His eyes must have betrayed his total lack of understanding because she smiled again, and this time she touched his cheek.

He leaned into her touch. "Wanted? As in past tense?" *Please, don't say yes. Tell me you meant something else. Certainly God wouldn't answer my prayers, then yank them away the next second?*

She nodded. "It won't work. I should have told you that a week ago when you said that you lived and worked in Minneapolis." Her eyes filled and she looked away.

He stared at her, grasping for comprehension. "What does this have to do with where I work? I don't understand."

But suddenly he did, and he wanted to groan. Oh no. Of course. The Phillips neighborhood, 2135 Franklin Avenue.

"I can't go back there, Noah." Her voice was so small he had to strain to hear it. "Not even for you."

This wasn't about *his* past . . . it was about *hers*. Her fear didn't have anything to do with who he'd been but who he was now. His job, his future . . . her past.

"Anne." He curled his arm around her despite the fact that she sat as if frozen. She was probably turning into an iceberg under all those sopping clothes. "Anne, I know."

She looked at him then, her eyes big, round, and full of disbelief. "No, Noah, you don't understand. It's not about my life here or my job or my plans . . . it's something that happened."

"I know." He nodded, wishing he didn't have to tell her, wishing he had nothing to do with her fears. If she was afraid of him now when she thought him only a man who happened to have a burden for the lost street children, what would she think when she realized he'd been there, unable to stop the moment her life hung in the balance? Guilt felt like a ten-ton anvil in his chest. He fingered her wet hair, summoning his courage.

"Noah, about a year ago, I was . . ." Her voice trembled.

"Shot." He flinched when he said it, remembering every ugly, deadly nanosecond. Her scream echoing off the walls of his heart, the shot that shattered so many lives, her eyes holding on to his gaze for dear life.

"How did you know?" Her voice dropped to a whisper. "Did Katie tell you?"

He lowered his forehead to hers, wondering if she could feel him shudder or hear the sorrow in his voice. "No." He swallowed a ball of sheer grief. "I was there."

23

God wasn't fair.

Anne stared at Noah, the living proof that miracles happened, and knew that God had played upon them a horrible joke. Didn't He have a heart?

She should have seen it. What kind of blinders had she donned to convince herself that Noah wasn't exactly the man for whom she'd hoped, wanted, prayed?

Here he sat, a flesh-and-blood, dream-come-true apparition from the past. It seemed too wonderful, too awful, to be true.

Anne closed her eyes as memory swept through her. The soft touch of a stranger, the haunting melody of "It Is Well with My Soul." She opened her eyes and studied Noah: the worry knitting his beautiful face; the small, round scar on his cheek; his incredible honey brown eyes, so warm, so riveting . . .

2135 Franklin Avenue.

She tried to breathe through her vise-gripped chest. *No. God, don't do this to me.* How cruel was He to give her the very materialization of her dreams—then wrench it away by giving her a man sold out to God and to the lost souls of the street? Not. Fair.

God should have warned her He was going to start answering prayers like manna from heaven. Then she might have qualified her request for a man with a passion for the hurting and lost with a specific location.

She clenched her jaw, but tears burned her eyes. Noah was her nightmare, in devastating proportions. A heart-breaking, impossibly gorgeous dream man she couldn't have.

Shaking, she turned her tearstained face away from Noah and everything he symbolized. "No, Noah. Please don't say that to me. I don't want you to be him."

Her voice seemed pinched. As the waterfall hissed in the growing darkness, horror spiraled out of her thoughts. She began to shiver from the inside out.

If God had heard her prayers about her hero and answered, then what did that mean? Had God also heard her petition for peace and safety from the far reaches of her childhood? Could it be that He'd sent her to 2135 Franklin Avenue for a reason?

To teach her, exactly . . . what? That peace and safety weren't in the ingredients of this mortal world? Ouch. The sheer devastation of that thought and the harsh lessons of God made her press her hands to her trembling lips. She felt the fabric of her flimsily reconstructed faith begin to rip.

Noah's close presence raised the tiny hairs on the back of her neck. She wanted to turn toward his strong, solid chest, dig her hands into his T-shirt, and force him to deny it for the sake of her shattering soul.

"You weren't there. You couldn't have been there. Katie told you, didn't she?" She stared hard into his eyes. The sadness in them confirmed the heartrending truth.

"You were shot while answering a call for my foster mother. Anthony Debries was strung out on drugs and had taken us both hostage. You and your partner walked into it." His quiet, clinical explanation made her wince. His

voice dropped so that every word seemed a groan. "Tony
shot you from five feet away."

She closed her eyes, wishing the words away, aching with
the assault of memories.

"I was there. I tried to stop him but I couldn't." His voice
broke. She opened her eyes and saw he'd covered his face
with his hands. Then the big, tough street punk began to
tremble, his grief so palpable it plunged right through
Anne's frozen body to her heart.

Noah was crying . . . for her. She stared at him, stunned.
Her throat tightened. She couldn't believe she'd actually
said the three little words aloud, bared her heart to him,
knowing he wouldn't echo her words. But now her street-
tough warrior was suffering because of her pain, broken
over the fact that he hadn't protected her. Something thick
and warm filled her chest. He wept for her. She couldn't—
wouldn't—dare to think that it might be because . . . he
loved her too.

As she watched him, something inside ripped; then in a
rush, a year of grief burst free. Fear, agony, even self-pity
spilled out, like the lancing of an infection. Anne moaned
with the enormity of the emotions.

In a movement that they both needed, Anne wrapped her
arms around Noah.

"I'm so sorry," he said, not surrendering to her embrace.
"I should have stopped him. Then you came in and I tried
to warn you, but . . ."

"I didn't understand your warning." She nudged closer.
When he finally settled his arm around her, she nestled into
his wide chest. "Noah, it's okay." He continued to weep as
if he had been the one shot, the one whose life had been
crushed. "I'm okay."

Her own words startled her. Since when was she okay?
Thirty minutes ago, her hideous scars had made her bathe
in her clothes rather than her swimsuit. Ten minutes ago,
her traumatic memories jerked her out of the embrace of the

man she loved. Suddenly now, seeing his tears, she was okay?

Oh yes. A divine breath filled her chest, one that should have been accompanied by angels singing and heavenly trumpets, and she realized why God had brought her to this moment, this hero. No one in the entire world could understand her pain, her grief, better than Noah Standing Bear, the man who'd seen its inception.

God hadn't been cruel.

He'd been merciful.

He'd been gentle.

He'd touched her battered soul by delivering to her the one man with whom she didn't have to be afraid. The one man who cried for her scars.

And just maybe, yes, God had heard her prayers for peace and safety, the exact emotions she felt when enfolded in Noah's arms. Who better to keep her safe than the one man, the very man, who had risked his life to save hers? If he'd nearly sacrificed himself to save her before, he'd do it again.

Certainly, Noah, better than anyone, would understand why she could never return to the inner city. He'd even admitted it. *I know,* he'd said, when she opened up her black soul. *I was there.*

He had been there, had tried to stop it, and now he grieved for her pain. This man who trembled in her arms would cut out his own heart before he'd drag her back to her fears. She felt it to the core of her heart.

A wave of pure delight filled her chest, and she spread her hands on his wide back. "Noah, it wasn't your fault." She leaned back, willing him to meet her gaze. "You saved my life. Don't you know that?"

He shook his head. "Because of me, you were nearly killed. I should have stopped him, but I was waiting, trying to figure out a way to disarm him when you walked in. If I had been faster . . . or smarter . . ." Tears continued to etch trails down his handsome face.

"No. You're not to blame for that kid's actions." Anne wiped a tear off his cheek. "You tried to stop him. If you hadn't jumped him, he would have shot me in the face." The memory of that moment, of Noah flying across the room in a full-out tackle, came back vividly. "You saved me, Noah, more than you could ever know."

He studied her, his sweet brown eyes full, glistening, unbelieving.

"You sang to me, remember? You sang 'It Is Well with My Soul,' and I never forgot it. You were with me during my rehab, during all the pain. God used that song you gave to me to hold me up. I've never forgotten you, Noah. I've been dreaming about you for a year."

His mouth moved as if trying to find words. They came out in a whisper. "Oh, Anne. I . . ." His words stopped, as if caught in his throat.

His eyes roamed her face with a longing so vivid it made her heart gallop through her chest. He touched her face gently with the tips of his fingers. A glorious, delicious smile broke out, as if he realized for the first time the meaning of her words. "Anne."

She lifted her face for his kiss, relishing it. His lips trembled as he kissed her with such tenderness, such thoughtfulness. While his arm curled around her, the other hand cupped her face and he ran his thumb along her cheek.

The moment was so beautiful she wanted to cry all over again.

"Noah," she murmured, finally putting a name to the man of her dreams.

Softly, his breath a whisper on her skin, he asked, "Are you still afraid of me?"

He felt her stiffen in his arms. *Please, no.*

"Noah!" The sound of panic laced the voice. As if slapped, Noah released his hold and searched the forest.

"Noah!"

"Over here!" He glanced at Anne. Her eyes, brimming with alarm, were fixed to his. She'd let go of his shirt and scooted away. He missed her already.

"Noah!" Latisha emerged from the trail, running at full power. Her eyes were huge white orbs in her tear-streaked face. "We need you!"

She skidded to a stop and, without a pause, grabbed Anne's arm and pulled. "Come. Now. Darrin's stuck on the wall of death and he's going to die!"

What had those kids done now?

Noah dashed past them, up the trail, his worst fears leading the way.

Twilight had turned menacing. Dark shadows cloaked the ground as Noah ran, tripped, stumbled, his mind already seeing Darrin a crumpled mess of blood and bones at the summit of the wall of death.

He heard screams, the echo of his own panic as he raced to the cliff edge. Over the lake, the sky was a bruised canopy, showering darkness over the rock wall. Noah dropped to his knees and looked over. His heart nearly stopped in his chest. "Darrin!"

The kid was clinging to the face of the wall like a monkey, both hands fisted white with effort. His feet spread-eagled—one toe in a foothold in the rock, the other on a two-inch ledge. He was pinned to the wall by sheer terror.

Darrin looked up at Noah, desperation etched in his plump dark face and terror in his eyes. Thirty feet below, scattered like squirrels on the rocks, the campers had taken positions to urge Darrin up or down, Noah didn't know which. Melinda, ten feet back from the cliff, huddled with Ross. Both looked as if they knew the inevitable.

Darrin was going to fall.

And kill himself.

Noah kept his voice calm, easy. "Hold on, Darrin. I'm coming to get you." Noah backed up slowly, praying he

didn't send debris over on the kid. He turned around in time to see Anne and Latisha emerge from the trail in a dead run. Anne had a fierce look on her face. For some reason, it gave him hope.

"He's stuck," Latisha said, gasping. "He climbed about halfway up and can't get down."

Latisha shook, and Anne pulled the girl to herself and held her tight. Latisha's voice hiccupped between sobs. "George dared him. He told him that if he could climb the wall, he'd get Shelly."

Noah made a face that betrayed the sick feeling in his gut. Get Shelly? Like she was a prize? He clenched his jaw. Right. This was a dare, a sick game. Noah grabbed his climbing harness that was still there from this afternoon's climb. He snapped two carabiners into his D ring and attached a rope to one. "I need someone to belay me!" Thankfully, the ropes had been secured under the light of the afternoon sun. He ran toward the edge and called, "Bucko, I need a belayer!"

"I'll do it." Anne had already hitched her webbing tight.

Noah looked at her, a shivering, soggy ball of grit. "Okay. I'll strap you in." Doubt lodged thick fingers into his chest, but what choice did he have?

Anne sat on the ground. He hooked her into the secure line, a rope fixed around a tree that would anchor her to the tree and keep her from sliding forward. Then he looped the belay rope around her. "You remember how to do this?" He'd given her a rudimentary lesson on belaying during the ropes course, but then again, she'd nearly plunged to her death. He wondered if she remembered anything from that day. He certainly would never forget the second he'd lost his heart.

Obviously she was more astute than he gave her credit for. "Yes. Don't worry. I learned how to belay while I was an EMT."

Oh yeah. Sitting there, gripping the rope, her feet planted, he nearly forgot that she was a city girl with an aversion to bugs. Her eyes glittered when she spoke. "I won't let you fall."

Oh, how he needed to hear that. Because right now he felt like he was teetering on the edge of an ugly plunge into darkness. He nodded at her, unable to speak. Noah picked up another harness, hooked on a carabiner, and clipped it into his rig.

"Noah, help me!"

With Darrin's frantic words, Noah's gaze riveted to Anne. Her calm, you-can-do-this expression centered him. Jaw tight, he looped his rappel line through the figure-eight rappelling carabiner and snapped it onto his harness. Fisting the rope in his right hand, he hesitated at the edge of the cliff, eyes still on Anne.

"I won't let you fall," she mouthed.

He could hear Darrin sucking in breaths, moments away from hyperventilating. Noah stepped over and moved down the rock wall swiftly, thankful for the months of classes he'd taken. He stopped beside Darrin, close enough to reach him but far enough that the kid couldn't take a diving leap at him. Noah anchored his rappel line around his leg, then unhooked the harness.

"Darrin, very slowly we're going to get this on you."

Sweat glistened on Darrin's face. His body shook, a bad sign that time ticked his life away. Noah held the harness at Darrin's foot. "Put your foot in this."

"I can't." The boy's voice was so weak Noah could barely hear it.

"Yes you can. You got this far; you've hung on this long. You can do this."

Darrin shook his head, and for a wild second, Noah thought the kid would spring off his position and into his arms, dragging them both down the cliff to a messy splat on the rocks below. "Calm down. You're gonna be fine."

Darrin sniffled.

"Listen, pal, pull it together." The last thing they needed right now was for Darrin to loosen his hold, to surrender to his fears. "You have three secure points. Just lift this foot and I'll slide the harness on. C'mon. We'll go slowly."

"I'm . . . gonna fall."

"No you're not. I'm here, and I'm not going to let anything happen to you."

When Darrin met his eyes, Noah saw fear so deep it went right to his soul. This was about more than clinging to a ledge. Why hadn't he seen it earlier? Darrin had turned away from him a week ago. But now Noah realized that Darrin had wanted Noah to run after him. Wanted him to prove that he was tougher than Darrin's rejection.

Oh yeah, Noah was up to that fight.

"Put your foot in here—now."

Darrin lifted his foot, just an inch, and Noah slid the harness under it. "Good. Now the other one."

Darrin hung on with white fists and complied. Noah slid the harness up his leg and tightened it.

Sweat dripped off Noah's forehead, into his eyes. Unhooking the belay line from the D ring, he clipped it onto Darrin's. "You're hooked in. Now I want you to climb up."

"What?"

Noah narrowed his eyes at him. He felt his heart beat for the first time in ten minutes. "Listen. I know this started out about a girl. About Shelly. But I want you to finish it. For yourself. You can do this."

Darrin's eyes were huge with terror.

"I promise you that we're not going to let you fall. But you gotta climb up. Don't let this thing beat you. You be the man it takes to overcome." Noah backed away, far enough so the kid couldn't touch him even if he jumped. "Climb."

Darrin blinked at him. Then with a flicker of determination that lit Noah's soul, he looked up, pushed with his legs, and reached for the next hold.

"Yes." *Yes!* "You have a hold to your left. A crack. Wedge your hand in and make a fist."

Darrin inched up. Noah's hands were slick so he fought

for holds as he climbed up beside Darrin. He heard movement and saw Bucko leaning over from the top. His expression betrayed guilt.

C'mon, Darrin—make it. For all of us.

Darrin moved with quiet desperation. Creeping up the rock face, Noah urged him on in low tones. Thank the Lord, Anne was on the other end of Darrin's line—if anyone could secure the kid, it was his Anne.

Who loved him.

Noah fought a wave of emotions and found a toehold. He could hear several voices at the top now, angry tones. Obviously the group from the bottom had scrambled up the path to the top of the cliff and were pointing fingers at each other. Street kids were blamers, and this near tragedy had serious potential to detonate into catastrophe. Noah tensed when he heard words he'd outlawed at the camp rippling the fabric of the night, echoing foully across the lake.

Darrin clawed his way up the cliff face, dragging Noah's heart along. When he reached the top, Bucko hauled him up by his harness as if he weighed no more than a few ounces and clasped the kid in a bear hug that made even Noah dizzy.

Darrin finally collapsed onto the ground, breathing in great gusts.

Noah plopped down beside him, totally unraveled. "You okay?"

Darrin nodded. "Thanks."

"You did well getting up that cliff. I'm proud of you."

Darrin looked at him with a hungry look, devouring Noah's words.

"Darrin, you loser!" George came up behind him and hit the kid hard on the back. "Man, you had to have Noah go down and baby-sit? What's with that?"

Noah turned, and the expression on his face must have scared George because he backed away, hands up. "I'm cool, man. Just funnin' with him."

"It's not funny, George," Shelly said, looking every inch

a dangerous she-cat about to pounce. "You goaded him into it and he nearly died."

"Listen—" The word that came out of George's mouth made Noah flinch. "You back off. You've done nothing but tease and flirt this entire time. I'm sick of your mouth."

Shelly looked slapped and, in a move that sucked Noah back a decade, she clamped her hands on her hips, straightened her shoulders, and jutted out her jaw. "You weren't so sick of it a few days ago."

Dry mouthed and sick to the center of his chest, Noah stared at George. What had these two been up to?

Anne had leaped to her feet, strained at her belay anchor toward Shelly. Her expression looked ferocious as she looked at George, then at Noah. "Calm down, George." There she was, the EMT from a year ago, looking trouble straight in the eye, too gritty to back down even though she was fixed to a solid oak tree like a dog on a leash.

"Hey, baby, I'm cool." George shrugged, but his black eyes glittered, cold as steel. "I don't like white girls, anyway. They're skin and bone and nothing but chitchat." His look ranged to Latisha, standing behind Shelly like a warrior. "But Latisha, now she's yum."

Noah heard Darrin's verbal reaction a second before Darrin rushed George. Noah didn't have time to stop the big kid from tackling George. They went down hard. Bucko immediately hauled Darrin up around the waist. Noah grabbed George, who littered the air with his filthy language. He pinned the kid's arms back. "Settle down, George. Just chill."

"Let go of me, man. I'm sick of him. He's either with us or he's out."

Noah froze. "With us?"

George wrenched out of his grip. "Yeah." He glared at Noah. "Man, you're so brainwashed, you can't even see brothers." He flicked a hand sign, physical graffiti that sunk Noah's heart to his toes. "Vice Lords, man. I'm family."

"No. You're. Not."

So this was the basis of Darrin and George's friendship. It wasn't about Shelly, not really. This dare had gang initiation written all over it.

Noah balled his fists, fighting a wave of fury. Words, accusation, names boiled in his chest, but to open his mouth would be to spew forth ugliness. *God, help. Give me self-control. Wisdom.*

Bucko released Darrin. The kid was wild-eyed, breathing hard, glaring at George.

George flicked Darrin a smug look.

Darrin exploded. He ran at George, hit him with a smacking blow across the face. George stumbled, stunned, then lunged at Darrin like a panther. Bucko dove in, grabbing at George, and got kicked in the face.

Noah grabbed George's shirt and heard it rip as he yanked back hard.

George whirled and hit Noah—a surprising, brain-rattling blow for a thirteen-year-old. "Get away from me!" Then he dove at Darrin again, landed two hands against his chest.

The air in Darrin's lungs puffed out as he stumbled back toward the edge. His eyes widened, his hands clawed the air, searching for purchase.

Noah lunged for him. *Please, God, no!* His hands closed around Darrin's deathly scream as the boy fell over the cliff into the night.

24

Anne knelt beside Darrin, her heart in her throat. He'd fallen at least thirty feet and landed in a pocket of brush, his head dangerously near a jagged boulder that would have split his skull like a cantaloupe. Anne squashed that image and braced Darrin's head with her knees, pulling back slightly with her fingers on his jawbone, nudging the base of the jaw upward to open his airway.

"Is he dead?" Noah's voice emerged in a throat-tight whisper.

Anne leaned over, her ear next to Darrin's mouth, her eyes glued to his chest. A thin, raspy breath. She pressed her fingertips to his throat and found a thready pulse. "No, but he's hurt badly."

Noah dug his hands into his hair, as if trying to keep calm. "What do you need?"

A back board, an IV, a blood-pressure cuff, and how about a helicopter? She blew out a breath and fought for calm. Darrin's body lay at an ugly angle, and even from this position, Anne could see he had at least a broken leg, if not a skull fracture or a broken back. "We need to stabilize him so I can assess his wounds."

Still attached to his rope, Noah had rappelled down the cliff after Darrin, moving like lightning while Shelly, Latisha, and the rest of the campers screamed. Bucko tackled George, but he didn't have to pin him. The kid had gone weak with what he'd done. Completely ashen.

Katie had had the good sense to unhook Anne from the anchor rope so Anne could run down the path as fast as her hiking boots would carry her. Poor Noah was still barefoot from his dip in the water. She didn't want to guess what his feet looked like after running up the trail and scraping down a cliff.

She had found him kneeling next to Darrin, his face twisted with worry. She hadn't paused to try and assure him, not knowing what to say but fearing the worst.

"Listen," she said to Noah, the man who, ten minutes ago, had looked like a bona fide hero as he climbed up the cliff with a triumphant Darrin. How quickly life could explode. She kept her voice low and steady, hoping to keep him centered. "I don't know how badly he's hurt, but we need to get him to a hospital and fast. Call Dan. Have him send a chopper in."

Noah stood. "What else?"

"I need my medical kit. And a flashlight. And, let's see, a towel. We need to immobilize his spine."

"Oh no."

Anne stood and gripped Noah's shoulder. "It's just a precaution. I'll need sleeping bags, at least two, and sturdy poles—use paddles—to make a gurney." Her touch must have galvanized him, for the look in his eyes steadied. "I think his leg is broken. I need Bucko and Katie. Tell the others to stay away. The last thing we need is for the campers to go into shock."

Noah nodded. "I'll be right back."

"And, Noah—" she turned back to Darrin, her chest tight—"tell the others to pray."

He scrabbled away as she knelt and rubbed her knuckles

against Darrin's sternum. "C'mon, pal, give me a pain reflex."

Yes! The kid jerked involuntarily. So maybe his spine wasn't crushed. *Please, God, give me wisdom. Help me think.*

Katie ran up, the beam from her flashlight flickering against trees and the jagged rock face. She skidded to her knees and dropped the medical pack next to Anne. "How is he?"

Anne shook her head. She dug out her stethoscope and scissors and cut open Darrin's shirt. "Point the flashlight on his chest." Anne listened for sounds of breathing, abnormal heart rhythm. She probed his chest and his abdomen for spasms or broken ribs. "Give me the flashlight." She scanned his body, looking for darker patches that might indicate internal bleeding. "I don't know."

She handed the light back to Katie and leaned over Darrin, speaking loudly. "Darrin, can you hear me?" She opened his eyes. Reactive pupils. A hint of relief tugged at her.

Footsteps thumped down the path. Noah emerged, holding a flashlight angled away, lighting the path. His face was a mess of emotions, sweat dripped off his chin. "Is he still alive?"

"Yes." She grabbed the towel and dug in her kit for an Ace bandage. "Where's Bucko?"

"Here." His voice pushed through the foliage ahead of him. A second later he appeared, looking like a grizzly. She was instantly glad she hadn't been on top of the cliff, witnessing Bucko's confrontation with George.

"Okay, listen. We need to immobilize him, put him onto a board to keep him stable."

Silence.

She turned, seeing the fear on their stark faces. *Keep them busy.* "We can do this. I need you all to take deep breaths and do everything I say. Get me something to keep his spine straight." She looked at Noah and wished for a second that she could rewind time and cling to him one second longer, one more golden moment to strengthen them. "Where are the paddles? Katie, Noah, run and get all the paddles you can."

Noah dropped a towel at her feet, turned, and sprinted into the darkness. Anne heart's spiraled after him, wishing she could ease his pain.

She cut the towel, ripped it in half, folded it into a long rectangle, then eased it under Darrin's neck, winding it around as best she could, careful not to make it too tight. Then she unwound the Ace bandage and repeated the gesture.

Darrin didn't stir.

"Here are the paddles!" Katie burst out of the darkness, holding two paddles.

"Okay, listen. We've got to support his spine. We're going to turn him slowly so I can get one of these under him. Katie, you take his hips and keep him straight. Bucko, I need you on his chest. All hands at once, on the count of three."

Anne braced Darrin's head. "Please, God, make this smooth."

Bucko sucked in his breath, kneeling beside the broken Darrin.

"One. Two. Three."

In one slick movement, they rolled Darrin on his side. Anne had the paddle in place in seconds. "Roll back." They settled Darrin on the handle. Anne could hear Katie sniffle as Anne secured Darrin's head with medical tape. "Katie. We need more paddles. Four of them, at least, to make a back board. Go."

Katie wiped her tears on her sweatshirt and raced off into the night again.

Anne became more tortured with every moment Darrin stayed unconscious. "Wake up, pal, please."

"Are these enough?" Noah was back with a handful of paddles. Katie ran beside him, breathing like a windstorm.

"Yes." Anne rubbed her head, trying to think. "Make me a back board."

"Right." Noah dropped them on the ground with a clatter that made Anne wince. Moving like a man under fire, he shoved them side by side, four in a row, opposite ends together, with another at the top and bottom. "Will tape work?"

Anne handed him the medical tape, thankful to see the color had returned to his face. His expression was a grim line of fierceness that told her he wasn't going to let Darrin fade without a fight. "Leave room in the middle for the paddle along his spine."

Noah readjusted the paddles, then deftly taped them together.

"And a sleeping bag," Anne added.

He reached into the pile he'd dumped at Anne's feet earlier and tugged a bag out of a stuff sack.

"Good. He needs to keep warm." Anne helped him spread out the bag over the paddles. "Now, let's roll him on. Bucko? On three, again."

Katie and Bucko manned their positions, their faces strained. They rolled him again, this time settling the back board underneath him.

Anne felt a surge of relief when Darrin groaned. "Darrin? Buddy? Wake up." She tapped him lightly on the face. He didn't move. "I gotta take a look at his leg." It pained her to see the grotesque angle of his left leg. At best, a simple fracture; at worst, compound.

She cut open his pant legs and wanted to cry aloud at what she saw. His thigh was swollen nearly spherical in shape, the thigh muscles in spasm—obvious indications of a femur fracture. If she didn't splint it, with traction, the bone ends could overlap, dig into the muscle, and cause not only pain but more internal damage. Even if his neck wasn't broken and his organs weren't bleeding, this femur fracture could send the kid into shock and kill him.

"Darrin needs to be airlifted out." She left the "or he'll

die" part off but read in Noah's grim expression that he understood. Noah crouched beside her. He wore only his sweatshirt and swim shorts, and the night had laced the air with chill.

For the first time, she noticed her own damp clothes and started to shiver. "I need to get him into traction." She gripped Noah's shoulder. His tortured gaze found hers. "Call for help."

"I can't get a signal on the cell. I don't know what's wrong. When I came through here this spring it worked fine."

She refused to surrender to despair. "We can't carry him out, Noah. He won't make it. Not with that leg injury and the possible trauma to his spinal cord."

"I know." He stood up, a veritable wall of guts and desperation against the dark hues of night. "I'll go for help. Pastor Dan and some other volunteers from town are on standby. They'll be here as soon as I can get ahold of them. You just keep him alive."

Anne nodded.

Noah turned to go but stopped at Bucko. "Get the kids together and pray. I'll be back with help to take them all home."

Noah had done two things right. He'd found his boots and he'd grabbed a flashlight. As the night sky pressed down on him and a million eyes watched him paddle across the inky lake into the darkness ahead, Noah fought the demons roaring about his soul.

Why hadn't he seen it coming? Anne surely had. Thundercloud Annie. He grimaced at the way he'd teased her. She'd warned him from the first that these street kids couldn't shake their colors. Not their gang colors at least. He wanted to scream, to punch something hard. Instead, he

forced power into his paddling and prayed with every stroke.

He nearly ran with his canoe up the stairway portage, the link between Rose and Hungry Jack Lakes. He made record time across the second lake, adrenaline numbing his body against the cold and ache in his shoulders.

Please, God, don't let Darrin die!

Noah rammed his canoe onto the shore. Throwing his paddle onto shore, he climbed out. Before he hoisted the canoe, he dug out his cell phone. *Please, work. Please. I need a signal.*

The phone had juice . . . and as the light blinked on, praise God, the signal flickered. He turned and the signal kicked in. Noah dialed with shaky hands, guessing it was about midnight.

"Hello?" Dan's voice, groggy, but so beautifully clear.

"Dan, it's me. We've had an accident."

Thank the Lord, Dan was a man of action. As a volunteer firefighter, he knew how to jump-start his common sense and make a frontal attack on a problem. As a pastor, he did it bathed in prayer.

"Where are you?"

"I'm on the Hungry Jack portage, headed toward Bearskin Lake. I need a helicopter. Can you call Dr. Simpson?" From his research, he knew Deep Haven had one very ancient medical chopper, an early BO-105 Eurocopter donated by Duluth's St. Margaret's Hospital. "One of our campers is down, and I need him airlifted now."

"Right. Okay. What campsite?"

"We're at the cliffs on Rose Lake."

Dan's silence hurt. "Okay," he said softly. "Consider it done. I'll meet you at the Bearskin put-in."

Noah nearly ran the portage to Bearskin Lake. Kneeling in the middle of his canoe, he paddled until his arms burned and sweat beaded along his spine. The night wind, frigid and suddenly violent, tangled his hair and fought his progress. He leaned into the breeze, smelling storm. *Please, God, protect them. Give Anne wisdom.*

What would he have done without her? She'd attacked the tragedy like a she-bear, a direct assault on death. Relief swept through Noah when she ordered him to get paddles. His utter helplessness had almost knocked him to his knees.

Thank the Lord, the churches had demanded her presence. Obviously others had seen past his enthusiasm to the realities of dragging twenty gangbangers out of the hood and into the wilderness. Seen the danger. The foolishness. One of them had been Anne. Why hadn't he listened to her?

Noah plowed into the water, his own stupidity fueling his efforts. Anne had been totally correct, and if he had half a brain he would have listened to her warnings. Hope had fogged his common sense, waved him off like a red flag to a bull. He'd certainly charged right into danger.

Just like he'd charged right into a relationship with a lady who didn't want him. *Wanted,* she'd said. Past tense verb. Even though she'd kissed him, told him she loved him, it didn't mean she would follow him back to her nightmares. He couldn't ask that of her. He hadn't stopped to think what his profession would do to a woman simply seeking peace. Hadn't she told him that night as he stood on the porch of her little cottage that all she wanted was somewhere safe to live?

Oh, what an idiot. A heartless, selfish jerk. He'd kissed her. He'd wanted more. All she had to give. But what was he willing to give her? His future? His profession? His calling?

His chest clenched at the thought. At the agony of wanting someone so badly and knowing that he couldn't have her. Not unless God released him from his commitment. Not unless he surrendered everything he was, everything he'd hoped to accomplish.

Then again, so far what had he accomplished? The list seemed pretty pathetic. He'd managed to endanger the lives of twenty kids, to trap a young woman into facing her

worst fears, and to permanently scar the barely beating organ in his chest.

The worst part was that he'd done it all without telling Anne how he felt. How he longed to be near her, just to see her smile, every moment of the day. How, when he thought about the future, he couldn't imagine her not in it, working so in tune with him that he wouldn't know where he stopped and she started. *I love you.* Yes, it had been on the edge of his lips, bubbling out from the most terrified, most hopeful recesses of his heart. He loved her—utterly, hopelessly, forever.

He'd known it the day she'd floored it into his camp, spent the day helping him construct his dreams, and sat with him in front of a crackling fire. Knew, even then, that Anne Lundstrom was the miracle he'd been waiting for his entire life.

But before he'd been able to force out the truth, lay his heart out in the open, she'd looked at him, her love clear and full and beckoning in her eyes, and he'd melted. He'd let his emotions run right over his words, and he'd kissed her. Without promises. Without any verbal vulnerability.

Oh, he was a real winner.

And he shouldn't forget—she was afraid of him. Or at least had been. She'd never answered him, and for some reason that omission sliced through him. Wanted. Afraid. Right now, their future seemed as iffy as Darrin's life.

The shore loomed closer, a dent in the haze of black treescape. Noah arrowed for it.

Maybe this accident was a giant "get real" from God. Noah Standing Bear, wake up and smell the looming antiseptic. Anne Lundstrom had a future here . . . Noah did not. If this accident didn't make that painfully clear, he hated to guess what God would use to get his attention. All he needed now was for his campers to draw lines in the dirt and drag out the Glocks they'd probably brought along and hidden in their packs.

Trust Me. The words beat inside him, keeping tune with

his pounding heart. Noah's throat thickened, unable to scrape up a response. It wasn't God who was inadequate . . . it was him.

It suddenly became as clear as the stars overhead. Noah should cut his losses and run. He should head south to the only job he'd had that he could do—and do well—and not try to be someone he wasn't. He should leave Anne to find her peaceful life in Deep Haven, one she sorely deserved, and exit her life before he caused her even more pain.

Headlights appeared on the landing. Noah recognized Dan's SUV. Dan shut off the lights, then got out, a fuzzy shadow of worry pacing the shoreline.

Noah couldn't let Dan see the failure written all over his face. The pastor would find out soon enough. Maybe Noah would be able to sell the canoes back to Courageous Outfitters. The lake property would probably rent to someone else quickly.

He already missed the smell of the forest, the call of loons across the lake. Already missed Anne's beautiful face in the soft glow of a campfire, as she tried to roast a marshmallow to perfection.

"Noah?" Dan's voice rang across the water. Noah lifted his paddle, then glided the canoe in. Dan caught the bow. "Chopper's on the way."

25

Anne felt a hand on her shoulder, dragging her out of her exhausted slumber into the hues of daylight. She lifted her head off Darrin's hospital bed. She'd fallen asleep in the padded chair next to his bed. The cotton sheets had embedded the wrinkles of sleep on her face. Grimy, bone-weary, and cold, she leaned easily into the one-arm hug Sandra proffered. "How are you doing this morning, kiddo?"

Anne cast a look at her patient. Swallowed in a cast up to his hip, with an oxygen mask strapped to his sleeping, oh-so-young face, Darrin was a picture of a miracle. Relief, or perhaps exhaustion, waxed Anne's eyes with moisture.

"I'm okay." She cast a look at her filthy clothes and grimaced. "I need a hot shower, my fleece sweatpants, wool socks, and a hot cup of tea."

Sandra laughed. Dressed in a lavender top and a pair of sensible white shoes, she emanated sanity and peace.

"It's good to be back in civilization," Anne added.

Sandra patted her shoulder. "Dan and some of the church members went in with Noah this morning to bring the campers back. With the adults at the stern, they should be home tonight."

"I'll bet the kids are pretty shook up. You should have seen their faces last night when the rescue team came in. Real-life heroes in the backwoods. Noah would have used it in a Soul Talk."

Sandra hummed, taking Darrin's pulse. She put his wrist down and adjusted his covers. The boy was still sleeping, but thank the Lord, he'd roused briefly around 2 A.M. when the rescue team hoisted him into the helicopter. Anne nearly collapsed in relief when the airlift team took over, established an IV line in Darrin, wrapped her in a blanket, and helped her into the helicopter. Sensitive to the fear of the surrounding campers, they'd even allowed Latisha to hug her brother.

Latisha had whispered a prayer before they'd ferried Darrin away, one that seeded Anne's heart with hope. "I pray the Lord my soul to keep . . ." Latisha barely choked out the last words, but Anne finished them with her. "And if I should die before I wake, I pray the Lord my soul to take."

But Darrin didn't die. His unsaved soul was still earthbound, not quite ready for its eternal destiny.

As if affirming it, Darrin had awakened midflight. On a fresh wash of morphine, he was coherent enough to tell Anne that riding in the helicopter was a "total bomb" and gave her a half grin.

That grin went right to her heart. She wished Noah had seen it. Poor guy didn't even know that Darrin not only survived but had let her pray for him as he drifted off to unconsciousness again.

Anne stood, stretched. Sunlight trumpeted through the windows along the sterile whites of the hospital room. It was a gorgeous Deep Haven summer day. Out on the Boundary Water lakes, the sunlight would be skipping off the ripples like diamonds kissing Anne's nose. The wind would carry with it the perfume of creation.

As Anne stared out into the parking lot at the sparseness of cars, she couldn't help but picture Noah, his strong arms paddling against the wind, his dark hair scraped back from his face, and his jaw set with a smattering of whiskers that only accentuated his dangerous, warrior aura. She couldn't wait to wrap her arms around him and tell him that Darrin was okay. Because Noah had refused to give up, to let an accident turn to tragedy.

Wasn't that the story of Noah's life? Foster kid, alone in the world, snagged by the lure of the gangs, fed by the intoxication of money, power. He'd gone to jail . . . and God had turned the street hood into a man with a heart for the kids he'd left behind.

Anne wished suddenly that she could embrace his vision. All of it, including his headfirst dive into the battle for the street. She felt so ensnared in fear that she couldn't possibly survive one battle, let along dodge the daily land mines that littered these kids' lives.

She glanced at Darrin, at his still unwhiskered face. Innocent in sleep, nothing remained of the raging bull she'd seen attack his buddy on the rock cliff. He'd scared her with the darkness in his eyes and the hatred in his cry, even if he'd been defending his sister.

In that gut-wrenching moment, she'd recognized herself. Darkness in her eyes, hatred in her cry. Even if it was self-defense, hadn't she hated these kids and all they represented? Had Noah looked into her eyes and seen darkness? She shivered at the thought.

How could she not have seen the lost, desperate children? Underneath their feet-planted, arms-folded, jaws-jutted, pierced exteriors lurked children who needed to know that they weren't forgotten. They weren't trash to be tossed into the streets for the gangs to scrape up and destroy. They were loved by Christ, and He could take even the stoniest heart and turn it into a soft, pliable organ.

It rocked her how much she wanted to see that happen. She longed to see Shelly fall to her knees and embrace her Savior. She ached to see Darrin grab on to salvation and become the man of God she knew he could be.

But how could she ever be a part of their future if she were locked away in Deep Haven?

Anne put a hand to her chest, pushed hard against her rising thoughts. *No. God, my life is here. You know that. I've been through enough. How can You even ask me to return? You know what life is like. It's dangerous and harsh and ugly. And I'm through suffering.* The deep pang of emptiness in her soul made her want to cry.

Sandra was inspecting the traction on Darrin's leg. Anne turned away from the window. "I feel like a hobo. I don't suppose you could get me a pair of scrubs?"

"Not a problem. I think I can even track down some shampoo and clean socks. Go sack out in that other bed. The bed count is light, and that one is yours."

Anne gave her friend a grateful smile.

The shower washed off a week of fatigue. Anne even managed a song, a hymn that had been pressing against her thoughts and now spiraled out, off-tune and glorious.

"When peace like a river attendeth my way, when sorrows like sea-billows roll; whatever my lot, Thou hast taught me to say, 'It is well, it is well with my soul.'"

The words reverberated through her like thunder, and she braced her hands against the shower stall in a sudden gasp. Was all well with her soul?

Something certainly felt different, as if in the past week—especially in the past twenty-four hours—a tendril of hope had pushed through the dry, cold soil of her heart. Something big and precious was about to bloom. Perhaps the beauty of windswept creation had burrowed into her soul, giving her the peace she'd longed for. Or maybe it was more. Maybe it was the realization that God had heard her unspoken prayers and had given her a man who would sacrifice even his dreams for her. She could hardly believe that Noah was the man who'd fringed her thoughts for over a year—the man with the voice of silk, the touch of tenderness. God had brought him back into her world.

Surely that meant God was finally on her side, finally

going to hold her in His hand and let her build a life of peace, nestled in the arms of the man she loved.

So what that Noah hadn't told her he loved her. She felt it and saw it in his heart-sweeping eyes.

So perhaps the little bloom in her heart was joy.

She hummed the rest of the song as she stepped out of the shower and tugged on the scrubs. Sandra was a true gem. She had even called down to the Footstep of Heaven and ordered a tea. Joe, the handsome author, had delivered it himself, with a hello from Mona, right before Anne escaped to the shower room. His warm smile made Anne remember the day she'd spent with them and their reminder that appearances could be deceiving.

Wasn't that the truth?

She returned to Darrin's room and was greeted by a hungry Darrin, slurping green Jell-O from his dinner tray. "Hey, ya."

"Yum." Anne winked at him. "Glad to see you got your appetite back."

"Want some?" He jiggled the bowl.

"Thanks, no." Anne cupped her hands around the mug of tea and sat in the chair. "How are you feeling?"

"Are you kidding? I think I should be feeling like I got hit by a Mack truck, but that old lady nurse gave me something and I'm feeling righto."

Anne sipped her tea. "Don't get used to it, pal. It's just until the healing process starts. But I'm glad you're feeling better."

"Yo, man. I wonder if you can buy this stuff."

"Percocet? Prescription only."

"No, Anne, I mean on the street. Like, I wonder what the street value is."

"I don't even want to guess." Anne reached over and checked his oxygen level: 20 percent. His lungs, thankfully, had been clear. The oxygen was purely to ward off shock. "Listen, don't even talk that way. Drugs aren't to be messed with, even these. People's lives can be ruined by any kind of addiction, even to prescription drugs."

Darrin finished his Jell-O, sipping the last bit loudly into his mouth. "I know."

"Yeah, well, do you know you're a lucky young man?" Anne rolled the food tray away. "You could have died out there."

Darrin played with the controls on his bed, raising, lowering. The mechanical bed hummed as the boy measured her words, evidenced by the hard look on his face.

Finally, he motored the bed back up and looked out the window. The sun had started to set, pushing the hospital shadow into the parking lot. Already the stark whites of the room had begun to gray. "I know. Thanks for saving my life."

Anne finished the last of her tea, then set the mug down, not looking at him. "It wasn't me. Noah paddled out and got help."

Silence. "He's full of surprises."

"Why are you surprised? He cares about you." Anne arched one brow, amazed that the kid couldn't see that.

Darrin didn't meet her gaze. "Yeah, I guess so . . ." He picked at his covers. "But I mean, why? He won't let it alone. He's like a pit bull. Chases me down after school, hounds me to hang with him."

"He doesn't want you to make the same mistakes he made."

Darrin harrumphed. "I ain't making no mistakes."

"Really?" Anne pursed her lips, weighing her words. "Like nearly killing yourself on a dare?"

Darrin shrugged.

Anne bit back a spurt of anger. These kids faced rage every day. They knew how to dodge it. She fought to be calm, compassionate, so that her words might find fertile soil. "You almost died. Twice. Noah risked his neck both times for you. Not only because he cares about you and wants to keep you out of the gangs but because he knows

that God has a great plan for your life and you're about to throw it away, just like you feel thrown away."

Darrin's eyes turned glossy.

"Darrin, what happened to your dad was an awful thing. It wasn't fair. But God doesn't deal in fair. He deals in hope. When life crashes around you, you can either hold on to hope or sink. And you're sinking. Fast. Noah's trying to keep your head above water until you decide to reach for God."

"And what's God going to give me?" The voice was tough, but under the layer of contempt simmered desperation.

"A new life. One with purpose. One with strength. One with hope." *One with love.* She blinked at her own words, wondering for the first time if she too hadn't been sinking. Had she let go of God's hope in that darkest hour only to drown in self-pity? Had Noah been trying to keep her afloat with his comments about hope until she reached for God? The thought stunned her, made her tingle.

Was this where she found joy when life assaulted her? By hanging tighter and finding that God reached down and hauled her out of the grasp of darkness?

She fought to keep her voice steady instead of betraying the tears filling her throat. "Noah told you about his past. That he'd been a Vice Lord. Did he tell you he also went to jail?"

Darrin shrugged.

"Then you know he could be doing hard time if God hadn't grabbed his heart and changed his life. Now he's got a purpose, happiness, goals, and—"

"You." Darrin interjected.

Anne felt a blush press against her face. She nodded. "That's right. He's got me. God can do all that for you too, Darrin. But you have to trust Him. You have to let Him change you, from the inside out. That starts with forgiveness. Start at the bottom and let God raise you up."

Let Him rescue you from the pit of despair and darkness.

A tear escaped, and she whisked it away. But Darrin wasn't watching. "I really miss my dad. I keep hoping that . . . that . . . he's in heaven." Tears glistened on his face when he looked up, thick drops of grief that reminded her that this young man remained so much his father's boy.

Anne took his hands in hers. "If he is, you can join him someday. And between now and then, you don't have to live in grief and fear. You can live a good life with that hope in front of you. Turn your life over to Jesus, Darrin. Let Him forgive you and make you a new person."

Darrin released her hands and scrubbed his face with his palms. "I'm not sure I can keep from running with the gangs." His voice was muffled, as if not willing for her to hear his worst fears.

"You can. With God's courage and strength, you can. I know that when you need Him the most, God will be there to rescue you."

Her words hung in the room, sifted against the hiss of the oxygen being pumped into Darrin's lungs. God had been there when they'd needed Him yesterday. And the day before . . . as far back as she could recall, every day of her life. Even the day she'd been shot, God had been there in the song and touch of a man she'd grown to love. He had been there as she'd dodged pranksters in school, as she'd struggled to finish her internship, as she'd fought for a new life.

"He'll rescue you," she repeated, this time to herself.

Darrin bit his lip. She didn't comment on the tears streaming down his dark, desperate face. Then he nodded. "If Noah really was the person he says, then I want God to change me too."

She had returned and made him hope again. Head in her arms, hair splayed out like a halo, his own rescuing angel.

Just in time.

He walked down the hall, his sterile prison, loathing the pinch of antiseptic, the telephone shrilling, death embedding the rose-papered walls.

His death.

But she'd returned, and if he stayed smart, ignored the sneers from the past, he'd be free. Finally. Dues paid.

A rush of desperation rattled through him, shaking out his muscles.

She held the key to his freedom.

He needed her.

Now.

"Are you sure you want to do this?" Granny D.'s raspy voice, weary from her wee-morning activities preparing breakfast and packing bag lunches, deciphered Noah's thoughts.

Noah crossed his arms over his chest and pushed back a wave of regret. Yes, he wanted to do this. Had to do this. Should have done it weeks ago. "Yes."

He watched as Shelly lugged her duffel bag to the center of the compound and pushed it into the pile of ratty suitcases and army duffel bags. Her shoulders were bowed, and somehow the disappointment on her young face salved the ache in Noah's chest. At least some of the kids were going to miss this place.

Stepping off the porch, he strode toward Bucko before his emotions could manhandle him. "You sure you can handle driving these kids home?"

Bucko looked as sleep-deprived as Noah felt. Bags of exhaustion hung under his red-streaked eyes. His massive, slumped shoulders betrayed the beating they'd taken yesterday muscling the campers, the canoes, and all the gear back to camp. Noah's entire staff deserved a long vacation in the tropics or at least in some five-star hotel equipped with a hot tub and sauna. Troopers with a capital *T,* they'd also unpacked their gear and prepared the kids for their trip home.

"Yep." Bucko slapped Noah's back; his knees nearly buckled. "Don't worry, boss. We'll get them home safely."

Noah nodded, his chest tight.

Bucko gave him a grim look. "Are you going to the hospital?"

"Later." Much later, after Anne was long gone. He owed her a debt of gratitude, but he couldn't face her after all she'd done and tell her it was over.

Wilderness Challenge had folded.

As soon as he could pack his gear, clean the kitchen, take down the tents, and lock up the outfitter's shack, he was headed to Minneapolis.

Back to his life. The one he should have never left.

Sure, Wilderness Challenge had been a credible idea—on paper and in his mind as he had sat in the Sculpture Garden and dreamed of lives being changed, of street kids bringing home hope from the north woods—but reality was flesh and broken bones and blood.

He noticed George dump his stuff into the pile of baggage and went over to talk to him. George still had a heart of flesh, evidenced by the silent horror of his actions. Thankfully, Bucko kept him close, and the rest of the campers were warned to keep their hands off and mouths shut. Noah still didn't know what to do with the kid. God had spared Darrin, and now Noah desperately wanted second chances for them all.

"How are you, pal?"

George shrugged, turned away.

"Listen, I'll see you round, okay?" Noah held out his hand. George stared at it. Noah didn't comment on the sadness in the kid's eyes. Slowly George slipped his hand into Noah's grip and gave him a limp shake. Well, hope had to start somewhere. "Super."

Latisha stumbled up, under the weight of a duffel bag. "I'm all packed but ain't goin' home. Not with my brother in the hospital." Her jutted chin told Noah she still packed a dangerous amount of attitude.

She'd been sneaking out with George on the sly, something they both admitted to later. Something Noah dearly hoped Darrin would never know.

What other things had been going on behind Noah's very naive back?

He found a compassionate voice, willing to take some guff from her, knowing she was torn up with guilt. "Latisha, Bucko needs your help with your mother. Keep her calm. Help get her packed. Bucko will bring you both back here in a few days to see Darrin. He'll be fine, and when I get to the hospital, I'll have him call home. I've already talked to your mother, and she needs you."

"Just so you know that I'm going to be back." Her chin began to quiver.

"I'm not going to tell Darrin about you and George." Noah lowered his voice. "That's your business."

The relieved smile she gave him nearly broke his heart.

"I'll see you in a couple days, okay?"

She nodded. "Thanks, Noah. Until yesterday, it was a great summer."

He yearned to agree with her. Yes, parts of it had been spectacular—the camaraderie, the Soul Talks, the wonder of the campers as they beheld God's creation up close and personal. The magic of meeting Anne. Oh yes, it had been the best—and most painful—summer of his life.

As if to remind him of everything he'd lost, Bertha bounded up, followed by three of Ross's campers. "She's got my shoe!"

Noah caught the dog's collar, the momentum nearly ripping off his arm. "Whoa there, honey." He grabbed the Nike in Bertha's mouth, wrenched it free, and tossed the slobbery mess to the kid. "Yum."

The smile the boys returned said Bertha had made a hit. As had Anne. She had been elevated to some kind of superwoman after her EMT save of Darrin. Noah's heart twisted. Oh, how he wanted to see her dive into these kids' lives . . . she obviously had the touch. Had the compassion, the kindness, the skill . . .

All she lacked was the guts.

That was something he couldn't help her with. He would never ever, not in a million painful years, leverage his love to get her to move to Minneapolis with him.

It was better that she never knew how he felt. That he'd wanted her beside him more than he wanted to breathe. But she'd come to Deep Haven to find peace, and he wasn't about to destroy that by pulling on her heartstrings. Even if he did manage to convince her that she'd be safe, it would only take the first drive-by shooting for her commitment to shatter. No, if he had any hope of Anne in his future, God would have to put her there. Wholly committed. Wholly at peace. Wholly trusting in His grace to be sufficient to conquer her fears.

He wouldn't hold his breath. Not after scraping open her scars and giving her fears new ammunition. She deserved more than anyone to live a life in a war-free zone.

Noah watched the kids load their belongings into the bus. His heart felt as if it had been bludgeoned.

Katie helped Shelly toss her gear into the back of the bus and hugged the young woman. Tears streaked down Katie's cheeks. She held Shelly at arm's length and mouthed, "I'll call you."

Noah smiled. So the camp would close. Maybe God had other plans. Still, standing in the middle of his crumpled dreams, Noah fought to see how. "Katie, could you come here?"

Katie winked at Shelly, then sauntered over. "What's up, boss?"

Noah looked away. "Can you gather up Anne's stuff and bring it down to the hospital? Take Bertha too."

Katie narrowed her eyes. "Why? Aren't you going?"

"Of course." If he had his druthers, he'd be gunning down the Gunflint Trail right now, not only to check on

Darrin but to hand his heart to the woman he loved, beg her to come to Minneapolis to join his lifework. And they'd get about as far as Duluth before he'd come to his senses and realize he was dragging her back to the lions' den. "I have some things to do at camp first." *Liar, liar.*

Katie's expression told him she knew exactly what he was thinking. Her silence made him shift, swallow. "What?" he said.

"Tell her yourself."

"What?" He pursed his lips. Did she read minds too?

"Tell her that you're quitting. Tell her that, after everything she's worked for this summer, the camp is cancelled. Kaput. I dare you."

Noah studied his boots. "Okay, you're right. I'm a giant coward." He gritted his teeth. "I don't want to see her because . . . because if I do, I know I'm going embarrass us both. I want her to come to Minneapolis so badly it hurts. But if I tell her that . . ."

"She's liable to agree." Katie nodded. "And, excuse me for being blind, but where's the tragedy in that?"

"She's worked for years to move here and start a new life, and she's never going to—"

"Give it up for a guy like you?"

Ouch. Noah flinched, angry that Katie could read him so easily.

"Listen, Noah, I don't know what you see when you look in the mirror, but Anne sees a man of honor. A man of courage."

"You don't know everything."

She laughed. "I know what she said. She said she thought you were a great guy. In fact, I'd even guess that she's in love with you."

Noah clenched his jaw against a rush of pain. *Thanks, Katie; that's a big help.*

"Anne's a smart woman," Katie continued, her voice rising. "Let her decide what she wants to do. If you don't ask, you'll never know."

Noah closed his eyes and shook his head. "I can't ask."

Katie sighed. "Then you'll never know."

"I know what her answer would be." Best-case scenario involved tears and heartache. And wouldn't that be fun for both of them? He ran his hand through his hair. "Please pack her stuff. Take her dog down and tell her . . . tell her good-bye for me."

If looks could kill, he'd be a smoking pile of cinders.

"Fine. But don't you ever complain about being alone, because I'll be around to remind you that you had the woman of your dreams right here, and you blew it."

26

Shh. She's sleeping."

Anne roused at the harsh sibilant sounds and tried to place the voice outside the drawn curtain. Katie. Verbal sunshine. She hadn't seen the staffer since waving good-bye in the wee hours from an aerial and oh-so-frightening view of the cliffs while riding in the helicopter.

Anne felt as if she'd been mowed down by a wrecking ball. Her hair had dried on the pillow, and as she sat up she could actually feel it rising from her scalp in an askew halo. She rubbed her eyes; her stomach roared to life and growled. She'd slept long—late afternoon hued the room in shadow, dim rays slanting through the blinds and lining the tile floor.

"How are you feeling?" Katie asked Darrin as Anne whisked the curtain aside. Katie glanced at her, guilt on her face.

"I was awake," Anne said as she finger combed her hair. "Although I know I don't look it." She slid off the bed. The tile against her bare feet sent a cold jolt to her brain.

Katie grinned, but sadness edged her eyes. "You're a sight for sore eyes." She patted Darrin's head in the next bed. "As are you, pal. You scared the wits out of us."

Darrin shrugged, but a blush touched his face. Anne could hardly believe how his heart had softened in a mere twenty-four hours. She bit her tongue and rocked on her toes, itching to tell Katie the good news.

Darrin was a new creation in Christ. Saved. Transformed.

Just wait until Noah found out. The thought put a silly grin on her face.

Katie sat down in a nearby chair. "Latisha will be here soon. She's heading home with the rest of the campers today. Bucko will drive your mom and her back tomorrow."

"The campers are leaving?" Anne said, panic in her voice. She fought to hide her dismay. Noah wasn't sending everyone home, was he? After they'd fought to open the camp, after Darrin's life had been transformed? "Why?"

Katie sighed. Her eyes told Anne everything, including how she felt about the decision. "He asked me to bring your gear down. It's in the car, along with Bertha."

Anne tried not to gape, but she felt as if she'd been slugged. Noah had tossed her out on her ear without a thank you . . . or an I love you. She blinked back the tears biting her eyes. "Um . . . thanks." She smoothed her scrubs, dying to ask Katie if Noah was on the bus, heading south . . . taking her heart with him.

How could he just leave? Turn his back on Wilderness Challenge, on his dreams, his kids . . . on her?

Her chin quivered, and she turned away, listening to Katie answer Darrin's questions about the campers. Of course Noah could leave. She might be wildly crazy about him, but he didn't love her. What a fool she'd been, declaring her heart. She'd practically taken it out and pinned it to her sleeve for him to wallop. Oh sure, he'd been kind; he'd made her think his feelings mirrored her own. Perhaps she'd mistaken the emotions in his eyes . . . perhaps it had been pity.

Her heart felt like an anvil in her chest. Yes, of course.

He'd seen her fall. He'd seen her bleed. Without knowing it, he'd dragged her right into the middle of her fears. Of course he felt guilty. And sorry for her.

Pity. Noah didn't love her. He was simply trying to shore up her emotions. All those tender looks, those nights sitting in front of the campfire listening to the song of the forest had been nothing more than Standing Bear pep talks.

Good thing she was in a hospital. She felt as if he'd torn her heart right out of her chest and stomped on it.

She turned to Darrin and Katie and interrupted them. "Excuse me. I'm going to go get something to eat." As if she could put anything in her pitching stomach. But she needed to move around.

She strode out of the room and down the hall, her body stiff and heavy as if moving through mud. At least she hadn't told Noah she'd follow him into his dreams. At least she hadn't sacrificed her future for his affection and pity.

She slumped into a chair at the end of the hallway and buried her face in her hands, fighting tears.

"Anne, honey? You okay?" Sandra sat beside her, materializing like an angel. "You look wrung out."

Anne forced a smile. "You're looking pretty ragged yourself. What's this, thirty-six-hour shifts?"

Sandra had bags under her eyes, and her shoulders carried a weight of exhaustion. Even her uniform looked like it had seen better days. She leaned her head against the wall and closed her eyes. "I got a catnap at the nurses' station. But we're short on nurses and Kelly called in sick this morning."

"They can't expect you to stay on."

Sandra didn't open her eyes. She just shook her head in a silent editorial.

"Listen, you go and get some sleep. I'll watch the floor for you." Anne reached for Sandra's stethoscope. "I feel fresh, although I may not look it." Maybe a few hours tending patients would drag her mind off her own fatal wounds.

Sandra leaned forward, bracing her elbows on her knees. Her voice sounded ancient, distant. "Are you sure?"

"Yes. Go. I'll get my ID badge."

Sandra closed her eyes as Anne ran down to the lounge, retrieved her badge and keys from her locker, and punched in. On her way back to the ER, she noticed a new picture hanging on the wall, an updated view of the Deep Haven lighthouse. So Garth Peterson hadn't been lurking around town in pretense while he mugged nurses at night. Anne allowed herself a moment of shame that she'd suspected him.

"Meds are due soon." Sandra angled her a weary look when Anne returned. "We only have three patients, but you'll need to do rounds in a few minutes."

"I can handle it. Let's do charts."

Sandra trudged over to the nurses' desk and grabbed the list of patients and trolley of charts. "Do you still have your keys?"

Anne jangled the keys in her hand and nodded.

"My guess is that they'll confiscate them after your shift. New policy is to only have one set per floor." She handed hers over to Anne. "Lock these up, please."

"Don't tell me they're still losing meds?"

Sandra shrugged. "Could be clerical, but Chief Sam has been prowling around like a lion. He thinks there's a connection between the missing meds and the attacks on nurses."

Anne tried not to imagine Peterson's soft hands on thin throats. She obviously had to work on her propensity to falsely accuse strangers. "How is Jenny, by the way?"

Sandra perched her hands on her hips and stretched. "Recovering. But it will take a while for her to shake the emotional wreckage from the attack." Sandra's eyes spoke her sympathy. Anne understood too well what kind of road Jenny would have to tread to find her way back to the living.

As Anne went over the patients' charts with Sandra, the twenty-bed unit became as quiet as a church on Tuesday.

Sandra finally crept into an empty room, and Anne made sure the door was closed.

Anne couldn't escape the feeling of loneliness as she locked up Sandra's keys, then slouched at the nurses' station, counting down minutes until rounds. She flipped through the charts: Mildred Larson, recovering from a myocardial infarction; Olin Karlstrom, in for a double bypass surgery. She checked their meds, then went in search of the med cart to fill the orders.

The pharmaceutical closet smelled faintly of antiseptic and plastic. The scent of medical science at its best and worst. So many different drugs. It made Anne both grateful and leery. She never escaped the sense of responsibility when she measured out the medicines. The wrong dose could kill.

She prepared the meds, levered the cart out of the closet, locked the door, and wheeled it down the hall. She knocked in warning, then entered Mrs. Larson's room. Anne hated to rouse the sleeping woman, but missing her meds would be worse than losing rest. Gently she took the woman's pulse, recorded it, then slipped on the blood-pressure cuff. By the time she'd recorded the results, Mrs. Larson had groaned and started a litany of complaints.

"Let me get your temperature; then I'll give you your meds."

The elderly woman grumbled but opened her mouth.

Anne took her temperature, then handed the woman the small container of pills and some water. Mrs. Larson drank them down with gusto. Anne checked her incision. "I think you'll be ready to head home soon."

"I hope so. My bones are weary of being in this bed all day, and I have a garden to tend."

"Oh, that sounds lovely." Anne took a peek at the remains of the woman's lunch, recorded it, then wheeled the med cart to the door. "What do you grow?"

"Tomatoes and squash. Some peppers. The growing

season is so short up here, they need all the lovin' they can get."

"I'm sure your plants miss you."

"Best garden I ever had was in north Minneapolis. Just a little inch of land, but my tomatoes grew like weeds. And the zucchini! Couldn't give them away. Here I barely get enough to make a decent loaf of bread."

Anne cradled the chart in her arms. The elderly woman's complexion improved as she talked. "Hmm."

"The ground's too cold up here to grow anything decent. I love the north country, but I sure do miss my little patch of garden. Sorry to give that up when I moved here. The tomatoes don't taste the same." The woman folded her hands on her blanket. "But I suppose when you choose one thing over another, you always lose something."

Anne nodded. "I'll be by to check on you later." She nearly ran out of the room.

"Whoa, Anne!" Dr. Jefferies caught her shoulders before she plowed into him.

"Sorry." Anne fought her beating heart and smiled at the doctor. He looked slightly disheveled today, as if he'd been jogging or working outside. His brown hair tangled in a mass, and definite lines etched his usually clear face. Sweat beaded his forehead. His gaze darted past her, down the empty hall, and back. "I need to get into the supply closet. Seems that I left my scrubs at home and I need a new pair." He smiled, but she noticed the edge of his lips quiver.

"Are you on today?" The chart had listed Dr. Simpson as the doctor on duty, although she hadn't seen him yet.

Dr. Jefferies nodded quickly. "And I'm late. Can I borrow the keys?"

Anne pulled the keys out of her smock pocket and dropped them in his palm. "I'll be down in room 102."

He turned and strode down the hall, around the corner.

Olin Karlstrom quizzed Anne for ten minutes on his upcoming surgery. The poor man looked pasty and she didn't like the hue of his lips. She took his pulse and made a note to track down Dr. Simpson.

Wheeling the medical cart out of the room, Anne headed toward Darrin's room. The soft click of a door closing made her pulse jump. She stopped and scanned the hall. Nothing but the ticking of the overhead clock and her own paranoid heartbeat.

She rolled the cart down to Darrin's room. Katie had the kid in stitches, retelling some story about Bucko wrestling two Duluth packs.

"Time for your meds."

Darrin shot her a wicked grin and sat up. Anne gave him a mock glare as she took his vitals. "Listen up. After today, your dosages go down. The last thing you need, believe me, is to get addicted to these." She spilled the pills into his palm and gave him a drink. He sucked them down.

"Are you on duty?" Katie asked.

Anne nodded. "Sandra is whipped. I was going to ask you if you could take Bertha over to my place. My aunt will keep an eye on her until I get home." She dug into her pocket to grab her house keys, then remembered she'd hooked them onto the floor keys. "Just a second; I'll run and get them."

Striding down the hall, it occurred to her that perhaps this moment delineated her future. Working endless shifts—double or single—in this tiny county hospital, taking pulses, administering meds. If she got lucky, she'd land Jenny's position and her world would expand to doing pregnancy tests and drug screenings at the Indian reservation.

Her heart suddenly weighed a million pounds.

One month ago the thought of living in this peaceful community gave her reason to rise each morning. It pumped hope into her veins, administered the grit to face rehabilitation, and supplied the energy to finish her internship. Nursing was a noble profession, worthy of every ounce of dedication. Hadn't she been desperately grateful for the nurses attending her while she clawed her way back to health?

But somehow this life dimmed in the face of all she'd seen recently. Shelly, craving for God's word. Latisha, laughing as she braided Katie's hair, precious trust rich in her voice. Darrin, crying as he confessed his sins and turned his life over to Jesus.

Spiritual nursing at its best.

The thought of spending her life dispensing the medicine of the gospel to these children sent a charge right to her soul. Never had she felt so alive, so pulsing with hope as she had this past month. Yes, facing these kids had nearly scared her out of her skin, but some sort of spiritual metamorphosis had changed her viewpoint. She'd seen past the tattoos and the body piercing to the aching, wounded souls within.

Perhaps this was how her father had felt that day as they sat at their kitchen table while the sun waxed it golden. His voice had shaken, his eyes alight, his very aura suggesting that they stood at the threshold of a great adventure, a life-altering purpose that would change their lives. And more.

Someone has to go, Anne.

These kids' souls needed tending from someone who understood their illnesses and the cure. Someone like Noah. Someone like Anne, who'd grown up among them. A street-toughened woman who faced their battles, in their language, and didn't surrender.

Someone with guts.

Anne marched down the hall with her hands fisted, wishing for the thousandth time that fear didn't streak through her every time she thought of Minneapolis. Wishing the past didn't imprison her, locking her away from the ministry she longed to dive into . . . from the man who already swam in those deep, dark waters.

She walked past the nurses' desk, down the corridor, and had just passed the medical closet when she heard . . . something coming from inside. A breath—no, heavy breathing. In. Out. Quickly.

The memory of the soft click of a door closing made her pause. She stood silently, listening to her heartbeat gather in her ears.

Again, breathing. Then the slap of something landing on the floor.

She grabbed the door handle and pushed it open.

Dr. Jefferies stood in the middle of the room. His brown eyes widened and he held a box of . . . Percocet?

"What are you doing?" Her voice sounded pitifully weak. She frowned at him to compensate.

His mouth opened. No sound fell out. Her heart jumped. This scene suddenly felt so . . . familiar. Perspiration beaded his forehead; his hands trembled.

She moved back.

Then his eyes narrowed. "Come in, Anne. Close the door behind you."

Yeah, right. Anne stiffened. Adrenaline pumped through her, and she told herself to run. Instead her eyes fixed on the doctor as he finished stuffing the box into a fanny pack around his waist. "You're stealing from the hospital."

His look told her he wasn't impressed with her assessment. "Come here."

Her head shook of its own accord. She felt for the door handle behind her with whatever feeling remained in her cold hand.

He took a step toward her. She noticed his pupils for the first time. Dilated. Black as night. He reached into his pocket, his gaze holding her like a steel trap. Her breath caught when a second later he pointed a gun at her nose. "Come here."

The air whooshed out of her.

No.

Not again.

"Help!" She flung the door open and ran. "Help!" The sound echoed down the sterile hall like a gunshot. "Help!" Her heartbeat thundered out before her.

"Anne!" Dr. Jefferies's voice came a breath behind her. "Stop."

Oh, sure. Anne's legs couldn't work fast enough. She rounded the nurses' station, heading toward the door—

He grabbed her hair.

"Ugh!" The pain speared right into her brain. Down her neck. Into her legs. They buckled and she fell to her knees.

He yanked her hair again. "Get up."

No. This was *not* happening to her again. She slammed her fist into his jaw. Pain exploded in her knuckles. "Ow!"

"C'mon," he growled. The man before her couldn't be the same person she'd sat beside in church, the man who had whizzed her around town in his Lexus. She stared at him dumbly.

"Anne, are you okay?"

Anne twisted around, crippled by his hold.

Katie stood in the hall, her eyes huge.

"Katie! Run!"

Anne heard Dr. Jefferies shout. Saw fear cascade across Katie's face. The gun whisked past her vision.

Katie whirled.

Ran.

When the gunshot shattered the air, Anne went dead inside.

27

The wind slicked Noah's sweaty skin as he drove down the Gunflint Trail to Deep Haven. His first stop after visiting Darrin would be the municipal pool. He needed a real shower if he intended to live with himself any longer.

He motored into the hospital parking lot and grimaced. Anne's dog, Bertha, had her massive head poked out of Katie's Mazda, completely dwarfing the driver's seat. She barked in hilarious greeting. Noah waved at the dog as he parked his bike, trying to keep his heart from settling into his knees.

Bertha's presence meant that Anne was still here. He'd have to face her and somehow confess that he'd failed her. He'd sucked her into a project that had burned to ash around them. He didn't want to think about the accompanying death of their future.

"Here, Bertha." He freed the dog. She jumped out, then slammed her huge paws on his chest. He nearly toppled over. "Okay, okay, I love you too." He rubbed the dog behind her ears while she slobbered his chin. "Go, run." Maybe killing a few minutes watching Bertha torment the seagulls would bolster his courage. He knew Anne wasn't going to give him the same reception. Not if Katie had delivered his message.

He folded his hands and tucked them behind his head, stretching. Bucko and the kids were probably past Hinckley by now. Their farewells, some with tears, tugged at his heart. He drew in a breath of the pine-scented air and tried to—

"Help!"

Noah whirled.

"Help!" Katie tore out of the hospital as if it were on fire. "Help!"

He sprinted toward her, caught her arms. "What's the matter?"

"Anne . . ." She hiccupped. Tears streaked her face. "Someone with . . . gun. Inside."

He didn't mean to shake her. "What? Is she hurt?"

Katie covered her mouth with her hand, terror in her eyes. "I don't know."

"Go. Call 911." He raced toward the building.

The utter silence in the hallway made him halt.

Swallow.

Breathe.

He cast a look toward the ER and saw a shadow move against the wall behind the nurses' station. "Anne?"

"No. It's Sandra." A head popped up. Fear emanated from her expression. "I saw him. He took her that way." She pointed, not steadily, down the hall the opposite direction as she ran toward him. "They went into a room. I don't know which one."

Noah grabbed her shaking hands. "Get out of here. Go."

Sandra tore out the front doors.

Noah stalked down the hall, nerves taut. Every instinct told him to burst into each room and mow down Anne's assailant with pure fury. He reined it in. It wouldn't help her if he got shot. *Lord, give me wisdom!*

He circled the nurses' station and ducked behind the

desk, listening. He heard muffled voices, one of them
Anne's.

"Is Katie dead?" Anne sat on a hospital bed, hands in the
surrender position, staring at Dr. Jefferies. He paced the
room from end to end like a caged tiger. She could hardly
believe that she'd once thought him handsome.

"I didn't want it this way, you know." His tone hovered
barely over a mutter. He stopped, looked at her with
reddened eyes. "I didn't have a choice."

"There are always choices."

He gave a sardonic laugh. "You don't know anything.
You don't know what it's like to be . . . trapped." His
speech started to slur. "I just want him to stop. Hurting.
Me."

She kept her voice soft. "Who's hurting you?"

He shook his head, his eyes wild.

Anne watched Dr. Jefferies draw into the fetal position
and morph as if suddenly a child, a terrified child.
"Doctor?" She eyed the door. *Right now. Run!*

He snapped up his head, his face twisted. "Don't. Move."
He smiled, looking like a wolf. "Are you afraid? Get in line,
Anne. The world feeds on fear. It's all around us, pulsating,
waiting to devour." He burst out in insane hilarity.

She gulped back a paralyzing spurt of terror. "And
getting strung out and killing me is going to destroy that
fear?"

He stumbled, then leaned against the wall. "I'm fine." He
slumped down. "Just fine." He angled the gun at her; it
wavered in his hand. "I'm tired."

She edged off the bed. "Let me help you. I'll get you
something to eat. You can take a nap right here—"

"You're so stupid," he snarled, but his eyes couldn't stay

fixed on her. She noticed the way his grip spasmed on the gun, dangerously close to the trigger.

She swallowed. *Oh, Lord, I am stupid. How did this happen to me again?* Her throat grew raw at the irony. Here she'd been building a refuge and the enemy lived right inside the gates. She blinked back tears. *God where are You?*

Here. I am here.

She stilled. Breathed. In. Out. And felt a presence so thick it filled the room and settled in her soul. *Here.* Peace reverberated through her as if two hands rested on her shoulders, holding her down. *I am here.*

Her heartbeat slowed. She closed her eyes and words flooded her mind: "*When peace like a river attendeth my way, when sorrows like sea-billows roll; whatever my lot, Thou has taught me to say, 'It is well, it is well with my soul.'*"

It is well with my soul. God had her soul, was keeping it . . .

Suddenly with a wash of pure, brilliant clarity, she understood.

God hadn't brought Noah into her life so she could hide in his muscular embrace. He'd brought Noah into her life to answer the pleas from her childhood . . . to show her, indeed, there is safety, peace, in this world.

The memory of Noah's song infiltrated her thoughts.

For me be it Christ, be it Christ hence to live.
If Jordan above me shall roll.
No pang shall be mine, for in death as in life,
Thou shalt whisper thy peace to my soul.

God had been with her as she bled on that bedroom floor, present in Noah's song, in Noah's strong hand holding hers.

God, there, watching over her bereft, terrified soul.

Keeping it safe, on both sides of eternity.

God had heard her prayers and answered—through Noah and his song. God had brought Anne to 2135 Franklin Avenue for a reason—to teach her that, yes, whether in death or life, even when storms and sea billows roll, all was well with her soul.

Tears fell in a torrent. *Yes, Lord. It is well. It is so well.* She may be a doomed hostage at the business end of a pistol, but Dr. Jefferies couldn't kill her soul.

Whether in fear or in triumph, God was with her. Just like He'd been a year ago in the soft song of an unnamed hero. And before, in the protection of her parents and their heritage of faith. God never left her.

She'd left Him. Katie's voice returned to her: *We will find God if we turn to Him. And in that surrender, He'll turn it into something both for His glory and your eternal good, according to His will.*

Anne had taken her eyes off her only source of healing. Her source of hope.

"For to me, living is for Christ, and dying is even better. Yet if I live, that means fruitful service for Christ. I really don't know which is better. I'm torn between two desires: Sometimes I want to live, and sometimes I long to go and be with Christ."

Anne comprehended for the first time what her father had meant. The fullness of Philippians 1:21-23 swept through her, taking with it the final residue of grief. The joy of her faith didn't come from living in safety on earth. It came from living in safety in her Father's hand, wherever He put her, among the living or the dying.

Anne couldn't construct a world without pain. But she could trust a big, capable God who would be there, holding her when trouble invaded her world. God's grace was sufficient to hold her in any circumstance. And in this—this reality, this character of God—dwelled the joy of her faith.

Joy wasn't a reaction to God's blessings. It was a state of being because of salvation through Jesus Christ.

She stared at Dr. Jefferies—his brown hair askew, his

eyes drooping, his gun hand quivering—and a wave of pity swept through her. A cleansing flow that left peace in its wake. Fear lingered at the recesses, but in the deepest place of her soul she felt the touch of the Almighty.

The embrace of grace.

The caress of eternity.

She began to laugh, a hysterical wonder that, even to her, felt just on the lee side of lunacy. But it bubbled out until she had to cover her face with her hands. Then the laughter turned to tears.

Only God could make her face her worst fears and, in that moment, heal her of her wounds.

"What's so funny?" Dr. Jefferies's eyes were half closed, but somehow he made it to his feet. "What's so funny?"

She stared at him. "Nothing is funny," she answered honestly. "I'm sorry that you won't let me help you."

He laughed, a sickly, throw-his-head-back puff of disgust. "Yeah, you can help me. C'mon." He staggered toward her and dug his fingers into her arm, causing her to wince.

"Where are we going?" Her voice came out surprisingly calm. God was holding her tight.

"Outside. Home. Away." He wobbled toward the door, then pushed her in front of him, curling his arm around her neck. "No fast moves, honey."

"I'm not your honey."

That endearment belonged to Noah.

"Stop it! You're hurting me!"

Anne's angry voice drilled into Noah. He gritted his teeth, fighting the urge to tear her assailant apart like a grizzly.

"Let go. It won't help you to kidnap me. They'll catch you."

"No they won't. Not if they want you to live."

Her quick intake of breath dittoed Noah's gasp. He remained behind the nurses' counter, watching the duo shuffle by. *Good girl, Anne. Fight him. Distract him.* Noah's legs tensed as he crept around the side of the station.

Sirens blared, a low moan in the background piercing the air.

Dr. Jefferies? Noah recognized the man from church, and a streak of white-hot fury shot through him. What kind of deceiving rat posed as a doctor one moment and took lives the next? It was like watching himself, only inside out. Dr. Jefferies looked like a man people could trust with their lives. Noah looked like the local thug down the street.

Well, a thug might be just the person Anne needed at the moment. Like Pastor Dan had said, God had made him exactly the way he wanted him.

Noah moved quietly. Swiftly.

He sprang like a cougar, arms out toward his prey. When he landed on Dr. Jefferies, they went down in a bone-cracking tackle. Pain spurted into Noah's shoulder. Dr. Jefferies rolled and jabbed an elbow into Noah's chest.

"Anne, run!" Noah grabbed the doctor by his shirt as the man bounced off the floor. "Run!"

He saw Anne turn, stand transfixed. He thought he heard his name. The physician wriggled out of his grip. Momentum propelled Noah off the floor, and he tackled the slimeball again. "Run, Anne!"

Dr. Jefferies roared in anger. Manic in his fury, he slammed his knee into Noah's ribs. Noah shoved his forearm into the man's neck. "Calm down!"

The man's eyes bugged out, his breath rasped. Noah pushed harder. Where were the cops?

"Noah, look out!" Was that Anne? His every muscle zeroed in on pinning the doctor to the floor. Arm across his neck. Knee in his gut.

"You!" Dr. Jefferies grunted, as if recognizing Noah for the first time.

A pistol knifed into Noah's ribs. Noah pressed harder,

praying for precious time. The doctor's eyes dimmed. Rolled. His body stiffened.

The gun reported. In a blast of white fire, pain speared through Noah's body.

"No!" Anne screamed as he fell into blackness.

"Noah, don't you die on me."

Noah clawed through a blanket of heat, to sheer bone-spearing pain. Anne? Darkness pressed him down.

Voices punched at the swaddle of agony.

"BP's ninety over fifty and dropping."

"IV line established."

Hands on him. Cold. Fear like shackles, pulling him into a black place. He fought it.

"I see an exit wound."

"Please, Noah, stay with me!"

A hand in his. Warm. Tight. He focused his energy on squeezing it.

Light in his eyes, flickering.

"He needs surgery—now."

Pressures, lead weight on his chest. Pushing. Suffocating. *I can't breathe!* Rasping.

The cocoon of darkness enfolded him. *Help! Help me, Lord!*

A sweet melody, like a swath of sunshine through a cloudy sky. "When peace like a river attendeth my way, when sorrows and sea-billows roll; whatever my lot, Thou hast taught me to say . . ."

Pain, tentacles stinging every nerve. A moan—his voice? The song. Cling to the song. Yes. It is well, it is well with my soul.

Falling.

Soft arms. "Anne?"

Peace.

Well.

❧

"Can I get you another cup of tea?"

Anne raised her head from where she'd buried it under her arms. Mona crouched before her, her eyes ringed with a compassion that made Anne want to dissolve in a puddle of fresh tears. "Yes, thank you." She might as well add another gallon of the spicy liquid to her stomach—pure caffeine and heaps of prayer were the only things keeping her glued together while waiting for Noah to pull through surgery.

He *had* to pull through. She wasn't going to lose him when everything in her heart told her that he was her future.

Pools of lamplight pushed the midnight shadows into the edges of the waiting room. A summer rainstorm fogged the dark windowpanes, sending a thread of chill into the tiled room.

Please, Lord.

Across the waiting room, Pastor Dan and Joe Michaels stood in a tight huddle. Praying? Good. They all needed to barrage heaven.

She'd read the solemn, grim expression from Dr. Simpson seconds before he'd whisked Noah away, tracking Noah's blood down the hall in deathly shoe prints.

Please, Lord.

The man had jumped in front of a gun for her. Again. She loved him so much it hurt. She didn't care if he'd done it out of pity. Didn't care if all he'd been trying to do was keep her in the hub of his ministry. It was time to go toe-to-toe with her fears—all of them—and beat them to a pulp.

She loved Noah Standing Bear. The second Noah was out of surgery, she would grab him by the lapels and shake the truth out of him. He loved her—she knew it. It had only taken her name on his lips as he faded into unconsciousness for her to realize it. Only taken the repeat performance of

303

his diving on her assailant and taking a bullet this time for it to take root in her heart.

But what if Noah . . . died? Her throat thickened. New tears welled, coursed down her face. Then his work wouldn't have been in vain. Suddenly, the thought of moving to the armpit of Minneapolis to minister to the dregs of society sounded like a glorious, God-filled future. For the first time Anne knew exactly why her father had packed up his family and moved them next door to pimps and drug lords—because his joy of salvation overflowed and nothing could stop him from sharing it with the most needy. If she didn't go, who would?

She'd pick up Noah's cross—*her* cross—and continue. If being with Noah, a man who grabbed hope with both hands, had taught her anything, it was to face fear and prejudice with the life-giving truth of grace. In fact, she had a sneaking suspicion that the girl her father had raised knew better than anyone how to stand up to gangbangers with sass and street smarts.

Oh yeah, she was going to take that job offer.

Regardless of what the next hour held.

Unfortunately, as she'd held Noah's hand and stared at his pain-twisted face, she hadn't uttered one hint of that glorious intent. Not "Noah, I love you!" Not "I'm not afraid of you!" Not even "I want to work beside you, to love you until eternity."

No, those words had lodged in her chest, stymied by the urge to sing. Softly. She and Noah needed the words of the hymn more than they needed emotional declarations that might never come to fruition.

Please, Lord.

So she had sung the hymn that told her God had brought her full circle. Answered her prayers. Given her, finally, her deep haven of peace and safety—in Him.

Please, Lord, I can't lose Noah now. Not when she wanted, more than life and breath, to partner with him for the lost kids on the street. To hold him when tragedy hit

them broadside, to dance with him when kids like Darrin chose life.

The door at the end of the hall creaked open.

Everyone froze.

Anne's heartbeats reeled out, one at a time, in rhythm with the heavy footsteps of Dr. Simpson. He clutched his surgeon's cap, his head down, shoulders horribly slumped.

Behind him plodded Sandra.

She was crying.

28

The hiss wheedled through the cotton of darkness, snaring him, bringing him forward, through the shadows.

Light. Explosions of color and warmth. Noah forced his eyes open and blinked.

Stark white ceiling. Blinds, half turned to allow sunlight to stripe the pink walls. An IV bag dangling above him and sweet, cold oxygen rushing into his nose.

Anne, asleep at his knees. *Oh, thank You, Lord!*

Her chestnut hair stuck up in a fuzzy helmet around her head. In relaxed slumber her freckled face looked amazingly young, innocent. Utterly beautiful. He wished with every aching cell in his body that they had a future together.

His mouth felt dry, his tongue gummy. His chest burned as if someone had plunged an ax through it. When he took a breath, fire seared his lungs. A moan escaped and, to his dismay, Anne stirred. He held his breath, which made his eyes tear.

Her eyes blinked open. Then she stared at him, a slight smile on her lips, her amazing hazel green eyes searching his face as if hoping to find a treasure there.

He grinned.

"Noah." His name on her lips—verbal sunshine to his cold heart. "You had me worried."

He reached out to her, wincing at the burn from the IV taped to his hand. She took his hand with both of hers, rubbed it with her soft fingers. "You're going to be okay."

"What happened?" His voice sounded like sandpaper.

She grabbed a drink, held the straw to his lips. He drank greedily, then felt nauseous.

"You . . . died." Tears trailed down her cheeks, telling him exactly how horrible it had been. "You were shot. In the ribs. The bullet missed your aorta but it hit one of your lungs."

No wonder he felt like an elephant had stomped on his chest.

"You had surgery, and during it your lung collapsed, and your heart . . . it stopped." She took a deep breath, and he noticed the way she fought for composure. "But Dr. Simpson restarted it, and Sandra prayed . . . and . . . and . . ." She kissed his hand, and this time the smile came easily, filling his broken chest with delight.

"Did they get him?" He had sketchy memories of Dr. Jefferies, manic, a gun in his hand. He didn't linger too long on the image of the scum doctor forcing Anne down the hall at gunpoint.

"Yes. He crumbled fast and confessed. Evidently, he's the point man for some drug ring, flushing prescription drugs onto the street. Chief Sam worked a trail back to Duluth, and they're looking at connections in Minneapolis." She smiled ruefully. "I guess you can't escape the snare of sin, even in Deep Haven."

He nodded. "Good thing God is there to cut us free."

Anne ran a hand down his cheek, and his heart confirmed, indeed, that it worked just fine. "Noah, you saved my life." The look in her eyes turned very, very warm. Tender. "You're my hero."

He looked away, unable to face the love he saw in her eyes, knowing that in about three seconds he was going to

have to tell her it was over. Then Katie's words filtered through his foggy memory. *Anne's a smart woman. Let her decide what she wants to do. If you don't ask, you'll never know.*

Didn't Anne deserve to know that she filled his life with sunshine and song? That she made him feel like a man of character, a hero? She was so pure and kind it made him long to be next to her so it would rub off. She made him a better man simply by smiling in his general direction, and he loved her so much it made the gaping hole in his chest feel like a scratch.

Maybe, just maybe, if God could take a man with a past and give him a future, He could give them hope also. Noah found Anne's gaze and held it, hoping she could see the emotions written in his eyes.

He opened his mouth, willing his feelings to spill out.

She spoke first. "That's twice you've been in the right place at the right time. It seems like God is using you to protect me."

Those words burrowed deep, fertilized courage. "I hope so. Because I promised Dr. Simpson that nothing would happen to you under my watch."

"Oh." Her face fell, a shadow across it.

No, that didn't come out right. He touched her chin. "But it was my pleasure. I'd do anything for the woman . . . I love."

She stared at him, and the joy on her face made him want to spring from the bed and dance. "You love me?"

"From the moment you walked into my life a year ago. You've never left my thoughts. You're such a gift to me, Anne."

She looked away, and for a second, he thought he saw her flinch.

He tugged at her chin and added earnestness to his voice. "No, not because you helped me this summer. Because you're kind and thoughtful and wise. You make me want to be a hero. For you."

She bit her lip, her eyes landing everywhere but his face.

"When I'm with you, I don't feel like a man with an ugly past. I feel whole and hopeful, like my entire future is golden."

She finally looked at him. A single tear trailed down her cheek. He gently wiped it away and said, "But we still have a problem."

Her face darkened with a trace of worry. She glanced to his wounds.

"No, not that. You said you were afraid of me." He felt grateful for the painkillers flushing his system, numbing him, hopefully, from her brutal answer. "Is that true?"

She shrugged, and a sly smile tweaked her lips. "Well, maybe a little. I'm deathly afraid that I might die from the way my heart is racing, or the fact that I can't seem to breathe if you aren't in the room. I think I have a life-threatening condition."

Now he was the one having trouble breathing.

Her expression turned serious, the EMT who fought death with her bare hands. "Noah, when I look at you, I don't see a gangster. I see a man with a heart after God. A man who has been transformed. I see a man with whom I'd like to work. As long as you'll let me."

He blinked at her. "In ministry? In Minneapolis?"

She nodded. "In Minneapolis or wherever God sends us. Maybe even back to Deep Haven next summer. Give Wilderness Challenge another good run." Her eyes lit up when she said it. Then her expression turned solemn again. "I learned something this summer. I can't escape trouble. Not really. Life is hard. But God is good, and His grace is sufficient for every situation. He is big enough to carry me through any tragedy if I trust Him. And I can find true joy in my faith because of God's faithfulness. Wilderness Challenge did exactly the thing you hoped—it pushed me to the end of myself, and I fell right into the arms of the Keeper of my soul."

A spark of mischief glinted in her eyes when she continued. "And, by the way, I'm not the only one who found
salvation. Darrin 'hooked up' with Christ, as you would
say. We had an enlightening conversation yesterday about
his fears and your past. He saw the light in the darkness, so
to speak." Tears clung to her lashes, and it moved him
deeply. "I'd say your camp was a roaring success."

Anne bit her lip, as if trying to hold in all the emotions
that played on her lovely face. Noah rubbed his thumb
along her lower lip, dying to kiss her. Instead, he found the
words he'd been yearning to say for a month. "I love you,
Anne."

Her gaze turned so tender he felt as if he might turn into
a pile of Granny D.'s oatmeal, a messy glob of emotions.
Suddenly Anne took a deep breath, and her words came out
in a flood of fervent passion. "I've loved you since that
moment last year when God used you to keep me from
drowning in despair." She touched his cheek. "Only God
could design my dream man from my deepest fears and
needs. A man who understands my sorrows, who can share
my happiness. A man who will risk his life to protect me.
Noah, you're the man I want."

Want. Present tense. He could feel a goofy smile taking
over his cheeks, lighting his eyes. "You sang to me, didn't
you?"

She wrinkled her nose. "It was the only thing I could
think of at the moment."

"You have a beautiful voice."

"Liar." She blushed and he relished it.

"So, when you say you're moving to Minneapolis—" his
chest tightened, but he pushed words through—"do you
think you'd consider . . . I mean . . . what do you think
about . . . Anne Standing Bear?"

Her breath caught; her eyes became luminous. A smile
tugged at her mouth. "There's a certain ring to it. Let's see
what God has in store."

Somehow he found his voice. "I think that's another one of your brilliant ideas."

"Kiss me, Noah." Anne leaned close, her face expectant.

He thought his heart might combust from mind-blowing joy. *God, You did this! You brought this woman into my life, not once, but twice. You let me protect her and love her. You gave me the partner I needed—in life, in love, in ministry. Now our future belongs in Your very capable hands.*

"Anything for you, my sweet thundercloud." He grinned, then drew her closer, kissing her. He poured out his love for her in his touch, gentle yet brimming with promise. She tasted as sweet as the morning, as delicious as hope. He savored it, hating when she pulled away. "Or maybe I should call you my sunshine."

She laughed, a giggle of delight. Then she touched her forehead to his, her eyes glistening, her fragrance pouring over him like an embrace. "I came here looking for peace. I never thought that God would help me find it in the arms of a born-again gangbanger with a heart for the inner city."

"I have a feeling He's just getting started."

Anne sighed, an audible swell of contentment that filled even his chest. "So you did keep me on staff to make all your dreams come true."

"What?" He frowned at her, confused by her quirky smile and her delicately raised eyebrow.

She ran her fingers lightly over his face. "Just a hunch I had." She kissed him again, softly, perfectly. He had to agree.

When she pulled away, he laced his fingers into her silky, chestnut hair. "Are you sure about this, Anne? I know what you've been through—"

She stopped his words with a kiss that made him nearly forget his name let alone his fears. "Noah . . . don't forget. It is well with my soul," she murmured against his lips.

Noah's heart swelled. "Oh yeah," he whispered. When she looked at him, he saw a wonder in her eyes that he

Tying the Knot

hadn't seen since the first day they'd met, when he'd tried to tell her—through his touch, his song, his eyes—that she could trust him.

And, finally, her response told him she'd read him perfectly.

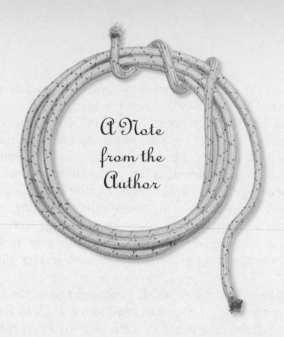

A Note from the Author

On March 1, 2002, at 1:00 P.M., three men broke into our high-rise apartment in Russia and brutally attacked me and my children. By the grace of God, our lives were spared and we were not terribly injured—physically. But the masked attackers had left deep spiritual and emotional wounds. We were sent to a trauma center for counseling for a month, then returned to Russia, our field of service, to complete our missionary term. Four months later, burned-out and spiritually empty, we packed our bags and returned to America for our scheduled one-year home service.

I had no plans to return. Secretly, I harbored deep in my heart a resolve to never again set foot in Russia, with its many dangers. I had done eight hard years of service there and felt that I had given the best part of myself to a country that didn't care. And no one—not even God—was going to change my mind. Yes, He'd spared my life, but I had serious doubts I could ever trust Him again.

But God knew better. Not only is He gentle, but He understands and can handle my pain and my questions. I dove into the Psalms, finding hope in David's cries to the Lord and healing in his praise to the Almighty in the darkest hours. I observed God's goodness to me, providing for my needs in the past—and present—and I allowed myself to be embraced by the body of Christ, who loved us well. Finally, as time and distance began to heal me, I was able to look behind and see God's grace embracing me every moment of the difficult journey. He reminded me that He would meet me in my future with the same abundance of grace.

I wrote Anne and Noah's story while struggling through the dark night of the soul. Amazingly, many times I felt as though the words that appeared on the page were more for me than for Anne. I journeyed with Anne until I, too, could see God embracing me in the darkest hour. Her victory is mine.

On New Year's Eve 2003, I surrendered to the Lord my future, agreeing to continue missionary work in Russia if God so chose. The peace that flooded my heart told me that His grace would carry me wherever He took our family. His grace is sufficient. For every heartache, every fear, every wound.

Thank you for reading *Tying the Knot*. I pray that somehow Anne and Noah's journey of faith and love will encourage and bless you. And that you will know, above all, that it is well with your soul.

In His grace,
Susan May Warren

About the Author

SUSAN MAY WARREN recently returned home after serving eight years with her husband and four children as missionaries in Khabarovsk, Far East Russia. Now writing full-time as her husband runs a lodge on Lake Superior in northern Minnesota, she and her family enjoy hiking and canoeing and being involved in their local church.

Susan holds a BA in mass communications from the University of Minnesota and is a multipublished author of novellas and novels with Tyndale, including *Happily Ever After,* the American Christian Romance Writers' 2003 Book of the Year and a 2004 Christy Award finalist. Other books in the series include *Tying the Knot* and *The Perfect Match,* the 2004 American Christian Fiction Writers' Book of the Year. *Flee the Night, Escape to Morning,* and *Expect the Sunrise* comprise her romantic-adventure, search-and-rescue series.

Reclaiming Nick is the first book in Susan's new romantic series.

Susan invites you to visit her Web site at
www.susanmaywarren.com.

She also welcomes letters by e-mail at
susan@susanmaywarren.com.

 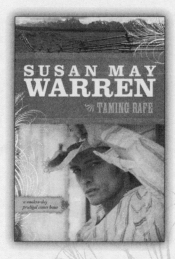

have you visited
tyndalefiction.com
lately?

Only there can you find:

→ books hot off the press

→ first chapter excerpts

→ inside scoops on your favorite authors

→ author interviews

→ contests

→ fun facts

→ and much more!

Sign up for your **free** newsletter!

Visit us today at: **tyndalefiction.com**

Tyndale fiction does more than entertain.

→ *It touches the heart.*

→ *It stirs the soul.*

→ *It changes lives.*

That's why Tyndale is so committed to being first in fiction!

TYNDALE FICTION